Also by K.F. Breene

A Kingdom of Ruin

By K.F. Breene

Contact info:

www.kfbreene.com

books@kfbreene.com

"I will love the light for it shows me the way, yet I will endure the darkness because it shows me the stars."

– Og Mandino

CHAPTER I

FINLEY

I SLID OFF the demon king's shoulder and crashed down into the soggy mud and weeds. My left hip struck a rock, and pain exploded through me, adding to the aches and bruises I'd accumulated on our three-day journey to this accursed place, the demons' kingdom. My sword was still sheathed at my side. The demon king, Dolion, had allowed me to bring it, knowing I didn't know how to use it. It was his little joke.

"Yeah, sure, just put me anywhere," I mumbled, wincing as I pushed away from the rock.

The large, magically powered boat that had borne us to this dark and rain-streaked island bobbed in the murky sea behind us, anchored. Rowboats floated from it, washing onto the sandy shore and unloading the demons and various cargo.

Boots squelched in the mud next to me before Jedrek, my dipshit betrothed, crashed down beside me, crying out.

"Quiet," I told him in a low voice.

Too late.

His previous transportation, a hard-faced demon with plenty

of strength hidden within his wiry frame, swung a foot into Jedrek's middle. Jedrek cried out again, rolling through the mud and weeds to get away.

"It's fine. He's just getting used to this." I put out my hand and leaned toward Jedrek, doing very little to shield him with my body. I'd learned by now that if they really wanted to lay into him—or me—they were going to do it. Still, I couldn't help trying to intervene. The only reason Dolion had lifted his magical suppression spell from our people was because I'd agreed to marry Jedrek. Which meant he needed to stay alive for the time being.

"Welcome to my castle, princess." Dolion looked down at me with a smirk on his blue face. Rain slid down the dark horns curling from his head. "Your new home."

Sorrow rose and squeezed my heart. The hollow pang of loss threatened to bring tears to my eyes as I remembered the way Nyfain looked at me before I was taken away. His utter despair. His desperation to keep me with him, in his kingdom and in his life.

In the end, he'd let me go. I knew he believed it would be forever. He thought I would break free from the demons, something he was confident I could do, and live my life elsewhere. My happiness mattered to him, and he didn't think he had anything to offer. Idiot. I would absolutely go back to him. The only reason I'd agreed to this farce was to get the suppression spell lifted. I would suffer anything to free my kingdom and my mate. With that spell gone, Nyfain could use his alpha magic to pull out everyone's animals. He could give our people a fighting chance... Because I *would* escape—straight back to Nyfain—and we would break the curse together. Then it would be time to fight.

I held on to my resolve with everything I had and looked up

through the driving rain, determined that Dolion would never see my pain. He would never know what all of this was costing me...or Nyfain.

"Quite the welcome mat you've rolled out," I said, lifting my hands and turning my palms up to look at the mud now caking my skin. "Did you do the landscaping yourself?"

He scowled at me, his gaze roaming my face. Darkness cascaded around his narrow shoulders like a cloak. "So strong. So stupid." He stepped forward and kicked, his heavy boot landing on my upper thigh. Pain vibrated through me. "*Look at it!*"

I tsked, but did as he said to stave off another kick. He'd done a good job at acting suave and balanced within Nyfain's castle—except when Nyfain was thwarting his commands—but he had a volatile temper. Not just directed at Jedrek and me, either. He doled out harsh punishments to his own people if they didn't follow his commands quickly enough. Do something wrong, even by accident? The punishment was worse still. He used his power and position to bully others. He led through fear.

I knew from history books that those types of leaders often had precarious perches on their thrones. I wondered how easy it would be to topple him.

"It's nothing like that dragon hovel you're so fond of," he said, and I could hear the smug pride in his voice.

He's got that right, my dragon murmured.

A formidable castle sat on top of a hill. Pale moonlight peeked through a break in the heavy clouds, washing across thin spires, bulky towers, and the castle's sprawling, disjointed architecture. Arrow slits punched through the first two levels, giving way to more modern rectangular windows for the next two. The fifth level looked like a sort of fortress, with sleek stone walls and a fresh feel that suggested it had been built sometime in the last hundred years.

The overall effect was grotesque. The designers had clearly been drunk.

The murky sea wrapped around the island fortress, the sandy shore we'd landed on turning rocky and then jagged as the land rose. At the other side of the castle would be cliffs, something I remembered from the maps I'd studied and descriptions I'd read. The only way in or out would be this heavily guarded shore. That or flying.

"It's enormous," I said in a level tone.

He puffed up a bit, his smirk turning to a grin.

I finished my thought: "It looks like you're compensating for something..."

His grin dripped off his face and his eyes sparkled with menace. "Welcome to your nightmare, highness."

"Cheers!" I said with a smile, raising my hand. "Actually, I need a drink for that toast, I believe. Fancy getting me one? You've left my butler behind. Oh, and I'm not anyone's highness. I'm a commoner. I thought someone would've told you..."

"You are the true mate to the dragon prince, or didn't he mention it?"

Nyfain's letter felt heavy in my back pocket. I didn't comment. Dolion was a cunning bastard who would use my weaknesses against me. One of them being that I was a blunt bitch who sucked at keeping secrets. But I *would* keep quiet about the important things, like how much I knew regarding Nyfain, his kingdom, his people, and breaking the demons' curse.

"But no, you're right," Dolion said. "You will never be royalty. You will die in my dungeon or at the hands of my court. Eventually, your dragon prince will also die. Your death will be his ruin."

"He's already ruined. We both are. But I admire your spunk." I winked at him.

His eyes narrowed as he stared down at me. He wasn't quite sure what to say to that. I supposed it wouldn't make much sense to him. He hadn't had everything stripped from him, like Nyfain had. He hadn't spent sixteen years watching his beloved kingdom crumble around him. And he certainly hadn't grown up poor and trapped like I had. Unable to reach the magic I was born with, fighting a curse that was slowly stealing the lives of those I loved.

No, he didn't know what *ruin* looked like. And he didn't know how to rise from the ashes. I'd make sure he never did.

Because I would be the bitch that burned down his whole world.

He pursed his lips and glanced at his minions behind him. "Take them to the dungeons. Around the side, mind. We'll need to do something about the stench clinging to her before any of the court can see her." He turned his attention back to me. "Clever of the dragon, to coat you in his scent. He is a conquered beast, but he still has his alpha legacy, it seems. But it won't protect you for long." Dolion studied me a moment. "Instruct the guards not to mar her face. I want my court to watch Beauty as she breaks."

"What about her arms?" asked the demon looming over Jedrek. "What skin will be visible?"

"Yes, good point. Do not mar the arms, no. No neck, even though we will want to cover that ridiculous bite mark on her shoulder. *Shifters*," he spat. "So barbaric, marking their mates. Disgusting."

"And this?" The demon stepped forward again, kicking at Jedrek's legs. Jedrek curled up a little tighter.

"That one is somewhat handsome for a shifter, no?" Dolion said, assessing Jedrek now. "I can think of a few ladies who might like him as a pet. Tell the guards to go easy on him if he cooperates."

"But not the princess?"

Dolion sneered. "She won't cooperate. Her dragon will forbid it."

He's not wrong, my dragon thought.

Dolion made a signal, and the demons around him moved forward. Two grabbed Jedrek and hauled him up, hustling him toward the castle. Two others grabbed my arms and yanked me to my feet, one tweaking my shoulder painfully.

Dolion's gaze traveled my face, and he reached out. I struggled not to jerk my head away as he lightly fingered the hair draping my cheek and then ran his manicured nails along my jaw and down to my chin. He applied pressure to tilt my face up a bit.

"So pretty, even disheveled as you are. I wouldn't mind using you as a pet myself. One mighty dragon on my leash, and his mate at my beck and call." A ghost of a smile crossed his lips, and my dragon thrashed in my hold, wanting to break free and crush some bones. "As soon as we can get that stench off you, it will be so. I promise. You will beg for my cock. I'll let your dragon prince watch as you do so…right before I kill you. It'll finally break him. I know it will."

"Hmm. What an offer," I said, winking. "Very tempting. I'll need to pass, though. I'm partial to dragon-sized cocks. I don't beg for appetizers."

He huffed out a laugh. "Even dragons break. In the end, you will be my little lamb, eager for affection. And my entire court will watch you fall."

A chill arrested me, but I kept myself from squirming. "Promises, promises."

"Time, *your highness*," he said as his gaze roamed my body. "All one needs is time. Even the strongest beings will crack and crumble given enough time and pressure." His eyes turned hungry. "And I have all the time in the world."

His hand drifted lower, toward my breast. I braced myself for the touch, but his hand stopped right before touching down, a wrinkle worming between his eyebrows. His jaw set, and a glimmer of fear sparked in his blood-red eyes.

Touching my face was one thing—Dolion had a lot of power and could withstand Nyfain's aromatic presence for such a benign gesture—but my breast was altogether different. Touching me there would be more intimate, erotic. And so he felt the full weight of the dragon's protection. It didn't matter that the golden prince wasn't here in the flesh.

Dolion pulled his hand away and turned. A burst of movement and he was walking toward the castle, a group of his strongest minions, similar in color to him, following at his heels.

"Let's go." A black-scaled demon gave me a shove.

As we crested the rise, the wind slammed into us, knocking me sideways into Jedrek. He huddled down into his sopping clothes, glancing beyond me. I followed his gaze, taking in the stark vegetation atop the hill—nothing but a few bare trees permanently bowed by the roaring wind, sickly bushes, and weeds. Beyond, the sea stretched out into the darkness. My dragon's power meant I could see in the dark with a black, white, and yellow color spectrum, but not at great distances like that. In the day, it would probably look like that part of the sea carried on into eternity.

Dolion's crew continued forward toward the grand front entrance of the castle, with a large gate arching over what had to be the door. It was too far away for me to see much detail. Of course, we weren't headed for the front entrance, and after we reached the windswept hilltop, our captors veered us right. We plodded along the side of the structure, likely aiming for a fast track to the dungeon.

As we neared the castle, I looked up at the monstrous thing, reaching far into the rain-soaked sky with multiple towers practically piercing the thick, sodden clouds. Or so it seemed from the ground.

My legs ached by the time we reached a little berm at the base of the wall. The metal door nestled within it clearly led down into the bowels of the castle. The hinges squealed as one of the demons bent and pulled it open, no key needed. He looked down into the dark depths, the blackness giving nothing away.

"Did his majesty say anything about the magical lock?" He hesitated a moment before asking in a louder voice, "Does anyone know if they stripped the *obice* covering this entrance?" He looked at the demon holding Jedrek, his flat face lined with wariness. "Did anyone ask?"

Obice. Ah. No key needed because the lock was magical in nature. Shit. In all the reading I'd done about the demons and their castle, trying to prepare myself for this moment, I didn't recall anything regarding this type of demon magic.

"Govam can release the *obice*," someone said. "He has the magic to do it."

The crowd shifted around, looking for whoever that was.

"Not at present," a deep, somewhat bored-sounding voice said from somewhere behind me. "I had that ability and others, but they were suppressed as punishment while I'm on this detail."

A few grumbled at that, turning back to the demon standing near the gaping blackness.

"Test it out," someone called from the back. "Walk down a bit."

"What, and lose my foot? Fuck off." The demon at the door looked through the crowd that had gathered around us. "Sonassa, try it."

A female laugh sounded behind me. "I don't want to lose my foot any more than you do, Ressfu, and it won't be me his majesty punishes for dereliction of duty."

The demon by the door, Ressfu, licked his pale yellow lips, the color a little lighter than the rest of his face. Like all demons, he was capable of using a human form, but he clearly couldn't be bothered. Then again, why would he? He was among his kind, the rest of them in their natural forms as well, ranging from nearly human looking to leather or scaled or even feathered.

"Zurgid, run around and find out whether the defenses are turned off," Ressfu said.

I heard shuffling in the back. "That would take forever. You know what it's like in the dungeons. His highness doesn't enforce any sort of regulations down there. He lets the officers run wild as long as they make his creatures."

The demon by the door looked down into the hole's depths, clearly debating. He lifted his gaze again, zipping over Jedrek and then landing on me. My stomach flipped at his sudden look of decisiveness.

"You, shifter woman, come here." He gestured me forward. Tingles of warning spread across my skin.

Well, shit.

CHAPTER 2

FINLEY

"**N**OT HER, IDIOT," a familiar voice said from behind. Sonassa. "She's the dragon prince's mate. The king has plans for her. Besides, didn't you hear? He'll want her as a pet eventually."

"His highness just said not to mar her face or arms," Ressfu said. "He said nothing about her legs."

"He'll want both of them to be there," Sonassa replied.

Ressfu looked beyond me, probably at Sonassa, clearly thinking it over. Anticipation rolled in my gut, and I got to work planning what I would do if they called on me to be the fall guy.

No problem, my dragon thought. *Grab that fuckstain Ressfu and toss him down the hole. See if he dies. They might beat the shit out of us, but that's better than losing a leg.*

This was true.

"Fine," Ressfu said before spitting to the side. "Luru, come here. You have the least seniority. Dip your tail in and see if the coast is clear."

The demon beside me grunted as if he thought it a fine idea.

Luru, a leathery-skinned demon with a hunch, didn't seem to agree. He slunk closer with a slack face, looking between Ressfu and the gaping door at his feet.

"I think it's probably fine," Luru said in a weak voice, stalling at the edge of the door. "The officers may not be regulated, but they are always punctual. They're always eager for fresh prisoners, especially dragons. They'll know the king was planning on bringing prisoners in at about this time."

"How would they know that?" Ressfu said. "These shifters weren't planned for."

"Not *these* shifters, no, but his highness almost always brings back *some* shifters from that kingdom, doesn't he? And he always sends them around this way to get cleaned up. Right?"

It didn't sound like he was entirely sure of what he was saying. Still, the words pinged around inside my head. Were some of the people from my kingdom—maybe even my village!—down in that dungeon?

Heart pounding, I waited as Luru argued for a moment longer before two demons stepped out of the crowd and roughly grabbed him.

"I'll go around!" Luru hollered as they marshaled him down a step, into the doorway. "I'm fast! I run fast! The officers like me. I'll just go—No!"

They lowered him. He pulled up his thin tail and bent his legs, suspended above the blackness.

"No. Please," Luru pleaded.

"Drop him," Ressfu said.

Luru started screaming and writhing as his captors released him over what was surely a staircase. He dropped down squirming, hit at an awkward angle, and screams turned into painful grunts and then screams again as he rolled down the stairs.

"Coward," someone spat.

Sonassa laughed. "You think *you* would've approached the situation with more decorum, do you? I didn't see you volunteering."

A few others snickered.

"We're good," Ressfu said, motioning everyone on.

The two demons already at the opening descended the stairs one at a time, darkness swallowing them as they went.

The demons holding me started forward, jostling me to keep up even though I wasn't resisting. They got to the mouth of the doorway.

"Wait," Ressfu said, eyeing my face. His mouth curled into a sinister grin. "You got lucky, dragon. You must know it. What will make you squeal, eh? I like to watch your kind quiver."

The two beside me chuckled darkly.

Ressfu reached for me, taking my arm in a clawed grip and jerking me toward the mouth of the stairs. Darkness covered what lay beneath—the kind of thick, impenetrable darkness that suggested magic was at work.

The demon's breath smelled like dead things. "Are your kind bred to feel no fear? Let's see."

He shoved me out over the lip of the doorway and into nothingness. Gravity snagged at me immediately, yanking me down.

Protect your head, my dragon thought-hollered, blasting me with power. The sweet fire filled me up and rushed through my blood. My senses heightened and my thought process sped up as blackness washed over me, cutting out my sight. It was clearly magically induced.

I closed my eyes so it wouldn't distract me, focusing instead on my other senses and the need to survive. Pungent aromas assaulted me, vomit and piss and decay wrapped in a musty scent like mold. I twisted and bent, making sure my first point of contact would be my side. A moment later, my hip hit a hard corner, half on and half off my sword scabbard. My upper body slammed down on stone steps.

I grunted and tucked, wrapping my hands around my head, forming a shape as close to a ball as I could manage.

Hang on, folks, we're about to do a little acrobatics, I thought desperately, speaking to my imaginary audience the way I always did under dire circumstances. My dragon must have felt the pressure, because she didn't call me an idiot.

I slid a little before the momentum lifted my feet and threatened to send me the rest of the way down on my head. My dragon continued to beat power into me, pulling it from Nyfain's dragon. Even all this distance away, we could still feel each other through the bond. It would play hell on Nyfain's nerves, knowing I was in trouble and he couldn't come to my aid, but for now I'd take what I could get.

The added power dulled the ache of the first landing, lessening the feel of stone scraping off skin. I tucked in harder, angling, and my bottom half flipped over the top. My ankle struck a step, and agony shot up my leg as my other foot caught. It was now my upper body's turn to fly over the lower. I was out of control. Careening.

Metal tinkled beside me and then below. My sword had somehow gotten loose and was now racing me to the bottom. Fantastic. As if I needed one more thing to worry about.

My other ankle smashed into a step. *Crack.* Incredible pain filled my world, forcing out a cry. Broken ankle, probably. Fractured, at least.

The fall seemed to go on forever, the pain threatening to overwhelm me with each agonizing bounce, each jostling of my newly busted ankle.

A breathless few moments later, my upper body crashed onto something somewhat soft. My legs didn't fare so well, though, smashing into the stone landing with enough force to send hot sparks of pure anguish racing up my body.

With my eyes still squinted shut, I sucked in a shuddering breath. I allowed one small tear to track across my pounding cheek. At least it didn't feel like anything was sticking into me. I must've missed the sword.

The world stopped spinning, and wet warmth seeped into my hair. I blinked my eyes open, afraid to move lest I jar my ankle, and looked at rough-hewn walls around me, not illuminated but not magically coated in darkness. My dragon's ability to see in the dark was strong enough for me to make out my miserable surroundings.

"What the fuck was he thinking?" I recognized that deep voice from above. Govam, they'd called him.

He grabbed my arms, unceremoniously hoisting me up. My foot caught on something and dragged over it, my busted ankle screaming at me. My sides ached, my back pounded, and my body was covered in stings from where I'd scraped stone. But I was alive. I'd made it down. "He was worried about her losing a leg, but then he threw her down the fucking steps? He could've killed her."

A tug on my hip registered before I heard the slide of my sword against the scabbard. Govam pushed it down to make sure it was secure. He must've grabbed it when it landed, possibly saving me from impalement.

"Not our problem."

A strong smell drifted from Govam. He had a decent amount of power. More than the other.

I grunted as I spied what I'd landed on. Luru, who hadn't fared as well as I had. He lay with a cracked skull and a chest glistening with blood. Something must've broken internally and punctured his skin.

Govam pulled me back to the wall at the other side of the landing, forcing me to step on my injured leg and nearly dragging a strangled cry from my throat.

"There, see?" Govam said as the second demon, a broad-faced creature with a wide nose, stepped in front of me and looked me over.

Broad Face zeroed in on my ankle, held off the ground and throbbing. "She's fucked up," he confirmed.

"Ah, well. She'll heal. When their magic isn't suppressed, dragons heal quick."

"What's to stop her from shifting? I never had the guts to ask the higher-ups on the way here. Seems stupid to let a dragon shift. They're enormous and mean."

"This particular one hasn't ever shifted before, I guess. She'll need to be guided through it or she could die, from what I understand."

"What about the dragons in the dungeon? How are we going to stop them now that the magic has been released?"

Govam, more human looking than the other but with slightly gray skin, scratched his chin. "Only some of them are from her kingdom. From what I've gathered, the suppression magic is gone, but they still need their alpha to draw out their animals. They won't get any shifter benefits until that happens. She may smell like the alpha, but she's not him. And even if she *could* free their dragons, they'd still be trapped in the dungeon, and we'd have them killed before they made it far. They aren't indestructible."

I stayed very still and ensured I had an entirely blank face. They'd just confirmed there were dragons in the dungeon. The ones from our kingdom must have been taken without Nyfain's knowledge. That or he hadn't been able to tell me because of the magical gag woven into the curse. Regardless, this meant I had help. It meant I'd have allies.

Broad Face shook his head, eyeing my body and then my face. "It's going to take an awful lot to clean this thing up. She's a mess."

"Not our problem, like you said."

Legs appeared in the blackness crowding the stairwell, the magic hovering like a blanket. Jedrek came into view with a fresh welt on his cheek. He'd probably tried to resist, and they'd slapped him around. The magic above must've deadened sound, though, because we hadn't heard any of it.

The leader, Ressfu, emerged on the stairs, his hand on Jedrek's shoulder. His gaze darted around the landing, pausing on Luru's broken body. Panic crept into his expression before easing into plain anxiety. He must've realized who it was. The next moment, his gaze hit me and a look of relief followed. He'd clearly regretted giving in to his stupid impulse. That was good. I hoped a lot of them gave in to moments of stupidity. Dumb creatures, even if they only acted foolish sometimes, were easier to fool.

The rest of the demons followed Ressfu, a good few of them looking me over for damage as they descended. When Ressfu reached the bottom, he reached for me.

"Her ankle is messed up," Govam said, still holding me up. "Like her face and a handful of other issues from her fall."

His voice didn't hold accusation, but Ressfu bristled all the same.

"She'll heal," Ressfu said, grabbing me and jerking me toward the tunnel. I tried to step-hop, but to keep from falling, I had to put weight on the bad ankle. Agony blasted through me, and I couldn't stifle a cry as I hopped on the other foot, trying to keep from going down. But I could already tell it was too late.

As I pitched forward, I threw out my hands to catch myself— just as a strong arm wrapped around my middle and pulled me up and against a chest.

"Fucking idiot," Govam mumbled softly, holding me so I could put my good foot on the ground. "Denski, get her other side. Let's get this done. I'm sick of this journey."

A thin demon emerged from the gathering, his smell suggesting his power was about the same as Govam's, which was higher than that of Broad Face and probably Ressfu, though it was hard to tell with so many of them gathered around.

They each took hold of one of my arms, and I hop/hobbled with them down the corridor, the sound of shuffling feet behind me indicating the others were coming along.

We followed the curve of the hallway, everyone obviously able to see in the darkness except for Jedrek, who stumbled within his captors' hold. The curse's suppression had been lifted from him, just like the rest of us from Wyvern, but I hadn't used my power to help yank his animal out of the darkness. I was worried he'd freak out and try to shift.

Up ahead, the low-hanging domed ceiling had an opening at the top that let in a slice of dusty, crimson-tinged white light. I looked up as we passed, but couldn't see anything through the hole. Onward we walked, darkness crowding in once again.

A bit farther in, the tunnel narrowed slightly, seemingly ending at a set of bars, the gaps between them slightly illuminated in that same reddish light. Through them were more rough-hewn walls, no difference from the hallway we'd walked down.

Govam stopped before it, saying nothing. In a moment, Ressfu walked around us, a key in hand. He glanced down at my feet before unlocking the door. He gave Govam a hard look, then headed through the opening and turned right.

Govam and Denski started forward in unison without so much as glancing at each other. I hobbled between them, my ankle pounding and sweat coating my skin despite the chill.

Torches lined these walls, few and far between, but they cast enough light for me to see without my dragon's intervention. I had no idea why torches had taken the place of the electrical or magical light in the previous area. At a crossroads we turned right, only to reach another one, where we turned left. I noticed subtle variations in the walls that would help me find my way back, and my dragon cataloged the various smells. After one more turn, the hall ended at a giant skull, the top of its head dusting the ceiling and its chin resting on the ground. Its cheekbones spanned the width of the hallway, and its eyes glowed a sparkling red. Each tooth was pointed in its slightly ajar mouth, giving it a more sinister look and feel.

Ressfu walked right toward it. Once there, he reached to the side and opened it like a door. I belatedly realized it was flat, only giving the illusion of protruding into the hallway.

"Cool," I said softly as we passed through.

The demons beside me acted like they hadn't heard.

On the other side, the smell intensified until it felt like I was swimming through it. The pungent aroma was equal parts musty and acidic, perfumed with sweat and death and decay. Its thickness coated my tongue and made my eyes water. My dragon recoiled within me, our senses blasted.

An orange glow filled the hall up ahead before it opened up into a large room. A suspension bridge spanned a chasm full of what looked like molten lava, glowing oranges and yellows and reds oozing and shifting. No heat rose, but the air shimmered with it.

"She'll need to be carried," Denski said as we stopped before the bridge.

Ressfu continued across, holding the chains on either side and making the bridge swing slightly with his movements. His clothing rippled with the air currents.

"I'll do it," Govam said. When Denski stepped away, Govam addressed me in a low voice. "Now, dragon, I know that you are hurting, but you have been on your best behavior. Now is not the time to act up. There is nowhere you can go. If you try, you won't get far. Killing us both on that bridge will serve no purpose. You'd best stick with good behavior. Do you understand what I'm saying?"

What does he think we're going to do, pitch us both into the demon lava, or whatever that stuff is? my dragon asked.

Seems like it. Are the other dragons here so desperate that they try to end their suffering in any way possible?

The thought filled me with sadness, but I pushed the emotion away. If they were desperate, I'd use that to help get us all out of here.

I nodded at Govam, then waited as he studied me for a moment. When he was apparently satisfied I was telling the truth, he matched my nod.

"How would you like to be carried?" he asked me.

I quirked an eyebrow. "Comfortably?"

His brow furrowed.

"Govam, what is the hold-up?" a female demon said at his back.

Ressfu stepped off the bridge on the other side of the chasm and looked back.

Still Govam waited, looking at me.

"Piggyback, then," I said.

Without a word, he turned and bent, flaring his arms behind him so that I could climb on. Denski stepped up to help me, and Govam curled his arms around my knees and straightened.

"I'm right behind you," Denski said, and I felt his hands grip my shirt at the center of my back.

"How many people have tried to pitch over the edge to their death—"

I barely finished getting those words out before a wave of vicious anxiety swept over me. Raw terror gripped my heart as he stepped out onto the bridge. A cold sweat ran over me, and suddenly I was desperate to escape. To run. To fling myself off the bridge and end it all.

CHAPTER 3

FINLEY

*S*HIT HAS GONE *sideways, folks,* I said to the invisible audience, clutching Govam with all my strength. *Something is amiss with this chasm.*

It's magic, my dragon thought.

No shit, huh? You don't think I just suddenly went batshit crazy?

Suddenly? No. You've always been batshit crazy, or you wouldn't speak to an imaginary audience...

I squeezed my eyes shut, battered with more terror. Horrible thoughts swelled and tried to take over my motor skills. Then I peeled my eyes open and forced myself to loosen the fists clutching his shirt. I had to get used to this. I had to push on in spite of the feelings battering me. To escape, I might have to cross this bridge again, which meant I had to withstand its magic.

"What's happening?" Govam asked, slowing. I thought I heard a tinge of panic in his tone. "She's loosening her hold."

"I don't see any change from back here," Denski replied.

"Does this not affect you guys?" I asked, forcing myself to look over his shoulder. A wave of vertigo made my head spin. The urge to fling myself toward that glowing, shifting orange nearly undid me.

"No. Demons are not affected, or how would we make the trip?" Denski answered.

"With iron will, perseverance, and practice?" I gritted my teeth. The world spun around me, Govam's body the only thing that felt solid. The good news was that I no longer registered any of my pain. That was a blessing, such as it was.

Denski huffed. "What do you take us for?"

"She's a dragon," Govam said. "They aren't right in the head. They think danger is a challenge. They like facing it."

Not entirely accurate, but it made me sound like a badass, so sure, why not.

Screaming sounded behind us, loud and high. I turned to look, my vision wavering. Fear liquifying my courage and making it drain away little by little.

Jedrek shoved and thrashed between the demons preventing him from climbing over the chain railing at the side. Another demon tried to crowd in, grabbing him and yanking him back.

"Just knock the idiot out and carry him," Denski grumbled, facing front again.

"They should," Govam agreed softly, nearly at the end now.

A moment later, the screaming cut off. They'd done exactly what Denski said.

I blinked my watery eyes and looked away, hating all of this. Hating my fear and the stink and the magically induced desperation to fall to my death and end it all. I breathed deeply, filling my lungs with oxygen.

The second Govam crossed the threshold onto solid ground,

the clenching fear dried up. The swimming, wobbling vision straightened out. Courage surged within me, and I had a mad desire to fight. To cradle Govam's head like a lover and crack his neck. It would be so easy. Effortless, really. They hadn't cared about killing Luru; would they care about losing another demon? Ressfu might even thank me. He'd been waiting for us with what was clearly annoyance.

"Get her off," Govam shouted suddenly, jerking backward. "Quick, get her off, *get her off!*"

Denski ripped me backward, throwing me to the ground. My butt hit stone, and I just barely kept from rolling onto the Bridge of Doom. The heel of my bad leg hit the ground and pain vibrated up, not quite so bad as before. I did benefit from faster healing, even if it didn't produce miracles.

Govam turned and looked down at me, thunder clouding his expression. He didn't say a word. He didn't have to. He'd somehow known what I was thinking.

"I wasn't going to do it," I said quickly. Defensively.

My dragon snickered.

It might be true! I told her. I honestly wasn't sure.

I struggled to get up. "I realize there'd be no point, even if no one cared."

He leaned down, wrapped his fingers around my upper arm, and hoisted me to my feet. Denski resumed his place by my side, and they walked me away from the mouth of the bridge. The others followed us, bringing Jedrek across.

"Come on. Time's wasting." Ressfu scanned the demons before turning and continuing down another hall.

"How'd you know?" I asked Govam softly. I took notice of a few pockmarks in the wall before we turned right.

He didn't comment.

We left the tunnels, and the chamber opened up around us. The smell intensified, if that were possible. I felt the breath leave me as I took in my surroundings.

Stone lined the floor like it had in the halls, but the ceiling was much higher, spanning the height of two or so levels. A main walkway led down the center of the space, and steps on either side led up to raised platforms. The steps broke around large, bulky stone columns that were amazing to look at and reached up to the smooth stone ceiling. Multiple arches were embedded in the walls in the raised areas, closed off with bars. Cells. But I didn't see any faces pressed against the bars, looking out. No hands gripping metal.

"It looks like dwarfs built this," I said in a hush.

Ressfu looked around as though expecting someone. He raised an irritated hand to keep us put before walking briskly down the center path.

I glanced at Govam, stoic at my side. "Not much of a talker, huh?"

He pretended not to hear me. Wondering if he'd crack, I decided to harass him a little. "Are you a screamer? You pop a nut and sing out your praise of the mighty orgasm?"

Almost as one, Govam and Denski turned their heads toward me slowly, wearing identical expressions of confused bewilderment.

"No one's ever asked you that before?" I gingerly touched the ground with my bad foot, testing it. Better, but still not good enough to walk on. "Probably because they've already heard you screaming. I bet you really get into it, huh? You act all calm and stoic now, but when you get your hump on, you're singing soprano. I've seen your type before."

Govam tilted his head to the side as though suddenly noticing a strange, brightly colored, possibly poisonous bug. I turned to Denski, also staring at me with a tilted head.

I lifted my eyebrows and nodded knowingly. "You know what I'm saying."

A crooked smile worked up his greenish skin, revealing slightly pointed teeth I hadn't noticed before. A smile from a lighthearted jest was a good sign. It meant they weren't all monsters—not all the time, at least. I didn't know if that would help me, but the more information, the better.

"Well, well, well."

The booming voice filled the space, drawing my attention. A slim demon sauntered down the center aisle, a white silk robe hanging off his bony shoulders.

"What have we here?" His voice was singsong. From the way he was moseying in, moving slowly, it was clear he had some power in this place. The message was clear: he wouldn't be rushed.

Maybe I should be freaked out, but I couldn't get over the sight of him. His face was discolored, like someone had tried to tie-dye his skin, fucked up, dabbed at it, and left it in a warm, moist place. I assumed it wasn't actually mold growing out of the side of his lips and down his neck, but I couldn't be too sure.

He got within five feet of me, and suddenly his entire body tensed like he'd had a spasm. He put two thin fingers to his nose and backed up a step.

His tone changed immediately. "What is this?" Alarm bled through each syllable.

"We got two, but they need to share a cell," Ressfu said. "A dragon and a... Some other kind of shifter. No one knows what, but it's a weaker beast, at any rate. If he cooperates, you need to go easy on him—his highness's orders. He'll be a pet in the high court. They both will."

"I know my role," the newcomer said tersely. He hadn't moved his eyes from me. "What is *this*?" He pointed at me.

"The dra-gon," Ressfu bit out slowly.

"It's an alpha's mate," Govam said in a bland tone.

"We have alphas, and we have mates, and *none* of them smell like that," the newcomer replied.

"You have powerful dragons. You don't have alphas," Govam said. "Not alphas like this one."

"She was claimed by the dragon prince," Ressfu said quickly, clearly trying to reclaim control of the conversation.

The newcomer blew out a breath, taking me in. This wasn't sexual. He was sizing me up. Assessing me. His gaze zipped down my body and stuck to the sword.

"I applaud you all for your…bravery, but we are not fools in the dungeon," the newcomer said, his tone sickly sweet. It made me feel like insects were crawling across my skin. "Remove the sword."

"Now, now, first officer," Sonassa said from somewhere behind me. "Is his highness not keeping you in high comfort? You have to steal from prisoners now? Surely that is beneath you."

"Not from prisoners, from *us*," Ressfu said. "If we take it off, we keep it."

Govam's voice cut through the muttering of those behind us. "His highness said to leave it on."

Ressfu waved him away. "Yeah, yeah, I know." He glared at the first officer. "She keeps it. The king's orders."

A crease formed between the first officer's eyebrows. "Is that so? And I assume he will provide us with the needed protections when she is to be moved to the whipping post?"

The whipping post? my dragon thought softly.

Neither of us liked the sound of that.

Govam's tone was disinterested. "We don't answer for his highness. He wants her to keep the sword. That's all I know."

"She doesn't know how to use it," Ressfu said. "He's mocking her by allowing her—"

"His highness's reasons are his own." Govam didn't take his eyes off the first officer. "And those reasons have clearly not been passed on to the dungeons. Who is to say what his real intentions are?" That sounded almost like a threat. It was clear the first officer and Govam did not like each other. "She keeps the sword."

"For now," the first officer said, matching Govam's stare.

Govam didn't comment.

"Fine." The first officer turned his attention to Jedrek, still out cold and being carried. "What of that thing? Is he also armed?"

"No," Ressfu said, his gaze darting to Govam and then away. "He's no trouble."

"Hmm." The first officer took a step back and waved his hand. Four identical figures in red robes strode forward from behind him, walking down the center of the columns, two holding thin red clubs and the other two armed with whips. They had the same sickly, moldy appearance as the first officer and nearly the same facial features, only with thinner, flatter noses. It was like the first officer had attempted to duplicate himself, hadn't gotten it exactly right, but thought it passable enough to continue using the same mold.

"Remember, they need to be put in a cell together." Ressfu motioned for Govam to bring me forward. "Don't mar her face or arms, and don't cut anything off. She might end up being a pet for his highness eventually. They need to get the smell off first, though."

"Keep her pretty for parties, yes." That horrible smile was still on the first officer's face. "There's a lot we can hide with clothes. But they won't get that smell off." He giggled to himself, touching slim fingers to his plump lips. "How silly to even think it. Once a shifter claims its mate, the stink is forever. Usually it's tolerable, but this… Well, it'll take a nose plug to be with her for any length of time. I doubt his highness will ever take her as a pet."

"Since when did you become an expert?" Ressfu curled his lip at the first officer.

Two of the red-robed demons took me from Denski and Govam, pulling me to the side and ripping my arms up and away from my sword. When I hobbled and nearly fell, they dragged me.

"Out of all of us, who is with them the most?" the first officer asked with a simpering smile. "Who knows how far one can go before they break?"

Ressfu narrowed his eyes. "Torturing them doesn't make you an expert."

"He'd need brains to be an expert on anything," Govam murmured.

The first officer's smile stretched wider as he took Govam in. "I noticed you are not in charge for once, captain. Instead, this fool of a guard is taking the lead. Interesting." His voice took on a boyishness that was off-putting in such a foul-looking creature. "What did you do to deserve this level of punishment? Not a large crime. No, no, not a large crime. That would get you in my stocks or licked by my whips. This is just a grievance, nothing more. An infraction." His wide-set yellow-green eyes slid to Denski. "And your second-in-command is with you. Hmm. I am *dying* with curiosity. Pay attention, Ressfu—the captain here spends nearly as much quality time with dragons as I do shifters in general. Maybe it is *him* the king should be asking for advice."

The first officer was obviously trying to get a rise out of Govam, but no such luck. Govam looked on placidly, ignoring him as he did me. As he did almost everyone, it seemed.

"Yes, well." The first officer motioned for Jedrek to be brought forward and set on the ground.

"Remember, he's a pet." Ressfu pointed at the unconscious body. "Don't drag him on his face or anything. I'm going to put in my report that I dropped him off in perfect health."

"You dropped him off unconscious and with a bruised face." The first officer entwined his spindly fingers and rested them on his protruding girth. "I know how to do my job. Do you?"

Ressfu scowled. "C'mon," he said to the room at large, turning. "We're done here."

The demons peeled away, Govam with one last glance at me before he left. As they moved back the way they'd come, one demon was left standing her ground, looking at me. She wore her human glamor, a beautiful redhead with full red lips and a little dot of a nose. A sparkling pink dress hugged her generous curves and accentuated her perfect display of cleavage.

She didn't utter a word. Just winked, turned, and sauntered away.

The sass conveyed by those few simple movements curled under my clothes and crawled across my skin. A succubus—she had to be. I wondered what she wanted with me.

The first officer watched her leave. Afterward, he regarded me with a slightly quizzical look that quickly turned to deviousness and menace.

"Welcome, dragon. Your captors have been fooled, haven't they? That potent scent isn't from the alpha alone. It is your power mixed together." He closed his eyes and smiled serenely. "It will be so sweet to taste. And what a delicious irony. I will use your pain and suffering to fuel my creatures and send them against your dragon prince. I'll be using his mate's own power against him, as it were."

So these were the demons that made the twisted creatures in the wood. Since they looked like the kind of thing you'd find in the back of an ice chest after two years of moldering, it fit.

When his eyes opened, he beheld me again. "You are quite young. Prettier than most. Softer. I'll have to be a bit more delicate with you so it lasts longer."

The first officer made a signal with his hand and turned, walking toward the far wall.

Four red-robed minions who hadn't been there a second ago stepped out from the sides. It was like they'd appeared from thin air. Literally. They didn't move forward, just waited and stared, letting us know they were there. Two of the other four yanked me forward, forcing me to step on my bad ankle before I could get the other in front of me. I limped, but the pain didn't vibrate like before, thank the goddess.

"I would like to get my hands on Ressfu," the first officer murmured as we walked, Jedrek hauled up and all but dragged with us. "I would like to torture him to death. The guards' bodies make the best creatures. I will watch with glee as he transforms into a hideous little creature that the dragon king could kill in his sleep."

So apparently they used dead people to make their creatures.

No wonder no one had cared much about Luru's fate. He'd still be useful down here, even in death.

I glanced around with raised eyebrows. The minions didn't seem to be listening. Was this for my benefit?

"They are all so stupid." The first officer reached a set of wide stone stairs that curved down into the darkness. He trailed his fingers along the wall as he descended. "You must've seen that, dragon."

Ah. For my sake, then.

"And stupid demons do stupid things and get in all kinds of trouble. Do enough stupid things, and the demon king will be happy to hand them over to me. Most of them are worth more as building blocks for my creations than they are as guards, surely."

We kept spiraling down at the next landing, and the stairwell slimmed down until the gangly minion to my right had to escort me solo. The stairs stopped at the third sub-level, the ceiling hanging low and dampness soaking the stone walls around us. There was no grandiosity down here. No columns or impressive stonework. It was exactly the kind of dungeon I'd envisioned.

The first officer stopped at the bottom of the steps and pushed his finger against the stone at his side. A click preceded a flood of light. It turned on with a loud buzz, raining down from the ceiling.

I couldn't help smiling. I was very young when the lights essentially went out in my kingdom. This felt like...a present. This place hadn't been trapped by a curse and cut off from the world. Even though very few modern conveniences could be found in this shitshow dungeon, the demons had access to them.

I didn't, of course. Not down here. Old stone and caked dirt covered the surfaces, and the bars were attached to the walls with metal contraptions that looked centuries old. Rustic old keys were clearly used in the large keyholes at the side of each cell.

The first officer turned to me with a smile that didn't need an explanation, and the minion at my side shoved me, forcing me to stumble down two steps and brace myself against the rough wall. The minion was on me in a moment, grabbing me and flinging me farther into the room. Lights and stone swirled in my vision as I stubbed my toe and went down, skidding my palms against the floor.

I knew from being in Nyfain's castle that demons fed off their victims—off their fear or desire or sadness. The first officer had mentioned power. He was probably trying to get a rise out of me. Maybe he even wanted me to fight back. Hell, maybe he was just being a bully. Whatever the reason, the end result was the same.

I had to take it.

There was no point in fighting back. Not here. Not on my first day when I had zero knowledge of this place. They had weapons they were capable of using, larger numbers, and they were blocking the exits. They'd stacked the odds, and only a fool wouldn't realize it.

Thuds and a grunt caught my attention, and I looked back over my shoulder to see Jedrek had been dropped off the last step. He lay crumpled on the ground, groaning and slowly flailing like a turtle on its back. I doubted it was a very pleasant way to wake up.

"Hmm," the first officer said, stepping in front of Jedrek and watching me. "Most unusual for a *dragon*."

He'd amplified his voice, and it boomed unpleasantly across the space.

Movement in front of me caught my eye. Thick forearms reached through the bars about halfway down the cell row. The hands came together and the fingers entwined, as though the owner was waiting patiently.

More limbs or hands or fingers threaded through the bars of the cells lining each side. Still, I didn't see any faces pressed against the metal. No noses peeked out, trying to see what was happening. The lack of curiosity suggested this wasn't an abnormal occurrence. That or maybe they had learned the art of patience in this miserable place. Maybe both.

A *crack* sounded right before a blinding white light of pain exploded in one single point against my back.

"Holy—What the fuck!" I skittered forward as the pain seemed to drip down into my body and set my blood to vibrating uncomfortably. Standing, I turned on my good leg and watched the world crystallize around me as my survival reflex kicked in.

One of the minions stood in the center of the space, whip handle in hand. My other escort stood behind the first with a polished red club.

The others stood back, watching. Waiting. Ready to step in if need be. Jedrek lay forgotten at their feet.

I wondered if there were more at the top of the stairs, waiting out of sight—and if they had other magic that would help them if I got through their little friends.

I wondered if I could get through them all.

Rush them, my dragon urged. Fire bled through me. *Take that fucking whip and strangle him with it.*

Fuck, I wanted to. I wanted to so badly.

Then what? I asked myself as well as my dragon. Hell, I'd ask the invisible audience if they'd actually answer. *They know what they're doing, these demons. It's obvious. They didn't mess with me upstairs, they did it down here, where I don't have as much space.*

Where the exit's not accessible. I'll get through a couple, but they'll inevitably take me down, and then they'll be on their guard around me.

Are you blind or something? Look at them. They are already on their guard around you. Give them something to fear.

I stood in indecision. Power pumped through me.

Jedrek lay at their feet, curled up, looking my way.

I need to be Jedrek, I thought, licking my lips. The minions watched, waiting for me to make the first move. *I need to be out of sight when I'm in plain view. To do that, I need to appear weak.*

Even if you appear weak, you don't smell weak. You don't feel weak. We are the mate of the golden dragon prince. Do him proud.

Fire ripped through me as the gangly minion's arm rose. The tip of the whip slid across the ground and then went airborne.

The pain of the last strike was a fresh memory. My rage was a palpable thing.

My brain said, *Take it.*

My logic said, *Play dead, be weak.*

My body said, *Fuck this shit.*

I threw up my forearm without meaning to. The slap of the whip flayed my skin as it struck and then wrapped around, stinging my arm. It should've hurt more. This situation should've hurt a lot more.

On instinct or maybe impulse, I twisted my arm and grabbed the whip, yanking it away.

So much for seeming weak.

The first officer's eyes gleamed, like maybe he'd expected me to do that. Like he'd *desired* it.

"Fuck," I said to no one in particular.

"You're in the stink now, lady," one of the prisoners on my left said, humor in his voice.

"What happened?" a woman called.

"She took the whip," another said.

"Who hasn't?" a man at the end mumbled.

"Fuck," I said again.

"Don't bother trying to kill them all and run," the first guy said. "Those fuckers pop out of thin air and make sure you don't get far. It's a real ball shriveler when they haul you back."

"She has a sword, though," someone said.

"Why isn't she using the sword?" another asked.

A deep baritone voice echoed through the space. "Give the whip to me." The man who'd spoken was behind me, but I didn't dare tear my eyes away from the minions for long enough to look. The feel of his command whispered over my body. "Let me spare you," he continued. "Let me take their wrath."

His power and authority tugged at me. His proposal stopped me short for a moment, the idea of sparing myself a sweet one after the hard journey to get here. But I hadn't come all this way to shirk my duties. Besides, he was obviously behind bars. How would he actually help me?

Fight, my dragon thought. *Let the others see that you have no fear. They'll respect you more for it. Show them your worth. The dragon is ready to supply us with all the power we need.*

As if her words had summoned it, a delicious hum rose through my middle. Heat and love and a soft devotion crept through my tired limbs and aching joints. Pride and strength straightened my back.

My lungs tightened as my heart squeezed.

Nyfain. He was lending me his support through the bond. He

was by my side even from all that distance.

I took a deep breath as my eyes filled with tears.

"Fuck it, let's do this." I ran-hobbled forward.

The minion with the club stepped around his buddy and lifted the instrument into the air. I punched forward, connecting with his throat and making him bend. I grabbed the club as the other raked my side with his claws.

"Sure would be fucking great if I could use this goddess-damned sword, huh?" I said in a series of grunts as I slapped the club against Mr. Claws's head. I went back to the first and knocked him in the head too.

"Incoming," one of the prisoners yelled.

The other two minions ran forward, and I grabbed one of them and ripped him closer. Mr. Claws raked forward, scoring the front of the demon I'd grabbed. I looped my arms around my demon shield, pulling the club against his neck. Mr. Claws tried to get at me around the one I held, and I turned, blocking the way again.

"He's dead," a prisoner called.

Helpful.

I dropped him, grabbed Mr. Claws, and pulled him close while spearing forward with my will, a physical manifestation of my power. It sliced right through his gut, opening a gash and making him scream.

Feet thudded against stone. A stream of red descended the stairs, whips and clubs in hand. They'd brought in reinforcements.

Fuck, my dragon thought.

I had to agree.

The demon horde reached me. A whip crack shot blinding pain through me as a club crashed down on my shoulder. More came with it, weapons and claws and fists. I could strike out with my will, but against all of this, I wouldn't get far.

I took what they had to offer without a sound. I did not cry or call out. As blow after blow fell, I wrapped myself in the feeling of Nyfain through the bond—in his strength and power and comfort. In my love for him, which I'd never gotten to express. In my thankfulness for our time together. I ignored all that was happening around me and took solace in the memory of his muscled arms wrapped around me. With him for support, I was strong enough to endure anything.

When the demons were satisfied, they dragged me to a cell at the end of the room. Jedrek was thrown in with me a moment later. Someone said something that was likely a taunt. I couldn't say. I ignored it. As one, they receded whence they had come, clicking out the light before trekking up the stairs.

Darkness blanketed my dank, dirty new home.

"This is a nightmare," Jedrek said with a tremor in his voice.

I couldn't help the laughter that bubbled up. I choked on it, on blood maybe, and let more come anyway.

Into the silence I said, "Cheers! Now get me a drink."

CHAPTER 4

HADRIEL

I FLEXED MY fingers and then wiggled them around, adjusting the positioning of my dick in my annoyingly tight black trousers. Fucking Cecil and his shitty work whenever I needed something. He was the worst seamster in the known world. When it came to my stuff, anyway. And he was the only one who worked on my stuff because of some bullshit deal he made with the sweeter, easier-to-work-with seamstress.

"Do you know what I would love?" I whispered to Leala, who was waiting beside me at the closed door to what had been Finley's tower. I really hoped the master couldn't hear me. My volume control was honestly the shits at this point in my tenure in the sex-demon-filled castle. "I would love a pair of jeans again. I used to love wearing jeans. I think the master is the only one with some left."

"I'd rather electricity or proper coffee. But sure, jeans would be great." She paused for a moment, waiting for me but not pushing. Neither of us wanted to do this. "I never wore jeans."

"That's because you're proper. I wore jeans. Horseshit didn't stick to jeans like other pants."

"What about leather?"

"I didn't get leather, are you kidding? I got jeans, and I got ignored." I puffed out a breath and thought about turning the door handle. "Fuck, why am I here? I'm a stable handle. I shouldn't be trying to talk to the fucking prince!"

"Stable *handle*? Are you still drunk?"

"*Still* drunk? I didn't drink earlier tonight. I stayed in the library and fretted. That's what I do now. I fret. That's *all* I've been doing for the last three days. But yes, I'm a little drunk. I took a couple swigs to bolster my courage, and then I got carried away." I pulled my hand away from the doorknob. "Why? Do you think it's noticeable?"

She rolled her eyes, which wasn't a particularly helpful response. Would the dragon pull my head off? He'd been unhinged since the demon king took Finley away. More so than usual. He wasn't safe to be around.

"You're the butler," she whispered.

I stared at her for a solid beat because fuck her, that wasn't helpful either.

"But will the dragon pull my head off!"

"*Shh!*" she said.

Right, yes, that was too loud. He probably heard that.

I stepped away from the door and took a deep breath. Finley always said oxygen helped the brain. She'd take deep breaths when facing danger.

I took another deep breath.

It wasn't fucking helping.

"Right, okay, let's go over this again." I rolled my neck. "I'm going to go in there and tell him that he needs to get his head out of his ass."

"But respectfully."

"Sure, yeah. And then I'm going to tell him that Finley left him with a job to do, and he needs to do that job or what was the point of her leaving..."

"Except don't mention her leaving."

"Because he might explode into a rage and kill me, right. And I'm going to..." I stalled because that was about as far as I'd gotten in previous practice sessions before I ran out of courage. "Why the fuck does this fall to me? Have I asked that yet?"

"You're doing this because Finley made you promise to keep the master on track," Leala said. "He's lost his way. You need to live up to your end of the bargain so that he can live up to his."

"Right, yeah. The thing is, I always felt a helluva lot more courageous when she was around. The woman gives literally no fucks about what people think. Zero fucks. It's inspiring. Without her, I remember that I am a sad-sack, mediocre butler who used to get picked on by dragons."

"That was only because of your smart mouth."

"No, it wasn't only because of my smart mouth! It was because they have a tendency for random acts of rage."

"When someone mouths off, yeah."

I took a deep breath, hoping this one might be the one that helped.

It wasn't.

"Fuck it. If I'm going to die, I'm going to die." I stepped forward, grabbed the handle, nearly lost my nerve, but then found myself walking into the tower room.

The familiarity of it was like a gut punch. Finley hadn't been at the castle all that long. Months compared to the years that I'd been cooped up here. But in that short time, she'd left a mark. I *missed* Finley. I missed our banter. I missed her passion for plants and her company. Everyone who knew her felt her absence. This room had utterly been claimed by her. Her favorite weapon—a dagger—lay on the bedside table. Slinky but plain dresses peeked out of the half-open wardrobe. Her spicy smell permeated the air.

I might've just imagined the last one. I still didn't have access to my animal. Actually, the master hadn't pulled out *any* of our animals. He was supposed to be preparing our kingdom for war, curing the people who still needed it and reuniting all of us with our animals, but none of that had happened. He'd shut down instead. Which was why I was here. He needed to get moving, and apparently I needed to be the kick in his ass.

He sat nude on the bed, facing the window as the sun crept over the horizon. A gash marred his back and dried blood crusted against his skin. He hadn't bothered cleaning himself up after battling in the Royal Wood the previous night, and I doubted he was worried about tending his wounds so they wouldn't scar. He'd started doing that when Finley came, I thought because he wanted to stop adding to his collection of scars for her sake, but it was obvious he didn't think she was coming back. He didn't *want* her back. He wanted, above all, for her to be happy, and for some fucking reason, he didn't believe he had anything to offer her. He was an incredibly powerful alpha prince, hot as all hell, with a stellar body, had the sort of rage she liked (she was insane), gave her mighty orgasms (quite loud ones, too), and he didn't think he had anything to offer. He was a real dipshit when it came to women, that much was clear.

He was bent over with his head in his hands, his fingers pushed up through his unruly dark brown hair. The force of his power and status shoved at me, uncomfortably strong, and I didn't even have the primal kick of my wolf to tell me that I should watch myself because a big ol' alpha was in the room.

Releasing the suppression magic had given him access to his incredible reserves of power, even if it hadn't given him his wings back. Not yet, anyway. A bunch of people surmised that when the curse was broken, life would go back to the way it had been, and not just in terms of electricity and running water and all that modern goodness. They believed anything that had been damaged because of the curse would be fixed.

I wasn't so sure. If the curse was broken, would all my memories of shame-fucking demons go away? Somehow I doubted it.

I sidestepped a little closer. And a little closer still.

"Sir." I cleared my throat. "Sir, might I have a word?"

"No. Leave."

His blast of power stung my eyes, but a command hadn't ridden his words. He clearly didn't want to be alone. Fuck. I wasn't sure I was ready for this. I should've had another drink.

I inched a bit closer.

"Yes, sir. Only, I was tasked by…" I pursed my lips because I didn't know how to do this without saying her name and setting him off. "I was tasked by…the woman who is sacrificing herself for us—"

The blast of power made me yelp this time. I looked back at Leala, haunting the doorway with a worried expression. She gave me a thumbs-up, like that might help.

I took a deep breath, like *that* might help.

"She was very clear, sir," I said, inching ever closer. Trying to will myself enough courage to stand in front of him. I didn't really *want* his full focus, but Finley would expect results, and I didn't want to let her down. I'd already let her down by not finding a way to go with her. "You need to pull the animals out of suppression. Only you can do it. There isn't anyone else strong enough. Not with her gone and your court cleared out."

"They're hurting her," he said, his voice gruff and filled with enough misery to prick my eyes with tears. "She must've arrived there recently because the type of pain has changed. It has increased tenfold. She's hanging on to my power with everything she has just to stay afloat. The pain is drowning her. I can feel it. I shouldn't have let her go."

My stomach twisted, and my heart ached for what she must be going through. But she'd known it was going to suck. She'd chosen this path, and regardless of what she was going through now, I knew she'd choose it again if given the chance. She was not a woman who took the easy way out, not when people were counting on her. He couldn't have kept her from going.

He wouldn't want to hear any of that, though. He was a man of action, and right now he probably felt as helpless as I did. He needed a way to support her.

"Okay, then…" I inched closer, level with him now and working my way in front of him. "So what can you do to help her? Obviously you can't go to her, not with the curse's magic forcing you to stay within the kingdom's borders. You can't fight her battles. So what can you do *with the resources you have* to make things easier for her?"

He dropped his hands, hunched over, and shook his head, at a loss.

I glanced back at Leala and lifted my eyebrows. *Need a little help* here, I thought.

"Do you know what is very confusing for people?" Leala said, walking into the room like she was as comfortable as could be. How the fuck did she manage it? "My kink."

My mouth dropped open.

"Love, it's not really the time," I said through my teeth.

"I like pain," she continued, coming to stand right beside me. She wrung her hands, her knuckles white. "I get off on it. Most people do not understand that. It makes them incredibly uncomfortable."

A blast of power had Leala and I both hunching for a moment. Alphas at full power were no joke.

"She is not you," he said.

"No, but she *could* be." She held out a hand, indicating the master for some reason. "Right now she is feeling your misery, right? It is making her pain worse, I should think. All due respect, sir, but it is probably acting like a weight on her ankle, pulling her down deeper. It's not helping. Instead…maybe put aside how much it pains you to feel what she's going through and feed her uplifting emotions. Feed her your love and support—"

"I'm doing that. I'm trying to ease her suffering as best I can."

"Okay then…" Leala stalled for a moment, shooting me an anxious look.

"Pleasure," I blurted. "Not just love and support, but downright pleasure. Right, Leala? Isn't that where you were going with that?"

"Yes." Leala smiled. "Yes! Feed her pleasure. Make her pain mix with pleasure, and it won't be as gruesome for her."

I squinted as I nodded. "It'll probably be a mind-fuck for her at first, but if she can feel it's you—whom she trusts more than anyone in the world—yeah, I can see that working, sir. It's worth a shot at any rate, right? It'll dull the pain somewhat. And it'll help her think about you, which is to think about home…"

The master's face came up slowly, his eyes bleary and soaked with guilt and misery. He focused in on Leala, and I'd be damned if she didn't stand straight and tall before him. That woman was majestic.

Suddenly, though, he let out a breath and sagged, bracing his hands on the bed.

"It's over," he said softly, his deep, gravelly voice thick. "She has passed out."

"I've passed out before, sir," Leala quipped. "I've gone so hard with it that I have passed out from pain…while still deriving pleasure from it. I think you can help her, sir. I really do. But you'll have to be strong, sir. You'll have to completely shove away your own pain so that you can give her only your purest pleasure."

Ooh, she was good. She was giving him a way to help *and* making him feel like he was powerful and strong for going for it. Great goddess and her kinky men, she was the most valuable player in this little meeting of minds.

He looked up again, his fierce golden eyes taking her in. I could barely remember the blue they'd been before the curse— before he'd forced a shift and his retinas retained the original color of his dragon's scales, which had been burned black.

He nodded once, curtly. He'd do it. Hopefully he'd succeed, and it would help both he and Finley.

Leala nudged me with her elbow. Whoops, shit, my turn.

"And the other way you can help is to prepare an arsenal for when she finds her way back here," I said quickly. "She asked me to make sure you were freeing the shifters. That you were monitoring the efforts to cure your kingdom of the sickness unleashed by the curse. She made a deal with the insufferable demon king so that you—"

"Yes, yes, I heard you outside the door." He stood, and I realized I'd gotten much too close. The prince absolutely loomed over me. "I hope that she does not come back—for her sake—but I will honor her wishes. Of course I will—looking after my people is my duty."

"Yes, sir." I rammed Leala with my shoulder so she'd get moving and we could get some breathing room. "Absolutely, sir. Perfect. She would be proud of that."

"You will come with me. Get some rest. We'll start at noon." He rolled his shoulders, and power oozed from his mighty frame. "And every time they hurt her, I will brutally kill one of their demons. I will not suffer her ill treatment without some sort of recourse."

I wasn't sure whether that was a good idea—I'd need to think on it—but it was certainly a *satisfying* idea. I wanted to watch. Those demons had had it coming for too long.

It wasn't until I got outside of the door that my brain zeroed in on what else he'd said.

"Wait, *I* have to go?" I stopped and turned to look through the open door. It shut in my face, and the lock clicked.

"That went well." Leala pulled me along. "I hope that pleasure thing works. It might have been a long shot."

"*I* have to go?" I thunked down the stairs on wooden legs. "Why do I have to go?"

She clicked her tongue. "Of course you have to go. You're supposed to keep tabs on him for her."

"Which I just did. I don't actually have to look over his shoulder."

"It'll be fine. Now, you heard the master—go get some rest. He's finally about to be the prince he needs to be. We just have to hope the miss finds her way out when she needs to."

46

CHAPTER 5

FINLEY

I LAY SPRAWLED out on my back in the straw, looking up at the low ceiling pocked with shadow. The lights had been turned on earlier, waking me up, but we were all the way in the back of the long room, and there were plenty of pockets and patches of darkness around us. None large enough to hold another stairwell or some sort of escape hatch, though. This area was a dead end. The stairs I'd come down seemed to be the only way back up.

The last traces of pain slowly left my body. Last night's beating had been a real doozy. I shuddered to consider how long it would've taken me to heal naturally. Or if I would've at all.

The dungeon festered quietly around me. Until Jedrek realized I was awake.

"This place stinks." He sat in the corner with his nose crinkled. Dirt marred his face, and his hair was matted in clumps. I doubted I was much better off. "It's dirty."

"I hate you."

I figured it needed to be said.

"Nice," he mumbled.

I thought about sitting up. Didn't.

"It's supposed to be dirty, you shit-eating fuckstain."

It might take me a moment to manage rational communication that didn't involve intense profanity.

I tried again.

"It's a dungeon. What were you expecting?" I took a deep breath. Then, because I just couldn't stop myself, I added, "Fart-box licker."

Someone barked out laughter down the way.

"You never did have any class," he grumbled.

I gritted my teeth so hard I worried I'd chip a tooth.

Just kill him, my dragon thought. *You're healed enough to kill him. It won't be hard.*

"You're part of the stink," he said, pushing closer to the bars on the other side of our fifteen-by-ten cell. It seemed quite a bit larger than all the others. Then again, the others didn't house Jedrek and all his drama, so mine was probably smaller by comparison. "I can't believe the demon king allowed that...beast to claim you when you're promised to *me*."

"That *beast* is your prince and uncrowned king, and I can't believe you think a woman can be given to you like a commodity."

"Obviously they can, or are you confused as to why you're here?"

My rage was an endless red sea. It was hard to even think. To form words.

"I know why I'm here." I thought about sitting up again. Didn't. "What's absurd is *you* don't know why *you're* here. You're delusional if you think all of this happened because you wanted to mate me."

He scoffed, and I couldn't tell whether I'd gotten through to him. "There's not even a proper toilet."

I barely stopped myself from looking at the single bucket in the corner that I had not used yet. I'd never wanted to stay dehydrated so much in my life.

"What are you going to say next, that there isn't a proper bed? It's a *dungeon.* You are in a dungeon, Jedrek. Why is any of this a surprise to you? What the fuck were you expecting?"

"I cooperated!" He stood in a rush, pointing at the ground for some reason. "I made a deal, and I cooperated. I shouldn't be here. This *place* wasn't in the deal!"

"You didn't make a deal, Jedrek. You're along for the ride. The sooner you realize that, the better."

He stared at me with a red face, confusion shimmering in the depths of his brown eyes. "What are you talking about? You were promised to me. You are going to mate me. He said he'd make you mate me."

"My deal was to marry you—not mate you. Marriage is a demon custom, and it isn't forever, unlike my actual mating with the guy whose smell I wear. You're a pawn, Jedrek. Your 'deal' is superficial. *You* didn't actually agree to anything. You offered something, and he turned it into a way to torment me. That's it." I thought about it for a moment. "I have to hand it to that demon king. It is a really effective torment. You are the absolute fucking worst. Literally the worst. I hate you more than ever, if that is even possible."

He shook his head and looked away, staring at the wall beyond our cell.

A moment of blessed silence passed, and I hoped that was the end of the argument. Or his complaining. Or even just his desire to talk to me. I really didn't think I could handle any more of his chatter.

"Hey, Strange Lady…"

I frowned at the singsong male voice. Silence rode the wake of his words.

Jedrek turned his head, looking out over the dungeon. His brow furrowed.

"Strange Lady…" the man repeated.

"A man in the cell near the stairs is looking down this way," Jedrek murmured, his gaze flicking to me for a moment.

"You there, in the last cell. I'm talking to you."

Feet scraped stone. Fabric rustled. People were moving around.

I thought about sitting up. Nearly did this time.

"Yeah?" I said instead.

I angled my head that way. A few pieces of straw marred some of my vision, too near my face, but the big forearms were jutting out of the bars again, leaning on a crossbar of iron. A few bars down the way had fingers wrapped around them, people up close and looking out or listening.

"I was intently eavesdropping on your conversation just now," the man said, "and I have a few questions."

I rolled to the side and finally sat up, looking through the bars and down the way. Movement caught my eye, a figure waving to me from the other end of the chamber, somewhat spotlit from above. He sat along the bars with his shoulder leaning against one and his back to the far wall. Our gazes met, and while I couldn't tell his eye color from the distance, I could tell he had dark eyebrows over deep-set eyes and dark brown skin.

"Hello, Strange Lady," he said with a smile, and pulled his arm back in, draping it over the top of his knee. "It is both lovely and sad to see a new face."

"Are they…" I glanced at the stairs. "Are they listening?"

"Nah. They don't lurk down here." He shifted a little, his face closer to the bars now. "They come for specific purposes and leave shortly thereafter. Your hope is that they don't leave with you."

I grimaced.

He wrapped long fingers around a bar. "Let's start with that creature in the cell with you. Did I hear that—"

"Out of everything, *that's* where you are starting?" a woman cut in. She stood opposite the person with outstretched forearms. She had wide-set eyes in a tan face. Her dark hair was pulled back, and clothes hung off her thin frame—she was starved from her time in here, no doubt.

"All good things come to those who wait, Tamara," the man at the far end said. "We have to set the stage first. It makes for a more pleasing picture."

She peeled her gaze off me to turn and look his way. I was sure her expression wasn't a kind or patient one, though I doubted he could see it from his vantage point.

He stuck out a finger. "Strange Lady, did I hear you correctly that you are promised to…marry the creature sharing a cell with you?"

"Yes."

"But you are mated to another?"

"Yes. Claimed by another, promised to marry this guy. They marry instead of mate—demons, I mean. It's a different custom."

"And your mate is okay with this…arranged marriage?"

"Yes. I mean…no, but… It's complicated."

"My goodness," someone murmured.

"Yes, Jade," Mr. Eavesdropper said, "my goodness, indeed. I

am confused already. Okay, let's back up." He paused. "I don't even know where to back up to."

"Where are you from?" the woman opposite Forearms asked. Tamara, Mr. Eavesdropper had called her.

"Ah yes, good question. That's a good starting place," Mr. Eavesdropper said.

"Wyvern," I replied.

"Aaaaah. The mysterious Wyvern that no one can seem to remember."

"Vemar, we've gone over this." Tamara's frustration was evident. "It's not mysterious to most of the people in this room. Right? Three-quarters of the people in this room are from Wyvern." My heart beat faster. "It is only mysterious to those of you who have magically forgotten its existence, and you're the only one who won't admit that the place is real."

"Just last blackout you told me about a huge worm creature that eats children. Everyone played along, and you all had tales…and come to find out you were making it all up. I know I am slipping into madness, Tamara. You don't need to hurry me along."

"We were joking that other time. This is real," she said.

"How should I know the difference?" he replied.

"Will you stop with this?" A woman's disembodied voice floated along the cells. I couldn't tell where she resided. "You aren't mad. You're just too gullible. You're fun to mess with."

"No, no." His hand dropped down to the ground outside his cell. "I'm pretty sure I went mad somewhere along the way. I haven't broken yet, though. You know how I know that? Because they don't dare send me off to the fine parties without a cage. They keep me caged and chained until they want to use me, and then they goose me with magic before they get me naked. It's fun when it's happening, may the goddess slap my heinie. I feel dirty when I'm done, though, and filthy for having enjoyed it, but damn it all if it isn't fun in the moment. You all know what I mean, don't say you don't. But one day their magic won't work so well, and that is the day when they will all die. *That* is how I know I'm not broken."

"It's called shame fucking," I murmured. "There was an awful lot of shame fucking where I came from. The demons ruled the nights. Not many fine folks left by now. Mostly mediocre, if you hear them tell it…"

"Maybe you have gone mad, too," he replied in the singsong voice before I could ask about those from my kingdom.

"If you're from Wyvern, why did I never see you in the court?" Tamara asked. "I knew all the dragons of the court, especially the females. I would've noticed you."

"I wasn't in the court. I'm common. Time didn't stop for me. I was seven when the curse struck. I only recently learned I was a dragon. I've never shifted."

A shocked silence descended. Forearms pushed a little closer to the bars, and his pointed nose peeked through them.

"Then how do you know you're a dragon?" someone asked down the way. A woman, but I couldn't tell which one.

I opened my mouth to respond but froze when I heard footsteps scrape against the steps.

All other sound ceased as everyone's focus snapped to who was coming.

Shiny black boots over tight black pants came into view, their steps slow and sure. Another set came right after, descending.

"Ah, fuck," Vemar said, rolling his head. "Here come the dignity thieves."

Govam and Denski came into view. They had different clothing and seemed a little fresher, like they'd bathed and slept, but they had the same resolute or blank expressions. The same coiled form of movement.

More boots came behind them, a host of female and male demons tramping down the stairs. One woman I recognized: Sonassa, the succubus who'd taken an interest in me. Her hips swung a little more freely than the others, and a little smile curled her lush lips.

They hit the bottom of the stairs, staring straight at me. They bypassed the others, clearly one destination in mind.

"No rest for the wicked, eh, Strange Lady?" Vemar said as he watched them.

"There is a time to fight and a time to wait." I knew that voice. It belonged to the shifter who'd volunteered to take a beating in my place last night. His baritone voice washed through the dungeon like a tranquil summer's day, warm and comforting. "Pull within yourself and wait for it to end. Whatever happens, there is no judgment here. Dragons stick together. Remember that. We are with you every step of the way. We will be here when you get back. Just make sure you *do* come back."

Murmurs of assent drifted down the way as the stream of guards in black continued their approach.

Govam reached my cell, coming to a stop in front of me. He glanced down at the sword, then over at Jedrek, huddled in the corner.

"You two are coming with me," he said. "Stand."

"I'm cooperating." Jedrek put his hands out. "See?"

"Put your back to the bars, dragon," Govam barked.

In a new twist of an old tale, she will show them her back, folks. Hold your breath and hope it doesn't go wrong.

Please kill that audience, my dragon intoned.

"You too," Govam said, and Jedrek stepped over toward the door and turned, giving me a nervous look. "Hands through. Two hands through the same set of bars, up to the wrists."

My belly coiled in unease, but I took a deep breath and did as ordered. Jedrek did the same, still looking at me anxiously.

Cold metal encircled my right wrist and tightened. My left wrist got the same action, the weight of the metal dragging them down. Cuffs.

"Step forward, dragon." Govam's voice was terse, official. He was in his rightful position again, I guessed. Captain. "You too…"

"Muskrat," someone called out. "I bet he's a muskrat!"

"He ain't no dragon, that's for sure," Vemar drawled. "Dragons don't play dead. I'd go with possum."

"Yeah, possum," a few people shouted, snickering.

"My parents were wolves," Jedrek grumbled. "I should be a wolf."

Govam ignored them all. "To the door, prisoners."

Denski fit the key in the lock, his eyes on me. He twisted, popped the lock, and opened the door slowly.

"Dragon first." He put out his hand and beckoned me closer. "Turn around and walk backward toward me. If you make any wrong moves, you'll get the whip and be tied up and dragged."

"Haven't we been through this already?" I asked, but did as he'd said. "I didn't make a move the last time you transported me."

"You killed an officer," Govam said, meeting us at the door.

"Yeah, but he started it."

"He did start it," Vemar called down. "I saw the whole thing."

"Quiet there," one of the guards barked. "Quiet down!"

Denski placed a hand on each of my arms at the elbow and guided me out of the cell before handing me off to Govam. He took hold, pointing me toward the stairs.

"Now you, possum," Denski said to Jedrek, and snickers sounded within the other cells.

"Here we go." Govam pushed me forward.

Four guards stepped toward me, two on each side. Sonassa was one of them, giving me a fond smile I didn't much like. Another couple of demons walked past us, heading for Jedrek. He wasn't getting as many guards as I was. I mentioned it to my dragon.

Can you blame them? My dragon sounded smug.

It would've been much better for me if I'd played dead, too. If they thought I was weak. Fewer guards would make it easier to escape.

"Look at that, Micah," someone called. "That little dragon is getting as many guards as you do."

"That new dragon got you nervous, boss?" Vemar asked with a grin, watching Govam.

Dragons react to strength, my dragon thought. *You are show-ing yours. Getting their support and respect is worth being stuck with a few more guards.*

As I passed the other cells, I saw the truth in what she was saying. The people I passed nodded supportively or gave me a thumbs-up.

"Stay strong," Tamara said as I passed, her hand resting on a crossbar, fisted. "We're with you."

"You are not alone," Forearms said, the same baritone voice

that had asked for the whip when I first got here. His soft brown eyes tracked me solemnly. "Distance your mind from what is to come and think of returning to us. We are dragons. We will always be here for you."

"Not always, I shouldn't think," Sonassa said with a small chuckle. "You will die eventually, Mr. Dragon. I might even mourn your passing…a little. You're my favorite."

Fear bit down deep, but I kept my head high as I walked out, everyone up at the bars now, watching as we walked past. They murmured their encouragement, but worry coated their expressions. Whatever was about to happen was obviously going to be bad.

CHAPTER 6

FINLEY

T HE GUARDS WALKED us up to and then through the main floor, ignoring the officers loitering around a little seating area with couches and chairs. One of them was pouring some sort of pink liquid into a huge copper canister, steam issuing from a little pipe near the back. The other officers, who all looked the same except for the one in white, gave us funny little smiles as we passed.

"Where are you taking us?" Jedrek bleated, fear making his voice quaver.

Don't speak, my dragon thought, watchful. *We'll probably sound like him.*

She has a very good point, folks. I'm shitting my pants right about now.

Again, her failure to comment on my invisible audience habit testified to how not okay she was with what was happening. Or, more aptly, what might be about to happen.

We were steered through a doorway opposite the one we'd used to enter the dungeon. It took us into a vaulted hall. There weren't any skull doors, scary bridges, or nondescript tunnels I'd have to struggle to remember. This path was cut and dried and easy to navigate. They weren't worried about prisoners getting out this way.

We reached a set of stairs in no time and wound up three flights, which somehow dumped us onto the second floor. That...was odd. I couldn't tell if it was intentional mind-fuckery or if their shoddy building practices were to blame.

"Where are we going?" Jedrek asked again.

No answer. The suspense of all this was starting to fray his nerves. Re-fray his nerves, maybe.

We finally stepped into a large room with two rows of gleaming copper tubs along each side. Two near the front were filled halfway with steaming water. Two human-looking demons wearing long black robes waited near each of them, holding little caddies for bathing.

"Strip them," Govam barked, not letting go of me.

The guards pushed in a little closer as the human-looking demons set down their caddies and stepped up. Now I was completely surrounded, still held by Govam.

The bath workers put out their hands, and claws elongated from their fingers. They planned to rip my clothes off and toss them away.

No, not my clothes. Nyfain's.

I belatedly remembered the note tucked into my back pocket. The piece of paper holding his elegant scrawl, his words of love. His assurances that I was both a dragon and his true mate.

Power roared through me. Emotion colored my thoughts, drowning out any sort of logic.

I would not lose that note. I would not lose these clothes or this sword. I wouldn't lose any of it. They'd all die before I did.

My dragon pumped more power into me. Power. Rage. *Action!*

"Freeze!" I could hear the panic in Govam's voice. "Everyone freeze! Dragon—Finley—give me a chance to figure this out."

"No, no, no, no, no!" Jedrek bucked and then kicked, trying to get out of his captors' hands while his bathing attendants waited in front of him, their claws out and ready. "No! I don't want this! *No!*"

He threw his body one way, then another, before arching back into Denski, trying to wiggle free.

"Take him down!" Govam yelled.

A guard to Jedrek's side pulled a foot-long rod from a holster. Flicking his wrist, he elongated it into a three-foot-long gleaming stick. The other guard did the same, advancing quickly, Denski still holding on. Their blows were fast and brutal, hitting Jedrek's sides and back, avoiding his head.

He cried out, quickly shrinking to get away.

"That's enough," Govam said, pushing me to the right to give them some room.

A last blow landed, and Denski let go, dropping Jedrek to the floor. Jedrek groaned and shuddered, shaking with barely held-in sobs.

"He is definitely not a dragon," Denski said, crossing his arms over his chest before giving Jedrek a prod with the toe of his boot.

Jedrek cried out and scooted away, shaking.

My chest constricted, pity washing away my dislike of him.

"He doesn't need all that," I said. "Don't react to him the way you would to me. He doesn't pose the same sort of threat. You know he doesn't."

"This is how we react to everyone," Govam said. "With drag-ons, it often escalates." He paused, his hands still tight on my arms. "Is this going to escalate?"

"I don't know." It was an honest answer.

"Denski."

Denski uncrossed his arms and stepped behind me to take Govam's place. His fingers curled delicately around my elbows, suggesting he wasn't a total idiot.

Govam stepped in front of me, his dusky gray stare digging into my eyes.

"Is that not a very dangerous place for you to be?" I couldn't help but ask, watching his hands.

He held them up and out, fingers spread. "Usually, yes. Very." His head tilted to the side. "But you're not like most dragons, are you? You're hard, and you're fierce, but you're not a trained warrior. You're a survivor. And survivors don't fight just to fight. Survivors aren't worried about ego. They're worried about seeing their next sunrise. Right?" He paused for a beat. "I know about surviving, Finley. It's why I'm still in this job. Tell me. What are you reacting to?"

I could feel my eyebrows pinch, wondering why he was asking the question again. Wondering if this was a trick of some sort.

"My clothes," I said, watching his reaction closely. "I want to keep my clothes intact."

"Your clothes are a mess. Your shirt is shredded in places and crusted with your blood. It won't last much longer."

I thought of the note, and my heart sped up. "My pants. They're leather. They're fine."

His eyes narrowed just slightly. He pulled back and glanced down at my pants, fine other than a few score marks from where stray whips had snapped them. As he looked back at my face, his brows pinched like mine were probably doing.

"Fine. I'll have them sent to your cell. Anything else?"

I shrugged. "Sure. Let me go."

He continued to stare for a moment before taking a step back. "Step out of your clothes. If you give us any trouble, we'll beat you and destroy your pants."

"I can entice her to behave." Sonassa leaned in a little to catch my attention, her magic crawling across my skin like it had when I'd arrived.

"Entice the possum." Govam gestured her away. "This dragon has a powerful true mate. She won't succumb to your power."

"No?" Her eyes glimmered. "Are we sure?"

Her magic flowed across my flesh like a whisper of satin. It curled around my nipples, tightening them, before slipping down to my core. I sucked in a breath at the blast of ecstasy, before my stomach flipped and then clenched. A feeling like acid dribbled through me, corroding the magic. Bile rose in my throat, and my head swam.

"No, thank you," I managed, trying to hold my stomach down. "That's a nope on my end."

"See?" Govam said. "Go use your talents on the man. He's not handling this well, and he needs to be presentable."

Sonassa frowned at me, her gaze roaming my body now. "If she can't be enticed, how will she be brought to heel at the parties?"

"Not my problem." Govam stared her down, and I faintly heard Denski say behind me, "We hope."

When Sonassa hit Jedrek with her magic, he loosened up immediately, becoming pliant with a dopey smile on his face. "Ah, yes, that's more like it. I cooperated…"

She undressed him herself, allowing him to put his hand on top of her head and push her head down his body. Her eyes were on me the whole time, her smile cunning as she lowered to her knees.

"Yeah," Jedrek muttered, his head falling back. "That's right. I cooperated. This is more like it."

This wasn't shame fucking for Jedrek. That much was clear. This was just fucking. He'd been with the demons in the village often enough that he was clearly happy for this brand of distraction.

I turned my back, disgusted, to finish undressing, but Sonassa called out, "Make her watch."

"That wasn't in my brief," Govam said, holding out his hand for me to take so that I could get in the tub.

Her slurping teamed with Jedrek's loud moans made my skin crawl. She was clearly being noisy on purpose, and he liked her all the more for it. Once he was in the water, she must've switched to a hand job, because the sloshing of water accompanied his groans and grunts—at one point, the guy fucking whinnied. *Whinnied!* What in the actual fuck?

"Does she have to keep it up through the whole thing?" I asked at one point, the attendants scrubbing suds through my hair. The bath might have actually been pleasant if not for the soundtrack. It wasn't the actual act that disgusted me—I'd been in the castle, after all; I knew how those things went—it was that the guy thought he fucking deserved it.

Govam stood beside me with his arms crossed over his chest, facing their way. His expression was dark. He didn't reply, but he didn't seem overly fond of the situation himself.

"Does it affect you?" I asked after getting out of the water. The attendants had dried me and were dressing me in a puffy pink gown that should've been used for curtains. They strapped the sword around it, which made the whole ensemble marginally more tolerable.

Govam glanced at me; he was still close but facing to the side, doing me the courtesy of not staring at my nudity.

His eyebrows shot up.

"The sexy magic," I elaborated. "Does it affect you?"

"No," Denski answered, standing near Jedrek. Sonassa was letting him grope her while the attendants rooted around in a chest for pants in his size. "Not unless their power is greater than ours. Which is very rarely the case, isn't it, Sonassa? Demons of your sort are best left for menial jobs, like jerking off possum shifters."

"It won't be pleasant for you to marry him, will it, little dragon?" Sonassa asked me in a sultry voice, ignoring Denski. It seemed the various demon factions disliked one another. At least the ones forced to work together. "You won't have magic to get you in the mood. You will have to be held, I think, when he makes an heir. Unless you make friends with me, of course. I have the ear of his highness. I can push off the wedding if you'd like me to…"

My blood ran cold. Was that what they were doing? Getting us ready for a wedding?

"The ear of the highness?" Denski huffed. "You don't have access to the cock of his highness, let alone his ear."

Sonassa glared but didn't comment.

A while later we were walking again, and despite Jedrek's repeated questions, they wouldn't tell us where we were headed. The hallways got finer and grander the farther we went, until it was obviously a place of royalty. Dolion had paid attention to the areas that mattered to him and clearly ignored the rest.

Through a set of double doors, we found a large room with gold and cream walls, a large crystal chandelier, and a huge rug adorning the floor. Red cushioned stools lined each side of a walkway up to a raised dais hosting a grand golden throne—empty—with purple fabric on the seat and back. Two golden posts rose beside it, draped with purple and red fabric. It was pretty impressive, I had to say. I didn't even know if Nyfain's castle had a throne room. Probably, I supposed, but I'd never seen it.

Govam directed me toward the dais and then stopped. Jedrek was guided to stand next to me, and the guards fanned out around us, Sonassa dropping her smirks and smiles completely.

I felt my eyebrows creep up as I looked around, not noticing the details so much as trying to keep my raging heart from breaking loose from my chest and skittering across the floor. My stomach tied in knots as I waited for whatever would come.

The door opened and admitted a handful of guards, all wearing loose black tops and tight black pants leading down into shiny boots, like Govam and his guards. They fanned out around the throne, a few standing in front of us, before Dolion walked out with all the arrogance and self-importance in the world. His long purple velvet cape dragged across the floor behind him, lined with puffy white fur around the edges. Two other demons followed, and I could smell them from the distance. Musty and gross, they were powerful, not terribly far down the power scale from the demon king himself. Their skin had the same blue tint, and similar horns curved away from their temples.

Dolion stepped up onto the dais and sat, swishing his cloak around him. The others took their places at his sides, a step down.

The hierarchy was clear, even for idiots.

Govam's hands tightened on my elbows as all the guards around us bowed, lowering their heads. His grip forced me to match the subservient posture.

Fuck this. My dragon thrashed against my hold, trying to steal control. *I will not bow to that donkey fucker.*

That's an insult to donkeys. I gritted my teeth but held the deep bow, looking up through my lashes with a bowed head.

Dolion watched me with an acute gaze, one elbow resting on the arm of his chair. He wanted to see me submit.

Fire raged through me. I could kill him; I knew I could. I had the power. I had the strength. More importantly, I had the anger. The *history* of anger, for what he'd done to my family. My village. For the people he had killed. For the injuries he had dealt my mate.

For the suffering he'd caused.

My animal pushed up, right beneath the surface. I felt Govam's fingers dig into my skin—a warning. Or maybe he was preparing himself.

Now is not the time, I barely got out, my thoughts tinged as red as Dolion's eyes. *I could kill him, but I couldn't kill them all. They'd take me down.*

I know, my dragon snarled. *But we will kill him one day. One day, we will rip his head off his neck, hollow out his eyes, and piss on his remains.*

A bit much, that. But in this case, I agree.

With incredible effort, I dropped my eyes. I bent my knees just a bit more. I feigned submission.

"Good," I heard from Govam, barely more than a whisper. His hands loosened on my elbows, his touch barely there now. The only thing that kept my anger from increasing was that he didn't sound smug or authoritative—he sounded supportive, like he knew the effort it had taken me to get through that.

Before I could wonder at it, I felt the tug of his hand, and everyone was standing once again.

"So." Dolion crossed a thin leg over the other. His gaze roamed me before he gave Jedrek the same assessment. "The happy couple has stepped before me. What do you think of your new home?"

Jedrek squirmed, drawing Dolion's eyes. I wondered why I hadn't pulled his animal loose yet. Then again, maybe he was still affected by Sonassa's magic. I wasn't sure whether I could pull the animals free if they were under any kind of demon influence.

"My goodness, shifter," Dolion said, tapping his thin lips. "I'd forgotten how nicely you clean up."

"He sure does," the demon to Dolion's right said, her horns thinner and a little more curved. "What is his animal?"

Dolion narrowed his eyes. "This one came from the villages. He wouldn't know."

"Submissive," Govam said.

"Hmm. I like the submissive ones," she replied.

"I'm not submissive," Jedrek grumbled.

"And delusional," Govam added.

The demons on the dais laughed delightedly, except for Dolion, whose eyes gleamed. "A handsome and delusional 'alpha.' He'll be a great favorite. How does he respond to your magic, Sonassa?"

"Like a little pussycat, your majesty," she replied, adding a little bow. "He welcomes it. I get the impression he was fond of the demons in his village."

"Yes, that was the impression I got when I first met him." Dolion tapped his lips again. "Get a suit that actually fits him. Bring him to dinner tonight. No other shifters. Just him. I want to see how he does. Sonassa, you take charge of him. You'll be more useful than Denski."

"My pleasure, sire." Her hips swung as she took Denski's place, offering him a smug smile as she did so. Apparently handling the prisoners was usually reserved for the higher tiers of demons.

Dolion leaned forward a little, peering down at Jedrek. "Remember, if you cooperate, you'll be treated well. Please me, and you'll be pampered. Displease me, however, and you'll find yourself in a worse place than that dungeon, do you understand? The pain you experience will have no comparison."

"Yes, sir—sire," Jedrek said, straightening up a little. He looked at me out of the corner of his eye, and I could just see his cheeks rising. He thought this was a hand out of his current hell. Or maybe he figured gaining Dolion's favor would get him married to me that much faster. Whatever it was, he had absolutely zero worry about what sort of duties would come next. He probably looked forward to them.

I kept myself from hunching, worried about my own fate. Worried about what duties would be coming for *me.* I'd be damned if I was passed around his demons. A great many of them would die before that happened.

Dolion flicked his fingers. "Sonassa, go find temporary quarters for him until we know where he will go."

"Of course, your highness." She offered a bow, and her magic swirled around us, licking down my body and attempting to settle between my legs.

I shivered and shrugged it off as Jedrek smiled broadly, liking the touch of her magic.

"Come on, pet," Sonassa said it to him, but her eyes were regarding me with hunger. The chick would just not let it go.

I gritted my teeth as they left, hating the feeling of vulnerability, being left on my own. He was the worst, but he felt like the only living thing familiar to me in this harsh and uncertain place.

"What about the golden dragon's mate?" Dolion asked. "Any trouble?"

"She is nothing but trouble, sire," Govam said. "We have to watch her closely. She's a dragon through and through."

"You filthy fucking liar," I seethed, spinning in outrage. His hands on my elbows locked me in place, and Denski quick-stepped toward us. His extendable stick came out of nowhere and crashed down on top of me. I withstood the pain as he hit me again, trying to cow me, to reduce me to a whimpering mess like he had with Jedrek.

The third strike hit me in my stomach, knocking the breath out of me. I bent with the blow but refused to let my knees buckle. Denski edged back, lowering his stick near his leg.

"Hmm, she's a strong one," the male demon beside Dolion said. "Quite pretty for a shifter. The smell, though…"

"Can you do anything about it?" Dolion asked. "She was claimed by the Wyvern alpha. I don't think severing the bond will be enough with her."

"We have never successfully severed a dragon's mating bond," the other demon said, entwining her fingers in front of her. "Only wolves so far. And the weaker ones at that. But…we can try to at least minimize the smell."

"Yes, that might be within our power," the other agreed.

Bear down, my dragon thought in sudden panic, clutching for the bond. *Hold on to Nyfain with everything you have. We don't want them to get lucky and somehow sever our connection. He's the only thing keeping us sane in here.*

"Hold her," Dolion said as the two demons on the dais drifted down the steps toward me, their expressions equally determined.

Guards gripped my arms and sides, three on each side, and Govam held fast to my elbows, his fingers digging in. The other guards pushed in close too—not grabbing me yet, but prepared to. As the powerful demons neared me, their magic dug in, burrowing into my skin and seemingly digging holes into my bones.

"No," I forced out through clenched teeth, the sudden pain overwhelming. Unimaginable. Quickly whisking away my logical mind. "No!"

I thrashed within the guards' hold. The demon magic burrowed deeper, clawing through my chest, hunting for my connection with Nyfain. My spine twisted, or at least it felt that way, bending down over itself. The magic dug deeper yet, shooting bursts of pain through every inch of my body.

I screamed, eyes squeezed shut. I kicked and thrashed at the hands all over my body. My power flailed out and slashed through flesh and bone. Those near me were ripped away, but more took their place as my dragon yanked at Nyfain's power. The gush came immediately, but it wasn't enough to lessen my agony.

Blackness encroached on my vision, and still the pain grew as they searched for our bond. Cutting and slicing. Turning me inside out.

A little tickle worried the bond, and terror bled through me anew.

Hold on to him with everything you are, my dragon wailed,

coiling around the bond to protect it. *Take the pain. That is nothing compared to losing him. Don't let them break us apart.*

The tickle increased, warming. Growing. Glowing.

But it wasn't the demons. It was Nyfain, reaching out to us through the bond. Trying to help us in our time of need.

No, not trying to help—trying to protect us in the only way he could.

His presence gushed through the bond. He must've realized what was happening in some way, because with his presence came one crystal-clear command: *Submit to me.* He pulled my consciousness toward him. Locked me into his hold, something I hadn't realized could be done through a bond. And then he wrapped his power, his essence, around us.

I didn't hesitate or balk. I fell into his dominating magic and let it consume me totally. I closed my eyes and drifted into the safety of his rolling, turbulent power.

The pain from the demons' magic drove down deep, but then it flowered into breath-stealing pleasure. I gasped—then groaned—as it curled through me and settled in my core.

Lean into it, my dragon said, fortifying her protection of the bond. *Give yourself to him, body and soul.*

No problem.

Another slash of pain shocked through me, turned quickly into a tidal wave of ecstasy that had my eyelids fluttering. Memories flooded me—hot nights in twisted sheets, slow, sensual mornings when he moved within me. I twisted them into a fantasy, focusing solely on the pleasure he was feeding me. Solely on *him.*

I imagined lying back, my knees spreading as he dipped between my thighs, his tongue flicking my fevered flesh. I groaned as he continued upward, his palms finding the insides of my knees before pushing them wider. I arched back and gave him more access.

A bite of pain made me wince, almost ripping me out of the moment.

I imagined his teeth tearing into my flesh, marking me brutally. But then his tongue swirled across the spot, pleasure curling into me and making my pussy throb. He worked up my body, biting and sucking, hurting me with his marks and then wrapping them up in delicious pleasure. His body pressed down onto me, trapping me pleasantly to the hard floor.

My bubble wobbled for a moment as the crack of a whip scored my flesh. The demons were trying to loosen me up with a beating.

More, Nyfain, I thought desperately, throwing myself back into his care. I imagined myself writhing under him—and fed those desires into the bond. *Yes, Nyfain, take me.*

Hard, throbbing pleasure pulsed back, and I imagined his hard cock rubbing between my slippery sex before pushing inside, filling me to the point of bursting. A delicious ache.

Harder, Nyfain, I said as the pain began to intensify, threatening to destroy my fantasy. *Quickly, harder.*

The pleasure surged, my mind turning it into his thrusting into me. Deeper. Filling my focus. His hips beat against mine, the painful pleasure tightening up my body. I felt down his back, imagining his scars into strips of golden scales. His cock pounded into me, and I hooked my legs around his hips, swinging up to crash into him.

Still the pain filtered through the fantasy, threatening my little oasis, the hold he had on me. It felt like the whips and demon magic were ripping my flesh from my bones piece by agonizing piece.

Please, Nyfain, I begged, unable to handle the onslaught. Tears streamed down my face. *Help me, Nyfain, please!*

His hold on me through the bond increased to a death grip.

His answering feeling was clear: *Mine!*

It felt as if the golden dragon were rearing up and spreading his wings over us. His power vibrated through the loose threads the demons had frayed from our bond, stitching everything back together again. He'd broken me and remade me so many times, it was muscle memory at this point.

His hard cock pounded into me, beating back the pain. Combating it with the hard crush of pleasure. The peaks of my breasts rubbed against his hard chest. I scratched down his back and heard his roar of pleasure. The sensations throbbed within me, harder, faster, bigger, and then I exploded, crying out with my orgasm and clutching him, the feelings so vivid they felt absolutely real.

In my mind's eye, I continued to envision two lines of gleaming golden scales down his back. I envisioned those protective wings shining in the buttery-yellow sun, the great golden dragon who would once again be the pride of Wyvern someday. He would do us all proud. A comforting hum vibrated through the bond, and I slipped into darkness.

CHAPTER 7
FINLEY

THE COOL STONE was a welcome relief against my overly hot front. Two weeks had passed since I was presented to Dolion. I'd blacked out from the pain of their...magical exfoliation? Whipping? Beating?

Apparently, they'd done all three.

Their goal hadn't been to beat me to death, but if I hadn't passed out, that was exactly what would have happened.

It seemed they'd never encountered someone like me before, with the ability to use her will as a strong physical presence and an incredibly powerful alpha dragon mate to feed her power. They wailed on me, and I guessed I'd struck out hard with my will, slashing and stabbing and maiming with the help of Nyfain's power boost.

I'd given them a bit of a scare.

They'd reacted by trying to pound me into unconsciousness. When they finally succeeded, they'd beaten me a little more for good measure. Govam was the one who'd pulled them off, and it had been universally agreed that they would need to try something else to get the stench off. Their magic wasn't gonna do it.

Thank fuck.

I'd heard all of this secondhand from Vemar, who had excellent hearing and made an art of eavesdropping. He'd heard Govam telling a guard about it when they dropped Jedrek off for a while before his big debut. Perhaps they thought Jedrek might calm me down or something. They really didn't have a clue.

It had taken three days to recover from Dolion's Great Cock-Up, and then the officers dragged me up to the top floor of the dungeon, strapped me to a whipping post in the back corner, and had another go. Those fuckers were good, too. They hurt me just enough for Nyfain to bring me to orgasm, then gave me a day or two to recover before they did it again. They knew I wouldn't intentionally lash out with my will due to the threat of being beaten to death.

My life was pain now, but Nyfain made sure it was always mixed with pleasure. What a crazy fucking afterlife I was living at present. Horrible but good at the same time. A fucking nightmare...and an exquisite daydream when in the moment.

Despite all the torment, I'd never once reached for the sword. Not in the height of danger, or when they were changing shackles and I had a few seconds to spare. That was probably why I still had it wrapped around my waist. They took it off for whippings and gave it back with a snicker afterward.

Ha-ha, fuckers. I don't know how to use this fine sword. Hilarious joke.

The guards didn't seem to take such enjoyment from their jobs, eyeing the sword warily before stoically carrying out their orders. I liked them much better for it.

I squeezed my hand around Nyfain's letter, which I held for

comfort when I got back from being whipped. Govam had returned my clothes as promised. Nyfain's letter had been replaced with a note of Govam's, indicating under which stone the letter was now hidden. Some were loose at the back of the cell, and one of them had a somewhat deep hole under it.

Why the fuck Govam was so cool about some things and a lying sack of shit about others, I did not know. Mind-fuckery, probably. A means of breaking prisoners. I had to be on my guard. There was no kindness here. Not from the demons, at any rate. I couldn't let myself think otherwise.

"You bring this on yourself, you know," Jedrek said, sitting in the corner of the cell with his legs pulled up and hugged close with his arms. His hair was mussed but recently cut, his clothes were plain but freshly laundered, and he didn't have any dirt streaks.

"Do I really?" I asked, catching sight of Vemar down in his cell, sitting with his shoulder propped against the bars, listening. A couple of others edged up closer to their bars as well, mostly quiet except for some rustling of straw or clothes. I was pretty sure my bickering with Jedrek, whenever the demons brought him back to "cheer me up," was a source of entertainment.

"If you'd stop talking back to them, they wouldn't have any reason to beat you, or whip you...or whatever it is they do."

"You know what, that right there is why our forced relationship is going to stand the test of time. It's your attention to detail regarding my affairs. I feel like you really *listen* when I talk, you know? You really pay attention to what's going on in my life."

"Your sarcasm is a little thick."

"Just a little? Huh. I thought I was really laying it on." I contemplated bringing my hand up to scratch my face...but that would hurt. For the moment, I'd take the itch over the pain. The slip of fabric covering me lay in tatters around my body. They only changed it when it was so ruined that it actually fell off. I'd stopped caring about nakedness. There really was no point. "They whip me, Jedrek, for the most part. Because I know you care so much—more sarcasm, by the way. And cut me with knives sometimes. You should come by sometime. I really draw a crowd. The officers drink in the power I exude, and then there are the pleasure seekers, who get off when I do, and the emotional turmoil and pain seekers—I'm quite the attraction. And no, it isn't brought on by talking back. They don't talk to me, and I don't talk to them. Unlike the guards, the officers crave power. They create their creatures with it and then celebrate with some sort of drink they tend to constantly. It's quite the party."

"I heard you make fun of them. The officers, I mean."

"Where'd you hear that from?"

"Sorry, Strange Lady," Vemar called. "I thought it was funny, the things you said when we were being whipped together. I didn't know he was going to be a douche about it."

Sometimes they brought multiple people up at once. Vemar had been very confused about the amount of people hanging around for our joint torture sesh, and even more so when I orgasmed at the end. He'd doubled down on calling me "Strange Lady." I couldn't really blame him.

"That's a more recent development," I said, a little drool escaping out of the side of my mouth. I didn't worry about it. It was better than blood. Or hell, maybe it *was* blood. Really hard to say at this point in the healing process. "They're going to keep bringing me up there regardless of what I do. What's a little banter among friends?"

"My thought exactly," Vemar said.

"Well, if you'd just cooperate, like I do, then you could spend time in the demon court," Jedrek said. "I've had dinner with them a couple of nights. I got to dress up and eat real meals and…have a nice night. It really wasn't so bad."

I let the air leak out of me for a moment. He'd used those words—"nice night"—a few times. From what I could gather, the guy was essentially passed around. The orgies here didn't sound as uncontrolled as the ones at Nyfain's castle, but Jedrek would have anywhere from one to multiple partners in one night. He wasn't with more than one at a time, it didn't sound like, but he still dipped his wick in more than one candle.

And he thought it was fucking awesome. Just like in the pub in the village back home, he was happy to participate in the shenanigans. He even boasted about not needing sexy magic.

He'd turned out to be a great favorite. His ego had gone through the roof, especially since I was still down here, dirty and bloody and using a bucket for a toilet.

"We have different interpretations of what constitutes a *nice night*," I said dryly. "Have you thought about what I've said?"

"What, about making maps and spying on them?" He snorted. "Why, so I can end up like you? The only reason I am sitting in this goddess-ignored cell is to improve your spirits. They want you to attend one of the upcoming parties—without making trouble. I told them it was a fool's errand. All you do is make trouble. You always have."

"Then why do you want me?"

"Everyone wants you. Even the demons want you. Despite your many faults, you're a looker. I intend to have you."

"Fine, but do you intend to stay here forever? Because if you don't make maps and help me find a way out, we're going to die here."

"The demon king will release us once he gets what he wants." Jedrek smoothed his hair, though what good he thought that would do, I didn't know.

"Jedrek," I said, somewhere between amused and incredibly frustrated. "What is it you think he wants?"

"What he was promised. My firstborn."

Frustration won out. "Are you stupid or something? Let's forget the fact that you are offering your *child* to a horrible demon. What the fuck would he want with a kid? He just steals whatever he wants. Which are adults, Jedrek. Dragon adults. Faerie adults. Shifter adults. He doesn't want a kid, and he's never going to let us go. He's going to try to break me, use me to hurt Nyfain, then kill me. Neither of us are getting out of here. Eventually you'll be used up, and then you'll be killed. You need to give me information so I can get us out of here."

"And do what?" he scoffed. "Go back to that hovel of a village? That golden dragon's kingdom is faltering. It's gone. He's not even golden anymore, and I heard he can't fly. Some dragon prince. There's nothing to go back to."

"Fine, then go to one of the other shifter kingdoms. *Anywhere*, Jedrek. Go literally anywhere else, where you will be free instead of being stuck in this nasty dungeon."

"I wouldn't be brought down to this nasty dungeon if it wasn't for you."

"Oh goddess help me, I can't—"

"Give up," a woman called. "He does not want to see the truth of his situation. I've known a few like him. All wolves, so maybe he *is* one." Her tone held disgust. "If his kind see the truth, they'll break. It's nicer for them if they live in their fantasies."

"Too bad he's trapping me in his fantasies with him," I mumbled, trying to think of another way to get through to him. He was in a prime spot to give me information. They didn't fear him. He was allowed to go places I couldn't, with hardly any guards. I needed him to get information.

Just kill him and be done with it, my dragon thought in annoyance. *Who knows how long we'll be stuck in this pit of shit? We don't need to make it worse with him. Just, like...blame it on the torturers. I'm sure they've killed a few people.*

I somehow doubt anyone will think the torturers killed him when they haven't once looked in his direction. Especially if his blood is all over me.

Some risks are worth taking, she replied.

Boots scraped against the steps, and I sighed and closed my eyes. Damn it all, the guards were coming. Their shoes had a different sound on those steps than the officers' did.

They came to take people for the demons. Shame fucking, basically, but at least Hadriel and the others had been allowed to skip the parties.

Though they kept to themselves for the most part, I knew the prisoners weren't happy to go, regardless of what they felt at the actual parties. I wanted to comfort them but didn't know how. It made me nostalgic for Hadriel, who had an easy way about him that had made life brighter for everyone at Nyfain's castle. He'd been my jester, and if anyone in this place would actually talk to me for more than a few moments, I could try to be theirs.

I turned my head to lay my other cheek on the hard stone so I could see who was taken. I didn't dare move any part of my body for a better view. It was too soon after my last dance with the whip. I did heal very quickly, but not quickly enough to ease the suffering. In all honesty, I probably didn't heal quickly enough to avoid some scarring. They were too aggressive in their ministrations. Too zealous to feel my agony. All my quick healing meant was that they beat me almost every day instead of every handful of days like they did with the others.

Govam and Denski descended with no other guards in tow. Huh. So they weren't coming for the dragons.

I wondered why the guards were sent at all. The sex demons were so much better at keeping everyone in check. Then again, the officers used dead bodies for their creations, and Dolion had made it clear he didn't give two shits about his people. Maybe the guards were just as useful dead as alive.

"Well, look at that, Jedrek, your ticket out of here." I turned my head and looked the other way again. I had no desire to see them approach. "Remember what I said."

They stopped just on the other side of the cell bars, their boots scuffing the stone, announcing their presence. Jedrek leaned forward but didn't get up.

"I hear they've been taking you daily lately," Govam said.

"You must be talking to me, or else my beloved Jedrek is keeping things from me."

"They're gonna kill her," Vemar told no one in particular. "I know we're heading into the blackout, but if they keep this pace up, they are going to kill that purty little dragon. What fun would their parties be then?"

The blackout, I gathered, was what Nyfain called the lull. It happened after the officers created all their twisted creatures to unleash in the Forbidden Wood in Wyvern and places unknown. We weren't the only unlucky ones, apparently, although I didn't have any details about that. I'd just overheard a brief snippet of conversation when I was being dragged away from the whipping post. The act of creation took a lot of power out of them, so after they finished their work, they drank that drink in the large copper canister and then passed out from exhaustion. That was what the dragons reckoned, at least. I'd gotten just as good at eavesdropping as Vemar. Not like there was much else to do.

"Nah, they won't kill me." I thought about itching my nose again. "They might think they can break me, and I must say they've put in a damn fine effort. Won't happen, though. Fuck 'em."

Silence rang out for a moment. Then Vemar said, "I think I like you, Strange Lady. I think I like you an awful lot."

In addition to being gullible, Vemar was notoriously easy to please.

"We're here for the male," Govam said, not having moved since he took up residence on the other side of the bars from my head.

"Yes, I figured that when you showed up without an entourage. I'm surprised they didn't send someone just to detain me while you grabbed him, though."

"You're in no position to fight."

"It is not polite to point out a lady's flaws."

The lock slid over, and metal groaned as Denski pulled open the door.

"You there. C'mon," Denski said, his voice hard.

Jedrek gave me a look that said, *See? I get treated well because I cooperate.*

"He's on the wrong floor," someone called out. "It enrages me to see him going with them this easily."

"They don't have a floor for possums," someone else said, the comment met with a smattering of laughter.

"He should be with the filthy wolves," a third shifter sneered.

"Why the hell hasn't she killed him by now?" the first voice asked. It was a commonly repeated question. "She took out a host of guards and one officer. She has the ability."

"*I* would've killed him by now," Vemar said.

"And now you will not be allowed near him, Vemar," Denski said patiently.

"I wasn't going to be allowed near him anyway. He's a prize, that one is. Real slick. I'll be in a cage, watching him on the arm of his new master."

"You're all going to rot down here," Jedrek said in a low tone as the cuffs snapped around his wrists.

Leather creaked, and I turned my head the other way to see Govam's boots creasing. His knees and hands came into view as he crouched down to be closer to me.

"I've heard that you barely speak or cry out when they whip you," he said. "You also don't swear at them when they come to get you. You don't berate them when they transport you… You take the pain stoically and let them put you back in your cell."

"Most of that is true, but as my blessed betrothed accused me of earlier, I do take the occasional shot at them. It breaks up the monotony."

"Your golden prince is helping you."

"What did he say?" someone asked.

"*Shh*," Vemar replied. "I'm trying to listen."

Govam lowered his voice further. "Maybe if he stopped helping you, the officers wouldn't call you up as much. They wouldn't go at you so hard. They're getting too much power from you to stop."

I didn't know how to tell Nyfain to stop, and I wasn't sure I had it in me to try. I relished our connection. I craved it.

Besides, I was working on the guards' muscle memory. Going up placidly and coming back placidly ensured they got into a rhythm. They pulled me out of the cell a certain way, clicked on the cuffs, walked me up, took off my sword—it was all becoming a routine. When I was ready, I'd crash that routine to pieces, and the shock of it would give me an opening.

Fighting and struggling didn't do anyone any good anyway. The other dragons did it, and they still came back all slashed up. What was the point?

A knee touched the ground, followed by a gloved hand, Govam getting lower so I could see him. His gaze settled on mine.

"You asked me some questions when we were bringing you in here, and I never answered," he said quietly. "I will now, while we have a moment." He paused as Jedrek was ordered to exit the cell. "I knew you were thinking about killing me because I know dragons. I've learned to read their subtleties. I've learned to understand what each small movement means. That's why I'm the only captain who hasn't been killed in this job."

"Yet."

"Correct. Yet." He paused. "It's clear that you barely know you're a dragon. You don't act like the rest of them, as I said. You've never shifted, and yet you are going to be the most dangerous of them all. I can see it in you. I can see the danger lurking. *See* it, not smell it. This doesn't have to do with the golden prince. You're trouble, Finley."

"That must be why they whip me with such gusto."

"I hear you exude more power than any shifter who's ever been in this dungeon. Only one of the faeries gives them the same dose, and that is when her sister is beside her."

So there was a powerful faerie in the dungeons. Interesting to know. I wondered if the demons were suppressing her power. Most likely. I figured it was how Dolion kept everyone in line. What handy magic for a sleazeball to have.

"The officers here love power above all else," Govam continued, his words barely above a whisper. "They're relentless. And they can be. They supply party favors and his highness's twisted creatures, but otherwise they're left alone. What happens down here remains here, for the most part, unless they need help in some way. They are not checked on by the rest of the castle."

I blinked a few times, letting that sink in. I lifted my head as much as I could, trying to study him a little more closely.

They weren't checked on? Meaning that if I timed my rebellion and escape just right, no one would be the wiser until Dolion wanted his party favors?

Why the fuck would the captain of the guard tell me this? *Me*, the dragon he thought was more dangerous than the others.

I narrowed my eyes.

"Don't go anywhere," I said as I dragged my arms up and braced my hands beside my shoulders. "I need to get up." I sucked in a breath. "This is going to suck."

Pain vibrated through me as I pushed my upper body off the ground. The skin on my back stretched, ripping at the fresh slashes and pulling open any scabs that had formed. I pushed back and then worked my knees under me, my legs aching, before trying to twist and plop onto my butt.

The pain was interrupted by a blast of delicious pleasure that soaked through my core and started to pound. It curled through my body, ripping a decadent moan from my lips.

Shit. Bad timing, I thought. *Better hurry this up before I climax in front of all these people.*

I twisted and sat, searing pain spreading across my skin. A feeling like a lazy tongue dragging across my taut nipple met the pain and conquered it, drenching my core with heat.

"Holy fuck," I said, my body pounding, not much pain this time to hinder the flow of pleasure. The feel of Nyfain shuddered through me, like he was shoving my legs wide and driving his cock into me.

"One sec," I managed, scooting to the wall, gasping with pleasure. "Maybe two seconds..."

My heat fanned higher. My ecstasy increased. My embarrassment was out of control.

My back hit the wall. I could barely think over the pulsing in my body as I imagined him between my legs. His hands on me. His cock pumping hard.

His pleasure poured through the bond, along with other feelings. His love. His devotion. His rage at what was happening to me.

The mark on my neck tingled as though a hot, wet tongue had slid across it. My legs straightened of their own accord, and pain ate at me, lending to the memory of when he'd bitten me and claimed me as his.

The orgasm forced out a strangled cry, tightening my jaw and stealing my breath. I shuddered, a wave of power blasting through me as sensation consumed me.

Shaking, breathing heavily, I rested my head against the wall for a moment. The silence of the room was deafening.

"Sorry." I gulped down air. "Sorry about that..."

Govam was staring at me with wide eyes in a blank face. He

clearly hadn't processed what had happened in front of the demon king, and no one had told him how I'd been handling the officers' whipping. Well, he knew now. He'd just gotten a front-row seat to exactly how that golden dragon was helping me through the pain.

Denski had stopped to look back, and Jedrek was scowling for all he was worth.

"Sorry about that," I said again with a flaming face. I probably still had spit dribbling off my chin, and I definitely had dirt and dried blood caked on every inch of me. I was not the epitome of sexy right now but…well, I just came in front of a bunch of people in the middle of a conversation. That wasn't something a person just shrugged off. Not outside of Nyfain's castle, anyway.

"You were saying?" I prompted when Govam continued to stare.

A guffaw trailed down the middle of the cells, Vemar finding great delight in all of this.

"What the fuck just happened?" I was pretty sure that was Tamara.

"Did she just…" A female's voice drifted away. Jade, I thought, her eyes as green as her name.

Silence settled again. Shocked silence. Silence no one could figure out how to fill.

"That was just my bond mate, helping me deal with the pain of moving around," I said with a grimace.

Govam held up his hand, his eyes shrinking back to normal size, and something new glimmering in them that I couldn't read. "I don't need to know."

"I kinda want to know," Vemar called. "It is fantastically filthy, Strange Lady, and I'm here for it."

"Thanks, Vemar," I said dryly as Govam went to stand. "No,

wait—" I held out a hand and lowered my voice, nothing but a soft hum so no one but the two of us could hear. "Why did you tell me that? About the castle?"

Govam didn't move, but I could almost feel him glancing over his shoulder. "I didn't tell you anything of note. Nothing everyone else doesn't already know."

But there was something in his eyes. A hooded sort of poignance.

"As to your other question when we brought you in," he said, "no, I am not a screamer. I can see why you'd be curious, given your display just now…"

Heat rushed to my cheeks.

He stood. "I have to get your…betrothed upstairs. He has made quite an impression. He has all the swagger of an alpha but none of the annoying stubbornness and power that comes with it. Not to mention he's handsome and easy to please. He's a great favorite."

"Knew it," Vemar said.

Govam's eyes turned hard. "Your first party is coming shortly. A cage has been cleaned out for you, so you'll get to see him in action."

With that, he turned and stalked down the dungeon, climbing the stairs with determined movements. Denski and Jedrek followed, Denski barely bothering to shove Jedrek to move faster. Jedrek already couldn't get out of here fast enough.

"Night-night," Denski called a moment before the lights clicked off and we were swathed in darkness. "*Obice* going active."

The *obice* was the magical lock. The officers usually applied it at the top of the stairs, though the head guards were capable of enacting it too.

My eyes adjusted immediately as I let out a soft breath and contemplated trying to lie down again. Part of me was tempted to move around just so Nyfain would have an excuse to bring me more pleasure, but I knew I would let little whimpers or worse escape, and I needed a break from embarrassment.

So I just sat there, looking out over the still stone, letting my mind wander. Without Jedrek around to annoy me, I should've known where it would go.

Straight to Nyfain.

An image of him materialized in my thoughts. He stood in the everlass field with the sun soaking through his tousled dark brown hair. His gorgeous golden gaze beat into me, and the air between us crackled with power. His straight nose cut through almost sharp cheekbones, hollowed at the cheek. I'd once thought him almost severe looking, absent the smiles that brought out his devastating handsomeness, but not anymore. I knew his rage, his moods, his tempers…they were all a cloak over his great, swelling, broken heart—a heart that had been broken anew when the demon king took me away.

But I'd be back. Unlike his mother, who hadn't been able to cheat the grave, I would not let the beyond claim me. If I had to crawl out of this place, freshly whipped and randomly orgasming, I would. I would make it back to him just as soon as I could.

And I'd bring the cavalry. The dragon cavalry.

Click.

The sound snapped me back into the moment.

Was that…a lock clicking over?

I stared in absolute bewilderment as the door to Vemar's cell slowly swung open.

What in the holy fuck, I thought as my dragon thought, *Holy fucking shit, did that just happen?*

He stepped out, facing my way. A cunning grin lit his face.

"Hey, Strange Lady…" he said in a singsong voice. "Time to see if you can use that sword, hmm?"

"Dragons handle their own problems," Mr. Baritone said as another click rang out. His door swung open next. My heart started pattering a little faster. "And we have a problem with you. Now that things are a little more settled, there are some questions that need answering. It's time you start talking."

CHAPTER 8

FINLEY

I OPENED MY mouth to ask what possible problem they could have with me when Vemar spoke again.

"You are awfully quiet, Strange Lady." He walked slowly down the left side of the main chamber, his hand out and fingers grazing the bars of the cells. Occasionally he hit someone's arms or knuckles. He gave a tiny jerk every time, as did the person being touched.

They couldn't see in the dark. Their animals were still suppressed. Whatever was happening now, whatever issue they had with me, I had an edge. I also wondered who exactly had the issue. Mr. Baritone had offered to help me that first night. Then again, he seemed like the alpha around here. He might've been using the collective *we*. And Vemar had been chatty with me this whole time, at least compared to the rest of them. He seemed to care about how much the officers were hurting me. What was his part in all of this? What had I done? Or was he just the muscle of the group?

Regardless, whatever was happening wasn't good. I needed to

make a move.

Gritting my teeth, I moved slowly and quietly to the opposite side of my cell. I braced my hands on the ground. Little sparks of pain erupted all over my body, but I ignored them.

Can you temporarily cut off Nyfain from feeling what I do? I asked my dragon as I pushed more weight onto my hands and got my feet under me before pushing to standing. More pain vibrated through me, not pleasant but endurable.

I don't know about cutting him off, but I can muffle what he feels. The dragon will know I'm doing it, though. He seems to keep a close watch on our connection.

Muffle it, then. It's fine if he knows. Maybe he'll realize I don't want to be interrupted.

Vemar reached the end of the last cell and paused. He tilted his head a little, and his other hand came out, as though he were getting ready to feel his way forward.

Back straight now, I took a few deep breaths, trying to work oxygen into my tired mind and aching body. Pleasure seeped into my blood—Nyfain was clearly on call.

I carefully stepped forward, aiming for little pockets of cleared straw so that I didn't make any noise. In addition to not being able to see in the dark, Vemar's hearing wouldn't be as acute as mine.

He can't smell Nyfain with his animal suppressed, my dragon thought. *Pull out his dragon and let that beast take a nice, big whiff. That'll slow this escapade a little.*

It also might have him changing shape, which would wreak havoc, bring the officers or guards to kill him, and probably get me slapped with nuptials to Jedrek so the demon king can once again suppress you. Remember how we forgot to stipulate that he had to keep the spell off our people even after the marriage?

Nyfain resisted the suppression.

Nyfain shifted to do so. We don't know how. Stop distracting me. I'm *the brains of the shifter pair, remember? You're the brawn.*

I reached the side of my cell and gripped the bars.

Now what, Miss Brains? my dragon asked.

Damn good question. I had no fucking idea.

Vemar's feet shuffled against the stone as he continued to move forward. Then he hit the rough stone wall to my left and felt along it in the direction of my cell, sightless eyes wide and staring at nothing.

"I know you hear me, Strange Lady," he said, his voice low and raspy. "Are you nervous?"

No, just fucking curious why you're coming for me, I thought, swallowing.

Mr. Baritone stood beside his opened door, head tilted to the side and down. Listening. Waiting. No one else had come out of their cells, but everywhere I looked, hands gripped bars or hung through them, everyone listening. Everyone waiting like Mr. Baritone. Clearly they were all in on this.

One thing I hadn't properly realized as I was walked or dragged past Mr. Baritone or even Vemar—they were fucking huge. They were the same kind of big as Nyfain, especially Mr. Baritone. He stood tall and proud and confident, shoulders held back and huge arms dangling at his sides. What must he have looked like before he was imprisoned? Even in the darkness I could see the scars running down his body, not unlike Nyfain's. He didn't have a powerful bond mate to help him circumvent the pain. His pain tolerance—all of their tolerances—would be incredible.

These guys aren't going to be any fun to tangle with, I thought miserably. *Especially in my current state.*

Deep breath. Another. My head cleared. Pleasure zinged around my body.

Muffle that bond, I told my dragon.

I did. Start trying a little harder to feel the fucking thing.

I grimaced and sent rage and annoyance through the bond. I *felt* a command for him to cut it out. I had no idea if he'd understand, but it was the only idea I had as Vemar worked closer, awfully slow now. Suddenly he was trying not to make any noise.

He stopped when his fingers touched the first bar of my cell. He lifted his hand until he was grazing the upper bars. He stood tall, about Nyfain's height, mostly straight-backed now but with a little stoop he'd probably earned from this place and would likely never see the end of.

He wasn't smiling for once. His dark brow was furrowed in focus as he carefully made his way past the bars, working toward the door. I pulled my hands back, but didn't move yet. He was close enough to grab. I could yank him in, turn him, and get hold of his neck before he knew what hit him. I could kill him a moment later.

Though what if it wasn't a key he had, but something to pick locks? I didn't know how to do that. It would be no good to me.

Then again, an attack from a mad dragon wouldn't do me much good either.

He edged along, his fingertips skimming above, his body coming evenly with mine.

I held my breath, taking his measure. From a distance, I'd thought him lanky. I'd expected him to be weak and frail. And, compared to his former self, maybe he was those things. But not compared to me. He might *look* starved, but he wasn't much smaller than a healthy Jedrek, and I knew his prowess and dragon rage would make him explosive in a fight.

Fuckity limp-dicks.

The breath almost went out of me. I'd always been larger than the other women in my village. Larger than many of the men, even. But I had the feeling I was not large for a dragon. Because I knew that Mr. Baritone was bigger still.

Watch, folks, as I very quietly walk with him to the door.

Even my inner commentary was a whisper. My whole body shook with the tension of the moment. They had me fucking trapped in here, and this was a dungeon—there were no rules.

No one in the dungeon made a sound. No one twisted or moved in impatience.

I heard the soft footfalls of Vemar, and I prayed he didn't hear mine as I gingerly stepped around the straw. Pain met the softest blossoming of pleasure as it radiated through my body, providing a strange sort of nulling effect.

Nyfain hadn't just understood the note—he'd done the situation one better. That guy was great in a bind.

I continued along, mostly keeping pace, careful of my step. Good thing Jedrek wasn't very good at housecleaning, and I'd never felt drawn to spread out the straw the way it was when we first got here.

Vemar reached the door before me and paused, his eyes narrowing, his head cocked. Listening.

I stopped one step away, a little straw between me and the door. The silence hung heavy with expectation.

His eyebrows very slowly drew in together, as though something wasn't quite right. He stood like that for a moment, his brow furrowed, his body still. Then his head slowly turned until his face was pointed my way even though his eyes looked a bit to my right. A smile stretched across his face.

"You are getting ready to kill me, aren't you, Strange Lady?" His voice was filled with held-back laughter. "You are a smart one."

I stayed where I was. This could be a trick. He could be guessing.

He didn't move forward. Neither did I. I wanted to see how he would try to get in.

He rolled his head, then his shoulders. He chuckled to himself before reaching forward again and grazing his fingers against the upper bars. He lowered his hand slowly, stepping back as much as he could while still making contact with the very tips of his fingers. When they reached about the height of my chest, they lingered.

There he stood, seemingly waiting. Testing me, I guessed. He clearly wondered if I'd step forward and grab his wrist through the bars.

Should I? I asked my dragon. *He is thin for his particular body type, but he's still bigger than me. Is he stronger?*

Not with my help, no, I wouldn't think so. I bet he's wily, though, or why would he be using himself as bait?

Yeah, good point. He'd expect me to grab his wrist and pull him forward. If he was expecting it, he'd have a counter for it.

Finally I decided to take the upfront approach.

"What are you doing?" I asked, my voice a little subdued.

He lowered his hand, and his gaze slid a little closer to me, the sound of my voice giving him guidance. "I was wondering if you would grab me and try to yank me closer. No, huh?"

"No."

"No..." He paused as though waiting for me to expand my answer. "Just no? No explanation, no cutting remark...just no. I'm not sure what to do with you, Strange Lady. How did you move so quietly? I was listening, and I didn't hear a sound."

"I stepped carefully."

"Which means you either know the exact placement of every last piece of straw in your cell, or you can see in the dark. I am going to guess B. Which means it must be true—you have access to your animal. When you were fighting that first night, a few of us felt the tug of your magic on our dragons before the suppression spell popped them back into place. Then there's the fast healing. Why do you get access to your dragon *and* a sword? It is such a curiosity. Is that why Govam thinks you are dangerous? Or is he saying those things for our benefit? You never know with those demons. They run hot and cold. Are you working for them...against us?"

"Definitely not. I don't know why he says the things he does."

"Don't you? Hmm. Do you know why they allow you to wear that sword and have access to your dragon?"

"Yes."

"You have not tried to kill anyone with your very pretty, very fine, likely very sharp sword."

I didn't respond. Saying nothing sounded so much better than admitting the demon king was mocking me for all to see.

Another click sounded within the dungeon. Metal tinkled against metal from several other locations simultaneously.

Mr. Baritone turned and walked toward the stairs. Doors swung open and people stepped out. My heart picked up speed. This wasn't right. All these dragons could get out, but they weren't escaping—their focus was on *me*.

Maybe unmuffle that bond, I thought with shaking legs.

Light washed through the dungeon. Mr. Baritone had clicked them on. He didn't mount the stairs, though. He started walking my way.

Vemar squinted and blinked, getting used to the difference. His gaze drifted downward over my body, settling on the sword.

"Open that door, Vemar," Mr. Baritone commanded. Although his voice was deep and the command was intentional, it was threaded with none of the power usually carried by an alpha's command.

Vemar chuckled again and stepped closer to the cell door. "You haven't even taken it out of the sheath. I was trying to get as far away as possible so that you wouldn't stick me with it, and you haven't even reached for it."

"I could've stuck you with it when you were walking toward the door. You were close enough."

"This is true, Strange Lady, and yet you didn't. Does that mean you like me? I see that mark on your neck. Will you choose me to lay mine on top? I'm sure I could dominate you."

My dragon huffed and didn't even bother to comment. If it had been Nyfain saying that, she would've purred and preened and tried to kick his ass. I could only assume an alpha of note would at least raise her hackles. Cleary she wasn't worried about this guy.

A sly smile slid across Vemar's face. "No, huh? Now I am curious about who made this claim if I am not enough. I wish Micah could scent it. I wonder if he would be driven mad with the desire to force his claim."

"He would die if he tried," I said without thinking.

Vemar's onyx eyes darted up, taking my measure. That smile stretched a little wider.

"Hmm" was the only sound he made.

He worked the lock as those who were leaving their cells congregated in the middle of the dungeon. The *obice* meant no one could escape.

Metal clicked, and Vemar extracted his tools, sliding them behind his ears and essentially making them disappear in his mass of tightly curled hair. He grabbed a bar and pulled the door open, filling the doorway so I couldn't get out.

"Now what?" I asked.

He shrugged. "Now we see what you will not show the officers, I think."

I frowned at him. I wasn't sure what that meant.

He stared at me placidly.

The people in the middle of the dungeon moved, the small crowd curling in on itself and then stepping away to the sides. One figure walked toward me.

Tamara, shadows moving across her deeply tanned face the closer she got. Ragged shreds of clothes hung over her somewhat bony body, much like Vemar. Much like all of them. But it would be a mistake to assume they were as weak as they looked.

"Come out, come out, little dragon," she said.

Vemar peeled away to the side, leaving the doorway open for me to step through.

No sense hiding in the cage.

No, no sense at all. Rush to meet them, my dragon bit out.

I breathed through her rush of power, refusing to succumb to the fire sizzling in my blood.

I didn't know if they were my foes yet. Not for sure. Maybe

there was still a chance I could work them around to my side. Get them to fight *with* me.

Through the door, I stepped left, away from Vemar. He made no move to crowd me.

Tamara continued toward me, in no hurry. Her deep hazel eyes sparkled with intelligence and something wild and vicious that made my stomach flutter.

I barely stopped from swallowing the sudden lump in my throat. I felt like I was in trouble, but I had no idea what I might have done. I only knew the consequences would be incredibly severe.

CHAPTER 9
FINLEY

THE SMALL CROWD at Tamara's back moved with her, organizing as they did so. A few women formed a line right behind her, moving in sync as though they'd been fighting together all their lives. The rest fell in behind them, Mr. Baritone keeping to the side, the tallest of them all. He took up a post at the corner of the last cell to the right as the women stopped in front of me.

I pegged Tamara at early thirties. The women behind her varied in age. They didn't glance down at the sword, but I could feel the weight of their focus on it. Tamara didn't bother looking at me, looking over my shoulder instead. It was like she'd already taken my measure and found me wanting.

"Where'd you get that sword?" she asked, the edge in her voice giving me chills.

"It's like I said. I'm from the Wyvern kingdom—"

"I didn't ask where you're from," she said, finally looking me in the eye, "I asked where you got the sword."

I returned her stare, not sure how forthcoming I should be.

"It was a gift," I said.

"A gift? That right?" She laughed, but the women behind her didn't laugh with her. Their eyes said they'd like to be cracking their knuckles against my face, and the only thing keeping them from me was my interrogator.

"A gift from who?" she asked.

"The prince. Nyfain."

The faux-smile dripped off her face. Her eyes narrowed. "You're telling me the crowned prince gave you that sword?"

"Yes."

"And those clothes you came in here with? Did he gift you those, too?"

"Yes," I said, and a murmur rippled from the crowd. The women lined up rocked from side to side, clearly wanting action. And now I knew why—they thought I'd stolen the sword.

And yeah, I was pretty clear on how absurd it sounded.

"Honestly, there is a logical explanation for…all of this…" I grimaced because every unbelievable story started along those lines.

She took a small step forward.

Power simmered low in my gut. My dragon started pulling it from Nyfain and storing it. I didn't stop her. I hadn't come all this way to get killed because of a misunderstanding.

"I served as the captain of the queen's guard," Tamara said in a low tone. "She was kindness and grace, steel and might. She held that kingdom together. We would've died for her, all of us would've, oath or no. And I *will not* see her prized possessions parceled off by those disgusting demons and paraded through here to torment us. Give me that sword, and I will leave you to your cell."

The fire within me started to flicker.

"No." I meant to say, *You have this all wrong,* but the look on her face—in her eyes—stole my words. Pain. Loss. Grief. Seeing this sword again, worn by the likes of me, was reminding her of all she'd lost. It was reminding her of a life that had been stolen from her. A monarch that she'd loved.

I was obviously the bearer of bad fucking tidings.

Out of the corner of my eye, I saw Vemar scratch his nose. He wore a smile.

"No…" he said softly. "No reasons, no explanations, just no."

I still didn't know why he was the one who'd come to me first. Maybe he'd volunteered, crazy enough to risk getting skewered for his efforts.

Tamara ignored him. "You have one last chance, and then I will take that sword," she said.

The fire within me pumped higher. Hotter. Power bristled. Stretched my skin. Still my dragon pulled more from Nyfain. More and more, readying for this. I'd kept my cool with the demons, for the most part. I'd been using my head…as much as I could. But all of that rage had built up, stored within me, until now I just wanted to explode with it. I needed to explain, but something told me she wasn't interested in hearing far-fetched stories. She was interested in the dragon way of doing things— violence.

Who was I to say boo?

When I finally spoke, my voice was low and mean and filled with the rage they all did so well. "Well…you can certainly try…"

She lunged for me, but I was ready. I made a wedge with my arms, worked inside of her grab, and slapped her hands wide. I darted in and peppered her middle with punches, then ducked under a flailing arm, pushed it over my head to turn her, and launched her to the side.

Yes, with my dragon's power, I was definitely stronger and faster than these malnourished, suppressed shifters.

The line of women advanced, and I rushed forward to get right into their business, hammering home punches and kicks, careful not to do too much damage. It seemed like they were justifiably angry about the sword, and anyone with allegiance to Nyfain's mom…

They were my kinda people. I wanted them as allies.

Still, they'd started it, and I wanted to kick a little ass. Needed to. Thankfully, they'd respect me more for it.

I kicked out and then shoved with my foot, sending someone sprawling. Then I swiped the legs out from under another woman and kicked her as she fell.

A fist sailed through the air, and I turned my face to take it in the cheek instead of the eye while I clotheslined a woman and broke through the line to punch a man in the throat. I tossed him and grabbed the next person, hurtling them behind me too.

The problem was that because I wasn't hurting anyone too badly, and because they were stubborn dragons, they popped back up like they were on springs and rejoined the fight.

End it hard, and then explain yourself, my dragon thought as I hammered my fist into a man's sternum, then tit-punched a woman. That would hurt. I didn't envy her.

Okay.

I tossed another man, felt a hand grab the sword and pull, and knew a moment of horror when the sword was yanked halfway out of its sheath.

Without thinking, I sent a shock wave of power all around me, *shoving* with my will and layering it with a stinging slap that wouldn't be soon forgotten. Power gushed from me but filled right back up, singing with Nyfain's essence. Begging to be used. Urging me to unleash more of my rage. He was joining the fight from a distance, and he would have his say.

I smiled. Tears came to my eyes. Fuck, I missed him. I hated being separated.

I pumped out power again, blasting it.

People fell back, stumbling over themselves to get away now. A man fell and then started crawling along the stone, no apparent destination in mind.

Mr. Baritone appeared in front of me like a phantom. A fucking enormous phantom with his broad shoulders and thick chest.

He flexed and leaned toward me. A blast of his power sandpapered my face, rich and heavy. It commanded me to back down. To submit.

Nyfain and I had clearly released his dragon. He wasn't from Wyvern, I didn't think, so it was only a matter of time before the suppression spell kicked back in. In the meantime, he thought he'd pull alpha around these parts.

He thought wrong.

I cut through his power with my will, slicing his skin with it on the backstroke. His eyes widened and jaw dropped. Surprise!

He barely lost a beat, though, before grabbing me and swinging me around. He walked forward and shoved my back against cell bars, so quickly I didn't have time to react. His power beat into me again: *Submit!*

Kill this motherfucker, my dragon said, and I was pretty sure this last week had made her a little too hungry for blood.

Before I could respond to her with thoughts, or him with will, a great tide of power welled up in me, the likes of which I had never experienced before. Ruthless and volatile, vicious and uncompromising, it made my body quiver as it coursed liquid magma through my blood. A scent curled around me as the power gushed into my middle, pine and lilac with a hint of honeysuckle, a delicious, balmy smell that I knew as well as I knew myself.

Nyfain had felt another alpha try to pull rank with his mate, and he was losing his fucking mind.

I used it, pushing aside Mr. Baritone's command and then hammering into him with my will. I didn't lift a finger. I didn't try to get out of his hold. Nyfain had always said male dragons had the upper hand with physical force, but females had the power of will. I could manifest that will physically, and I wanted to prove it beyond a shadow of doubt.

Gush after endless gush of power battered Mr. Baritone, pounded against him, sliced his skin and pummeled his ribs. Still, Nyfain sent more, his dragon joining the show, turbulent and wild, as they pummeled this other alpha to prove their dominance.

Mr. Baritone seized up, his fists locked in a hard grip around my upper arms. Sweat broke out on his face. His eyebrows stitched together. His eyes kept increasing in size, fully rounded and a little panicked. He'd had no idea what he was messing with.

"Let go," I said, loud enough for everyone to hear. I stuffed magic into the command.

Mr. Baritone didn't struggle with the command like Nyfain always did. He didn't make me wonder whether he would ignore me.

No, his fingers peeled away almost immediately, and he dropped his arms at his sides.

"Step away," I said, making that command a bit spicy. It

would race down his spine violently and tingle his balls uncomfortably.

He took two halting steps, giving me space. His chest rose and fell quickly, and his eyes had taken on a wild edge. Accustomed to being the dominator, Mr. Baritone was now being dominated.

"Submit," I told him, my dragon right near the surface, riding me hard to make a statement. I could feel Nyfain's dragon through the bond, pumping in more power, wanting to make a statement just as much as my dragon did.

Mr. Baritone stared at me but didn't act or comment.

Tell him to kneel, my dragon thought. *Saying he's submitting won't be enough. Not after the way he manhandled you. Make him kneel, and make sure you don't have to tell him twice. You've already fucked up, allowing him to resist your first command—you need to make this one count.*

That seemed a little extreme, but this wasn't some milquetoast human interaction. There were dragons in the mix, and they were crazy.

I summoned the power. I straightened my body. If there had been any pain left over from the whipping earlier, there was no way in hell I'd feel it with all this power running through me.

"*Kneel,*" I barked, giving the command everything I had.

My dragon made an *ohhhhmmm* kinda thought, which typically meant she'd fucked up somehow, and the entire dungeon of people crashed down onto their knees. A few cried out in pain, busting their kneecaps in the process. Some tipped forward with the blow, landing on their faces.

Nyfain's dragon swelled in pride, which was a pretty solid tip-off that I'd gone too far.

Too much power, my dragon thought. *You were supposed to*

make *them, not* force *them.*

What the fuck is the difference? I thought-shouted at her.

She retreated, slinking away and leaving me to deal with the fallout. What a shithead.

"Damn it," I muttered, facing the other shifters, all of whom looked up at me with wary and/or pain-filled eyes. "Sorry, everyone. Sorry! Honestly, my dragon has been suppressed most of my life. I've never even shifted! Remember me saying that? It's true. The only reason I know she's a dragon is because Nyfain, the prince of Wyvern, is my true mate. We have a bond, and his dragon and my dragon are a couple of real assholes. I'm serious. They said to make a statement and…sorry."

"It can't be true," Tamara said softly, her gaze rooted to me. "It can't be true."

"You can smell me now, right? You know it's true."

"But…" Another woman with a gap in her teeth blinked at me, intense longing in her eyes. "The curse. If…"

I pointed at her. Clearly Dolion had only lifted the magical gag from Nyfain. "You have the magical gag, right?" She nodded. "I don't, because I was born in one of the villages. I'm common. Basically, as a sum-up…" I glanced at the stairs and licked my lips. I doubted anyone was listening…but still. I continued in an undertone. "The curse hasn't been broken, but the suppression has been lifted. If you are from Wyvern, I can give you access to your dragon. Or…I probably just did. But since the curse is still in effect, it might hinder your ability to shift."

"So that's what that feeling was," someone muttered. "It felt like something magical had shifted or changed, but I couldn't figure out what."

"The prince had his wings shorn off," said a man with a large forehead and pointy chin.

"Yes, exactly," I said. "It doesn't matter anyway, because if you shifted, they'd just kill you. It's better if you keep all of this to yourself and relish in being with your dragon again. Unless your dragon is an asshole like mine, and then…sorry about the return to drama."

You're just as much of an asshole, my dragon thought.

Not even possible.

"He's your true mate, but you didn't…" Tamara bent her head a little, willing me to finish the sentence.

"Imprint? No. The curse hasn't been broken." I showed her my teeth, not sure how much to say. "The demons took me away before it could happen." Close enough and mostly true.

"But, Strange Lady, *why* don't you use the sword?" Vemar said, lying on his side with his head propped up on his elbow. He hadn't stepped into the fight, but he hadn't been able to escape my command to kneel, either.

I lifted my hands and then dropped them in defeat. "The sword *was* a gift. I was dealing with some trouble—from Jedrek, actually—and Nyfain was trying to help. He gave me a bunch of weapons, most of which I could use. The sword never worked for me. I can work a pocketknife like a motherfucker, but a sword? No. We didn't have enough time to train with it. I wear it now because the demons apparently think it's a great joke that I can't use it."

"No," Tamara said softly, pain in her eyes. "You aren't wearing it as a joke. You are wearing it to remind us of what we lost. You are wearing it because the demon king knew the effect it would have. He's not taunting you—he is taunting us."

Her words hit me like a sack of bricks. I sagged a little, digesting them. Faces fell around me. Tamara's pain was shared.

I took a deep breath. Part of being a hero was building people up. Probably. It was about all I could do right now, at any rate.

"Well then," I said with determination. "Fuck them. They don't get to decide how we feel. Let it serve as a symbol for a future we will regain."

Fire sparked in their eyes—all of them, hearing the call for any sort of future, not just for the Wyvern kingdom. Heads nodded. Backs straightened.

"And, hell, maybe someone can show me how to use it!"

A few people smiled, and even more chuckled. They might not have realized I was serious.

Tamara climbed to her feet, that fire still raging in her eyes.

"A villager." She huffed out a laugh and offered me her hand. "The golden prince's true mate is a villager."

I could hear the irony singing through her words.

"A really poor one, too," I replied with a grin. "The mad king is probably turning over in his grave."

Tamara laughed. "Probably."

"There is nothing wrong with growing up in a village," Vemar said, and many nodded.

Tamara sobered a little. "The queen was from a village in the Flamma Kingdom. A village in a different kingdom, with a lot more status, but a village nonetheless. I wonder if she would've been pleased. She also wanted humility for her son. She wanted him grounded. A poor villager who unabashedly kills officers and comes in front of guards must surely keep him on his toes."

I pinched my face without meaning to, my cheeks flaming red again. She laughed.

"So, I have a few questions," I said to quickly change the subject.

Mr. Baritone rose, walking closer. His gaze flicked to Nyfain's mark, and hunger flitted through his eyes. A push of his power made me bristle.

"Ooh-wee," Vemar said, sitting up and rubbing his knees. "Micah's dragon smells another alpha and wants to accept the challenge."

Mr. Baritone was clearly Micah. Nyfain had told me there would be shifters who saw his mark as a challenge rather than a threat. He'd told me one of them could give me a future— something he thought he could not.

Don't you even think about it, my dragon warned me, and I rolled my eyes.

"It won't be a problem," Micah told me. "I can already feel the tug of the suppression magic yanking on my dragon. I'm not from Wyvern. I haven't been freed. When my dragon is suppressed, he won't thrash at me to take the challenge and work to claim you."

I wanted to ask how his dragon intended to meet a challenge from another dragon who wasn't even here, or stake his claim on a woman who wasn't interested, but it was irrelevant right now. There were larger issues at hand.

"If you can get out of your cells, why aren't we leaving?" I asked.

"They have a magical lock at the top of the stairs." Micah glanced behind him at the stairs. "Try to go through it and get something cut off."

"Ah," I said, having forgotten that in all the commotion. "And the lock-picking tools?"

"Stolen, obviously," Vemar said, scratching his head. "When we are...*treated* to their fancy parties, we grab anything we can.

Sometimes there are useful things, but most times not. They watch us closely, so there's very little we can sneak out, especially given the state of mind we usually leave in."

"I hate to say it, but the wolves are our saving grace," Micah said. "They are generally thought to be more compliant than we are—"

"Because they *are* more compliant than we are," said a woman with light brown hair soiled with oil and grime. "They show their lack of worth where it counts the most."

"They don't raise such a ruckus." Vemar winked at me.

"The more submissive of them act cowed and broken and eager to please, and they do a damn fine job," Bad Hair Year continued, her lip curling. "It's kind of their *thing*, I guess."

A few people snarled at that.

"They also work as a unit better than most other shifters out there," Micah cut in. "They've cased the castle, taken what we've needed, and gotten to know all the players better than we could've managed. It's too bad we only see them fleetingly at the parties."

People fidgeted and a few murmured, unhappy to agree but needing to. Despite the need to work together, apparently dragons thought they were better than wolves. And wolves likely thought the reverse.

"How long have you been working on all of this?" I asked, hope curling through me.

"Years. Since he got here." Vemar pointed at Micah. "He's the one who got us all organized. How long you been here, Micah?"

"Time is hard to judge, but...half a decade, maybe? A bit more?"

My hope shriveled up, and an uncomfortable weight lodged in my stomach. "That long? If the wolves have cased the castle, surely you have most of what you need. What's the hold-up?"

"It's hard to get opportunities to talk with them," Micah said. "We are only pulled out of here for larger engagements, and then we are heavily guarded. There aren't a lot of opportunities to touch base."

"We tried to escape once," Tamara said. "We thought we had everything ready. We got as far as the banks, ready to force our way to the boats…"

"What happened?" I asked.

"Govam happened," Bad Hair Year said with a grim set to her mouth. "Somehow he knew what we were planning. He had a team waiting. Without our dragons, we had no hope. They dragged us back and beat us to within an inch of our lives."

I let out a breath, thinking about my interactions with the demon. He was clearly dangling carrots in front of me to get me to act, and then he'd be waiting to step in and catch me. Mind-fuckery, all right, and he was damned good at it.

"Huh," I said, running my thumb over the hilt of the sword. "Well then. Maybe we need to do a little study on Govam and make sure we're anticipating him more than he is us."

"Already underway," Micah said with a glimmer in his eyes. "We will make a second attempt, and next time we will win."

"Next time," Tamara said with a shit-eating grin, "more than half of us will have our dragons."

"What if we don't want to leave?" someone asked from the back, a skin-and-bones man in his late thirties, I'd guess.

His eyes had a sheen over them in his gaunt face. His lank black hair fell down over a pronounced forehead.

"Why wouldn't you want to leave?" I asked.

"Because I'm in no hurry to rush to my death. Like the alpha said, it's been tried. It failed. My dragon has already been suppressed again. I don't have access to healing. When they put me back in my cell the last time, they cracked my head and broke all my limbs in multiple places. I nearly bled out. I'd rather not suffer that again. They'll kill me this time, I know they will."

I stared at him incredulously.

He looks like he's nearly dead now, my dragon murmured. *What is he holding out for? Why does he wish to go slowly?*

I glanced at the cells lining the squat room, the ceiling pushing down over us. I worried the cold, grimy stone with my toe and curled my nose at the thick, putrid smell that hung heavy in the air.

"*This* is living?" I asked, taking two steps and pulling the door to the nearest cell wide. I pointed inside while looking at him. "Being forced to rot in this cage? Being taken out and beaten so they can consume our pain and fear?" I glanced in, intending to point out the light covering of straw, nothing more than an illusion of bedding. Or the bucket in the corner for waste that usually overflowed before it was emptied.

But something caught my eye. Something I hadn't seen when being dragged in and out of the dungeon.

Dotted here and there, creeping through the stone, somewhat wilting and laden with dead leaves, sprouted five everlass plants. They'd found a way to keep us company, even in hell.

Everlass, the very plant that had provided the people in the villages healing from the sickness the demons had unleashed on us.

Everlass, the plant that had brought Nyfain and me together.

Emotion welled up through me. Tears blurred my vision.

I choked out a laugh and walked into the cell immediately,

avoiding the straw piled up on one side, and bent to the first plant, immediately pruning.

"What is she doing?" a man asked.

"What do you have in there?" a woman replied, obviously speaking to the owner of the cell.

"Nothing. Same as you. Probably less," the man said.

Tamara appeared outside the cell door, quickly followed by Vemar. Micah filled in behind them.

"She's pruning the everlass," Tamara said softly. "Like the queen used to do. And the lady's maids. She knows how to work the plants."

"Lotta good that'll do us in here," someone murmured.

"Where there is everlass, there is hope." I stood when I was finished and walked to the next cell, finding four plants huddled in the shadows near the back. "Because where there is everlass, there is life." Heart in my throat, I went from cell to cell. Finally, in one, I felt my chest tighten and my hope flower. "And sometimes"—I bent toward the crowded plant—"There is death."

CHAPTER 10

HADRIEL

"OOPS." I PUT up my hand even though my mare was walking steadily behind the master's bad-tempered stallion. "Sir, you took the wrong trail."

I stopped at the fork in the beaten-down path within the Royal Wood as the prince went right instead of heading left toward the castle.

"Sir…" I stared longingly in the direction we were supposed to go, then up through the straggly, twisted tree cover to glimpse the darkening sky. Now that I had access to my wolf again, I could see in the dark for the most part, but that was beside the point. I didn't want to be stuck in this hellhole of a wood after dark. I definitely didn't want to battle the horrible creatures that populated it.

In all honesty, I also wanted to be released from the master's company. He wasn't good for my bowels. The guy was much too intense.

"It's rolling toward night, sir," I called, getting farther and farther behind. "Shouldn't we be getting—Damn it."

I leaned forward to get my mare walking after him. It was possible I wouldn't get in trouble for just leaving him and going back to the castle, but it was a risk I wasn't willing to take.

"I'm sure you remember, sir," I said as I caught up, "that *last week* was the lull in demon creature activity. Tonight will have demon creature activity. You need to get something to eat and a little rest before you face the threat."

Glenarm Village was just up the way, the first village the master had visited to begin pulling shifters out of suppression. Through a lot of diligence, he'd knocked it out in two weeks and promptly moved on. He'd spent this last week attending to the second-most-powerful village. At this rate, if the prince didn't drop dead from exhaustion, we'd have the whole kingdom sorted in well under the time I'd mentally allotted for Finley to break out of her cage.

I sure fucking hoped Finley broke out of her cage. Her plan had sounded so promising when we were discussing it at the castle. She'd sounded so sure she'd come back. The problem was that we'd been sitting in the middle of a sex demon orgy, full of weird demon cocks and pussies with teeth and all sorts of other crap. It was possible our view of reality had been skewed. I was starting to get a little nervous about it now, to be honest.

A lot nervous, actually. So nervous, in fact, that I'd started grilling the master every morning about the demon creatures he'd killed the previous night—where he'd found them and if they'd been running around willy-nilly, heading in a straight line, or hanging around like gobshites. With the information he gave me, I was plotting a map and trying to trace them back to their point of origin. The gate that let the creatures into the kingdom was said to move around, but how many entry points could there be?

Besides, this bullshit had gone on for so long that they were probably on some sort of schedule. All I had to do was brave my watery bowels, pepper the master for information, and eventually I'd have their access points. I knew I would. I was good at this silly shit.

Granted, I had no clue what I'd do with the information, but that could come later. Desperate measures always came later.

He didn't speak as he continued on, the village just up ahead and the sun lifting her skirts and stepping behind the horizon.

"Are you lost? Grunt once for yes, two for no..." I tilted my head and stuck out my ear, listening. Nothing.

Damn. He was in such a sullen snit that he didn't even want to berate me for being an idiot.

We broke the boundary line, and he didn't even flinch. The magic was deteriorating, and he was stronger now that the suppression had been lifted. Boundaries were mere suggestions to him at this point.

When we reached the village stables, the master swung his thick thigh over his stallion's back and hopped to the ground. I took a moment to admire the way his threadbare jeans molded perfectly to his high and tight ass. Goddess goose me, the man was a fucking vision. I couldn't even be jealous of his physique, he was that fine to look at.

I slid to the ground and followed the master as he handed off his stallion to a stable boy. I did the same.

"Sir, if you don't beg my minding—No." I scrunched up my face and tried again. The guy scrambled my wits. "If you don't mind me begging—asking! Fuck! If you don't *mind* me *asking*, what are we doing?"

His golden eyes flicked my way for the briefest of moments

before he started walking toward the village green. A host of people had assembled there, standing in a cluster with another few groups looking on. When they noticed the master, they fanned out, and a man and two women stepped forward to greet him.

"Sire," said the middle-aged woman with gray streaks at her temple.

Everyone on the village green bowed, some more elegantly and practiced than others. The castle wasn't the only place where a bunch of mediocre assholes had been shuttled into top positions.

"I got your note." The master stopped before her, looking around at those assembled. "What's this about?"

"Well...it's better if we show you." The woman stepped back, her gaze becoming intense as it held his. She grabbed the edges of her shiny green robe-slash-gown, a hideous sort of garment embroidered with fake pearls and bright strings and a few ill-placed tassels, and peeled it off her shoulders. It dropped and pooled at her feet, leaving her nude in the dwindling light of evening.

A swell of magic had me taking a step back. I'd rather not be randomly attacked because she mistakenly thought I was challenging her. Her form morphed into a sleek gray wolf with slightly glowing hazel eyes.

The breath went out of me. I found myself taking a step forward, my eyes searching her for deformities.

"But...the curse," I said as the master walked around her, clearly searching for the same thing.

"After you freed our animals," said another woman, this one in her mid-thirties with tightly coiled black hair and sepia eyes that matched her skin tone, "a few people couldn't control their animals' need to regain their fur. They shifted."

She stepped out of a plain white robe, her swell of power making me step back again. Her form changed into that of a honey badger, a damn good animal to have on your side and a horrible opponent if one was your enemy. Very similar to dragons, actually. Less moody, though.

"As you see," piped up a red-faced man, his eyes a strange fawn color and his features a little too close together, "shifting within the curse hasn't affected them like it did you, sire. It hasn't affected any of us like that."

His swell of power wasn't so great as the others as he transformed into a hawk-type bird and flapped up into the air. He swung toward me, battering me with the tips of his wings.

"What the—" I waved my hand at him, then ducked when he persisted, losing my shit just a little. When he still didn't fly away, I did a quick panic run in a circle, slapping my hands above my head, trying to get the accursed thing to bugger off. "Get it off, get it off!"

Surprised laughter rose from the crowd.

"He's trying to find a perch." A woman in the crowd stepped forward and put out her arm.

"A perch, fine." I slowed down from my hunched jog and smoothed back my hair, attempting for a little decorum as I straightened up. "Just leave me out of it."

The master was looking at me like he didn't know whether to be angry, annoyed, or amused.

I used the pad of my index finger to wipe each side of my mustache along my upper lip. Mediocre butler, on duty.

The wolf shifted back, breathing heavily but not too taxed from quick shifts. She picked up her robe and pulled it back on.

"It seems the only issue with shifting right now," she said, "is a change in eye color pigmentation. For some of us, the color has changed to that of our animal's fur or coat or scales, and others have developed pigmentation similar to their human skin. We have no idea why. It has changed for everyone, though. Like yours."

"Scales?" the master asked.

She nodded, looking to the side. A woman in loose, flowing garments like the others stepped forward, dragging a tall boy with a gangly body. His back was bowed, like he knew he'd done something wrong, and he stared at his feet. I was no master at guessing ages, but he barely looked sixteen, just old enough to shift.

"My son, your highness." She offered a slight curtsey and addressed the master through tight lips. "He was told not to shift. I told him twice, and he heard it from our council, too. I *told him* that it might kill him. But did he listen? No."

"It seems the boy is a dragon, your highness," one of the others said. "His parents are both in the big cat family, as were their parents—"

"His grandfather on his father's side, rest his soul, was a bear, actually," the mother said.

"And his shift?" the master asked, looking intently at the boy. "It went well? His wings were intact?"

"Yes, sire." The woman manhandled her son to get him to turn around before pulling up his shirt, exposing his back. An emerald-green stripe of scales cut down each side. "His eyes are now the same color as these scales, but otherwise he is fine. *He could've died*"—she took a beat to glare at her son—"but he succeeded in shifting on his own."

"It hurt," the boy grumbled.

"Yes, because you did it without guidance, you moron!" The woman slapped him upside the head. Clearly she'd been worried for her boy, and now that she knew he was fine, she was taking her fear out on him. My mom used to do that to me all the time when I was a kid.

The master leaned his weight from one foot to the other, looking intently at the boy. No emotions crossed his face, but my heart went out to the guy. This new dragon would need guidance to take to the sky, and the master could no longer offer it. He could no longer soar with his kind. He'd paid a helluva price for his father's mistakes.

"We think, your highness," the woman said, entwining her fingers in front of her, "that the suppression magic was what affected your shift. It stands to reason. Without it, we are free to shift without complication."

"I see." The master paused for another beat, looking over the gathering. "Give it a bit more time. Let's see what happens with the other villages. If it is as you say, we'll plan a first shift for the strongest of our youth. If all goes well, we'll lead more of them through it. Start educating them now. Talk to them of the shifter ways. We need to get them up to speed."

"Yes, sire. And…sire…" She squeezed her hands together before minutely rolling her shoulders. She'd had a good act going up until now, but suddenly her nerves were showing. It made me feel a bit better about the way my bowels twisted into knots every time I had to talk directly to the dragon prince. "Marcus—the boy there—is quite tall for his age. He's taller than his father was. We have a few more boys and girls like that. Taller than the others. Stubborn youths, some of them. I wonder…" She lost steam, her words fading away.

The honey badger shifted back into her human form, putting on her robe before taking up the thread of the conversation.

"Folklore suggests that when a people are in great peril, a swell of dragons are born to defend them. It is the goddess's way of defending her people."

"Wolves can defend just as well," someone grumbled, then grunted, probably elbowed to shut up. I would've agreed with him…if wolves could fly. Or breathe fire. The dragons had us there, and they knew it, the arrogant bastards.

"In times of peril, the dragons will rise," someone murmured.

"Most of these youths were already born when the curse came into effect, though," someone said.

The master slid his gaze my way.

I lifted my eyebrows in question, not able to read his…anything, really. I never knew what he was thinking.

"This kingdom was in turmoil long before the curse," he finally said, swinging his golden gaze back to them. "We'll know the truth of it soon."

"Yes, sire," the woman said, and she and her friend both curtsied. The gangly boy got shoved back the way he had come.

"Come." The master turned and strode back toward the horses.

It was the first time he'd given me an actual command all day.

I nearly fell over myself to do as he said. "Yes, sir. Right at your—Somewhat behind your heels, sir. Should I call you sire now? I'm not sure where we stand with the whole *don't antagonize the demons with your title* situation. I mean, you've killed most of the ones in the castle, so it hardly matters what they think…"

"Hannon, Finley's brother," he said after mounting, as though he hadn't heard a word I'd spoken.

"Yes…sire?"

But I didn't get an answer. He kept riding until we reached the stables at the castle, then put out his hand for the stable boy to bring his stallion. The boy scurried away to do just that.

"He is taller than his father, isn't he?"

I blinked a few times, thinking, then shook my head. "I don't think I ever saw them next to each other. He's big, though. Tall, broad. He's the biggest in their village, I think. And Finley was the tallest girl. I remember her saying that. She was tall for a guy in her village, even."

He grunted as his stallion came. In a moment, he swung onto its back before guiding it around and looking down at me.

"I'll need you shadowing me tonight," he said, and I was pretty sure my balls shriveled up into my body. "Finley has been anxious for the last couple days. She hasn't been punished for…whatever it is they punish her for. Right now, she is practically jumping out of her skin. I'll need to be available to help her should she require assistance. You can watch for the demons' creations while I'm…indisposed."

"But…" He walked on, and I had to scramble onto Bella's back and hurry her after him. "But sir, how can I keep up with a dragon?"

"You are a wolf, are you not? Don't wolves always pride themselves on how quickly and quietly they can get through a wood?"

"But I can't—" I gritted my teeth and internally swore. I *could* shift, apparently. Those village people had said so. And while generally that would've been an amazing thing, it wasn't so great if it meant I'd been forced to spend even *more* time in the moody prince's company.

"I can help you through the shift, if you're rusty," he said, suddenly chatty as shit. When it came to doling out terrible news, he was apparently full of things to say. "I can give you a boost of power to make sure the transition is easy."

"What about Urien?" That was his trusty valet, a relic from a time when people did the job they were trained for, and did it well.

"He's always on hand, but tonight...I want another set of eyes. You're doing it for Finley, Hadriel. Something tells me that tonight..." His voice turned into a hard growl. "Whatever is happening tonight...she'll need all the support she can get."

CHAPTER II

FINLEY

"THIS IS NOT going to be any fun, Strange Lady," Vemar called down, clutching the bars of his cell. "Just remember, we're all going through it with you. The rest of us have been through this before, and we all survived."

"If you get a chance to kill someone, go ahead and take it," Tamara said, pacing back and forth in her cell.

"You do that, they'll keep you in the cage," said Lucille, a somewhat petite woman for a dragon. "Like all of us."

"She'll want to stay in the cage." Micah rested his forearms on a crossbar and let his hands dangle outside of the bars as usual. "How many have you killed now?"

"Nineteen." Lucille grinned, showing the gap in her top row of teeth. Apparently she'd gotten that when a guard kicked her in the mouth. "I keep trying to round up to twenty, but they're onto me."

"How about you, Micah?" someone down the row asked. "Care to impress the new girl?"

"Kill number isn't as important as rank," Micah replied.

"He's killed every captain but one." Tamara smirked at him across the way. "You just need that clean sweep, and then you'll be bored."

"They keep elevating new guards to captain." Micah shrugged. "I have plenty to hunt."

The sound of boots thunking on stone reverberated down the row of cells. It sounded like an army.

"Here we go," Micah said in a low, calm voice. My small hairs stood on end from the level of menace dripping from each and every syllable. "Finley, we don't go to as many parties as the wolves or faeries because we're dangerous. We're unpredictable. Killing guards on these nights won't get you beaten like other times because they want to show us off. They'll sacrifice guards to do it. But what it *will* do is make them wary to call you up again. That's a good thing."

"Consider it open season," Tamara said with a small chuckle. "Kill at will."

One by one, the dragons stepped away from the bars. Those I could see drifted to the center of their cells, hands at their sides. All gazes were directed toward the stairs, except for Micah's. He looked my way and nodded once, giving me a wave of courage and confidence.

I glanced back at the corner where I'd stored the dried everlass leaves, staring longingly at the crowded ones. If only I could get those into the water source at this party, I could likely kill the whole lot of them. Then again, I hadn't tried cold-seeping them to see if they would have the same potency. Not to mention I doubted the demons would let me near their water source...

I flexed and relaxed my hands as the stampede of boots got louder. I stepped into the center of my cell as well. Other than me, it was empty, as Jedrek hadn't been brought down for a while. Black boots with a high shine appeared on the steps, Govam descending. Denski followed, and then came a line of hard-eyed demons with shackles in their hands and determination on their faces. These guards looked like they were ready for war.

"Why not the sex demons instead of the guards?" I asked the others. The thought had occurred to me a few times, but I'd always forgotten to ask.

"A bunch of lustful, grabby dragons aren't any easier to move," Tamara said, still staring in the direction of the stairs as the guards descended.

"I think it is actually something to do with their hierarchy," Micah said in a low voice. "I've asked out of curiosity, but no one's given me a direct answer. The sex demons are somewhat looked down upon, it seems."

"I'm not complaining," Vemar said.

The guards filed into the dungeon, three to five guards each congregating outside of the various cells.

"Looks like we have a lot of new faces," Vemar called out. "Do we have a new captain leading a new team, perhaps?"

Govam didn't spare Vemar a glance, nor did he walk as far as my cell. He stopped outside Micah's cell and stared in for a moment, not speaking.

"I get this one, then?" A sallow-skinned demon with two large horns curling from his head stopped outside of my cell, looking in. He gave me a once-over, pausing for a long moment on my sword. When his eyes met mine again, there was something not quite right with the gleam in them. Something hostile and unbalanced. Heat sparkled there, too. Desire. "Just a pretty little girl dragon. What a nice treat for my first time in this position, hmm?

Breaking me in easy…while I break you in hard."

I ignored him as Vemar continued to call out above the din. "Think you can survive the night, Govam?"

The demon in front of me looked back as more guards joined him, five in all.

"Who's the new guy?" Tamara asked, looking my way. "He looks like a dead man. An ugly dead man."

"Ooh-wee," Vemar said. "Fresh meat."

"A new captain, what a treat," someone else called as metal tinkled within the sounds of boots scuffing and people moving. All the guards were taking their positions, staring into the cells of the dragons they'd be managing.

"There used to be five captains assigned to the dragons, didn't there, Govam?" another said. "Micah has been bad for the health of your organization."

The lip of the sallow-skinned demon curled as another guard stepped up to the bars in front of me, holding cuffs.

"Let's go, dragon," the guard with cuffs said, the metal tinkling between his hands.

"Strange Lady," Vemar called out in his classic singsong voice. "Now would be a terrible time to behave. You have a lot of catching up to do if you want to match Micah."

The squeak of metal hinges announced a cell door opening. Then another. As I turned around to put my hands through the space between the bars, shouts erupted. Another door opened, and then one clanged shut. Over my shoulder, I saw a cluster of guards at the end speed up, some rushing forward and some shoving back. A long arm swung through the air, the fist smashing into a demon's face. Through the crowd I could briefly see Vemar, his face red with exertion and anger as he fought his way into the demon horde.

Sticks came out, slashing down at him. He laughed as he got his hands around a demon's neck. He adjusted his hold. I didn't hear the crack, but I didn't need to. The demon dropped like a stone as a crowd swarmed Vemar, taking him to the ground.

My wrists were grabbed and yanked through the bars. My shoulders screamed from the rough treatment as my arms slid against metal. I winced, cooperating, waiting for the cuffs to be applied.

"Okay," the guard said.

My hands were pushed again, and I went to step forward. Before I could, I felt a fist in my hair, yanking my head back. My skull banged off the bars as lips neared my ear between the bars.

"You best be good, dragon, or I will make you regret it," the sallow-skinned demon whispered. His grip on my hair tightened, and he shook it a little before releasing me.

"Get 'em out and lead 'em up," Govam yelled over the crowd.

"Back up to us, dragon," my guard said, three of them waiting on the other side of the door. "Back up—what's the deal with that sword, captain? Can we leave it here or what?"

"Govam said she's supposed to keep it—the king's orders." The sallow-skinned demon looked at my hip, indecision in his eyes. "She doesn't know how to use it, I guess. She hasn't ever reached for it. The demon king isn't worried about her having it."

The guard in front of me furrowed his brow in consternation, clearly not convinced. "Since when does one of these dragons not know how to use a sword? I've heard most of them are proficient."

"Come on, let's go." The new captain looked toward Govam, who had Micah out of the cell, surrounded by guards. They started him toward the stairs, working around the other guards extracting dragons or still trying to subdue Vemar.

The key turned in the lock and the door swung open before rough hands grabbed me and yanked me backward. I stumbled, nearly falling, before more hands took hold and ripped me around to face the stairs. A shove had me nearly stumbling forward, but then the hands secured me between two demons a bit shorter than me.

Tamara's deep hazel eyes zipped my way as she was pulled from her cell. She held my gaze for a tense beat, and I could feel the power swirling around her as my guards pushed me near her. She looked downward poignantly, her gaze stopping at my hip. When it came back up, holding mine, I didn't need to be told what she was after.

I might not know how to use the sword, but *she* did.

Time to be naughty.

As I passed her, I let my will pulse outward, shoving the guards back. I spun and kicked, getting the new captain in the sternum.

Tamara's power ballooned, and then she ripped her hands wide and forward, snapping the chains on the cuffs and propelling the guards off their feet.

Holy shit, my dragon thought.

Holy shit was right. Tamara was half starved and out of practice, yet when she had access to her dragon, she had some serious strength and power.

My guards rushed forward to grab me. Tamara got there first.

She grabbed the hilt of the sword, yanked it out, and pushed me out of the way. Then she slashed to the right before lunging forward, her pose absolute perfection. The strength and power wove into an intricate dance. This dragon absolutely *did* know how to use a sword.

The point of the sword dove into the middle of the new captain. She pulled it free and made quick work of the three guards near him, slashing and stabbing like a motherfucking master.

I have a girl crush, my dragon said.

We were on the same page.

Hands grabbed me from behind. I surged my power in an attempt to break the cuffs like Tamara had, but the blows started to fall, one hitting my head. Black spots appeared in my vision. I speared with my will, digging into a demon as I stepped to the side and turned. I drove my head forward, using my forehead to break a nose. I was already dizzy—what was a little more trauma for a good cause?

An extendable stick cracked down on my shoulder. Another swung from the side at my thigh.

"Give in," Tamara said, downing another demon as a group of guards tackled her. I could barely hear her voice over the shouting and grunting. "They'll stop if you do. They won't if you won't."

Two demons piled onto me and shoved me to the ground. My cheek hit stone and their weight knocked the breath out of me.

My dragon's rage fanned higher, but I stopped struggling. With my hands behind my back, there wasn't much I could do. I could kill them with will, but more guards would just take their places. I didn't want to waste the energy that I would surely need later on.

Someone pinned their knee in the center of my back. Others knelt around me, leaning over and bracing their hands on me to keep me still. I lay there, waiting.

"Fucking dragons," one of them muttered, sitting back. "I wish we could just kill the lot of them."

"We'd all be better off," another replied, grabbing one of my upper arms. Another did the same with the other arm, and they dragged me up, their movements coarse.

"Leave that sword behind," Govam commanded from a quarter of the way up the stairs, looking down. "Leave it in the cell. The sheath, too."

The guards wasted no time in unstrapping the sheath from around my waist. They wrestled the blade away from Tamara. Without cleaning it, they unceremoniously tossed it into my cell and slammed the door. Rough hands shoved me forward as Tamara was hauled up, her eyes shining with smug excitement.

"Let's go." Govam continued up the stairs with Micah, who was looking our way with pride.

The dragons lived for these moments, that was clear. They were stuck in this hell, but they'd figured out how to start a few more fires.

The way into the upper part of the castle was the same, and the officers waited where they had the last time I was led this way. I barely heard Govam mentioning the fresh blood down in the lower dungeon that the officers might use for their creations. I didn't miss the first officer's response, though: "Another captain goes down, huh, Govam? And when might your turn be?"

Things slowed down at the baths. The other dungeons had been emptied as well, apparently, and the other prisoners were easier to handle. Which was why they were the first to bathe. When our turn came, we all stayed locked up as the attendants ripped off our clothes and scrubbed us down.

After I was dry, I was prepared the same way as before, with an ugly dress and bad hair. We were led through another set of doors, although not to a throne room this time. We all waited in a line, the dragon handlers occasionally using their weapons to beat a dragon into submission.

"What is that now, a full dozen guards lost?" said Tamara, standing in her cluster of guards in front of me, looking around at them. "When are you going to learn that we don't like going to your parties?"

"The second you're not needed, I'll take great pleasure in killing you," replied the surly demon holding her.

"You won't last that long," Tamara answered, her confidence a great balloon around her.

The line started moving faster, our guards shoving us along. At a large double door, demons were checking people in as we came up. A green-skinned demon to the right, wearing a silk gown that matched the color of her skin, eyed me as we approached the front.

"Cage," a guard said as we stopped in front of the attendants.

Tamara was beside me, her guard telling the male demon in a tuxedo the same thing. It was something they'd probably repeat about all the dragons.

"What is that smell?" the green demon asked, crinkling her nose.

"It's something to do with her shifter mate or something, I don't know. I'm just supposed to get her from the dungeon to the cage. Which one?"

With a pained expression, she took a step to the side, out of the way. "Put her in the fifth cage, next to the alpha dragon. They'll be a nice spectacle."

"Tenth cage," the male demon said to Tamara's guards. "Strip her."

I could see Tamara's jaw clench as we started through the

door. She lifted her chin defiantly, though. She was refusing to let this get to her.

I let out a slow breath, my gut twisting. But at least she'd be in a cage, away from groping hands. Also, she was a shifter—she was probably mostly fine in her skin. Nyfain always had been.

Why would they bother dressing her up if they were just going to strip her? I asked my dragon as we were escorted into a huge room with crystal chandeliers dripping down in several places. Raised golden cages encircled the floor, mostly near the walls, although two were pushed a little closer together on the far right, just off the stage where a band was setting up. Those cages were a sort of focal point, like an attraction. I already knew we'd be gawked at as people sauntered to and from the dance floor.

Govam stood just beside one of the "show" cages, watching four guards pushing Micah in. Micah stared at Govam the whole time, and I could tell it was an intimidation tactic for the smaller-statured demon. If Govam was worried about it, though, he didn't let it show.

My guard yanked and shoved me toward the second cage, acting as though I were resisting for some reason, and I wondered where all the wolves and faeries had gone. There was no sign of them. Only servants scurried around the huge rectangular room, seeing to the large food tables and fixing the various decorations.

The golden cage holding Micah clanged shut, and the guards stepped back, looking at him.

"You'll want to behave yourself tonight," Govam said as the golden cage next to Micah's was opened for me. "The king has some important guests. He won't take kindly to one of them being killed."

"Then he better warn them to stay away from my cage," Micah responded, his voice soft, his tone terrifying.

Govam glanced at me as my guards shoved me into my cage and closed the door.

"Turn," Micah's guards said, echoed by mine a moment later.

I did as Micah did, backing up and sticking my hands out through the cage. Our cuffs were removed at the same time. As I stepped forward, rubbing my wrists, he shoved farther back and grabbed the front of one of the guards.

"Watch out," one shouted as another yelled. Govam didn't so much as step forward to help.

Micah surged forward, the guard in his hands, and rammed the guard's front against the cage. Incredibly fast, he turned and adjusted his hold, turning the guard toward him and wrapping his large, strong hands around the creature's neck. Staring at Govam the whole time, he ignored the clubs whacking at him as he calmly choked the life out of the guard.

I stood, transfixed, my mouth hanging open.

He doesn't fuck around, my dragon said, in awe.

Only when the guard stopped struggling did Micah release him and step away, out of reach of the guards and their clubs. His stare was still on Govam.

"Someday that'll be you," he said in a voice out of a nightmare.

Tingles coated my flesh, and my dragon stirred, a soft purr winding through her at the display of power and violence.

Govam blinked placidly. "Maybe, but it won't be you who gets to me." He pointed at me. "It'll be her."

Two of the guards grabbed the feet of the newly fallen and dragged him across the floor and out.

Govam turned his attention to me. "Mind yourself. This isn't the place to act up."

"This is exactly the place to act up," Micah said.

Govam turned and walked toward the far door as the last of the dragons were put into cages. Four cages stood empty around the perimeter of the room.

"Those will be for three wolves and two faeries," Micah said, leaning against the bars, noticing my scrutiny. "The faeries get put in the same one."

"Where are the wolves and faeries?"

I noticed Tamara in the center of the room, scars crisscrossing her deeply tanned skin on full display. She stood straight and proud, her pose strong and her shoulders squared. It looked like she was daring someone to come near her cage.

Actually, that was probably exactly what she was doing.

"The ones that go in the cages should be out any moment," Micah said. "The rest come out after the guests are here."

Three other dragons were also nude, all in the center of the room. Everyone around the perimeter wore a prisoner's version of finery—puffy, ridiculous dresses or ill-fitting suits or tuxedoes.

"How the fuck is this allowed?" I asked, anger burning brightly. "Dolion spoke of a magical council. And even if there weren't one, these people are from other kingdoms. Mine is conquered at the moment, sure, but yours isn't. The wolf kingdom isn't under demon control, right? How are they okay with all of you being in this situation?"

"They don't know." Micah brushed some lint off his suit as he leaned toward me, the fabric hugging his sturdy frame and large shoulders. Despite the situation, he cleaned up like a champ, the clothes bringing out his striking good looks and hiding all the scars from years of abuse. "We're missing persons. All of us were essentially kidnapped, and they bring us here to rot. The only escape is death."

"You can't actually believe that."

His frame didn't droop, but his eyes held sorrow. "I don't know what I believe anymore, Finley. We were so close to escape. We thought we had everything figured out. Turned out we'd been two steps behind all along. I keep up the illusion of hope for the others, but... Even if we have access to our dragons, it's too far to fly to the mainland. The boats are closely guarded, and they're magically steered in a way I don't understand." He shook his head. "I really don't know if there is a way off this island. Not with our numbers. No one has ever escaped that I've heard of. Certainly not in my time here, and I've been here for what feels like five lifetimes."

The little cracks within him were showing. This strong dragon wouldn't be broken by the whippings or these ridiculous parties...no, it was the thought of no way out that would do him in. A thought that was clearly eating him alive.

I strengthened my resolve. Firmed up my determination.

"We *will* get out of here, Micah. Now you have backup to help lead the charge. I'm bringing you fresh energy and new ideas. We'll get out because I *have* to get out. The fate of a kingdom is riding on my success."

His eyes traveled my face. He looked at me for a long moment before finally nodding. "Okay."

"Okay."

Movement caught my eye, guards escorting more people. I could distinguish the wolves right away, prowling forward like they were on a hunt. A male and female each had two guards escorting them, and a third shifter, who looked around the room with eyes cut from granite, had three. He noticed me immediately, and from the way his gaze then flicked to Micah, he recognized the importance of my proximity to the alpha dragon. As he passed our cages to get to his own, his nostrils flared. Sparks of menace lit his eyes, and his gaze bored into mine.

"Same team, friend," I called out.

"Shut up, dragon," a guard barked, and I grinned, because fuck him.

The wolf noticed it, and his eyes narrowed a little before he turned his gaze front-facing again, not a hitch in his step.

"He's in the same position I am," Micah said softly as I noticed the two fairer folk being escorted up the other side of the room. They almost glided, like they were skating on ice. Their slight frames lent more grace to their movements. Each had pointed ears and what looked like baby-soft skin. They looked alike, and I wondered if they were the sisters who had been mentioned.

"We're all in the same position you are," I replied as one of the faeries turned to glance my way. Beautiful indigo eyes speared through me.

"I mean, he was with me during the escape. He had as much riding on it as I did. And now...he's trying to keep his people motivated. He's having a harder time of it than I am. Wolves aren't so goddess-awful stubborn as dragons. They aren't as willing to kill guards for no real benefit."

"What about the faeries?"

"I don't know about the faeries. They mostly keep to themselves. But those in the cages—I've heard they are very tame. Very soft. And yet they are still kept in cages. I think their magic scares the demon king. They are powerful, and I've heard the suppression magic wobbles when too much power is unleashed around them."

I watched the women get into their shared cage. "What kind of power?"

"That I don't know. I assumed demon magic."

"Why don't you know every last detail about them?"

"Because I am not of sound mind when I get close to them. My mind is swept away by demon magic. And also because…we don't play well with others. Never have. I technically live—or lived—in a wolf-run kingdom. But the dragons have their own part of it carved out, and we don't follow anyone's rules. They call us wild, and I think we're a thorn in their sides, but they leave us alone. In turn, we keep to ourselves."

I stepped closer to him and wrapped my fingers around the golden bars. "Not the Flamma Kingdom…"

He glanced my way and then did a double take. His brows pinched. "Of course the Flamma Kingdom."

"My mate—his mom was from there. The queen. She was our queen. She died."

His eyelids fluttered, then he looked away. He shook his head. "It's like you're stirring up memories that fade before they can surface. Something about that rings a bell, but…damned if I know what."

"I wonder if you knew her." I put my hand to my chest as the other cages were slammed shut. The attendants roamed the room, organizing flowers and straightening the chairs around the edges of the room. "I was common and young. I barely even remember people speaking of her. But I've heard a lot of stories since then. She was well loved, and I know she came from that village. The dragon one in the wolf kingdom."

His expression fell. "There are a collection of dragon villages in my kingdom. We mostly control the mountain country at the southeastern tip. I don't recall hearing about someone from our village leaving to become a queen, but as I said, some memories refuse to take root."

I pulled my lips to the side. True enough.

Several of the dragons sank down to sit on the ground, settling in to wait. Two of the wolves did the same. No one spoke or even exchanged looks. Everyone either looked at the ground, their postures tense, or stared straight ahead at nothing, refusing to allow their feelings about the situation to show.

Nervousness coiled in my belly. We were in cages—how bad could it be? But clearly something terrible would happen.

I kept talking to distract myself. "Why do they call it a dragon kingdom or a wolf kingdom based on who rules? We have a lot of different types of shifters in our kingdom, and now we *only* have non-dragons, since all the dragons were either killed or brought here. I heard that shifters like to be with their kind of animal, but that doesn't seem to totally be the case."

He looked at me funny.

"What?" I asked.

"It's like you've never been around our kind."

"Our... The curse... It's complicated."

He shrugged. "Those with the most power tend to stick together, yes. Those without much power just kinda...file in. But when it comes to why dragons are spread out... We're not really pack animals. We need more space."

"Except you are in a wolf kingdom instead of the dragon-ruled kingdom..."

"Ah. I see what you're saying. Yes, historically there was a divide that happened long ago because of a…" His brow furrowed again. "I want to say a king who was not equipped to be on the throne. I don't remember the particulars. Or even…the kingdom name…" His voice turned wispy, and he shook his head. "Goddess help me, I've been here too long. Even history lessons aren't sticking."

"It's not history lessons." I moved back to the front of my cage as Tamara glanced my way, her eyes tight. I gave her a thumbs-up, my stomach coiling with anticipation. Her smile was slim but thankful, and she straightened up a little more, ready to take on what came. "You're probably talking about my kingdom, and the curse is making the memories slippery."

"Possibly. I seem to remember the rulership being a question, in any case. I believe they shed some dragons long ago that created a home in my collection of villages and elsewhere in the world. Maybe Tamara knows more, or can remember that page out of history. Then there are those born naturally, elsewhere, and sometimes they seek us. Or did."

The curse kept trying to erase his knowledge. The magic was trying to unravel our history.

He shook his head. "There are other dragons, too, from other places or that are from the parents of different creatures, but now they come to us or stay elsewhere."

A wave of despondency and sadness nearly overwhelmed me, but it was immediately answered by a rush of love and support riding a wave of power.

"We will get out of here," I said softly, meeting the indigo gaze of one of the faeries across the room. "We'll get out of here, and we will bring this fucktacular ass-basket of a kingdom to the ground."

CHAPTER 12

FINLEY

A N HOUR LATER, the demon guests moved into the room, all of them in some sort of human-esque glamor. They held glasses of deep red brandy-wine or flutes of a yellowish sort of elixir as they perused the cages and pointed at those inside. The tamer prisoners walked amongst them, wearing blue robes open in the front, showing off their wares. What I could only think of as handlers accompanied the loose prisoners, sex demons using their magic to keep everyone agreeable and eager to please or be pleased.

The more I watched, the angrier I became. Nyfain had gone from trying to support and balance me to soaking up my anger and feeding me power. Through the bond, I got waves of his own rage. Given the time of day, he was probably in the wood taking it out on the officers' creatures, using my anger and unease to fuel his own aggression.

"This is the best party I've ever been to," Micah commented, standing in the middle of his cage and looking down at two female demons with elaborate hair. They huddled together, staring up at him with fearful yet heat-soaked gazes.

"Is my company really that intoxicating?" I said sarcastically, staring at my own audience. Three male demons and a female looked up at me with unease on their faces. The female held her nose.

I grinned at them.

"First, yes. But you knew that."

I frowned at him. It didn't seem like he was being sarcastic.

"Second," he continued, "you're pumping enough power at me to…ensure I am not alone through this."

I knew he was talking about my effect on his animal. The demon suppression magic would continually try to punch it back in, but apparently it wasn't working at the moment. Which meant he got a little company.

A familiar face caught my eye, and my heart sank down to my feet.

Jedrek.

Dressed to the nines with his hair slicked back and an air of importance, he strutted around like he was the richest, most important man in the room. The female demon beside him, in a human glamor, wore a sparkly black dress with a neckline that plunged down to her navel and gaped at the back. He smiled and swaggered, sipping his wine before bending over to kiss her neck.

"It seems he'd like to have a harem," Micah said, following my gaze. "Or maybe he's traded you in for someone willing?"

Jedrek's hand slid down her bare back before settling on her butt. He gave her a gentle squeeze, and she turned, pushing her front against his side. Her hand lowered to his stomach.

Gross.

"They look like a couple," I said. "He's treating her like she's his girlfriend."

"Does that pain you?"

"Emotionally? No." I glanced at the crowd of female demons now ogling Jedrek. "But any sort of watching and reporting from him isn't going to happen. He won't have any incentive to get out of here."

Micah nodded and turned his face away, surveying the clusters of people moving around the room. Most of them ignored the creatures glaring down at them from the cages, opting instead to invite the nicer, less aggressive blue-robed people into their midst.

"His...decisions are not unusual." Micah nodded to the right. "The brunette in the mauve dress is a wolf. She's been here nearly as long as me. Didn't take long for her to cooperate. She's passed around, but she's usually only with one person at a time. When one tires of her, someone else takes her."

"It's not her choice who takes her?"

"No. Prisoners get no choices. You know that. There are two other wolves like that, a man and a woman, and a few faeries." He paused for a moment as Jedrek noticed me. "He's handsome. They'll have set him up with a nice life. As long as he's fine living in a cage with no obvious bars, he'll be looked after."

Jedrek rolled his eyes at me and then bent to say something to his date. She looked around him at me, and her eyes widened. She nodded, letting him step away.

He moved through the room like he owned it, swinging his shoulders and straightening his suit. When he passed the blue-robed prisoners, he gave them pitying, condescending looks. He might've been back in our village, but with finer clothes and more delusions.

"A lotta swagger for a prisoner," Micah growled.

"No shit, right?"

"I thought I'd find you in there," Jedrek said as he reached me, glancing at Micah, now leaning against the bars closest to me. He crinkled his nose and took a couple steps back, away from my scent.

The demons ogling me gave him a smile before slowly sauntering away, heading to the next cage down the way. I had no idea why we were such fun to look at.

"And I bet you didn't do a damn thing to keep me out of here," I told him.

"I told them not to hurt you, but honestly, Finley, what do you expect? You fight and kill guards and—you were always wild. Well? This is what you get. Now you see. A little obedience training will go a long way, I think."

"It truly amazes me that you haven't killed him yet," Micah said, pushing off the bars and straightening up, looking down at two demon females who were walking toward his cage.

Jedrek huffed and pretended to ignore Micah.

"Learn the lessons they are trying to teach you," Jedrek said, "and then you can get out of there. You can move into my rooms."

He said it like *roomzzz*. Like he'd moved up in the world and had a standing place in the hierarchy here.

"Where do you think this leads?" I demanded of him, pushing to the side of the cage. "Do you think they're going to welcome you into their society as anything other than a pet? Get a clue, Jedrek. There is no way that you get a happily-ever-after like this."

He shook his head a little. "Why do you insist on learning the hard way?" He tossed up his hands. "Well, enjoy this. When you're ready to see reason, let me know."

My anger grew, turning into blistering power. It scratched against the inside of my skin, wanting to escape. Searing pain erupted along my back before I heard a dull *clang*. A hand fisted in my dress and yanked me. The bars of the cage knocked into my head. Snapping my eyes open, I almost lashed out, but Micah was staring at me with his deep brown eyes.

"No," he said, the command shocking into me and freezing me up. "Not here. Rein it in."

He was flattened against his cage so that he could reach me, holding my dress in a tight grip.

"Break them up," I heard, and it sounded like Govam.

Micah's voice was low and intense. His eyes held mine. "I know you weren't lying—you've never shifted before. You have no scales on your back. Do not start now. I can guide you when the time comes, but it can't happen here. They'll kill you inside of a minute, do you hear me? No matter who you are."

I swallowed loudly as guards ran to our cage. They carried a sort of pole with a fizzing end, lightning in stick form.

Micah grinned at me. "They never learn."

The first guard jabbed the stick through the bars. The end rammed into Micah's thigh, and I heard a loud buzzing. He gritted his teeth, and the muscles on his face tightened. Another guard jabbed Micah's lower back. He jerked against the bars like he was being struck by lightning. Still he held me.

"Let go." I tried to rip loose. "What are you doing? Let go, and they'll stop!"

He huffed out a laugh as his body convulsed, another jab. "Gotta…reel…them in."

Without warning, he spun, grabbing two of the poles and yanking them closer. The guards didn't have the foresight to let go, not wanting their weapons stolen. They held on, their arms ramming against the cage as Micah released the poles and reached through the bars. He grabbed them by their throats, his large hands reaching more than halfway around each. His hands squeezed as he bent, cutting off their air.

The guards dropped their poles and grabbed Micah's wrists, trying to wrench away. They gaped like fish, their faces turning red.

Other guards rushed closer, but they'd wised up enough not to get too close. They darted in to jab Micah and then quickly away again, afraid he might drop his current victims and go for them. He dealt with the prodding, keeping his grip on the guards' necks. They struggled, twisted, and thrashed, but could not break free. Finally, their breath all dried up, they went limp in his hold.

"I didn't see you trying to free your men, Govam," Micah said in his deep baritone, shoving the guards away. They dropped to the floor, unmoving. The others half danced outside of the cage, their poles in hand and their expressions wary.

"I know better." Govam made a signal, and the guards pushed back.

"And yet you send your men in…"

"I also know better than to go against protocol." He waited until the limp guards were carted away before turning and heading back to the corner.

Breathing heavily, clearly fired up, Micah stared after them for a moment. Loud laughter drifted across the shocked silence of the ballroom.

"Another few notches for your wall, Micah," Vemar called out, waving a hand.

A small group opened up, and I caught sight of Dolion on the other side of the room. He hadn't donned a human glamor like the others, so he stuck out among this crowd with his blue skin and horns. A small smile graced his face, and his eyes sparkled. He'd liked that showing. He'd liked seeing evidence of our ferocity.

I drifted back to the center of my cage, thinking, wondering what Dolion was getting out of us losing our tempers.

"That Govam is a slick one," Micah said softly, watching the last captain standing take up residence in his corner.

"He says he knows dragons."

"He really does. It's infuriating. I've been trying to kill him for years." He sucked in a breath and noticed the crowd of demons nervously smiling his way. "Looks like I'll fetch the king a good few pennies tonight."

"What do you mean?"

He glanced my way before shifting his attention back to the room. "We're up for auction. This is the preshow. They'll bid on us before too long. The winner takes their choice. A sex demon gets us in the mood, and then…"

"Shame fucking."

A crooked smile worked up his face, and he glanced at me again. "I remember you saying that. It doesn't sound quite so bad when you give it such a succinct label."

"I learned from the best."

My anger fanned higher. My dragon still sat right near the surface.

"So that's why Dolion is pleased," I murmured, watching him work the room, saying a few things to each guest before moving on. Laughter and pleased smiles followed in his wake. "He's making money off us."

"Of course. His officers get power, and he gets paid."

I reached out and grabbed one of the bars. "I still can't believe this goes on. That no one does anything about it!"

"How would anyone know?"

I widened my eyes and indicated everyone in the huge room.

"People who are willing to pay for the privilege of fucking a shifter are hardly going to tattle on the people who provide them their entertainment," Micah said. "They wouldn't want to get implicated in all this."

I ran my lip through my teeth, power still pumping through and around me. My desire to do something violent ate at me.

"If you get me off this island, Finley…" Micah said in a low, rough voice. "If you can somehow get me home, I will personally make sure you have a dragon army at your back. As the goddess looks down, I will help you."

I nodded slowly, watching the clusters of demons as they drifted past us. Watching the people in blue move among them, unhappy to do so. Watching Jedrek do the same, only with smug smiles and his infallible swagger. The injustice of it all choked me, bled away my reasoning until rage ate me from the inside out.

"You're scaring away your suitors." Micah chuckled darkly. "They aren't amused by the way you're enhancing that claiming scent."

"Enhancing? What do you mean?"

He gave me another funny look before shaking his head and looking away. "It blows my mind how little you know about what you are."

"You're powerful. Why aren't they worried about your scent?"

"Because mine isn't a claiming scent blasting off a powerful female who doesn't wish to be approached. Don't get me wrong, they wouldn't be eager to meet me without this cage, but a claiming scent is different. Quite a bit different. It warns them that your big, tough mate will kill them if they touch you…"

I've been thinking that, so…you're welcome, my dragon thought.

Not *my* unconscious warning, then. My dragon's.

Thank you, I thought, and then, *Keep doing it.*

"I don't think you'll get many bids," Micah said, leaning on the bars near me. "Unless Dolion assures them that the smell will come off."

"Which…it won't."

"Right. Maybe he'll just say you're off-limits because you're his. That'll make them interested. Still…he'd need to get that smell off to do anything with you."

"And…he won't."

Micah laughed. "Let's hope not, for your sake."

"But not for yours," I said, laughing.

"For mine too, I suppose, until we get out of here and I convince you that there are better alphas in the sea."

My stomach fluttered, although I wasn't sure why. I ignored it.

He pushed off the bars. "You've got company."

A woman in a blue robe wandered near us before stopping and bending to her foot. She adjusted the strap on her sandal, then straightened up slowly, looking out at the sea of happy faces.

"You have the guests nervous," the woman said, facing the crowd. I could just see her pointed ears peeking out of her soft brown hair. A faerie.

"It's my dad jokes," I told her, lounging against the bars like Micah was doing.

"You are from that forgotten kingdom, are you not?"

"You know of it?"

"Yes. Well…no. I know some who had claimed to be from there. They died of a sickness. A sort of plague. They said it was from a curse."

The breath went out of me. "Yes. It was. Are there any left?"

"No. The dragons don't have that sickness."

"Correct. Kinda. The people of the castle and court weren't afflicted with the sickness, and all the dragons were in the court." I didn't bother explaining the particulars of the curse. It likely wouldn't mean anything to her anyway.

She turned and walked a little farther before bending to her sandal again. When she straightened, she looked up into my face.

"Calia has noticed you. She has heard that you have power in plenty. You are our hope. We will be in touch."

"Who is…"

But the woman moved along, continuing her lap of the room before she disappeared back into the crowd.

"Calia is the faerie in the cage over there." Micah glanced right and then away again.

The faerie with the indigo eyes was staring at me from across the ballroom, her gaze acute even from so far away.

"She had powerful magic once, I've heard," Micah went on. "The suppression has locked it inside of her. She tried to escape after us but didn't make it nearly as far. It was a fool's errand."

"Anyone else? Tried to escape, I mean?"

"One more attempt, that I know of. A few wolves. That was after they strengthened the bridge over the lava pit, I hear. They never came back." Micah adjusted his stance. "I've heard that Calia thinks she can dissolve the suppression and then the magical locks, if she has enough power fed to her."

"Fed to her?"

He shrugged. "I don't know what that means either. I heard through Vemar, and he wasn't in his right mind when he got a moment to speak with her. Apparently an alpha shifter should have enough power to spare, but we've all been suppressed. Cut off from the majority of our strength."

"Until I came along."

He nodded slowly. "Until you fuck up and get your privileges stripped away, yeah."

Truer words had never been spoken.

The party continued on. More groups stepped up to ogle Micah, always keeping well away lest he reach through the bars and grab them. A few approached me, but they almost always crinkled their noses and quickly moved on. Only one man stepped closer and narrowed his eyes, studying me intently. Tall and thin, he hid his demon behind a false exterior. I didn't recognize his scent or face, and he didn't speak two words to me. In a moment, he walked past Micah and folded himself back into the crowd.

At the end of the night, Dolion took the stage with a sheet of paper in his clawed blue hand.

"I'll see you on the other side," Micah said with a note of finality in his voice.

I watched as Dolion announced the winners of the auction by the cage number of the captive. Sex demons oozing magic slunk out of the crowds with smarmy expressions. In a moment, the dragons had been turned into lust bunnies, and the wolves and faeries after them.

Blue-robed people walked away with those who had not been chosen. By the time my cage was called, only a smattering of people were left in the grand ballroom. Nervousness ate at me.

"And finally, my pet," Dolion said, waving his hand through the air to indicate me. "I'm sure you'll all agree that she's still a work in progress. The smell, first of all. You can wash the girl, but it seems you can't wash the dragon shifter off her."

A few people laughed at that, clapping politely for some reason.

"Now, without further ado, the after-party. Come—I have a treat in store for all of you." Dolion smiled at them and took the stairs at the side of the stage, only sparing one quick glance for me. In that look, though, his anger was clear. I was dead weight. If he couldn't get the smell off, I was no good at these parties.

If I'd thought I'd be returned to the dungeon, I was sorely mistaken. Instead, my home for the night was the whipping post—a post that would be my constant company for the weeks to come. Weeks that sailed by without presenting any opportunity for me to make contact with the shifter prisoners who had more freedom in the castle than we did. Weeks that stagnated my escape plans. Without being able to attend parties or move through the castle, I couldn't gain the information I so sorely needed.

I needed to figure out how to stop broadcasting Nyfain's scent, if only so I could socialize. My escape depended on it. Well…that or a miracle.

CHAPTER 13

HADRIEL

"**H**URRY UP, HADRIEL. We don't have all day, Hadriel," I muttered as I hunched on my trusty and spirited mare, who felt about as patient as I did. Bella pranced to the side, eager to get out of these goddess-pissed-on woods. The Royal Wood used to be such a lovely place, but now look. Shits-ville, wasted and twisted and creepy as fuck. I hated it.

Which was why I was more than a little perturbed when the master had to stop and jack off.

My heart twisted, but I refused to look away. He sat behind a tree off to the side, not even fully out of view, and yanked on his cock. He moaned and writhed, pumping into his hand and tilting his head back.

I should be used to this kind of thing. I *was* used to this kind of thing, when normal people were doing it. Not with him, though. Not like this.

Because he was only doing it to help Finley.

Tears glossed my eyes, but I continued to stare. I *forced* myself to stare. I was bearing witness. She was being hurt, he was doing a deed that must've ripped out chunks of his bloody heart to do while she was being hurt, and I sat here like fart stains on underwear doing fuck-all.

I hated this. I hated all of this.

It was killing me.

It was killing all of us.

Most of all, though, it was killing him.

What the master was doing was an act of selflessness and devotion to compensate for acts of violence and cruelty, and I'd had about enough. I didn't mind admitting that I was on the verge of breaking. He was breaking, I was breaking—we were all fucking breaking.

This had been going on for nearly two months, give or take. It felt like longer, it might've been shorter—I didn't fucking know anymore. However long it had been, it was too long. She needed help. Slap my ass and call me Betty, the woman clearly needed help, and that hot, big-dicked prince was just not enough. Someone had to do something more.

I didn't know how much longer I could hold out without doing something stupid, like trying to rescue her. I knew where those portals were. Studying the pattern for a few nights had been enough for me to crack the code. The rest was just overkill. Yet I still made a meticulous record of every demon creature killing. I put together maps and a schedule. And after the master realized what I was doing, he insisted on checking out the locations in person. I'd gotten it right, and now he no longer needed to spend all night hunting for the demon creatures. He just stuck close to the portals and ruined them as they came in. We'd also gotten proof that the curse still prevented him from leaving the kingdom. He'd tried to step through one of the portals and was seared by the magic. Thank the goddess he healed fast now, or he'd be one ugly sonuvabitch after that. He'd raged in frustration. He couldn't be the one to rescue her…at least not by those means.

It would need to fall to someone else. Like a mediocre butler who was also a master puzzle-putter-together.

If I went through one of the portals, assuming it didn't sear the skin off me, I could bring Leala. She would be happy for a little whip time. The master had killed most of the demons in the castle, so she needed a few more daddies, as it were.

Why the fuck was I talking myself into this?

If anyone was unqualified to play hero, it was me.

The master groaned out his completion, and I hoped to hell it had helped Finley.

He dropped his hands to his sides and leaned his head back, but I knew him well enough to know it had nothing to do with postcoital bliss. He was waiting until Finley passed out to allow himself all the pent-up terror, sorrow, and rage at what was going on.

We were all just so fucking helpless.

"We are getting really close now," I said to literally no one, looking out through the scraggly trees as if I enjoyed the view. It always helped him to yell at me when he came back from one of these heart-wrenching pleasure sessions. "All of the most power-ful shifters have been released from their suppression. They're helping the less powerful ones. We have people shifting all over the place—new people, too! Kids, even! Well, kids to me, anyway. Fuck, I feel old. Anyway, I call that a big win. We've moved at a breakneck pace, and I've had literally zero life, but we all have to do our part, hm? Those shifters took the most power. Now we just need to juice up the stragglers, and we'll be all set."

He pushed to his feet, his head bowed, and pulled up his riding pants.

A tear dribbled down my cheek, and my heart threatened to rip in half and bleed all over my ribs.

"And the amount of new dragons! Isn't that a fucking miracle?" I sucked in a shuddering breath and tried like hell not to sob. "That's one for the history books, that is. When we have paper in large supply, I might turn into a scholar, you know? I just might. I've seen things. And we're almost all cured of the sickness, too."

I nodded for no purpose. Bella pranced in impatience, ready to get moving. The master's great black stallion looked back with a hard glare, huffed in evident disdain, and then swished his tail. Awful jackass. It was as moody as his master.

"Have you seen the rosebush lately?" I asked. "Of course you have, since you spend a lot of time wallowing in your mother's room. Vibrant and alive, all elements of the kingdom. Sure, people continue to fall ill, but we've got it under control."

He stepped out of the brush, jumped up, and swung his leg over the back of his stallion. Without a word, he kicked his heels and they moved on. No barking at me. No biting my head off.

Shit.

He was in a bad way. This must've been a real doozie of a session.

Finley's sessions went in fits and starts. She'd need the master's help every day for a week, get a bit of time off, and then it would happen again. Sometimes there were breaks, but they never lasted long enough. And it shouldn't be happening at all.

None of us had thought the dirty ol' demon king would dare to treat the master's mate this way. I didn't know what he was up to, but he was really stepping in it. I wanted to rip his face off, and

I wasn't usually all that violent. Or I hadn't been, at any rate, before everything went tits up.

"Do you know what I love?" I asked a little too loudly. Nonsense usually snapped him out of his funk if an upbeat summary of current events wouldn't do the trick. "Tea. I really love tea. I love it just plain, with maybe a biscuit or two. I'll sit out in the sun or maybe the shade, sometimes at night but usually in the morning, and drink and dunk and drink and dunk…"

I let my words drift away as we wound back toward the castle. He hunched on his horse, and I knew he had dark purple circles under his eyes. He didn't sleep much anymore. He patrolled the Royal Wood, and he helped right his kingdom. Finley was counting on him, and he was giving his everything to his mission—to *her*—even though he mostly didn't think she would come back.

My heart ached again, and I blinked back tears as I looked out to the side.

"She is stronger than both of us, sir," I said softly, but I knew he'd heard. We both had full access to our animals now. Mine was mostly quiet these days, offering only soft and subtle support. I thought he'd gotten used to the darkness, and his voice was slow to come back. I hoped he'd continue to open up as time went on, but right now he was keen to watch. Which was fine. Just the feel of him was enough for now.

"You know her. She will not break. She will not veer from her course. If she sets her mind to something, she'll see it through. She's just as strong now as when she went to them, isn't she? Didn't you say that?"

He didn't answer.

"That first week was rough, but you're helping her now. And can't you two communicate after a fashion? You said that, I know you did. So that is good comfort for her." My voice broke, and I gritted my teeth for a moment to hold back the emotion. A tear fell down my cheek. "She'll get out, sire. She will."

"I won't stand for much more of this," he said as we left the gnarled trees of the wood. "I *will not* stand feeling her pain and being able to do nothing for her. My duty is to protect her."

"But you *are* doing something. You're certainly doing more than I am. I'm doing fuck-all. I can't even help by fucking myself."

He shook his head as we neared the stables. "I'm going to summon Dolion and make a deal. I'll give myself in her place. I'll put in a clause to ensure no one in the kingdom meets further harm. He'll take the deal because he wants to make a mockery of me. He still doesn't realize the only way to break me is to hurt Finley and my people. If they're safe, he has no power over me. And if he imprisons me in his court, I'll kill his people one by one until we are the only ones left or die trying. We'll see who breaks first." He dug his heels into his stallion's flanks. "Hah!"

They sped off at a gallop.

"What?" I said, following suit. We were no match for their speed. "Damn him and his top-of-the-line horse stock. Why the fuck did the horses in court join us in the whole *time's stopped* thing, when plants and flowers and other living crap haven't? Oh, that's good. I need to save that for one of my nonsensical comments."

But it does make sense, my wolf said. *It's a good question.*

I mean, yeah, logically it makes sense, but when he's in a temper, he hates listening to random shit with no relevance. It usually gets his rage up. That's a good one to use for annoying him. I have to hang on to it.

I slowed the horse near the stables as the master was pulling his leg from across the stallion.

"Sir, no. Wait." I swung my foot over Bella's back and hopped off while still moving, hitting the ground too fast and stumbling forward. I didn't fall, though. Ol' Hadriel still had it. "Sir, wait. No, you can't do that."

I caught up with him as he made his way across the brittle grass to the castle. Everything in me wanted to grab his arm and pull him around to face me, but I knew that would get me bodily tossed across the grass. I didn't much feel like going flying. So I half jogged to match his long-legged stride.

"Sir, all due respect, and usually you are a rock of sense, but your batshit crazy idea would undermine everything she has gone through."

"She isn't as strong as when she went," he bit out, taking the steps two at a time. "She's weaker. She needs more of my power to sustain her. She is hungry all the time—they are starving her. Not letting her get enough rest. She's wilting."

It felt like a hole had opened up in my chest and consumed me. I hadn't known that about Finley. He hadn't spoken of it.

"This is *my* battle, not hers," he continued, his voice hard and rough, filled with rage. "I will not let her fight it anymore. It is my pain to bear, and *I* will trade myself for her. She will understand in time."

"But sire..." I huffed and panted, trying to keep up with him. "Roses don't wilt, sire." I sucked in a breath and grabbed the door to keep it from closing in my face after he went through. "I mean, the bush doesn't. The flowers do, but those are just bee food. The actual plant gets brittle and shitty looking, but it holds up. It weathers the storm. And then, when you least expect it, those fuckers get three drops of water and come back to life and grow wild again."

"Roses do wilt. They do die. My mother was proof." He turned left toward the stairs.

"Your mother didn't have any support. She had a fuckstain of a husband who made her life hell and a son who was suffering. It was draining the life out of her. When you got out, she stopped fighting. She went to her room one night and that was it. She gave in. Finley is not in the same situation. She has a mate who would die for her. She is in hell, but she knows you have her back. So she will not wilt. She will not die. She'll go straggly and ugly and maybe all fucked up, but at the first drops of water, that bitch will grow wild, just you wait. She'll fuck up any garden the demon king has cultivated. I mean, I'm really running with this metaphor, but mark my words. She will make it back to us. If anyone could escape her cage, Finley can. That woman breathed life into this ruined kingdom."

He stopped outside of his door, his back straight and broad but his shoulders hunching just a little. I paused behind him, not sure where this was going. This was all new territory. I'd done a few pep talks, sure, but never this impassioned.

Then again, he'd never mentioned trading himself before.

"I'll give her two more months. If she's not back by then, I will summon the demon king and take control of the situation."

"Four more," I said, not sure any of us could last four more months of this torment. Actually, Finley probably could. She was stronger than all of us. "Give her four more months. She'll make something happen by then, I know she will. She just needs time. I can feel it."

He turned his head a little, as though he might look back. "Three. Three more months. That's it."

I opened my mouth to argue, beg, or maybe just cry, who fucking knew anymore, but he crossed the threshold and slammed the door in my face.

"Fuck." I turned and started jogging down the corridor. "Wait, why am I jogging? I'm not the one on a timeline. Where the fuck am I even going?"

I slowed as the master's valet walked down the hallway, chest puffed out, back straight, exuding an air of arrogant importance. He wore a tailored suit with a white waistcoat and white bow tie, old-school style. He was the prince's original valet, and the only reason he hadn't been killed or kidnapped was because he hid within the castle or the wood every night to keep an incredibly low profile. I admired the brass balls on the guy.

"He needs a pep talk," I told him as he walked by. "He's got some crazy ideas."

The valet didn't glance my way as he walked past. Not that I was surprised. He had zero time for people who didn't do their job well, and that was most of the castle at this point. I knew better than to rise above the level of mediocrity, however. Assuming I even knew how, which would be a terrible assumption.

"You going to the party tonight?" Maxine asked, standing at the bottom of the stairs. She had her needlepoint clutched in her right hand, clearly done with her hobby of choice for the day.

"Goddess punch me in the face, Maxine, there are bigger issues right now than parties!" I said, utterly losing my cool now that the master wasn't within earshot. No, I shouldn't take it out on her, but then again, she had put salt in my tea that one time, and I had a long-ass memory. "Besides, there are only two lower-powered demons still around, and they don't have enough juice to make my dick stand up. All that's left is you fuckers, and not to be a dick or anything, but I'm sick of fucking you people. I'm sick of this whole fucking horse ride, to be honest."

"You want a horse-fucking ride? *What?*" she asked, aghast.

I stopped a quarter of the way up the stairs, my hand on the rail, and turned back to see if she was joking.

No, her surprise and disgust and curious expression relayed that *that* was all she'd taken away from what I said.

"You need help, Maxine." I turned back up the stairs. "And you won't find it in needlepoint."

"Oh, go lick a sponge."

"I'd rather do that than go to another party, that's for damn sure. Great goddess blow me, this castle is all wrong. It is one hundred percent wrong."

Leala was in the tower, taking Finley's clothes out of the wardrobe, straightening them and dusting them off, and then returning them.

"Leala," I said as I walked in.

She startled, looking back with wide eyes. "Oh!" She let out a sigh and pressed her palm to her chest. "Hadriel. I didn't hear you, sorry."

"Yeah, yeah. Listen…" I started to pace, opening and closing my hands. "Okay, this is going to sound crazy…"

She pulled out another dress and shook it out, running her fingers across a crease. "I'm going to have to iron this one."

"Damn it, Leala!" I faced her. "This is serious!"

"No, Hadriel, that is hysterical blustering."

I tilted my head to the side. She had a point.

I went back to pacing.

"The master said that he'd trade himself for Finley."

She slowed in her movements. "What was that?"

"Yeah, right? It's fucking crazy. He's giving her three months, and then he's going to trade himself for her." I stopped and faced her again. "She might have three months—she might have three years—but he doesn't. He cannot stand feeling her suffer without being able to help her. It's breaking him as nothing else has been able to do so far."

"We're all breaking, Hadriel. It's worse for those of us who knew her the most. I visited her family not long ago. They've been hunting the wood for the portals. Hannon, her brother, has decided to go to her. He said they are a team, and he won't let her do this alone. Not anymore."

I gaped at her for a moment, at a loss for words. "What the fuck?"

"His animal has been released, but he can't shift. The master even tried to help him, to no end. He needs someone more experienced to coax his animal out, I guess, but if not even the prince can—"

"I don't give two donkey shits about that. What are you talking about, he's going to go to her?"

"He hasn't shifted, but he can still feel his animal. He isn't suppressed. His animal apparently has helped him decide this is doable."

"What's his fucking animal?"

She gave me a deadpan stare. "I just said that—"

"Yeah, yeah, sure, sure, we don't know yet." I waved her away. "When were you going to tell me this?"

She sighed and shook her head a little. "After I figured out whether I wanted to help him." She hooked the dress in the wardrobe, didn't take out another, and sagged where she stood. "I won't make three months either. Not without doing something.

What were we thinking, letting her go?"

I lifted my hands and then dropped them. "This is just fucking typical," I muttered, crossing to the window and staring out at the darkening sky. "That big...really nice guy, actually, just stole my thunder."

"What do you mean?"

I shook my head, then basically choked on the lump lodged in my throat. "I'm a fucking idiot, and I don't really have the courage for this, and I'm definitely going to get myself killed or bungle up whatever Finley is doing, but..."

I turned back to her, and I knew my eyes were pleading with her to give me a slap or stuff a dildo in my mouth—anything to keep the words from escaping. But they came spilling out anyway.

"I know where the portals are. Roughly. And fuck it, I'm going to her. I have no choice. I have to."

Tears welled in her eyes. "I know that you know where the portals are. You mention it every time you get drunk. And I knew you were going to decide on going eventually. But I still didn't know what I would say when you did. It's a really bad idea, Hadriel."

"No shit, Leala. *Obviously* it is a really bad idea. I haven't a hope of helping. I'm probably going to ruin everything. But...I basically talked her into leaving."

"No, you didn't."

"Well, I made it sound doable. I have to go. And I have to get her back before the three months are up."

"And now you have the possibility of Hannon helping," she said.

I nodded. "He's incredibly capable. And courageous."

"And probably knows how to fight, just in case."

"Does he?"

She grimaced. "No idea. I figured it would help your courage to say he did." She stared at me as tears ran down her cheeks. "I don't know how to fight."

"Neither do I."

"But I'll go if you go."

I shook my head. "Don't do that. Don't hang this on me. That's a bitch move, Leala, and I won't have it."

"If you go, I'm going. And if you don't go, you're a coward."

"What in the fuck?" I said, exasperated. Then the chafing of my shitty pants prompted me to say, "Think we can make that dickhead seamster go? I want payback for all the times he's made me bullshit clothes. He does it on purpose! I know he does. He's too good at his job to be that bad. I want to shove him in front of a demon and yell, 'This is for the pants!'"

"When?" she asked quietly.

I tried to swallow with a suddenly dry mouth, then shook my head. "I guess whenever Hannon is ready. Now if you'll excuse me, I have to go throw up, and then drink so much I can't stand up straight."

CHAPTER 14

HADRIEL

A WEEK AFTER Leala and I had decided on the worst possible idea in the history of bad ideas, I hid behind a tree in my maid outfit. A real maid outfit this time, without my ding-a-ling hanging out. Leala thought I was being stupid. Hannon thought I looked ridiculous. But this motherfucker knew how to coast along the mediocrity line, and the maid outfit was the perfect ensemble for when we got captured. And we would be captured. The alternative was getting killed, and though that would be a fitting end to this terrible idea, it wasn't part of the plan. A plan, I might add, that hinged on a lot of unknowns.

First, we needed to find some demons, preferably ones who worked in the castle. I hoped those types would be directly on the other side of the portal. I had no fucking idea what we'd do if they weren't.

Then we needed to act bumbling and stupid so they wouldn't get scared off by our sudden appearance and/or instantly try to kill us. If they *did* try to kill us, and we killed them first...bad news. (By "we," I meant Hannon, obviously. Leala and I weren't equipped to successfully kill anyone.) We'd need a Plan B in a hurry because the next wave of demons would probably also try to kill us. Eventually, the outcome wouldn't be favorable. There was only so much one man and his cringing companions could do against a horde of demons.

Once captured, we needed to hope they took us to the castle and then down to the dungeons where Finley was almost certainly being kept. Hannon didn't seem to think there were many other places they'd take us. Except to a shallow grave. He'd read up on what he could, so…we were going to trust he was right. We didn't have much choice.

If Finley wasn't in the dungeon…Plan B. Or maybe C…or F by that point.

This couldn't be a stupider idea if we'd actively tried for it. Essentially, we were winging it and trying not to die. Which was probably what Finley had been doing the whole time she'd been gone.

At least now she wouldn't be doing it alone. The master had given the mission a go-ahead even though he didn't seem to have much more hope than before.

"Where is he?" I whispered to Leala, who was hidden behind the next tree. She had on all black, down to her boots, and her blond hair was covered in mud. I had no fucking idea why the mud was necessary, but I was in a maid outfit. I couldn't really throw stones.

She gave her head a tiny shake as something roared off to the side. Shortly thereafter, we heard, *hunka, hunka, hunka.*

"Fuck," I whispered, clutching my knapsack tightly.

"I thought you said the master usually clears this part of the wood out by now?" Leala asked quietly.

"Usually he does, but it's been a bad week for Finley, and he's been burning the candle at both ends. Besides, he couldn't exactly roll out a red carpet for us, could he? The last thing we want is to draw attention to what we're doing..." I froze up with the creature's next roar, ending again in the strange *hunka, hunka, hunka.* "It's moving away from us. The master will get it. Or someone from the villages. They're super zealous lately about helping protect the woods, since they can shift—"

"I know, I know, *shh.*"

I clamped my teeth together as Leala peered around the tree. I followed suit, needing to know if danger was coming so I could run like hell. It was dark, but moonlight filtered through the dead and twisted tree canopy above us. They were everywhere, those twisted, ruined trees, blocking what I desperately hoped was a portal to the demon kingdom. I'd never been this deep into the wood, so the exact whereabouts of things was a little hazy to me.

"There he is!" Leala ran out from behind the tree, stooped over like we were under attack by an army of archers.

No dummy, I leaned to the other side of the tree and peered the way she'd been looking. Sure enough, Hannon's large frame moved within the patches of moonlight, a T-shirt stretched across his shoulders. He wore plain, worn-in baggy pants and boots, probably full of holes. He was scruffy and unassuming and super nice and still amazingly, incredibly hot. Hopefully also incredibly courageous, because Leala and I definitely needed a little help on that front.

I pushed out from behind the tree, trying not to be self-conscious about my choice of attire. Hannon noticed me immediately and had the decency not to look me up and down. He'd known what I was planning on wearing but had never seen it. The

visual was the arresting bit. Hopefully the demons on the other side would think so, too.

He nodded at me in greeting as I approached. The demon creature roared again, still moving away. Hannon barely glanced in that direction, not worried about it.

Courageous, definitely. Good.

"Are we sure we can cross?" he asked me, his red hair swirling around his head like fire. "In the wood to the other side of our village—the regular wood not haunted by the demons—there's a barrier that kills anyone who tries to cross."

"Yes…we can cross."

"He's not positive about that," Leala said. "The master couldn't, but the master is specifically governed by the curse. We're just caught in the crossfire."

"Thank you for ratting me out, my love. Much appreciated." I grimaced at Hannon. "Okay, technically no, I do not know if we can cross. But Finley and…that other guy from your village got through. If there was magic preventing us from crossing, they would've had a hard time of it."

"It's worth a shot," Hannon said, adjusting the belt around his hips. I belatedly noticed two sheaths hanging from it—one looked to hold an axe, of all things, and the other…

"Is that a kitchen knife?" I pointed.

He didn't bother to look where I was pointing. "Yes. I can't shift yet. I need weapons."

I was going to press, but…well, it was still a knife, so whatever. It was more than Leala and I had. Neither of us knew how to use weapons, and we didn't want to accidentally kill ourselves. Or get them taken and then used against us by people who were more knowledgeable. Our only useful weapons were our animals.

"Right, okay, are we doing this?" I got my bearings and started walking before my sense of survival could talk me out of it.

The others followed, thankfully, as I walked between two large trees and scanned the leaf-strewn ground. Brambles curled across it, many of them broken owing to several game trails.

No, not game trails. Creature trails.

As we continued to walk, the various paths in the area mostly converged into a wide thoroughfare of beaten-down plants. A glowing purple fog pulsed up ahead, announcing our certain death or the real beginning of our rescue attempt.

"Okay, what's the plan?" I asked.

"You know the plan, Hadriel," Leala whispered, edging closer to the slightly glowing fog. "You created it."

"Yes, love, but I'm so scared that my mind has gone blank, and it is taking everything in me not to soil myself."

"We go—" Hannon cut off, and in a terrifying moment, I saw why.

An enormous creature emerged from the fog, walking on all fours—its front feet ended in wicked black claws, while the back two were hooves. It had a great horned head with fangs and glowing red eyes, and it prowled forward like a wolf on some sort of growth magic, a long tail curving up over its back. The tail had another fucking face on the end of it, and my nightmares were complete.

"Fuck," I bleated.

The creature saw us at the same time that Hannon and Leala burst into action. Hannon ripped out his axe and threw, the weapon turning end over end in the air. It dug into the skull as the creature lunged forward.

Leala ran in a circle, yelling. I stood watching like an idiot.

Hannon ripped his knife out of its sheath and rushed forward, ready to meet the creature head-on. But the axe had done its job. The creature's legs buckled, dumping it down into the dirt until it skidded to a stop at Hannon's feet. He stood over it, seemingly calm as fuck, while Leala continued to run in a circle and I drooled a little, my face having frozen in fright.

Hannon slipped his knife into its sheath as gracefully as you please before bending to yank the axe from the creature's skull.

"Leala, my darling, stop running around like an idiot." I caught her arm. Then wiped my drool.

Hannon cleaned off his axe and re-sheathed it, looking at the portal like something else might stumble through.

Hell, maybe it would. I'd thought all the creatures would have come through by now, but clearly I was wrong.

"Right, okay. Good job, everyone." I gave a random thumbs-up because I felt like I needed to do something to help the team out. Moral support would have to do.

Leala breathed hard as she walked beside me, giving the (hopefully dead) creature a wide berth. Hannon, clearly the badass of the group, met us by the tail with the face on it, the thing randomly chomping with sharp little teeth.

"What the fuck?" I whispered, holding Leala's hand.

"Agreed," she replied.

We stopped in front of the portal, and she gave me a little nudge. I was supposed to go first.

"I should go in wolf form, probably," I hastened to say.

No, my wolf replied, the bastard.

"Go. I'll be right behind you." Leala nudged me again.

"Fuck." I clearly needed a thesaurus.

Taking a deep breath, willing Hannon to lend me strength, I

held my breath and darted through the portal. Anything worth doing was worth doing so fast you couldn't lose your nerve.

The landscape changed in an instant, the wood replaced by some sort of scary marsh. My boots sank down into squishy ground, water seeping up to the soles. The moon cast light down on murky waters in random pockets here and there. Bushes dotted the way, some on land, some in water, and thin trees with no branches stuck out at odd angles.

Leala bumped into my back as I surveyed what else was around.

A short distance off, three hunched figures made their way down a glistening path that looked like water. A large boat built in the likeness of a wooden serpent bobbed in what looked like a glistening strip of river. Cages sat around us, large and larger, many with odd-looking creatures stowed inside.

Hannon bumped into the back of Leala, forcing me forward. I took a step I didn't want to take, and my foot splashed onto the wet path, the water rising over the toe.

"Sorry," Leala whispered, her voice much too loud in the silent, desolate place.

"Damn it."

At least I'd changed it up from *fuck* this time.

A creature beside us growled, and one of the hunched figures slowly turned around.

"Here we go," I whispered.

Then I said, "Oops," really loudly, and wiggled in place like I would've turned and run back through the portal if not for the others in my way.

Another figure glanced back as the first slowed. The third eventually did too, the three of them stopping.

"Oh…no!" Leala said dramatically.

"Take a fucking acting lesson," I whispered to her.

"Says the guy randomly wiggling like he has crabs."

"The *I have crabs* wiggle is different, Leala. Where have you been?"

Hannon stepped out from behind us, giving us a clear path to dart back through the portal. We now had no reason not to flee to safety, which was a problem because we needed to get captured in order for Plan A (a.k.a. the only plan) to work. The hunched figures hadn't started running toward us yet. Actually, they weren't even walking at a moderate pace.

"I'll attack weakly," Hannon murmured. "You follow behind."

"No—but—that might spook them into killing us!" I whispered furiously as he ran forward with his kitchen knife.

At least he looked the part of "not warrior," except for the sheer size of the guy.

"Fuck," I said. What could I say? That word was ol' trusty. "Okay, yeah. Go, go!"

"You go!" Leala replied.

"Fuck!" I ran after Hannon, yelling because I didn't have a weapon and didn't want to change out of my clothes to shift.

The figures continued to stare at us, and I could see Hannon slowing a bit, not really sure what to do with that reaction.

"Here. I got it!" I caught up, my feet sloshing through the water, and then ducked in front and continued the charge. As we got closer, the figures finally started to back-pedal…and I dramatically tripped and fell right onto my face.

Hannon, not expecting it, or maybe just a better actor than Leala and me, got tangled up in my feet and fell on top of me.

"Don't stab me," I yelled before my face slapped the ground

and mud stuck to my cheek. "Gross."

"Oh no, don't capture us!" Leala shouted, *not* tangling in our feet and diving onto the disgusting, wet ground. It smelled like meat that had been sitting out for too long.

The hunched figures *finally* turned to action, however slowly. One bent over and *thwapped* my head with something hard, the feeling vibrating through my brain. I grunted and then went limp, figuring playing dead was a good way to keep them from doing it again.

I heard Hannon grunt, but instead of going limp, he tensed, like he was about to get revenge.

"I'll come quietly," Leala said, still speaking in that loud, dramatic voice. She had obviously *not* missed her calling for the stage. "We'll all come quietly."

Hannon grunted again. Leala must've kicked him.

"Should we take them in or kill them?" one of the hunched figures asked, his old boots caked with mud and gunk.

"The king likes his pets, and that one is pretty. The other one is sturdy."

I tried not to let their ignoring me go to my head.

"Take them," the third said, and his weight shifted on his feet. I felt hands on me and wasn't sure if I should keep playing dead or feign not-quite-dead-so-I-can-help-you-carry-me. In the end, to get things moving, I went for lethargic.

They hefted us up and moved us to the boat, throwing us inside and then finally binding our hands behind our backs. Once there, they took a short break before slowly walking back to the portal and releasing one more creature.

While we waited, it occurred to me that Hannon could've killed them all three times over in the time it took them to decide what to do with us. He could've killed them before they even figured out whether to take a step forward or back at his approach. For a moment, it seemed like I should've changed up my plan.

But then they settled into the boat, one at the back and the other two in the middle and front, and I realized there was no motor. The rig had sails, after a fashion, but they didn't do much out here in the still marsh. Instead, the demon put his hands on a sort of table at the back, and the boat shuddered to life. The thing was run on demon magic.

"Maybe we should've made boats or brought oars and stormed the demon castle that way," Leala murmured near my ear, lying on her side and facing my head.

But it took us five days to reach the castle, with a lengthy stop at an island where more creatures were stored and a camp had been set up. I realized storming the place wouldn't have worked. Not without an enormous army we simply did not have. A few bedraggled, out-of-practice shifters and a bunch of new, inexperienced dragons wouldn't do much against a demon horde in their fortified home. The only way to play this was from the inside. We had to get to Finley, and then we all had to get back out again.

Which very well might prove impossible.

CHAPTER 15
FINLEY

A STRANGE SORT of commotion roused me from my slumber. I lay on my stomach with my face against the stone, straw poking me in the temple. My eyes faced the wall with the stairs so that I wouldn't have to move when an officer came down to grab someone. It was our duty to give the poor sod who was taken some encouragement, although it felt pointless. This was our life. Whippings. Parties. And, for me, the fun times I was brought up to Dolion so someone new could try to eradicate the "horrible stink" on my skin. We'd all kinda gotten used to it.

Or maybe I'd just gotten used to it. The others had surely gotten accustomed to it long before I came into the picture.

The only good news was that I'd stopped worrying whether the demons could affect the bond. They couldn't. And while I had figured out how to stop boosting Nyfain's scent...I didn't. Fuck 'em.

The only thing I did worry about was time. The officers liked me for my power, so there wasn't much of a danger they'd kill me off, but without going to the parties, and especially the after-parties, I couldn't get in contact with the wolves or faeries. The other dragons were trying to gather and relay what information they could, but dragons were so often separated from the others. It was slow going, and I was running out of time.

I knew that because something had changed with Nyfain. I could feel his emotions winding up, as though he were readying to do something big. Something probably foolish.

Time was ticking.

"You don't have to be so rough. I was happy playing dead!"

The voice reverberated down the steps and across the open space, pinging around my mind and quickening my heart.

"What's up with this area? The top room was so nice and then, what, your builders decided they didn't care about doing a good job anymore? Fuck—"

I lifted my head as two feet came into view, covered in mud and grime. The person stumbled but caught themselves. Two bare knees came into view next, and then the body that belonged to them, covered in a sort of maid outfit caked with mud.

My heart stopped, and I couldn't process the face, with his hair mussed and dark brown growth all over his face. His thin mustache was longer now, not having been trimmed and taken care of.

Hadriel.

He'd come with me after all…in a maid outfit, as promised.

Tears came to my eyes, and laughing sobs racked my tired body. Then just sobs. No matter how good it felt to see him, I didn't want this for him. He couldn't handle the sort of life that this part of the dungeon endured. It would be a death sentence for him.

"Go back," I struggled to say, but whom was I talking to? It was too late. He was here now.

But…why? *How?*

He looked behind him, both hands free. "I am going, you red-robed fuckbumper. Can't you see I'm going? Eat a fucking carrot once in a while, and you'd see that." He straightened up and smoothed his maid dress down his front. Clumps of mud dropped to the ground. "First that fucking bridge of absolute terror—what the fuck was up with that thing?" he muttered, continuing down the stairs. "And why do all you fuckers look the same? What is going on here? And *if* you wanted to look the same, why choose ugly as the common theme?"

The first officer behind him shoved again, and he jumped two steps down to the bottom.

"Ha! Nice try, jackass. I didn't land on my head this time."

"*Shh.*" Leala came down after him, her hair covered in mud and sticking out every which way, her trim frame dressed all in black. She glanced behind her with a hesitant smile, her eyes tight. Her officer followed with his whip in hand, clearly not intending to use it. They'd already realized these two weren't going to harm them.

And then my world wobbled.

"No." Tears streamed down my cheeks. "Please, *no!*"

Hannon came last, his face hard and determined. He had two sheaths hanging from a belt, both empty. The second he could, he looked down the row of cells, finding me almost immediately.

My heart wrenched in my chest. Power pulsed out all around me.

"Damn it, Hannon." I struggled to get up, accidentally shoving an everlass plant. They grew in my cell now, and I'd be lying if I said they weren't helping me cling hard to my duty.

"Go." The first officer shoved Hadriel farther into the room.

"Every time you touch me, I feel like showering." He wiped off his shoulder with a glare at the first officer before slinking into the center of the dungeon, looking absolutely ridiculous and totally comfortable with that fact. I was back to laugh-crying.

Leala held back, as did Hannon, though I saw that Hannon's wrists had been cuffed behind his back, probably because of his size. His shoulders were hunched, like he was unsure about this whole setup. His aura of calm acceptance thrived even here, as he watched the goings-on with a still body and obvious patience. That had clearly given the officers, and maybe the guards before them, the illusion that he wasn't dangerous. It had kept him from being pushed down the stairs.

Of the three, Hadriel was the one they'd decided they needed to watch out for.

My laugh-crying intensified.

Micah reached through the bars, like he often did, and the movement attracted Hadriel's gaze. Startling, he scampered to the other side, finding Tamara standing in the center of her cage, staring at him like she'd seen a ghost.

"Ah, fuck *me*," Hadriel said with a groan, scurrying back to the center. "Please don't tell me this area is for the dragons."

One of the officers stepped forward, whip in hand. He moved his arm in a circle, and I wanted to shout for Hadriel to get out of the way, but I knew there was nowhere for him to go.

Crack.

The slash landed somewhere on Hadriel's front.

"What in the holy fucking hell, you goblin cumsplat! *Ahh!*" Hadriel scurried backward, fell onto his ass, and then crab-walked away as the officer stepped forward.

Hadriel stuck out his hand. "No! No more. I was playing dead! *I was playing dead!*"

"Stop." The first officer, not smiling, stepped away from the wall, approaching the whip-toting officer. "Leave him. He has no power, just a mouth. Try one of the others."

One of the other officers shoved Leala toward the center of the space.

"Yes, yes," Hadriel panted, turning over and crawling in my general direction. "Yes, she's the one who likes the whips."

I crawled toward the bars, wrapping my fingers around them and watching Hadriel come closer. The crack rang out, and I looked up as Leala cried out. My gut twisted. And then she murmured, "Mmm, yes, Daddy. A little lower."

Leala turned halfway and pushed out her butt. I could see that pain tightened her features, but the swell of pleasure in her voice was unmistakable. This was probably rougher treatment than she was used to, but she was going for it all the same, probably out of a sense of survival.

The guard froze, lowering his whip arm slightly, and flicked his gaze toward the first officer. Dragons came to the bars now, looking out, many with shocked faces.

"I. Am. In. *Love*," Vemar gushed, scooting over to sit in his favorite place next to the bars.

The first officer, his brow furrowed in concentration, gestured. "Try again."

The officer with the whip moved a little more slowly this time, as if unsure, then let loose. The point must've struck where Leala had desired, because after the initial pinching of her expression, a smile slowly soaked up her lips. "Yes, *please*. Again!"

The first officer's brow creased further. He shook his head in frustration. "No. No power. She needs to be a level up, too. Try the last."

"Hey."

I belatedly noticed that Hadriel had made it to my cell.

I sat back onto my butt, a wave of pain rising up, but my latest wounds were already healing.

"Oh, honey." He tsked, looking over my face and then down to my chest. "I can see your tits in that top. I thought we went over this? Running around showing off your tits is no way to go through life." He smiled sadly and reached out to grab one of the bars.

I closed my hand over his. "Why are you here?"

"Look at this! You're crying *for me*? I'm honored." He pulled at the hem of his outfit. "I told you I would go with you. When you took too long to come back, I decided to do just that."

"But...how?"

"Finding that portal wasn't too hard. The journey here wasn't great, but whatever. I am thoroughly knowledgeable about their whole boat setup now. Or...Hannon is. The master has apparently been delivering books to your brother—who knew? Sneaky fucker. Anyway, most of those books were about the demons. The master didn't have time to study up, but he knew your family would. Hannon was filling in the gaps of his knowledge on the way here without them being any the wiser. He doesn't say much, but he watches plenty. I do the talking, take all the focus, and Hannon...notices things. I'm pretty sure he doesn't think he and I are as great of a team as you and him, but he'll have to make do."

"But...why? Why did you come? I would've gotten out."

I didn't voice the *somehow* or the *someday*, and definitely not the *maybe*.

Hadriel's smile was still sad but determined. "I'm the brains, love. I'm the master puzzle-smith. I mean...I'm the fucking butler! Of course I had to be here. And don't worry, I excel at mediocrity to the point where that whip strike was literally the worst thing that's happened to me so far. It's been rotten, but not *that* rotten, you know?"

He glanced around as Hannon walked slowly to the center of the space, his eyes on Hadriel and me. He was giving us time to talk.

I started crying fresh tears.

Hadriel reached through the bars and wiped them away. "Where's that rat Jeddick? Or whatever his name was."

"He's playing pet. They keep him in his own rooms, plural. He's passed from one person to the next."

Hadriel's eyes narrowed slightly. "And that keeps him out of the dungeon? Gives him a bit of freedom?"

"Don't go that route, Hadriel," I said, worried. "It isn't any way to live."

He frowned at me. "Love, I beg your pardon, but which of us has been trapped in a nightmare sex castle these last sixteen years, you or me? I am well versed on what is, and is not, living."

"Turn around," the first officer barked. "No pleasure shot for you."

Hadriel spat out laughter and then wiped it off my face. "Sorry. Fucking Leala, she's my hero. Anyway, freedom is what we're after, right? I will shame-fuck my way through this whole castle, I do not give two shits. Gay, straight? Don't care. I'll be whoever they want me to be so that I can get us what we need. My brain is already stocked with nightmares—what's a few more? Cheers!"

He raised his hand, glanced around, and then scowled at Micah looking down the way at us.

"Fuck, that dragon is big," Hadriel murmured. "He'd give the master a run for his money. Also, I've overused the word 'fuck' on this trip. It's a problem. I need something new. Anyway—"

The whip struck out, slicing into Hannon. He staggered back a few places before bending slightly, catching his breath. In a moment, he straightened back up with obvious effort and stepped forward again.

"Yes," the first officer said, his eyes shining. My heart fell. "Yes, he can stay. Find him a cell. The others—put them upstairs."

"Okay, love. Gotta go." Hadriel paused and then dug in the side of his shoe. "Almost forgot. This might've gotten a little wet, but it should still be readable. He had to be careful what was said in case I got searched, but…well…"

He handed me a folded bit of dirty, crinkled paper. Through a wet spot, I could see familiar scrawl.

My heart started to race. Nyfain had written me a letter.

I quickly grabbed and stashed it, fresh tears in my eyes.

Hadriel patted my hand and then put his palm to my cheek. "I got this, okay? I hear we get used for party favors or some such shit. I can party-favor like no one can party-favor. People tell me things. And they tell Leala things. Don't underestimate her—she travels in weird circles where people are more likely to let down their guards." He winked and pushed to standing. "Thank the goddess for her bountiful gifts," he said loudly, turning. "Get me out of this hall of dragons."

"I thought you'd be dead by now, Hadriel," Lucille said with a sort of swagger I'd never seen in her before. Then again, I'd only known her here. "Nice outfit."

"I thought *you* were dead, Lucille. It was nice and quiet in the castle without you playing dirty tricks on me." He spread his arms and bowed. "I am glad you are in that cage. Nice dental work, by the way. It really suits you."

"We won't be behind these bars forever, Hadriel." Xavier leaned his pointy chin out through the bars. "Watch yourself."

"Yes, Xavier, because while I'm a prisoner in the *demon* castle, your slow wit is going to be my greatest concern." Hadriel passed one of the officers, walked halfway up the stairs without an escort, and gave them all a gesture they clearly knew. "*Adieu*, fuckers."

"Bye, milady," Leala whispered to me before jogging after him.

One of the officers escorted Hannon to an empty cell somewhat near me on the left side of the chamber. He removed the cuffs and clanged the door shut before following the others up the stairs. They left the lights on, incredibly blasé about the new prisoners. Or maybe that was how they usually acted with the wolves and faeries.

I stared through the bars at my brother, who sat down with crossed legs and looked around for a moment before his gaze settled on me.

"Oh, Strange Lady," Vemar called in his singsong voice, sticking his hand through the bars. "I have a few questions…"

"Was that really Hadriel?" Tamara asked, looking my way with wide, excited eyes. "I used to pick on that guy mercilessly. I couldn't help myself—he always pushed the wrong buttons, but not hard enough to warrant a fight. Just hard enough for me to—"

"Throw him in the pond?" Jade laughed.

"I stuffed his head in horseshit once," said Roarke, a quiet dragon with blue eyes so light they almost looked white. It was the first time I'd ever heard him speak. "He told me my pants made it look like I had two asses."

Half the people in the cells laughed.

"Was that a lady's maid with him?" a woman asked—I couldn't see who'd said it.

"The one who likes a little snap and sizzle?" Vemar grinned. "We've seen people grab the whip, we've seen people dodge the whip, and we've seen people take the whipping—but enjoying it? That's a first."

"Who is that?" Micah asked, and everyone quieted down.

I hadn't taken my eyes off Hannon, but I didn't need to look at Micah to know he was asking about my brother.

"Why are you here?" I asked Hannon, still crying, damn it. Still so happy and scared and mad. "Why did you come? *How* did you come? What's going on in the kingdom? Are the kids okay—"

I closed my eyes and pressed my lips together, trying to stop all the questions from gushing out, to stop the mad desire to ask Vemar to get me out of my cell so I could go to Hannon.

Hannon smiled at me disarmingly. "Hadriel mapped out the portals. They are pretty easy to get through, and there wasn't much waiting for us on the other side."

"They weren't easy to get through back in the day," Tamara said. "We were transported through there, and it felt like the magic was ripping my skin off. We lost a couple people who couldn't handle it."

"The demons peeled the magic back when my lot came through," Lucille said. "They put it back up afterward. We didn't lose anyone then. The sickness has taken them since, though. Those who weren't in court when the curse struck."

"The sickness…or the officers," another said, his tone solemn. Lucille nodded.

"They aren't magical anymore," Hannon said, glancing down

the way. "At least, not in a way that matters. We went through no problem. There were three workers on the other side, and we could've easily killed them if we'd wanted to."

"Then why didn't you?" someone asked. I was thinking the same thing.

Hannon shook his head slowly. "We never could've gotten to this island without a boat, and their boats are demon-run. They need their sort of magic to work."

"So even if we break out of here, we have no way to get across the sea?" Tamara asked, a growl in her voice.

"I know how the boats operate," Hannon replied. "Mostly. I just need a demon's magic at the helm. I can get us across the sea if someone can force a demon. And if we can get out of here, of course."

A shocked silence rang through the dungeon. No one so much as rustled their shreds of clothes or crinkled their straw.

Then: "But who *is* he, Strange Lady?"

I huffed out a laugh. "He's my brother, and he's apparently come to play hero."

"But Finley..." Hannon's face was tense. "Nyfain—the prince..." His eyes flicked to the side. Apparently he didn't want to sound overly familiar with Nyfain's subjects in the room. Something that probably should've occurred to me and never had. Not like I would've changed. "He can't handle what you're going through. Hadriel said it's breaking him down. He can handle pain, but he can't handle *you* in pain. It's breaking us all down, truthfully. He's given Hadriel three months, and then he plans to trade himself for you. For his kingdom."

A stab of fear hit my heart. That explained the impatience I was feeling through the bond. I'd figured he would do something foolish, and that was about as foolish as he could get.

"Well then," I said, a newfound determination steeling within me. "We better hope Hadriel can network."

"Our hope is in the hands of a stable hand?" Lucille said before thunking her head forward against the bars.

I grinned. "Not a stable hand, no. The most mediocre butler you'll ever meet."

I turned my back on everyone and unfolded the note with shaking hands.

My dearest Finley,

It's hard to know what to say.

I miss you.

I love you.

I think of you always, especially when I sit on that little hill in the wood and watch the sunrise. Or when I crawl under the bedsheets in our tower room. Or when I work the everlass fields. Your absence is a gaping hole within me, a hollow that I could bear if you were free, living your life in peace. One I struggle with because I know you are in pain.

If you get this note, the rescue party has reached you. I hope they can help. Hadriel claims he is not worth much, but he has greatly helped me with the kingdom. He is a good person to have in a pinch. He always seems to know what to say in order to shift the mood of those around him. I truly think he'll be useful. Leala seems to bolster him, so they will be a good team. Worst case, they will bring you a little comfort from home.

I have all the faith in Hannon, but I don't have to tell you that, of course. I did try to dissuade him from putting himself in harm's way—I know you would've wanted me to—but he wouldn't hear of it. I think he has a strong, determined sort of animal that thinks nothing of sacrificing itself for its loved ones.

It is clearly a family trait.

I will continue to help you through the bond in any way possible. Please, please take care of yourself as best you can. Try to escape, but do not take any unnecessary risks. Stay strong and stay alive. I will not let you suffer for much longer. I will ensure your freedom with my last breath, if need be, as is my duty. One way or another, you will be free of your cage, and then I need you to finally find happiness.

You are my heart, little dragon. Guard yourself well, because in so doing, you guard the most precious part of me.

Yours forever,
Nyfain

P.S. I would've liked to smuggle you in a book, but it seems Hadriel chose the skimpiest of clothing options available. I worried where he might stick the book in order to get it to you...

I laughed through my tears, the ache for him overwhelming. Through the bond, I felt an answering surge of warmth and love. He must know what I was doing.

I lay down and held the note to my heart. I had my family now. I had my friends. Together we could do this. Together we could make miracles.

CHAPTER 16

HADRIEL

AFTER REMOVING US from Finley's dungeon, the guards brought us to the next floor up. One of the robed, moldy creatures shoved me, but I was too shocked to verbally retaliate.

"Was that for real? Did you recognize them too?" I whispered to Leala, and the guard shoved me again. Turning to him, I said, "My darling, you can't look tough when shoving a man wearing a maid's outfit. It simply isn't possible. There is no toughness within the absurd. Just let it happen. It would be much easier that way."

I must've confused him, or made entirely too much sense, because the next shove was halfhearted.

"I thought they were all dead," Leala murmured as we walked down the center of a wide grouping of cells, most of them containing people sitting in the middle of their individual cells or leaning against the side. They watched us walk by, not one face I recognized.

We turned a corner and continued on to another block of cells. There were quite a few more prisoners in this area than in the one below.

"Hmm, yes," Leala said after a guard gave her a particularly hard shove. "How about you give me a spank to go with it?"

I glanced back at the demon, who looked confused and wary. Her kink seemed to make even the most vicious of creatures uncomfortable. Clearly we wouldn't be fitting into this establishment, which was crazy, since their kind had made us what we were. Well…maybe not *made*, but certainly brought it out in us.

"So did I," I replied. "So did everyone. The master is going to just *love* finding out that his people have been kept here like this for so long."

"It's probably better he doesn't know. He couldn't have done anything to save them. Not without damning us all."

"Too true."

We passed a woman sitting in the middle of her cell with her legs crossed and her arms resting on her knees. Her eyes flicked open, revealing a lovely and slightly startling indigo stare. I'd never seen eyes that color.

I stumbled and then paused, transfixed for reasons I couldn't explain. She watched me as Leala walked on and my guard debated whether this was a fine time to ignore my maid's outfit and shove me as he figured he should.

I waited for her to say something. It felt like I *needed* for her to say something.

She took my measure before looking to the guard. Her expression didn't change, but suddenly it felt like she understood my whole situation—why I was here and the role I needed to play.

She closed her eyes again, and I felt released.

I sucked in a breath and started walking right before the guard moved to shove me. He hit air and then stumbled forward, bumping into my back.

"See?" I told him. "That's why you don't try to shove people like me. You just end up looking like an idiot."

"You need to get that smart mouth whipped off you," the officer growled.

"Probably. But someone will probably end up fucking it instead. I give great head."

The guard sucked in a startled breath.

What was with this place? Did they not know the sex demons who'd been holed up in our kingdom all this time? Because chatter like that shouldn't be a shock to anyone around these parts.

"Woman. Here." The officer with Leala stepped to the side and opened a cell, a dingy sort of affair with a bit of straw spread across the floor and a bucket in the corner.

"Oh lovely, Leala. What a fine setup." I smiled at her in goodbye as they led me a little farther down the cell block, to a tiny chamber on the other side—rough stone with bars in the front. "And a fine establishment for me, too. Lucky, lucky."

The door clanged shut, and I had a moment of intense claustrophobia, squeezing my chest and curdling my stomach. I breathed deeply, trying to quell the panic, when I heard, "It'll get easier."

A man stood at the corner of his cell opposite me, leaning against the rough stone siding and the bars.

He saw me looking and nodded. "The first time that door slams is the hardest. It feels like your whole world is ending. But it gets easier. Eventually you look forward to coming back here. It beats the alternative."

"I know what the alternative is, trust me, and I don't think this beats it." I walked in a circle, feeling the walls. Then the bars, stopping at the lock.

"I don't want to scare you, but even if you've heard what the alternative is, it's much different when you're experiencing it."

It turned out he was entirely right. Just not in the way he thought.

THE FIRST PARTY—OR gathering, as they were called, since apparently parties were much larger and included the dragons—was held in a smallish ballroom decked out with pillows and lounges and couches. A slew of well-dressed and colorful "regular" demons moved amongst us, choosing whom they'd like and almost always calling over a sex demon to get their intended in the mood. The sex demons didn't even participate. There were no kinks. There weren't even any demons who thrived off pain. It was just regular, straightforward fucking. The demons only needed a few pumps to get off, then rolled away with a satisfied smile afterward.

What the fuck was the point in that? There weren't even any costumes!

The whole situation was entirely vanilla and, quite frankly, incredibly boring. I was fine with vanilla sex one on one— probably; it had been a while—but if everyone was in the same room, I expected an orgy. A three-way *at the very least*.

There was none of that, though. They didn't even share partners!

Honestly, I couldn't make sense of the whole thing. I couldn't fathom why they'd bothered getting me out of my cell for it. Worse, the (unchained and supposedly free) prisoners weren't allowed to chat with one another. We couldn't even pass notes! How the fuck was I supposed to network and get information if I couldn't speak to anyone?

And how the fuck was I going to relay all of this to Finley when dragons typically weren't invited to the gatherings because they always tried to kill everyone?

No wonder Finley had been here so long with very little to show for it. The situation was stacked against us.

We needed to vastly increase the level of debauchery. The regular demons needed a good goosing. It was the only way we were going to get anywhere.

After a quick meeting with Leala in the dungeons after the third gathering, which elicited gasps and shocked horror and some serious judging from the other prisoners, we decided this place needed some shame fucking. They'd forced us into it back at the castle, and it was time to return the favor.

Happy birthday, Dolion, you colossal prick. We're going to ruin the whole lot of you for any sort of sexual normalcy for years to come. Enjoy the therapy.

Now, the thing about getting shame fucking going was that you had to start small. It was like pushing a big boulder downhill—you had to be patient while it got going. But once that fucker started rolling, you just had to stand back as it moved faster and faster until there was no stopping it.

I was the guy who was going to give that boulder a shove.

Thank the goddess I had come, because Finley badly needed me.

This bitch was about to go down.

LEALA

I LAY ON the couch with a satisfied smile and draped my arms over the back, pushing my breasts into the air. The nipple clamps tightened between them, sending a shot of pain through me that flowered into delicious, glorious pleasure. I moaned and dropped my head as a flat-faced demon with large black horns bent over me, looking curious and wary and uncomfortably aroused.

My smile grew, and I looked over his head at Hadriel, who was lying between two male demons, a dick in each hand. He pumped each, moving in such a way that silently urged them to move a little closer. One of the demons felt up his inner thigh and cupped his balls, angling his face to be kissed.

Only Hadriel turned the other way, kissing and licking across the cheek of the other. That one caught on that something was wanted of him and turned slightly, finding Hadriel's cock and stroking.

I could hear their collective groan from here.

Hadriel lay back a little, his eyes drifting open as he did so. He caught my gaze and snapped to attention, clearly wondering if I needed something.

I winked, looked to the demon settling between my spread thighs and then back to my friend. *He's interested in my kink.*

A little smile worked up Hadriel's face, saying he'd caught my silent message, and his eyes sparkled. I knew what he was thinking: *Bingo!*

If you found one with your kink, you'd draw others. Mine was an actual kink, of course, and Hadriel's was a sexual orientation, but the demons here seemed to be strangely intolerant. It had taken Hadriel a little coaxing to get them to open up about liking cock.

Hadriel's grin turned wicked as he took his hand from one of the demon's cocks and put it on the demon's head. He pushed, easing the demon down his bare stomach to his dick. Then he turned and whispered something in the ear of the other.

The first demon resisted a little, his eyes getting tight, as Hadriel urged the other to scoot up. Hadriel quickly took the second demon's cock in his mouth, handling it like a sex-starved champion. The first, seeing that, hesitantly licked the tip of Hadriel's dick, testing it out. Hadriel pushed harder and thrust upward, pumping into the demon's mouth. The demon took it, sucking it in and still cupping his balls, groaning as he did so.

Heat settled in my core. I loved watching men get it on. I had no idea why, but it really fired me up.

"C'mon, baby, show Mama what that tongue can do." I leaned forward and grabbed my admirer's head by his shiny black horns.

I leaned back again and pulled his mouth to my exposed pussy, begging for action. I didn't need sex demons to get me hot—I thrived in the uncomfortable and perverse. Hadriel had been bored, but I'd found those first few gatherings fucking amazing. I'd come so hard each time that I'd almost blacked out. The tension, the wariness, the icky taboo factor of the setup—I took those demons for a ride they'd never experienced before. If I could've gotten spanked in the process, it would've been utter perfection.

And now here we were, helping them cross boundaries they weren't sure they even wanted to sidle up to, let alone step over. It was a fucking wet dream.

He traced his tongue up the middle of my slick folds, tasting. He moaned softly, and I pushed my hips up, grinding my cunt into his mouth.

"Yes, baby," I said, wondering which kink might be best for the situation. "I've been naughty…"

He sucked in my clit and then swirled his tongue around, gathering heat in my core. It felt fantastic, but I needed more. And so did he. This was normal fucking. We had to transcend normal.

"Come on, Daddy," I said, tugging on my nipple clamps and moaning at the burst of pain. "Suck off your nasty little slut."

He did circles with his tongue before he sucked again, doing as he was told.

Ah. Not a dominator, then—this guy wanted to be dominated.

Sure, I could work with that. It wasn't exactly my flavor, but desperate times, as they said.

"Suck harder," I barked, holding both of his horns and yanking his face into me as I pumped my hips up at him. "Harder!"

He shoved forward, his hands hitting the edge of the couch cushions and his movements turning harried.

That did it.

"Fuck me with your fingers," I commanded, drawing the eyes of a male and female demon chatting off to the side. The demon between my legs worked his hand up to my cunt and threaded in two fingers, thankfully without claws. I liked pain, but there were limits. He curved them up just right, ramming them into my growing wetness. "Yes, baby. Hmm, yes. Keep going. Keep sucking."

I yanked on the chain between my nipple clamps—where Hadriel had found them, I had no idea. That guy was the most resourceful person I'd ever met.

The pain dumped blissful pleasure into me, but I needed more.

"Bite my clit—don't take it off, bite softly," I said, breathing heavily.

The demon looked up at me warily.

"Bite!" I yelled down at him.

He thrust his fingers faster and bucked his hips, needing a wet cunt to stick that dick in. He bit down, not as hard as I wanted, but I didn't want to push the envelope and lose my clit.

"Yes," I said, winding up now. Pleasure gushed through my body like a live thing. It coursed with the pumping of his fingers. With the sparks of pain from my nipples. "Yes!"

I exploded, crying out louder than anyone in these things ever did. That was a sign that they hadn't been pushing themselves. Not in the way sexual people were capable of doing. And these demons *were* sexual, even if they didn't have incubi or succubi magic. It was obvious. They just hadn't been encouraged to express themselves.

I could help them with that...

Every sex demon in the place looked at me, desperate desire on their faces. Two drifted my way as the male demon standing with the female stepped closer.

"Now fuck me," I said, looking at the standing male demon.

As if in a trance, he walked closer, his eyes drifting down my body possessively. The other demon, the one who'd been eating my pussy, tried to scramble up my body.

"No, no." I brought up my foot and put it on his face. "Not you. You...can lick her pussy..." I pointed at the female. "While I suck you"—I pointed to the standing demon—"off."

The three hesitated in shocked silence. Out of the corner of my eye, I saw Hadriel lift a thumb into the air. I barely kept myself from laughing.

Here we go!

I slid down to the ground into the pillows. This was a risk. If they didn't come to me, the spell would be broken. But I couldn't do more than bait them, or they'd realize my manipulation and probably balk.

In a moment, I gave a tug on my nipple clamps before removing them. The blood rushed back to the sensitive area, pain and pleasure and... Holy fuck, I needed to come again.

"Join us, Eslin," the standing male demon said, reaching me and curling his fingers into my hair. He thrust his cock into my mouth harshly, ramming the back of my throat. I moaned around the treatment, my nipples still painfully tingling, now fingering myself to get there again. "You always say you want me to lick your pussy more often because you're not comfortable with animals doing it. Now you have one of our kind to do it. Win-win."

The female demon hesitated. She needed a harder push.

I looked up at the male demon as I bobbed on his cock. His hand clenched into a tight fist in my hair. He had me at his mercy. To prove it, I took more of his dick so that my eyes would water and I would look vulnerable below him.

Feeling the fire of control, he barked at the female, "Sit down and let him tongue-fuck your pussy!"

I groaned around his cock as a shiver of pleasure blistered across my flesh. He was going to be fun.

The female demon startled, but did what he said, albeit hesitantly. She lay back slowly, and I knew this was the big time. Getting these demons to fuck each other in naughty ways was opening the door to the great, wide world of "why didn't I know how fun sex really was?" and "this shit is going downhill fast" and, eventually, "how did I get here, and why can't I stop shame-fucking?"

I was thoroughly in control here, when back at the castle I'd never felt that way. So crazy. So wrong. So hot.

The male demon pulled me off his cock and looked down at me, his green gaze tracing my face. His grin was slight and eyes on fire with desire.

"Tell him to suck her pussy," he commanded.

He meant the other male demon, who was looking back and forth between her and me with unsure eyes.

I didn't have any time to waste. If that female decided she was uncomfortable and walked, it would break the spell for the other two. They were going to feel dirty later, and a little shameful, but if they'd all gotten off, no one would be able to take the higher ground and make the others feel worse. They'd all feel equally shitty but erotic.

"Lick her gently," I told him. I knew her type. "Tease her. Get her comfortable."

The male above me thrust his cock back into my mouth as he watched another demon go down on his...mate, or whatever their thing was. He groaned as he thrust into my mouth with long strokes, getting off on being a voyeur.

Ah. So he was the type who liked watching other guys fuck his loved ones.

I decreased my suction as she eased back a bit, watching her mate. The demon between her thighs played and sucked, and it was taking forever, so I reached over and pinched him.

"Ugh," he said, digging his tongue between her folds.

"Yes," the demon above me said, thrusting.

I took what he had to offer and then broke off, pushing him

away and diving for the other male demon's cock.

"That's right, suck his cock," Mr. Daddy said, kneeling behind me.

The female let out a little moan, and I knew we had her.

I grabbed the cock in front of me and put my lips around it as I felt two strong hands slap down on each side of my ass.

"Oh! Yes," I said around the dick, spreading my thighs.

"You like that?" He slapped me again with one hand while the other one disappeared, probably wrapping around the base of his cock. His blunt tip parted my folds, and then he filled me in one hard thrust while slapping my ass.

An orgasm ripped through me—I'd already been at the edge, and that was just the thing I needed to send me over. I bucked and yelled, shuddering.

He kept pumping into me. The other demon grabbed my head and pulled me closer as he licked and sucked the writhing female. She wrapped her legs around him, trying to draw him closer, and I nearly let him up so he could fuck her. But I wanted us all to finish on an orgy. I wanted to be the one they knew as the *bad one.* The one who made them do it. The one they would all secretly want to see again because while the sex had made them feel dirty, it had been crazy and new and felt so good.

I sucked as another slap landed. His cock slammed into me. His hips hit my ass. Another slap.

"Oh goddess, yes, I'm close again," I bleated before going back to the cock. I twisted his balls a little, and he jerked before thrusting, coming away from the woman to watch me take him in my mouth.

"What do you think you're doing?" I berated him, not feeling the dominatrix schtick while being dominated. It was very challenging wearing both hats. "Tongue-fuck that pussy until she comes all over your face."

I nearly grimaced, wondering if I'd gone too far. But he dove back for her with zeal, burying his face between her thighs and going to town.

The male behind me filled me rhythmically, speeding up. He spanked me, the pain heightening the pleasure, while his cock branded me. One more thrust, and I squeezed the cock in my mouth as I moaned around it. It erupted, filling my mouth and dribbling everywhere while the male behind me groaned out his release.

The woman hadn't come yet, though. Shit. She had to come for this to work!

I struggled up like a woman on a mission, shoved the useless male demon out of the way, kicked off the other, and shoved my head between her spread thighs. She jerked, clearly never having done this before, but her eyes were glazed with pleasure, and her need to finish beat out her uncertainty about letting another woman go down on her for the first time.

I wasn't a master at this, and I didn't much like doing it, but I would pull out all the stops for the occasion.

I swirled and licked and finger-fucked that thing with gusto. Hands touched down on my ass before a cock threaded into my pussy, and I didn't bother to look back to see who was joining the party. I pulsed suction on her clit as the large cock stretched me pleasantly—a new person, then.

Fuck, spreading a little debauchery around here was easy!

I tongued her clit and felt the cock pull out and move up.

Ah. He wanted to fuck an ass, probably for the first time, judging by his panicked movements to get inside.

Fine, whatever.

The woman screamed—literally screamed—out her orgasm as the cock dove in deep, no lube to speak of. As the pain consumed me, turning to fucking exquisite pleasure, I felt hands tearing me away from the woman, pushing me back, and then Hadriel's face swam above me as he sat me firmly onto the cock in my ass and shoved another demon to my front. He was keeping them rolling down the mountain of "wow, that got *way* outta hand." I'd gone from a little kink, to a little voyeurism, to a little orgy, to a full scale free-for-all in the space of an hour. They did not know what had hit them. I was going to ruin them all with my magnificent pussy.

This was the beginning of the end. Their days of reserved, vanilla sex parties would never be the same. They wouldn't really be shame-fucking, though. No way. They'd be feeding that spark of lust that existed in them all. They'd be in their element.

I didn't know what the demon king had been trying, keeping their appetites all caged up, but we'd just set them loose. Their deeds here would forever alter them.

Welcome to hell, demon castle. Cheers!

CHAPTER 17

FINLEY

"**H**ere, Hannon, drink this." I sat next to Hannon's head in his cell, holding a dented tin cup filled with cold-steeped everlass.

He lay on his stomach with his eyes closed and his head pointed my way. His shirt had been all but stripped away on his back, revealing angry gashes, welts, and tears in his skin.

He'd been here about a month and had received one to two whippings a week, fairly moderate in aggression by the look of it. It didn't seem that his power was a problem—the officers seemed all too happy with what they'd gotten out of him—but his ability to heal. He had access to his animal, which had given him power and sight in the dark and other enhanced abilities, but his body didn't seem to heal at accelerated rates. For that reason, they couldn't whip him as often as they liked.

"It's okay," Hannon said softly, his eyes closed and pain lacing his features. "Save it for someone who needs it more."

Vemar whistled, leaning into the open doorway and looking in. "That is one selfless man, right there. Brother, *you* need it more. None of us take this long to heal, even with our animals suppressed. Take the Strange Brew."

Tamara and Lucille sat cross-legged just outside the cell, looking concerned.

"Take it, Hannon," Tamara said. "It'll at least let us see if your sister is any good with those everlass leaves she picks and hoards."

"Well it's cold-steeped because we don't have access to a fire, and it's just everlass because we obviously also don't have access to a garden or herbs or anything, but it should ease the pain and speed the healing a little," I said. "The plants are happy and leaves prepared well. They'll help as best they can."

"The goddess only knows she's been talking to the things for long enough," Vemar said.

"It hurts to move," Hannon grumbled.

Vemar hung his head a little, and the girls wilted. It hadn't taken long for Hannon to earn everyone's love. My soft, calm brother—never ruffled, never complaining, always supportive—had a way of winning loyalty. His pain was their pain. His act of selflessness in getting here pulled on everyone's heartstrings. If I didn't love him so much, I'd be jealous as fuck.

Instead, I was just grateful. He needed the help. He shouldn't be here. I was the one that was supposed to take risks and get banged up, not him.

"I'll help." Micah stepped around Vemar and walked into the cell, glancing at the cup in my hand. "Is that your water?"

"Yes. I rationed, so it's okay. I've been cold-steeping it ever since I told the officer I lost my other cup and got beaten for it, remember? Everlass prefers hot baths to cold, so it's not at peak strength, but it should help."

"No wonder you know how to work that plant so well, Strange

Lady," Vemar said, following Micah into the cell. "It's as temper-amental as you are."

Hannon wheezed out a laugh and then started coughing, shuddering, and wincing. Everything in me tensed.

"Here we go," Micah said, exchanging a look with Vemar. The two of them pulled Hannon to sitting and then held him so that he didn't have to use his own strength.

My heart swelled so much it felt like there wasn't enough room within my ribs.

"Thank you," I whispered, my hands shaking as I lifted the cup toward Hannon's mouth.

"Here, let me." Tamara hastened into the now-crowded cell, putting her hand on my shoulder and taking the cup. "I don't have as much invested in his wellness. I won't shake as much."

She smiled to let me know she was kidding as Lucille pulled me out of the way.

"She was never very good at the bedside part of things," Hannon said softly. "That should be my job."

"Instead you jumped right into the fire with us." Vemar nod-ded. "No harm in that."

No one pointed out the obviously great harm in that.

"He doesn't have scales on his back," Lucille said softly as we watched the others nurse Hannon. "Which makes sense, since he hasn't shifted. But...did you notice that he doesn't even have the start of everlass in his cell?"

I blinked a few times because no, I hadn't noticed. I did now, though, looking at the creases in the stone and the patches where everlass might find its way into the world. All bare.

"My parents weren't dragons." I watched Tamara tilt the cup and then Hannon's throat as he drank the liquid down. "It's odd that I am."

"Not that odd," Hannon said after he finished. He breathed heavily as the guys set him back onto his stomach. Micah exited, brushing by me gently for such a big guy, and Vemar sat down on the other side of Hannon, back against the wall, and pulled up his knees and rested his arms around his legs. "I've meant to tell you this a million times, but the timing never felt right. Either I didn't feel up to talking or you wouldn't have felt like hearing it."

"Yeah, you two aren't settling in like normal," Vemar said. "Or…" He paused and thought a moment. "Maybe you are but it's been so long since someone was new that we've forgotten."

"The prince has nearly everyone out of suppression, and the people in the villages are shifting," Hannon continued. "There are a lot of first shifts happening, and there's an incredible number of dragons. Incredible, given they are coming from non-dragon parents. They say this happens when the people are in peril. The goddess, or the old gods, or nature—no one agrees on who or what—calls dragons into existence to defend their people and set things right in the natural order. Or the kingdom. Or something—again, there are a lot of views on this. Regardless, there are a lot of dragons who need flight instruction now, but the prince doesn't have wings."

Micah frowned. "Why doesn't he have wings?"

"He refused to let the curse and the suppression take his dragon from him," Tamara said softly, in the way of someone who'd repeated it often. "So he forced the change as the suppression was trying to take hold. It reduced his power and sheared off his wings, but he kept his dragon when everyone else lost theirs."

"If a lot of people are doing their first shifts, why didn't you, brother?" Vemar asked Hannon.

"I tried. Wouldn't happen. Everyone else in the village did. I felt the swell of power and all the other things I was supposed to, but it just wouldn't happen. My animal didn't seem frustrated by it. It felt like whatever needed to happen in order for him to come out hadn't yet, and he is content to wait. Neither of us knows what we're waiting for, though."

"Unlucky." Micah's voice was soothing. "That happens sometimes. We used to call that a late shifter."

"But at least you aren't suppressed anymore," Lucille said. "There's that. You know you have an animal, and you get most of its rewards, so that's good enough until we get out of this toilet."

"Speaking of. Strange Lady, when are we getting out of this toilet?" Vemar asked with a crooked smile.

I took my cup from Tamara and went to stow it under one of the loose stones in my cell. I had three cubbyholes now, which I'd dug out myself. They mostly held leaves, except for the one that held the cup and Nyfain's notes.

I sighed and shook my head. "They don't let us out. Me especially. I think we've fucked ourselves with our ruthlessness. I need to speak to Hadriel and see if he's made any headway, but I haven't seen him. They don't even whip us at the same time as the other dungeon."

"Have you practiced subduing your stench, though?" Vemar asked. "That'll help you get into the after-parties, and *that* will help you socialize with the others."

I leaned against the bars to Hannon's cell. "Yes, I have. It means I have to subdue my connection with Nyfain, and he goes a little crazy when I do it, but yes, I can get it done."

"Even though I rather like that smell"—Lucille licked her lips, then winked at me—"do it and let's see if it works."

Quickly, so as not to stress Nyfain out too much, I pushed down the feeling of our bond and muffled the connection, the separation from him immediately making my heart ache for his touch. For the slow smiles only I seemed to tease out of him, and the sparkling rage in his eyes that led to explosive sex.

Micah reached out and grabbed the bars, his large body tense and eyes blazing. "That's enough."

Vemar started laughing. "Makes it even more enticing to claim her, huh, Micah?"

Micah rolled his shoulders. "I've never felt that level of challenge before," he murmured. "When it's subdued, it's almost like the male is taunting me, hiding the full brunt of his power. It's...hard to explain."

"You're obviously powerful, even in suppression," Hannon said to Micah. "How did a powerful dragon like you end up in here?"

Vemar answered, "A storm blew us off our trading route. We ended up on foreign land. Faerie land, actually. We ran aground, and guess which creature owned the vessel that found us?"

"So they just randomly take people they find?" Hannon asked. "They kidnap magical people all over the world?"

"They host a collection of missing peoples, yes," Lucille said. "And stolen people. And conquered people. No one comes looking because why would they think to search in the bowels of the demon castle for people who were last known to be out at sea?"

"Or maybe they suspect, and they don't have any proof." My words came out like a growl. "But look—*we're* proof. We just need to get out of here to show people."

"We need to get to Hadriel and Leala," Hannon said.

"Or Weston, the wolf alpha." Vemar rubbed his slightly bearded chin. We hadn't been called up for a party recently, and everyone was looking a little worse for wear. They didn't bother grooming us if no one but the officers would see us. "I'm never fond of dealing with wolf alphas, but if anyone knows what's going on with the wolves, it's that guy. No one farts without his permission."

I released the smothering hold I'd put on my bond with Nyfain, and relief and love washed through me. I echoed it, closing my eyes to relish the feeling of him deep inside of me, then thought of his body deep inside of me, causing another ache that pooled heat into my core and tightened my nipples.

"Bedtime, I think." Vemar pushed to standing, stepped over Hannon, and closed the cell door behind him. "Strange Lady has that look in her eyes. She needs quiet time where she thinks no one can hear her moan."

My mouth dropped open. I worked my jaw, willing words to come out to deflect, but I didn't have a clue what to say. It didn't happen often, but occasionally I let myself fall into the feelings from Nyfain when I *wasn't* in pain, experiencing pure pleasure from the bond. From him. It eased some of my longing to see him again.

"Quick, let's all go to sleep so she won't be embarrassed." Lucille smirked at me. "Just think of how embarrassed she'll be when she is crowned princess and she knows her guards all listened to her climax."

"*If* all this is true and he's truly the one who holds her claim." Tamara gave me a poignant look.

Lucille rolled her eyes, because yes, there could be no doubt whose scent it was. Whose power blended with mine. Still, I was common. I wasn't officially a dragon until my first shift, and as long as I was stuck in this dungeon, I would never shift. The courts adhered to a certain protocol, and I didn't tick any boxes. It was a problem for a later day.

I was not happy with this conversation so near Hannon.

"You guys," I hissed. "My brother is here."

"Please leave me out of it," Hannon said, turning his head the other way.

I was determined to hold out just on principle, but when we were all locked back in our cells in the darkness and I lay on my bed of uncomfortable straw that did little to soften the hard stone...I *did* give in once again. I let the longing wash over me.

Desire spread through my body. I spread my legs and slipped my hand into my loose pants, careful to make absolutely no sound. An answering need flowed from the bond. Nyfain's desperation to touch me again was so strong that it nearly took my breath away. I stroked my finger through my wetness and rubbed it around my clit, sighing at the glorious sensation. Through the bond, I felt him stroking his cock. This was basically bond sex. We might be an incredible distance apart, but it wasn't so far that we couldn't make-believe-fuck each other.

I pressed the heel of my palm to my clit and plunged two fingers into my pussy, barely stifling a groan as I did so. I licked my finger and thumb of my other hand and lightly pinched my nipple, adding that sensation to the growing mix. My mind drifted deeper into the fantasy, images playing behind my eyes.

Nyfain's fingers took over for mine, plunging into me, stroking me just right. The tip of his cock dragged through my slick folds and paused at the entrance. Pleasure whispered across my flesh.

Heat turned to fire. Desire turned to desperate, aching need.

His big body lay over mine, all strength and muscle, and I ran my fingers down his broad back. This faux-reality had restored his gorgeous golden scales, two lines down the sides of his back. I stroked my fingers down them, causing him to buck into me wildly. I arched, cutting off my moan just in case it bled into reality, and wrapped my legs around his trim hips. I dragged my fingers down those scales again as his lips trailed along my jaw and then settled on my lips, opening my mouth so he could swipe his tongue through.

Fuck me, Nyfain, I thought, rocking my hips up. His slammed down, his cock driving down deep, filling me up in a way that felt like home.

He thrust on top of me, his perfect ass moving within my constricted legs. His kiss deepened, consuming, sweeping me away. His hard chest rubbed my nipples.

Pleasure surged through my body as he pounded into me, his hips slapping against my flesh. His kisses desperate. His love filling me up and flowing over, fusing with mine.

As though he were speaking them in my ear, I felt his words. I felt his possession. His drive to protect what was his.

Mine, I knew he thought, his cock branding me, his teeth moving over my mark and biting down, claiming me again. And again. *Mine!*

I came so hard that I lost my senses for a moment, confusing reality with this waking dream, losing myself to the pleasure of the moment. As I floated, not wanting to drift back to my body, I swore I could hear, *I love you, my little dragon.*

"HERE WE GO again," Vemar called out the next afternoon, sitting where he always did, idling the time away. "Party time."

Everyone pushed to standing and, sure enough, the sound of boots drifted into the space. Those boots appeared a moment later, followed by the bodies they belonged to, appearing beyond the lip of the low-hanging ceiling. Govam was in the lead, like always, with Denski right behind him. He walked down the center of the cells, eyes on me for a long moment before they found Micah. Denski kept going, coming for me. Apparently they hadn't named another new captain yet.

"Captain," Denski said, slowing by Hannon's cell.

"Stop," Govam said. The guards who'd been filing in slowed and then did as instructed, studying the cells to see what might have triggered Govam. By now they all knew that his word was law. To ignore it would be to die like all the others.

He joined Denski outside of Hannon's cell, and I pushed closer to the bars.

"Who's this?" Govam asked, his voice raised so everyone could hear. "I don't know him."

"Losing your faculties, Govam?" Vemar said in a bored voice. "He's always been there. Ol' fire crotch, we call him."

"Ew," Lucille said. "It's not cute when you know there's a dick hiding in that fire crotch. Kinda taints the palette."

"Speaking of taint…" Vemar started laughing.

Govam glanced back at Micah, then to me, his eyes boring into mine, and turned to face me.

"Who is this?" he demanded. "Why wasn't I alerted to his presence?"

"Are you under the impression I run this place or something?" I quirked an eyebrow at him.

His eyes narrowed.

"He's in rough shape," Denski said. "Should we get him up anyway?"

"No." The words were out of my mouth before I knew I'd thought them. "As you said, he's in no position to go. Leave him here."

Govam tilted his head a little. He didn't smile, his eyes didn't twinkle, but I knew I'd revealed my hand.

"Get him up," he said, still eying me. "He's handsome—he'll fetch a good price."

The power within me coiled to the point of pain as the rest of the guards burst into action, lining up in front of the cells of the shifters they'd be escorting to the baths. I heard someone bark for me to back up to the bars, and I did. Then I followed the guard's direction to step around so I could be let out. I didn't flinch when they unlocked the cell and rushed in to grab me. Didn't resist when they led me past Hannon, his expression screwed up in intense pain as he allowed them to manhandle him, ripping open his wounds so that they bled down his back.

I didn't act out, because I was waiting...

Waiting for when Micah slowed things down, as he always did.

Waiting for him to taunt Govam, as he always did.

Waiting for when he burst into movement, jamming the rest of them up behind him...

When it happened, the power within me exploded, white hot. Strength bled through my limbs in a way that was new and fucking amazing. Searing agony ripped down my back, my dragon wanting to come out, but I was in complete control of the situation this time. I had to be. Hannon depended on it.

I flexed and yanked my hands apart, breaking out of Denski's hold and the metal cuffs that couldn't contain me. In a flash, I grabbed Govam from behind and threw him to the right, against the bars of the nearest cell. Taller than him, stronger, fucking angrier, I grabbed his throat with one hand and shoved everyone else away, creating a bubble of power around us with the sheer force of my will. Nyfain flooded me with magic, fortifying me in this space with Govam, where no one could reach us.

Where no one could save him.

"If you force that man upstairs," I ground out, "I will do what no other dragon has ever done. I will fucking end you."

His eyes widened and a glimmer of fear sparkled within their slate-gray depths.

"You asked who he is?" I went on, my tone deathly quiet. The guards beat at my will, no more effective than a cloud of gnats. "He's my flesh and blood. I will burn this whole place to the ground, starting with you, if he is taken up to those parasites." I spat the last word, pausing for a moment to let that sink in. "Do you want to live or die, Govam? Decide right now."

I tightened my hold on his throat, but we both knew that wasn't how I would kill him. His hands were at his sides, pinned with my magic.

"You won't burn this place to the ground," he replied. "You don't have the people. You have a lot of power, but not enough. They'd kill you eventually. And him with you."

"Fine. But you'll die first. And I have the power to make it slow. Right here, in front of all your guards."

He licked his lips. His eyes changed—the intensity, not the color—and something new appeared in them. I didn't know if I should be scared or wary or worried for my future. But then, I'd decided not to think about the future just now.

"Can they hear me outside of this…bubble?" he asked.

"Yes. I'm not a faerie. I don't have that kind of magic."

There was an edge to Govam's voice as he raised it and said, "Leave him. Even if he was presentable, which he isn't, we don't have the guards. He's trouble."

"What about the dragon?" Denski asked, just outside my wall of will, his hands burned from trying to get in. That meant he was willing to take damage to help his captain. They had a tight bond. I wondered if this explained why Denski had never been elevated to a similar post—Govam didn't want his friend targeted by Micah.

Govam kept eye contact with me, never glancing away for even one second. "You can resume your duties, Denski. She and I have an understanding. Don't we, Finley? I will not include your brother in the parties if you play nice."

"Not quite," I replied. "You won't include my brother in the parties so that I won't slice off your dick and choke you with it. There was nothing in there about my playing nice with others. But yes, I won't cause any more trouble than normal if you leave him out of this."

Govam nodded. "We understand each other."

I pushed off him, keeping him put for a moment while I backed up and extended my hands behind my back. Apparently I could break out of my cuffs—I just needed enough motivation. I wondered if that was true of most of the non-suppressed dragons. If so, it made me wonder why they bothered with the things. Or why the other Wyvern dragons didn't break them on the regular. Then again, Govam had increased the amount of guards for each non-suppressed person so they'd be ready if we broke out.

Well…no, maybe not. They hadn't been ready for me.

Denski grabbed my elbows as Hannon was put back in his cell. They were a little rougher than I would've liked. Still, he was there instead of here. I couldn't spare him pain, but at least I could spare him the parties.

I just hoped Hadriel and Leala weren't too badly off.

CHAPTER 18

FINLEY

"WHAT IN THE hell?" Micah said softly as he looked at the demons coming through the main doors.

My jaw dropped. "What the hell" was right.

Costumes. Everyone had on costumes. It was reminiscent of a party back at Nyfain's castle. Although some of the guests showed next to no skin, others were nearly naked. No robed figures walked amongst them this time—the "tame" shifters and faeries wore sparkly briefs and body paint of all colors.

"Has this happened before?" I asked Micah, fighting a crooked smile. Even though no one really wanted to get too close to me, they continued to put us together as the focal point of the cages. I was going to try to pull back on that a little tonight. I *had* to get near the other shifters, even if it meant getting bought, killing my john, and facing the repercussions.

"No." Micah chuckled, then started laughing. "Absolutely not, no. Despite the fact that there is an entire faction of sex demons in this kingdom, the demon king likes to pretend their kind are civilized. Civilized in his mind means..."

"Vanilla," I said, my smile widening.

"Apparently they've had a change of heart." He sounded mystified.

Hadriel and Leala work fast, my dragon thought, full of pride.

"Are they…" Micah's words drifted away for a moment. "Are they wearing nipple clamp…pasties? Is that a thing?"

Really fast. I laughed.

"So it seems," I said, spying Leala in the crowd draped on a demon's arm with those nipple clamp pasties and a sparkly pink thong. The demon next to her held a leash attached to a collared male demon trailing along behind them.

I could not believe my eyes. Collars? Hadriel and Leala were miracle workers.

Then again, there were sex demons present, and this was the exact vibe they'd created at Nyfain's castle. Dolion might've been trying to show a certain face to his guests, but this depravity had always been lurking within them. Hadriel and Leala, true experts, had just let it out. I was sure the sex demons in his castle had helped. How could they not? This was their jam.

The night rolled on as it had in the past, with demons wandering closer to assess us and giving me a wide berth despite my attempts to muffle my scent. It wasn't until about halfway through the party that I spotted Hadriel, working the crowd with smiles and grins but toning down his usual flamboyance. It was almost like he was trying to blend in. No purple beast costume this time, although he did wear a fuzzy purple necktie and wrist cuffs.

He visited the cage of the indigo-eyed faerie, staying for a brief period before sauntering over to the alpha wolf. Putting his back to the cage, Hadriel looked out at the crowd of partygoers, his lips barely moving. To someone not in the know, it would look like he was just assessing the room. He was obviously networking, though, and the perpetual tightness in my stomach loosened just a little.

Not long afterward, he threaded his way through the crowd, stopping to chat a few times and allowing a woman to grab his junk. He grabbed a female demon and walked her toward Micah. At Micah's cell, after marveling about the large dragon's frame and muscles, he excused himself and sidled over to me.

"My love," he said quietly, his back to me as though he were still assessing Micah. "That dress is truly hideous. It is like they are trying to make you ugly."

"Any news?" I murmured, looking out at the crowd.

Dolion strolled through the double doors, his smile tight and his shoulders tense—I could see it from all the way across the room. He looked around, trying to take it all in, his movements getting stiffer and stiffer as he did. He paused next to a male shifter in a pair of tiny briefs and looked him over, a little crease forming between his eyebrows.

The woman next to him offered the shifter a beaming smile and then a pat-down, running her fingers over his chest and down to his stomach. She pulled her hand away before she could trail them over his bulge, but the look in her eyes suggested she would have liked to keep exploring. She continued walking with Dolion, her gaze seeking out more flesh, her desire plain. She evidently liked what she saw.

Dolion must've hated it, though, because he disentangled himself from her, putting distance between them. She hardly seemed to notice.

"How'd you do this?" I asked Hadriel as he worked his way back to the female demon checking out Micah.

He paused and turned to look at me, assessing me like any guest or "tame" shifter might. He waved his hand in front of his nose and screwed up his face in disgust.

"We don't have time to waste on questions like that, dove," he told me, his tone not at all matching his actions and body language. "We need to get you in a room with the indigo-eyed faerie and the alpha wolf. They've been collecting information for years. Years and years. But they don't have the power to break out or the knowledge to operate the boats. They need the way cleared, essentially. They need the dragons."

"They'll have the dragons. We just need a way to get out of the dungeons."

He nodded and turned again as the lady demon wandered over to him.

"The faerie thinks you can help her with that," he murmured, so low I barely heard. He rose his voice as the demon took his arm. "Do you know what?" He turned my way. "She is a vision. I think she'd be a great show for Tessau while you pleasure him, don't you? Or I can pleasure him—or you! If she were a little removed, we wouldn't be troubled by the smell."

The demon's beige-eyed gaze traveled over me, hesitating on my cleavage and roaming my face.

"I like the smell," she purred, tracing fingers across Hadriel's bare arm. "Maybe she could pleasure me while you pleasure Tessau." Her lips curled into a sultry smile. "He is ever so confused by how much he likes it."

"Yes, but then he turns violent. That's a job for the end of the night. Instead…what if you pleasure her while he fucks you?" He moaned softly and nuzzled her neck. "Now that sounds hot."

She continued to assess me as a somewhat short but broad

demon walked our way. He spotted Hadriel and the demon before shifting his attention to me. Appreciation filled his eyes until he got a little closer, then a spark of confusion eclipsed it, followed by aggression.

"Tessau." The lady demon turned to him, letting go of Hadriel. "Our new pet has the most interesting idea. Me licking the pussy of this divine-smelling shifter while you take me from behind."

The guy demon looked over me again, his expression shifting between arousal and wariness. He was trying to come to terms with the smell, I guessed. I hadn't realized females would enjoy it, though it stood to reason. Nyfain was power and dominance and strength, and anyone who liked those characteristics would probably appreciate his scent. When I wasn't adding my own "fuck off" flair to it, at any rate.

"Maybe," Tessau said, taking her arm and steering her away. "Or maybe I will take her myself."

As they wandered away, I clenched my teeth and refused to let anger show in my face or bearing. I might let a woman go down on me—it wasn't an unpleasant experience, something I'd learned in my experimental days—but I would not allow that wank-hammer to fuck me. He'd die first.

As if hearing my thoughts, Hadriel paused before following them. "Don't worry, love," he whispered. "A lot of these demons are in the impressionable stages of debauchery. I can talk them into and out of almost anything. That male demon is bi—he just doesn't quite realize it—so I can lean on his confusion if I need to. You might need to do *some* sex acts, but we'll try to limit that to your own digits, yes?"

I took a deep breath but didn't respond.

He nodded. "I have to go. Leave it to me, though. I know all the right people, and most of them think I'm ridiculous."

"How is that helpful?"

He frowned at me. "Because they aren't threatened by me, which means I get to move around pretty freely. The lessons in the master's castle are really coming in handy. Be thinking about your part—we need the dragons to get us through the castle and out. Where is Hannon, speaking of? He's our expert on those boats."

"He won't be coming to these parties. I made sure of it."

Hadriel glanced at my face with confusion before nodding and hurrying off.

"He's a valuable asset," Micah said after he left.

"Yes, and if you'd told him that a few months ago, he would have laughed in your face."

"Incoming," Micah said, moving to the other side of his cage as Dolion stepped out of the crowd and walked directly toward me. No one hovered around him this time. And as he distanced himself from those mingling on the outskirts of the party, his flat expression fell away, exposing the rage beneath.

"I cannot, for the life of me, figure out how you did this," he seethed, his tone low and vicious. It was clear he was talking about the drastic change in the crowd. "Is it that little shifter man-whore who came with you? I thought he was firmly in hand. More fool me, maybe. Not to worry—he's been returned to the dungeons. To *you*."

I was careful to keep perfectly composed, not giving anything away. "Don't degrade sex workers like that. They deserve better than your slurs. Or for Jedrek to be mentioned in the same sentence."

His lip curled in barely controlled anger. "I took you in order to keep that dragon prince in line. But I've received word that he has essentially cleared the kingdom of demons. You're of absolutely no use to me alive, but at least you might offer some potential as revenge. We'll see how tall he stands when he watches you and your family suffer gruesome deaths, hmm?" He took a step away, clasping his hands behind his back. "Enjoy the party. It'll be your last."

Cold washed through me as he strode away, every movement full of rage.

"Looks like we've run out of time," Micah said softly, watching him go.

"I have, at any rate."

"*We* have. There's one issue with what he said, though."

"What's that?"

"The officers. We can clear all the ones we see, but they have some sort of power to avert the eye. They can get away without being noticed...and then they'll alert the guards, who'll be after us in no time."

I gripped the bars as my heart clattered against my ribcage. "I have a plan for the officers. They drink that fizzy drink right before the lull—the blackout. My crowded everlass leaves are ready. I just need to cold-seep them to speed up the release of their power. I can drop them into the canister when I'm brought up with Vemar—he's great at making distractions. If the faerie and alpha can get us past those locks, and Hannon can manage the boats, I can get us the rest of the way. All I need is the opportunity."

"Then we must ensure you have it."

LATER THAT NIGHT, I was purchased for the first time. I would join the others in the private rooms reserved for the paying partici-pants and their "acquisitions." The couple Hadriel had tried to set up hadn't come through. Instead, I'd been purchased by a guy influenced by Leala. The details? I would need to wear leather, expose my tits and ass, and…urinate on someone.

Like…what in the holy fuck?

What in the holy fuck?

For the first time, I kinda wished the demon sex magic could influence me. It would make this task a lot less grim.

"You can't be serious," I told Leala when I met her in the changing room after the main party adjourned for the night. Govam had escorted me that far and then closed the door on us. I assumed he'd be waiting on the other side, ensuring I couldn't make a run for it.

With no help from me, she pulled chaps onto my legs. "I'm sorry, milady, I am. Hadriel told me the deal he could work out. But that couple didn't have a friend we could hook up with Calia, and she's the most important person for you to connect with tonight."

Calia was the indigo-eyed faerie, and apparently she'd been sold to Mr. Pee-body's friend, who was fine with partying in the same private quarters.

Apparently, they enjoyed watching too.

"Why do *I* have to wiz on him?" My stomach still churned after what Dolion had told me. I had precious little time. Micah had overheard that the next big party would be in a month. According to Dolion, I'd be gone before that, and I had to make sure it was by my own choosing. "Why can't you do it and I'll pretend to watch?"

"Because you are gorgeous and strong and he likes to be dominated. Your smell is going to drive him wild after we get him in the right mood. You won't have to do anything objectionable, milady. Except maybe whip him or shove something up his ass."

"No." I shook my head. "Please tell me you're joking. I mean, sure to the whipping. But otherwise…no. Nuh-uh. Nope."

"It's fine, milady, really. He's a lamb. You will only have to be the aggressor. He won't try anything with you. No one will. He doesn't share his nightly toys like some of the others do."

"Ugh. Fine, but how am I going to meet with Calia?"

"With some guidance from Hadriel and me, these after-parties have become a little looser, and I expect that'll hold, even with the dragons present. They'll probably try to work the sex demon magic on you to keep you tame, but we both know it doesn't affect you the same way it does everyone else. Here we go, here's a leather bustier."

It left my breasts open to the air.

"Trust me, this is the best way," Leala said, finishing up my outfit. "The only way, actually. We didn't have a lot of options."

No options, and no time.

"Fine. I mean, I can't believe this is even a thing, but fine."

"Neither did he. I am very good at assessing kinks, and I just knew this would do it for him. He is big into being humiliated. Here we go." She fastened me with a chain choker and then dressed herself in lace and satin, her breasts as bare as mine and her nether region equally uncovered.

I wished I could say the night was a good time.

I couldn't. It was fucking weird, top to bottom. Leala had definitely found a couple of people with serious kinks. I spanked, I dong-slapped, I choked (a little too violently), and yes, I straddled his body and let the stream flow. He came so hard that we thought he was dead for a moment. He lay there with his pointed tongue hanging out, staring sightlessly at the sky.

Leala gave me a *well done* nod. He definitely liked my scent, but he'd *loved* my aggression, even when someone had to pull me off him so I wouldn't kill him.

I'd really wanted to kill him. I didn't care about people's kinks…until they forced me to participate. And then someone really needed to die. That was just logic.

"Okay, milady," Leala said as the demon lay there recovering. She ushered me quickly to the side of the chamber, glancing behind her as she did so. "Take this." She pressed a folded piece of paper into my hand, no larger than my palm. "The alpha wolf asked me to pass this on. Hide it."

I slipped it down into the covered area beneath my breasts.

"Now." She glanced at the other side of the room, where people writhed and groaned, overseen by a sex demon that was supposed to follow me everywhere but clearly wanted in on the action. "Wait here for a moment. Don't draw attention to yourself. I'll grab Calia."

She hurried away, and I lightly touched my fingertips to the piece of paper hidden against my sternum.

"Dragon." Calia hastened up to me, completely naked and hands shifting back and forth between covering her chest and her crotch. She swallowed, incredibly self-conscious.

Clearly she wasn't whipped and left in tattered rags as often as the dragons were.

"We don't have much time, so I will be brief," she said, talking low and quickly. She rubbed a hand over her pretty face, her cheeks flushed and eyes a bit dazed. "The demon's magic is still wearing off. Forgive me. As background, I do not remember your kingdom. Maybe I never knew of it. But I know there is more of the world than meets our eyes or takes residence in our memories. I've met those who claim to be from Wyvern, and many of them sickened and then died. That sickness is one the demons often build into their magic, killing the victims slowly and painfully. I often wonder what other kingdoms have been lost. This castle is just a castle. It is not a kingdom. Where are the other citizens of Dolion's kingdom? Housed in ruined kingdoms the king is tormenting? I do not know."

She crossed her arms in front of her chest before putting them back at her sides. The effort it took to do so was obvious.

"I'm not used to having to…entertain without demon aid," she said softly. "It's not ideal. None of this is ideal. Being a prisoner is one thing—I've seen dungeons in all parts of this magical world. But I have never been treated like this. *Used* like this. It…" She clenched her jaw and took a deep breath.

I couldn't help myself. "Why have you been in many dungeons?" I asked.

She studied me for a moment. "Dragons." She shook her head slightly, a small smile gracing her lips. "Most people would be aghast by that revelation. Or horrified. Not dragons. That is why we need your kind to help us escape. We cannot do it without your ferocity."

"How can you help?"

She rubbed her face again. "I have a rare type of magic. In simple terms, I can pick locks, magically speaking. If there is a spell, I can disentangle it…up to a point. Spells that encompass a whole kingdom would be beyond me. But moderate spells, like those over doors, are within my power."

My heart started to beat faster.

She nodded, my reaction clearly showing in my expression. "If I have access to my magic, I can break the magical locks on the dungeons. Can the dragons pick the physical locks?"

"Yes."

"Yes, good. We'll need your help on my floor, too. The problem is—"

"Oh violet eyes," someone said in a creepy singsong voice. "Where is my violet eyes?"

A look of terror crossed her face. Tears came to her eyes, but she stood her ground.

"It's fine," I said quickly, patting her arm. "Their magic doesn't affect me. I'll kill him before I leave."

Her breath hitched. For a moment she just stared at me, then she put a hand on my forearm and squeezed gently. "I will consider that an act of friendship."

I shrugged. "I was thinking the burst of power might free up your magic, which would be a logical next step in our plan, but friendship is a good reason too."

"Dragons," she whispered again, her smile growing. Her expression cleared. "The problem," she said, talking faster now, "is that my magic is suppressed. Like almost everyone else's. Except yours, correct? And some of the other dragons?"

"Yes."

"I can use the power of other species to bolster my own. It's how I'm able to unwind their magic. If you are powerful enough, you might be able to pull my magic free the way you did with the dragons. It will work the same, even though it is magic and not an animal."

"But the magical suppression will just kick back in, won't it? That's what happens for the dragons who haven't had the spell lifted."

Her smile was slight. "Not if I can…pick the lock, as it were. If I can disentangle the magic spell before it suppresses me again, then I will be free. I will have the ability to help us escape the first level of the dungeons. After that…"

"The dragons will take over."

She nodded as the sex demon approached, her eyes on Calia.

"You think you can fully…unlock yourself from the suppression spell while dealing with that?" I nodded toward the mess of bodies writhing in the corner.

Her thin eyebrows pinched together. She licked her lips. "I will have to," she said uncertainly.

I was already in hot water with Dolion. He was *already* going to make an example of me by killing me in front of Nyfain. What did I have to lose? This was the next step in freeing us.

"How about you get ready to go, and we'll get this party started?"

CHAPTER 19

FINLEY

I PUSHED CALIA out of the way and walked directly toward the sex demon. He stopped, and his magic hit me, oozing over me like slime. My stomach churned. Bile rose in my throat. I barely kept myself from stopping and retching.

I plowed into him, grabbing his shoulders and walking him backward until I neared the others, and then I sliced into his middle with my magic and threw him. He smashed into the group of naked people.

Bodies flew to the sides in a tangle of limbs, some trying to get out of the way of the suddenly dead demon and some getting hit by the debris. The other sex demon was the next to go as power pulsed and pumped around me, throbbing into the room.

"Do not shift," I called out, throwing the second sex demon, quickly lifeless, out of the way.

The demon huddled on the floor, looking up at me with wide orange eyes in his brown-scaled face. "Guards!" he shouted, cowering as I stood over him. "Guards!"

I bent to take him out, then thought better of it. Why should I steal the others' opportunity for revenge?

"Anyone want my collar to strangle him?" I asked, removing it so the guards I'd eventually be confronted with didn't get any ideas.

"I don't need a collar." A lady shifter pounced on him, wrapping her fingers tightly around his neck. His hands flailed, caught by a faerie and held out of the way.

"I can feel…" A shifter pressed his hand to his chest. "I can feel—"

"Do not act on it," I barked, magic riding the command, shocking into him.

He jerked as though slapped, and he wasn't the only one. The rest were shedding the effects of the demon's sex and suppression magic, turning on their captors and brutally tearing them down.

A side door opened, and I realized I'd forgotten about Mr. Pee-body.

"Help," he yelled through the door. "Help!"

Guards streamed into the room, pushing him out of the way. Before I could get to him, I was surrounded, my power still pumping out.

Get all you can from Nyfain, quickly, I told my dragon.

On it.

Power surged into me, and it kept coming. As guards swarmed me, grabbing me and attempting to throw me to the floor, I blasted out a hard thrust of power at Calia, still standing in the corner. I didn't know if I could direct it like that, but it was worth a shot.

My chest hit the ground and someone put their hand on my head. My hands were wrenched behind me and secured with cuffs before I was yanked up and marshaled out of the room. As they turned to get me out of the door, I caught the rest of the shifters descending on Mr. Pee-body. The guards were so preoccupied with the dragon that they didn't seem to notice. Mr. Pee-body wouldn't be getting out alive either.

Govam's voice rang out. "Let's go, let's go."

They hustled me down the wide and luxurious corridor, then took a small arched door into what looked like the servants' halls.

"I've got her." Govam pushed his way through the others and took my shoulders.

"Just a tiny bit of trouble," I told him, out of breath. "They deserved it, though. Seriously. There is no way you'd fault me if you knew what they were getting up to. It was not my scene."

"I tried to warn them that you could not be controlled. I was ignored. That's why we were waiting outside of the room instead of inside. Part of staying alive around dragons is knowing when to get out of their way."

Smart guy.

"His highness blames you for the...change in...party dynamics," Govam said softly as they ushered me down a few flights of narrow stone steps.

"I know. He told me."

"He was correct, of course, just not in the way he supposed."

I tensed.

"Easy, dragon," Govam said. "My job is not to instruct his highness regarding his affairs. My job is to escort dragons. I am nothing but a minion in this castle, regardless of my title. No one listens to guards or officers. Not about anything important. We have our duties, and that is where our usefulness ends."

He walked me through the dungeon. Officers wandered about, smiling at me as I passed.

"She's back early again, hmm, Govam?" the first officer called. "I think soon I'll be given leave to use her as I see fit. There is yet more power I can wring from her."

"He's not wrong about getting free license with you soon," Govam whispered as we walked to the next set of stairs. "The demon king does not like acknowledging the incubi and succubi as beings that exist naturally among us. He values their ability to control and twist minds, but he'd prefer to have nothing to do with them. That's why they are used to taunt and torture kingdoms under his control. He likes to think they are the only demons who enjoy less-than-standard sex, even though he himself has some...peculiar tastes. The party tonight exposed a nerve. He will not let it stand."

"I know. As I said, he told me."

"He'll give them time to wring the last shreds of power from you, and then he will throw you at the golden prince's feet and kill you for good. The officers are only kind to those deemed useful. They can also be cruel."

"Whipping us is their version of kind?"

"You were deemed useful, so they were not actively trying to break you. Sometime soon, the demon king will want you broken. He will do it to hurt the golden prince—*and* you."

He slowly led me down the last flight of stairs, Denski and the other guards lingering behind.

"Soon, you will lose all traces of yourself, and when you die, that prince will die with you. At least the parts of him that matter."

His tone was so matter-of-fact. He didn't sound like he was warning me, or deriving any pleasure from our conversation. He was just giving me the current state of affairs.

"Why are you telling me this?"

He didn't answer, just sped up again and walked me through the rows of cells, all of them empty except for Hannon's and mine. Jedrek lay curled up in the corner, his clothes torn and stained with blood. They'd clearly beaten him for the part they thought he'd played in the most recent party.

Fear choked me as Govam shoved me into the cell and I backed up to get my cuffs removed.

Soon they would realize it wasn't Jedrek who'd made things so spicy. They would put together that everything had changed after the arrival of the two new additions from Nyfain's castle.

Hadriel and Leala were in danger. So was Hannon, given he was my brother and could be used to torment me. *I* was in danger. Jedrek, too, though it was a little harder to care about that.

We had to get out of here. *Now.*

I just hoped to hell the boost of power I'd given Calia would be enough for her to get moving. Otherwise we'd just have to force our way out through the officers and make sure we crossed the waters before the rest of the castle found out about it.

LATER THAT NIGHT—OR maybe it was early morning—I sat against the back wall and contemplated all I'd learned.

I'd read the note Leala pressed into my hand.

It had been written in all caps, the letters slightly slanted, which made it easy to read. Weston had been collecting information like a hoarder collected trinkets. He had boat schedules (there were none), guard rotation schedules (quite the clusterfuck in organization, that), information about where the officers slept and how many of them there were at any given time, plus knowledge of the magic that protected them. He'd drawn a map of the castle, and while there were several blank spaces, he had good intel on exit routes. He even knew where Dolion slept. He also knew there was no way to get to Dolion. Not for us. We'd never reach him through all the corridors and guards and staff.

Fine. We didn't need to reach him. We just needed to get out. Revenge could come later.

I pored over the information, connecting the dots, fueled by my sudden panic to get the fuck out of here. I was devising two plans—one that hinged on Calia picking the magical lock, and one that would have to work without her. I just wished I could some-how reach Hadriel and talk them over. He was very good at plan making, at looking at all the pieces and fitting them together.

"You okay?" Hannon asked, sitting up like I was.

"Yeah. You?"

"Shut up, I'm trying to sleep," Jedrek groused before turning over and curling up a little tighter.

He'd screamed at me just before everyone got back a few hours ago, too sore to do much more than turn over and yell, but doing that with all the gusto he could manage. It was the same old song and dance. He blamed me for everything, including the strange "weeds" now growing in the cell.

I hadn't meant to lose my cool and punch him, but…well, you could talk shit to me, but you didn't do it about the everlass. That was crossing the line.

He did mention something of note—he'd been told by Dolion that he'd get to marry me and sleep with me (if he could work his dick) before I was taken back to his kingdom to be killed. In other words, Dolion really intended to drive that last nail into Nyfain's coffin.

Or so he thought. I would be long fucking gone before any

nuptials took place, one way or another.

"That…concoction helped," Hannon said quietly. "A lot."

A scuffing of feet sounded from the steps.

"*Shh*," I heard, followed by a murmur.

Hannon scrunched up his brow. He'd heard it too.

A moment later, I saw two bare legs descend the stairs, followed by a miniscule pair of briefs and Hadriel's bent body. He paused when he was in full view, looking my way, before giving a little wave and continuing down the stairs.

I pushed forward, not believing what I was seeing.

Behind him, wearing a long slip, crept Calia, her fingers trailing on the stone and her other hand on Hadriel's shoulder. What must be her sister followed, in the same sort of drape. Unlike Hadriel, they couldn't see in the dark. The alpha wolf descended behind them, not using the faerie's shoulder for guidance but definitely feeling with his feet before stepping.

"Micah," I said, standing. "Micah, are you awake?"

"*I* am awake, Strange Lady." Vemar came forward to the bars. "What is that I hear?"

Hadriel reached the bottom of the steps and helped the faeries the rest of the way before waiting for the alpha wolf. Hadriel murmured something to them before leading the way down the center of the cells to me.

"Who is there? Who is sneaking?" A note of alarm had crept into Vemar's voice.

"*Shh*," Hadriel said. "The officers might hear you."

Vemar pushed a little closer to the bars, his hands coming through and resting on the horizontal support bars. "Did they lift the magical lock on this dungeon earlier than usual? Coming down here is quite a risk."

"Are all dragons as dense as you? *Shh!*" Hadriel waved at him, though Vemar couldn't see it, continuing to lead the others my way. "My love," he whispered when he reached me. "We've had a helluva breakthrough."

"Why are you down here?" I asked with a note of panic. "What if they catch you?"

Pulling on Calia's hands, he led her right to the bars. She gripped the cold metal, staring sightlessly into my cell. Her doppelgänger followed suit, the two of them pressed tightly together.

"We should have a few hours," Hadriel said, watching as the alpha wolf reached out and found the bars. He stepped a little closer but didn't hang on. "Tell her, Calia."

A metal click sounded within the dungeon. Vemar's cell door swung open, and he stepped out slowly, feeling his way.

"Oh fuck," Hadriel murmured. "Is he going to come kill me now? Fucking dragons."

"It's fine," I told Hadriel before patting Calia's hands. "What's the breakthrough? Did you take down the demons' *obice*?"

I couldn't help the excitement and hope in my tone. A slow release of curiosity and similar hope dripped down from the bond, Nyfain obviously wondering if I'd gotten good news. So did I.

"Your power release earlier was more than strong enough to bring me out of suppression," Calia said softly as Vemar carefully walked our way. "Then your...rather thorough distraction allowed me plenty of time to unpick myself from their suppression spell. It's a very simple spell. Simple but strong and effective, as I'm sure you know."

"So you picked the *obice* to this floor?" I asked in a gush.

A smile graced her lovely face. "Yes. That's also a simple spell.

Corrosive, and as dirty as those who set it, but easily manageable, not the least because it is an older spell. Demon magic decays rapidly. Newer spells will be harder to break, but what need would they have of newer spells with all of us suppressed?"

"Which means they can't know, or suspect, anyone outside of your kingdom has been released," the alpha wolf said. He stuck his hand through the bars for a handshake. "Weston, estranged from the Lake Forest Pack, Red Lupine kingdom."

"Oh, that's the same—"

"Nope," Hadriel cut me off, giving me an expression that said, *Shut the hell up.*

Apparently he didn't want an origin in common with the alpha. Although given the history of his parents, who'd been exiled or rejected or whatever from that kingdom, that made sense.

"Estranged?" I asked.

"You can't be an alpha of a pack," Weston replied with a growl, "when you are locked in a demon dungeon and loaned out as a sex slave."

I puffed out my cheeks with a breath I didn't expel. "Right," I said, finally releasing it. "I guess not. Good point."

"This is my sister, Felicia," Calia said, pulling her sister a little closer. "She acts as a booster for my magic. She's the one they took first, kidnapped right from the shores of our village. I saw it but was too far away to help. I knew who took her, though. I didn't prepare enough, thinking it would be as easy to escape this dungeon as any. I didn't account for the magical suppression."

"Hindsight, as they say," I murmured. "The dragons without suppression know they cannot shift or otherwise advertise that their animals have been freed. They might not have suppression, but I'm not sure Dolion realizes I am powerful enough to pull their animals free. I've tried to keep it that way."

Weston nodded. "Good."

"We need you to pull out his animal, dove," Hadriel said. "And probably the most powerful of the dragons—that big fucker, right? He's terrifying. Calia can peel away their suppression right now, before the officers open for the day, but then she'll need to rest. We can make a couple trips to bring people to release, but I have to be honest, love…I don't think we have all the time in the world. The demon king is not too thrilled with the current state of affairs. He'll be setting things back to rights and looking for the people who made it like that. Playtime is over."

"He's blaming it on Jedrek and me—"

"You did it." Jedrek rose like a man possessed, his eyes wild. "You did this!" He pointed at Hadriel. "You're from the castle, aren't you? I thought I recognized you from somewhere." He curled his hand into a fist. "You ruined everything I had. Well, not for long. The second his majesty hears about this—"

"Enough," Weston barked, but there was no power riding his words.

We need to release his wolf so that he can get Jedrek under control, my dragon said.

I did as suggested, blasting out power as Vemar stopped beside Hadriel and gave his shoulder a hard pat.

Hadriel did a sort of shimmy, trying to sidle away, something that made Vemar grin wickedly.

"Enough," Weston commanded again, this time with power and might curling through his words.

Jedrek jerked ramrod straight, his eyes growing intense, his mouth clenching. Fear lit his gaze. Another alpha was on the scene, and this one spoke the same language—wolf.

"You will be removed from this place," Weston said as Calia and her doppelgänger turned to Vemar, probably focused on lifting the suppression magic. They'd already helped Weston, and he'd just needed me to pull his animal free. "You will be placed in a proper pack where you belong. You clearly have not done well running solo."

Jedrek's hand came up to his chest. Shit. I'd unintentionally released his animal.

"Tell him not to shift," I told Weston quickly.

"What's going on?" Micah and Tamara stepped up to the bars of their cells, joining a few others who'd already woken.

Weston continued barking orders at Jedrek as the faeries did their job. Hadriel reached through the bars for me.

"We have to leave this kingdom soon, love. Let's talk about how to make that happen."

CHAPTER 20

FINLEY

THE WHIP CRACK sounded a moment before the pain registered, crawling across my back. Pleasure pounded through
me, overriding the sensation. I didn't soak it in, though. I didn't
soak in either feeling, actually. My mind was focused on the task
ahead—I had to give these bastards a big, powerful send-off,
courtesy of the crowded everlass, so they'd go retire for the night
and give the wolves a bunch of much-needed planning time.

Crack.

I stroked the grooves in the whipping post I was strapped to,
fingernail marks from those who had come before me. Maybe
even mine from previous sessions. It connected me to the others
who had stood in my shoes—or lack of shoes, I guessed. Today I
wore a loose slip, currently being shredded from my body.

Crack.

The tip of the whip sliced my flesh. Searing pain met pleasure.
My brain drifted away from both feelings.

I'd given Calia a week to free as many people as possible from
the suppression spell. Most of the dragons had been released, and

they'd also freed the more powerful shifters and faeries. We had about as much power as we would get.

Now it was my turn.

My interlude with the officers had turned out exactly like I hoped. I'd stuck my fists out of the cell to be cuffed, soggy crowded everlass in one hand (steeped to start the release of the poison) and dried crowded everlass in the other. Though a little liquid had dripped from my hand as we made our way, they hadn't appeared to notice. When passing the large copper canister of their brewing fizzy drink, I'd snapped the cuffs, killed an officer, and knocked into the large canister as if I'd tripped.

In reality, I used the distraction to drop in the leaves.

The officers, as hoped, ran to secure the canister as I pretended to try to escape.

That was when I got a refresher on the officers' ability to randomly pop out of nowhere, whips in hand. They had dragged a terribly weak me (my acting prowess was on point) to the whipping post, secured me in, and here we were...just waiting for the crowded everlass to do its job.

They wouldn't dip into their strange drink until tomorrow, according to Weston. After the drink would come the lull, their period of rest, and the length of that break apparently depended on how much power they'd poured into the process. The more power they harvested from us, the stronger their creations. The stronger the creatures, the longer the officers needed to recover from making them. The guards talked about it here and there, and over the years, Weston had paid careful attention.

Nyfain's job had probably been harder these last months because I'd been feeding the guards our combined power. My presence here was harming him in more ways than one.

Okay, pity party, keep it together, my dragon thought. *You can only go to pieces when you are back in his arms.*

I didn't understand the logic but agreed with the sentiment.

When the officers were resting or celebrating or whatever it was they did, they'd drink most of that fizzy stuff. They wouldn't know they'd been poisoned until they were dying. Crowded everlass worked quickly and didn't have a strong flavor.

Don't fuck with an everlass-loving dragon.

Crack.

I rubbed my finger across another groove.

I could feel Nyfain's despair. He was trying to hide it from me, I knew, but it kept growing. I also felt his impatience.

An imaginary clock ticked in my head. I barely felt the vibrating pain mingling with pleasure as it raged through my body. All I could focus on was tomorrow. There were so many moving parts to our escape plan, the largest of which was the Bridge of Doom.

I didn't have a fucking clue how we'd make it over that.

Crack.

Apparently the strength of the magic was now ten times what it was during one of the last escapes. That was guesswork on Micah's part, but it stood to reason. Our reactions when we went over it were much more severe than anyone else remembered.

I pulled more power from Nyfain, stuffing it into the air around me. A very distinct snuffling sound indicated the officers were eagerly consuming it.

The bridge was the only path we could take. Hadriel, Weston, and I had looked at every possible exit route. All of the others would run through guard stations, idling demons, or other groups that would sound the alarm. We could kill everyone we ran across, but eventually there would be too many of them. They had an enormous castle of demons ready to die for their king, and we had a cluster of weakened shifters and faeries. The odds weren't in our favor.

Bile rose in my throat, and my stomach swirled as my mind turned to Nyfain's kingdom.

We didn't have great odds of making a stand in Wyvern either, something Micah, Weston, and even Calia had said to me after hearing Hadriel's update on our general numbers. More dragons had been awakened in our kingdom, yes, but they were young. Inexperienced. They wouldn't help us in a battle. The rest of the shifters, experienced or not, were the mediocre or lesser-powered shifters who'd suffered years of demon abuse.

I'd seen the lengths the king was willing to go to get what he wanted. All he'd have to do was keep throwing demons at us until we were buried under the onslaught. There were too many of them.

But I liked our shitty odds better than the thought of spending another minute away from Nyfain.

Pain sucked at me, pulling me down.

"Two more and then release her," the first officer said, hovering around me.

"But first officer, I believe the king has no more use for her."

"That is true, officer," the first officer said. They never used actual names with each other. Not in front of us, anyway. They didn't even use nicknames. It was a shame, because I'd given them a few they could've adopted. Like Dickface Barney or Turd Goblin Sue. "But that kind of work must be savored, and the end of the cycle is upon us. We'll finish our other duties before we do his bidding. We have plenty of time."

"Yes, first officer," the minion said before doling out two

more lashes that stung like hell and then standing aside.

They hauled me back downstairs and to my cell. Jedrek sat with his back to the wall, watching as they dropped me inside.

"I have valuable information for the king," he told the officers, leaning forward. "Very valuable. About who has been messing with the parties and escape attempts…"

I tried to summon the strength to crawl over and shut him up, but my body wouldn't work with my brain. My dragon hissed, desperate to silence him. Tamara drifted to her cell bars, but no one else pushed forward with the panic I so keenly felt.

The closest officer laughed as he clanged the door shut. The other shook his head.

"I'm valuable," Jedrek called out, desperate. "I don't belong down here. I was falsely imprisoned. It wasn't me!"

The officers didn't comment, leaving by way of the stairs and clicking off the light as they did so. I'd be the last prisoner to give them power tonight.

"Lock it up," one of the officers said to the other as they disappeared from view.

"You are a disgrace to your kingdom," Tamara seethed, flashing her teeth at Jedrek.

"Nice try, possum," Vemar called down. "But they've heard that before. They've heard it all before. The whining, begging, promising the moon. They know better than to believe desperate prisoners at this point."

"But…" Jedrek scowled at me. It didn't seem like he was inclined to mate with me anymore. At least there was that. "You…"

I ignored him, belly to the stone, pain thrumming within me. Calia and her sister would take the night off too. We needed to save our strength.

Tomorrow was the big day.

I hoped we hadn't made several grave errors. We could work with one or two, but several…

ADRENALINE PUMPED THROUGH me the next night, and support and encouragement swirled through the bond. Nyfain must know what we were about to attempt.

The other dragons waited in their cells, idle and lounging, amazing actors. I stayed on my stomach because I *wasn't* a good actor, and my terror and apprehension was probably showing clearly on my face.

Fuck, what if I got us all killed?

What if we couldn't cross the bridge?

What if…

I sucked in a deep breath and closed my eyes, willing myself to relax.

"They'll believe me eventually when they see the parties don't change," Jedrek mumbled, scratching at his head and then his chest. "I won't have to stay in here." His voice cracked. "I can't stay in here. I can't do this. I can't be forced to live in this stench, sleeping out in the open with no food or bathroom. I can't…"

Sobs racked his body, overcoming him. He wilted where he sat, breaking before me. Before us all.

Despite myself, I pitied him. Being the demons' pet had clearly given him hope. And now that his position, such as it was, had been stripped from him, he couldn't handle imprisonment. Especially not with a strong alpha dragon pressing on his senses, something that had to feel much more intense now that he could access his wolf.

But the sound of feet on the steps pulled my focus. That would be the officers coming down to shut off the lights and engage the magic to lock us in.

Except shiny black boots descended the stairs, four pairs in total. Guards. Given the number, they were coming for one of the stronger dragons.

My heart sped up.

Govam reached the end of the stairs and looked my way. His gaze never wavered as he cut a path directly for me.

Micah, standing at his cell, snapped his head in my direction. Hannon was watching my face, unsure of what was happening but ready to react to it based on how I did.

Govam stopped at my cell, the other guards behind him, Denski not present.

"Let's go, Finley. The king wants to see you."

I stood slowly, going over my options. Obviously I could kill them all, but then we'd never make it to the king. He'd be wondering where we'd gone, and he didn't strike me as a patient man.

"Jedrek too?" I asked, backing to the bars.

"No, not him. Just you."

Well, that was good, at least. Maybe they'd make a last-ditch effort to strip me of Nyfain's scent. Or try to break me, since the officers had refused to do it. I could stand that. Time was a problem, though. It was of the essence, and I had none of it. The crowded everlass was in the fizzy drink. It was only a matter of time before the officers consumed it, if they hadn't already, and died. Even in a place like this, a bunch of dead bodies would be noticed.

Damn it, why today of all days?

Shaking all over, uncertain, I waited for him to put the cuffs on and then met him at the cell door. He opened it, his eyes on my face, a small crease between his brows.

"The king doesn't want to kiss and make up?" I asked with a grin.

Govam didn't respond, not that I'd expected otherwise. Instead, he took hold of me and marched me toward the stairs.

The others watched me pass. Most hid the trepidation from their faces, but not all. They knew what this meant.

I wondered if they would go without me.

"Step lively," Govam said, urging me up the stairs.

The second-floor landing was bare. It didn't take long to discover why. The officers were lounging around the top floor, goblets in hand or visiting the fizzy container.

"Now is not a good day for this, Govam," the first officer said, nestled on a couch within a bunch of pillows. "We will not be in a position to engage the *obice* and lock her in when you return."

"I can handle it. King's orders."

"You're higher powered, yes. Your kind usually aren't. Too bad you can't elevate yourself, hmm? Bad genetics. What a dismal life you do lead."

I heard Govam's huff of derision, but he didn't comment. I wondered what kind of life the officer thought *he* led.

In the washroom, I let the attendants clean me up without speaking, but I wanted to ask what this was about. What was happening. How long it would take. I just didn't think I could manage it without a quaver in my voice. Without giving away my urgency to hurry it up. I was a prisoner; I should have all the time in the world.

My hair was arranged simply, a change from normal, and very little makeup was applied to my face. The dress was hideous, as usual, and they stalled as they went to put on footwear.

"What would you like for her?" the attendant asked.

Govam frowned, looking at my feet. "Shoes…of some sort. I don't know."

"Well, we can go with a pump that matches the dress, or a sandal—"

"Sir." Denski hurried into the room, out of breath. He glanced at me. "The king has received some unexpected visitors, and the current guard staff are lacking. Those who were punished for the party have not been replaced. They've requested your aid."

Govam studied my face for a long moment. "You don't intend to cause trouble and be killed this evening, do you, Finley? Denski is just as capable as I am."

I tried to play it cool but couldn't keep the relief out of my voice. "If I don't have to see Dolion, I'll be a lamb."

Govam nodded at Denski and then strode away.

"Right, put her back in her usual clothes," Denski demanded. "Hurry, I want to be on hand in case I'm needed. I don't have time to dally with a dragon."

"We're out of fresh slips, sir," one of the attendants said. "There are men's clothes?"

"Fine," Denski said, and I stifled a laugh at how fitting that was. I'd come here in men's clothes, after all. Might as well leave that way.

"And her shoes, sir?" the attendant asked. "I have…slippers and…worn-in boots."

"I don't care. Boots." Glancing at me, he added, "That way you can give your cellmate a kick to stop him from sniveling. He was the most irksome pet we've had. He didn't seem to understand the power dynamic."

They gave me socks that had only one hole each, then

strapped me into boots slightly too small but good enough.

Denski grabbed my elbows. "Do I need cuffs?" he asked. "I'm not sure why we bother, since you can break out of them anyway."

"I was wondering the same thing, and no, I don't. I wasn't lying—if I'm not going to the king, I don't intend to cause trouble."

"Then let's hope he doesn't send for you after his guests leave." He shoved me forward, and I wondered if that was a possibility. If so, we'd have zero time to lose.

He spoke to me as he led the way along the corridor, his tone bored and conversational. "He's not at all pleased about that party, by the way."

"I've heard that from several people. It seems he doesn't like when the shoe is on the other foot."

"No, he does not. Interestingly, his guests all raved. I heard that attendance for the next party will be higher than any of the previous ones. Word has spread. That means purchase prices will go up. He'll disappoint everyone, including his treasurer, if he reins in the party dynamics."

"Maybe he'll rein in the parties but leave the after-parties untouched."

"Maybe. Hopefully not. It's tough to watch some of that. It puts me off sex entirely." He paused for a moment. "I heard you were requested to urinate on someone."

"You heard that, did you?" I said dryly.

"Yes. He's dead now, by the way. I'd say you got the last laugh but...well, I doubt you were laughing."

"No."

"Which is what I find interesting."

Huh. I'd had no idea he was capable of this level of chatting. Govam really dried up his words when they were working together.

"You are not appreciative of those party dynamics either. You didn't participate in the antics at your castle, if what I've heard is true. Why would you work to change the parties here?"

"Revenge?"

He was quiet a moment as we reached the top level of the dungeon. "Yes, I suppose there is that. Though that doesn't seem like your speed."

"No? And what is my speed, Mr. Jailer?"

We walked down the center of the columns in the grand room. Near the end, several of the officers were lounging in their chairs and on their pillows, their heads thrown back and their arms dangling to the sides, hanging limply. Another officer, holding a cup, lay on his side on the ground, his head behind the couch. The space was deathly quiet except for a high-pitched sort of keening echoing through the space.

"What is going on here?" Denski said quietly, slowing.

My heart started to thump. I looked at the scene in feigned confusion, playing it off like I hadn't poisoned them. Clearly the crowded everlass in our cells was much heartier than its free-growing friend. It would work in all settings and in all situations. Now I knew.

I loved it even more.

Too bad it might get us caught before we had even tried to escape.

CHAPTER 21

FINLEY

"THEY WHIPPED THE shit out of me last night, and then they do their creature creation and…hibernation or whatever it is that results from it," I said nonchalantly, as though I were an old expert on the subject. "Of course, I'm usually locked away by now. I've never actually seen it. I just know we're neglected for a day and a half after they finish."

Denski started walking slowly, and I could just see him nodding out of the corner of my eye.

"Yes, that's true. Though I didn't realize you were neglected."

"Would it matter?"

"We're not evil, Finley, whatever you may think. We have a job to do, and if we don't do it effectively, we are punished. Punishment around here can mean death. But would it matter? No, it wouldn't. Our job is to get you from one point to another. We try to do it without dying. Looking after you isn't our job."

"I would say that overthrowing your king is your job, but what do I know?"

"Nothing, obviously."

He walked me down to the base level and left me in my cell, closing the door after me. He glanced at a sleeping Jedrek, then at me again, nodded, and turned to go. The other guards, having remained silent this whole time, followed him.

At the bottom of the stairs, he stopped and let the other guards pass. He clicked off the light and ascended, not stopping at the top to initiate the magical lock. I tilted my head, continuing to listen. Anxiety tightened my chest. Maybe he didn't know how to do it. He might think he had to wake the officers, and then he'd find out that was impossible.

"What was that about?" Hannon asked urgently from his cell.

"They were taking me to see Dolion, but I guess Dolion got some unexpected visitors. Govam was called to help. They changed me back into non-fancy clothes, and Denski was asked to put me back."

Micah looked down the line at me. "Govam had to help the king?"

"Yeah. He left. The rest stayed."

"Govam solely handles the dragons. They don't waste him on anyone else. They know if they lose him, they'll lose everyone else. We'd kill them all too quickly without him."

I shrugged. "They said that there weren't enough guards because they were punished after the last party."

"Punishment here means death, typically," Tamara said to Micah, echoing what Denski had just told me. "It stands to reason that a great many people got punished. I saw more than a few guards take part in the…festivities."

"Yeah, so did I," Vemar intoned. "I killed three of them, even doped up with that slut-shaming magic."

"Shame fucking, you moron," Lucille said.

"Right, yeah."

"So, what now?" Tamara asked me. "And…are you wearing boots? And…tights?"

I looked down at the stretchy pants. "They were out of slips. I guess this is what they felt passed for men's clothes, I don't know." I looked at the stairs, pausing to listen for any movement. "Do you think they've actually gone?"

"Only one way to find out." Vemar disappeared from view before appearing again. Metal tinkled; he was going after the lock.

"What if they aren't, though?" I said as quietly as I could while still being heard.

"Then I will get quite the punishment. Here that doesn't mean death, since they need to keep siphoning our power. Aren't we lucky?" He exited his cell, incredibly fast at picking the lock after years of practice. He walked silently to the bottom of the stairs and clicked on the light.

"Nothing like a little stealth to get the job done," someone murmured dryly.

"I don't see anyone," Vemar said. "They could be lingering on the floor above us, I suppose, but I don't know why they would. Guards don't like to hang around here if they can help it."

"We need to wait for the officers to put that lock in place," Micah said, his deep voice rumbling around the space.

"Most of them are dead," I said, hurrying to empty my hidey-holes beneath the stones. I picked up Nyfain's notes, thankful that this clothing, odd as it was, at least had a couple pockets. Those stashed, I pulled the sword belt around my waist, fastening it in place. We'd never gotten to those lessons Tamara had talked about. There were a few opportunities, but we'd never felt well enough to take advantage of them. I wasn't planning on leaving it behind, though.

"What, already?" Hannon asked. "That seems awfully fast."

"It is. I couldn't do any testing, though, so I just guessed about time and potency, hoping for the best. One was dying as we came through."

Vemar stopped in the middle of the dungeon, a giant smile on his face as he looked at me. "And how did you explain that to the guards, Strange Lady?"

I told them about the conversation as I waited for Vemar to get me out of the cell. The lock clicked over, and he stepped aside as he opened the door.

"They believed that?" Hannon asked as Tamara helped him out of his cell.

"There is no love between the officers and the guards," Tamara said, glancing at my sword. "I'm sure Denski didn't care either way. He probably figured it wasn't his business."

But it would be if we escaped, and a bunch of dead officers was a pretty good tip-off of our plan. I wondered if he'd checked on them when he went back through. If he realized they were dead and called someone, we'd soon have guards to contend with. Which meant it was officially go time. It would be better to meet them up there, where there was room to fight, than have them cage us in down here.

"We need to get going. How can we check whether the *obice* is engaged?"

"I didn't hear him muttering the spell," said Vemar, ushering the slower dragons out of their cells.

I hadn't even realized any words needed to be spoken. My cell was too far back for me to have heard anything.

"Still, we should check before someone loses a head," I replied.

"I'll do it." Elex, the guy who'd been wary about escaping, limped toward the stairs with a pronounced hunch in his back. "I would rather go quickly than face what they'll do to us when we get caught."

"They won't do a damn thing if they catch us," I told him, "besides die."

Vemar laughed and threw back his head. "Yes!"

"Would you shut up?" Tamara scowled at him. "We don't need anyone to know what we're up to."

"Sorry," he muttered, wrestling with his smile.

"There has to be another way," I said as Elex climbed the stairs. "What if—"

Micah shook his head slowly, making sure everyone was out of their cells and getting ready to go. "Let him," he whispered as Elex passed.

I didn't understand why I should, but they'd all been in here much longer than me. I let it drop.

Elex bent toward the top of the stairs, half crawling under some sort of invisible line. Then he straightened suddenly, his whole body tense. Nothing happened.

Everyone released the breath they'd been holding.

"Jedrek, come on." I gestured him out of the cell.

He stared at me with mistrust in his red-rimmed eyes. "Why? So I can get blamed for something else you've done? Not a chance. Your attempt will fail. I don't want any part of it."

"Leave him here," Vemar said. "If he doesn't want to come, more power to him."

I gritted my teeth, knowing that wasn't in me. Hannon saw my expression and, without a word, stepped into the cell and punched Jedrek in the face. Jedrek went out cold. Hannon picked him up and threw him over a wide shoulder.

"That'll work," I said, turning.

"And he's always seemed so nice," Vemar said, smiling again.

"Why would he not set the magical lock?" Hannon wondered out loud as we all started jogging toward the stairs. "Has that happened before?"

"Occasionally," Micah replied as the others stepped aside so that we could take the lead. "Seldom, but mistakes happen. They don't get too fussed about it. They figure the officers would keep us from getting through the dungeon, and someone else would stop us if we went through the castle."

"We've stopped even trying to run when it happens," Lucille said.

"But you've gotten out before..." I went up the stairs. Elex waited for us at the landing.

"When they forgot to engage the magical lock, yeah. And you've heard how well that worked out."

"Not very uplifting, guys," Tamara murmured as we poured into the second-floor dungeon.

We jogged through the cells, everyone awake and confused as hell to see us.

"Why didn't they engage the *obice* spell?" Calia said, standing.

I explained as we jogged from cell to cell, releasing everyone.

"My love, you are early," Hadriel said. "Why? How?"

I went through everything again as cells opened quickly, everyone stepping out in much better clothes than most of the dragons. This lot was better taken care of than we were. Of course, they had more to endure.

"Are we positive the officers are dead?" Leala asked as we headed back to the stairs as a group. Once again, everyone stepped aside to make room for the leadership, which had swelled with this last stop.

"Positive?" I asked, hitting the stairs. "No. Reasonably sure that at least a good portion of them are dead? Yes. One should be done dying right about now."

"Wait." Micah grabbed my arm before we reached the top of the stairwell. "We need to make sure this lock hasn't been engaged either."

"Right, yes," I said, flattening to the side of the wall.

It was Calia and her sister who stepped up this time. Leaving their hands at their sides, they closed their eyes.

"Nothing," Calia said, opening her eyes and moving down a stair to give me room again. "No magical lock."

I took a deep breath and pushed forward, the others moving aside to let me go first. "Moment of truth."

It was time to see if I'd actually killed the officers, and if so, if Denski had realized it and told someone.

HADRIEL

I FOLLOWED FINLEY and the others as we surged up the stairs. Leala ran beside me, both of us waiting with bated breath to see what awaited us at the top. I hoped to hell the officers were dead. Guards weren't a concern—if there were guards anywhere up there, the dragons would massacre them in zero seconds flat and smile while they did it. But officers were tricky fuckers. I couldn't even smell them when they were using their magic.

Finley reached the top floor and sprinted forward without hesitation. We followed her into the glow of the large hall. More officers than I'd ever seen lay sprawled out on couches and pillows.

It took exactly one glance to gauge that they were stone dead. Not just that, but they'd died grotesquely.

Been killed grotesquely, more like.

Arms dangled. Heads lolled back. Tongues stuck out. Some had grimaces even in death.

"Ugh," I said softly, feeling a strange desire to grab a strand of pearls. I didn't even wear pearls!

Micah knelt next to the first officer, putting his fingers on the other man's throat.

"But do they have pulses under normal circumstances?" I asked softly. "Like...do they have hearts?"

A couple people huffed out shallow laughter, but I was actually serious. These things definitely weren't human, and they didn't seem like the other demons. In fact, they were a little like the creatures they made. I wasn't sure if their anatomy operated the same way as ours did.

"We're good. Let's go. Hurry," Finley said, motioning everyone forward.

Unease swam in my guts. Something wasn't right about this.

Actually, that wasn't true. Everything was *too* right about all this. There was no way a guard had passed through here without noticing these creatures were dead. No one was that oblivious.

Pieces started clicking together. The whole picture materialized.

Suddenly I wanted to throw up.

Finley had been taken up to the king, but the meeting had fallen through at the last minute?

Sure, that was plausible.

Then she'd gotten better clothes with *boots*, of all things?

Maybe. After a big party, it was possible they were short on spare garments.

But that, paired with the guard's lack of reaction to the obviously dead officers...

It set off every warning bell I had.

Sweat broke out on my brow.

Cuntpuddles, was this a trap?

But I didn't say any of that to Finley. I didn't want to spread doubt, because the reality was that we couldn't waste this opportunity. If we didn't get out now, quite a few of us would be killed. Of that I was certain.

There was only one silver lining. If it *was* a trap, and the guards or whoever were waiting for us somewhere, they didn't know that most of us could shift. They didn't know the level of firepower—literal *fire*power—the dragons could rain down on them. They would learn the hard way that you did not ever fuck with dragons. It just wasn't worth it. They were crazy, and proud of it.

Still, the puzzle in my head looked pretty complete, and adrenaline raced through my body. I took deep breaths and tried to focus on something else.

"Can you actually use that thing?" I asked Leala as she snatched up one of the officer's whips and jogged after the others.

"Of course I can," she whispered, squeezing the leather handle. "I'm not an expert, but I can get the job done."

"I thought you liked getting the whip rather than using it?"

"We do what we must. Now *shh*."

I wasn't sure what that meant, and I hoped I never had to learn. I was ready to leave all this sexual bullshit behind. I was ready for demons and curses and strange magic to fuck off. I had hit my wall on this trip, I really had.

The strongest of the wolves stripped down before stashing their clothes to the side in one of the little cubbies that held torture devices. They shifted into their wolf forms, the first time I'd ever seen them do it.

The breath left me when I felt a rush of power from the alpha, immediately followed by the brush of his awareness against my wolf's consciousness. It had been a long while since I'd felt that draw—urging us to connect to our new pack. Reeling us in, almost, the alpha's expectation that we should join him overriding any desire we might have to be contrary. The second we gave in, though, his grip on us as pack members would be complete.

We'll stay on two legs, I thought to my wolf as the group followed Finley, running down the center of the mighty columns.

But we need a pack, my wolf whined, the desire to join the alpha eating away at him. There was safety in a pack, especially with an alpha like that. There was family.

Finley is our pack. She is our alpha. She pulls us with respect and trust even though she can't pull us with her animal. We stay on two legs, and we stay with her.

My wolf didn't really understand—it was against his nature to push back when confronted with an alpha of Weston's stature, but I held firm. My wolf hadn't been back in the world long, and he'd understand soon enough. He'd see that there were no better leaders than Finley and the master, not when they were together. They made each other so much stronger.

We just had to make sure they got back together.

"This way is death," someone in the back said, hobbling along like some sort of stick man held together by rusty twine. A dragon, but one that looked half-dead. "It's an endless series of dead ends and tunnels. Anyone who has run this way without a map has died. We don't have a map this time."

"We don't need one," I replied, holding Leala's hand now because I needed a little moral support to keep moving forward. "When people are brought in, they are reeling from the shock of being kidnapped. They are panicked and afraid, or mad and fighting. They don't notice the fine details of their surroundings. They're too intent on escaping to worry about what will happen down the road. Finley, and us after her, didn't have the same experience. We made a point of taking in the fine details so we could come back this way if we needed to. We have…"

I paused as we reached the squat doorway that led toward what Finley called the Bridge of Doom. I still didn't know how we were going to get over the thing. I'd had a hard enough time getting across on the way in, and that was with the guards practically dragging me.

Breath held and heart in throat, we jogged through the doorway. I immediately looked right, in case no one else had. There was a little hidey-hole back there that someone could crouch in. I knew this because I had contemplated trying to break free and running back and hiding there, hoping they'd just forget about me. It was in a moment of cowardice. I'd had a lot of those on this trip. It was a little embarrassing how many, actually.

Nothing jumped out, though. Nothing moved or even flickered. My wolf didn't smell anything, either.

Continuing on, wondering if I would have a heart attack before we hit the surface, I finished what I was saying.

"We've compared notes and found they matched. We know the way. And this is the only way we can make it out."

I didn't know if any of that comforted him, but at least it shut him up. We couldn't afford dissenters right now. What we were doing was perilous enough.

Our footfalls were too loud for my taste as we made our way, but nothing jumped out at us. Nothing stabbed into us from behind. It was the calm before Doom.

We went around another turn, down a corridor I didn't actually remember because I'd been too freaked out by the bridge crossing, and the orange glow finally reached through the doorway up ahead. It seemed to throb, beckoning us closer. Laughing at us, maybe.

"I hated coming across this," Leala said quietly, tucking her whip into the back of her pants. She was readying for an internal battle.

She hadn't needed as much violence to get across as I had, but she'd also been dragged a bit. Shoved a bit. Carried a bit.

Fucking bridge.

Tension rose as we shoved in and pushed to the side, leaving room for Finley at the front, standing beside the rope bridge that moved at the slightest misstep and tore at your eyes and sanity.

I squeezed Leala's hand. "If I don't go down in history as the best fucking butler who ever lived, going above and beyond the job, I'm going to slap a bitch."

She squeezed it back. "You can slap me. Multiple times. Anywhere you want."

"You always have to ruin things."

She laughed, and it made me realize how much I'd needed that sound.

In a moment, all humor would be sucked out of us, along with the will to live.

CHAPTER 22

FINLEY

URGENCY RODE ME as I faced off with the bridge. This would be the hardest part of our escape, but if we made it across, we'd be home safe. I felt it.

"Calia, can you help with this?" I asked, standing beside the suspension bridge secured with rope. The lava below moved and shifted. Dizzying heat rose from the toxic stew.

"Only for my sister and myself. The magic is too immense. It's built into the foundation."

"Can you carry someone across who might be kicking and screaming?"

She eyed me dubiously. Probably not, then.

"Fine. Head across if you'd like."

She nodded and grabbed her sister's hand, stepping onto the bridge.

Let the animals cross the bridge, my dragon thought, desperate to break free and take over. She hovered right near the surface, giving me more strength and determination. *Animals don't think about throwing themselves to their deaths. That's a human thing.*

It's a brain malfunction. Animals rely on their survival instinct. They'll know not to veer to the sides.

It was worth a shot, I supposed. Though I would absolutely blame it on her in the event it went tits up.

"My dragon thinks the animals will have a better shot of making the crossing," I announced to the group at large, gripping the end of the rope to keep from shouting for everyone to just run across so we could get this moving. I still worried Dolion might send for me. We needed to be long gone before that happened.

"What about those of us who can't change?" someone asked from the back.

"Or those of us who aren't shifters?" The male faerie's eyes were tight with worry.

"I can carry people across," Hannon said, Jedrek still unconscious (or playing dead) across his shoulder. "This bridge doesn't affect me."

Micah turned to look at him with a hard stare.

"What are you?" Lucille asked, narrowing her eyes.

Hannon shrugged. "Maybe I'm a demon, I don't know, but I can run people back and forth."

"Big stone balls on that guy," Vemar murmured with a grin. "I like that. Could be a demon, doesn't give a shit."

"I completely missed that he wasn't affected the first time we crossed it," Hadriel muttered.

"He's not a demon," I said, exasperated though curious as to what sort of animal didn't succumb to the Bridge of Doom.

Tamara looked skyward. "There should be enough room to...sorta fly-hop over. My dragon is confident she can handle this."

"Mine too," said Micah, immediately echoed by the other

dragons who were capable of shifting.

Weston gave a soft yelp and moved closer to the bridge.

"He'll cross now," Hadriel said. "In case you can't read *wolf*. He has a connection with the other wolves. If he can keep his head, they will too. He's confident he can handle it. But then, you all are, so…"

In other words, there was ego, bravado, and reality. We had yet to see how reality would shake out, but Hannon couldn't run everyone back and forth. We had to trust the animals to make this journey.

"Okay. Go," I barked, pulling power from my dragon, who in turn pulled it from Nyfain.

The dragons shed their clothes and handed them off to anyone willing to hold them. I thought it better not to mention that the clothes would probably end up fluttering into the lava.

As the wolves crossed, hair standing up on their backs and teeth bared, Tamara jogged as far to the side of the gathering as she could. She looked up at the rock ceiling curving upward into a dome. A push of magic slammed into my dragon, and she roiled, scratching to rise to the surface.

"No, no, you fucking idiot." I clenched my teeth and bore down on her, struggling to keep her at bay. "We can't change here for the first time. We'll crush everyone, stumble, take out the bridge as we fall into the lava, and all will be lost. Get *down*."

Tamara's gray dragon rose into existence, smaller than Nyfain and able to hunch down a little so she didn't hit the ceiling. The dragon looked down at the lava before scooting back toward us, giving her more wing room. In a breathless moment, she jumped out over the lava and only then pumped her wings quickly, blasting us with air.

The wolves made their way across the bridge, the wind from Tamara's wings washing over them. One in the back hunched and turned, gnashing teeth at the air. It shivered, then shook, lowering its head and starting to whine.

Tamara rose a bit, but there wasn't much room. Tilting her wings slightly, she shoved forward, aiming for the larger landing on the other side.

Weston, nearly to safety, ears flat against his head, turned back and let out a savage growl.

"He's losing one of them," Hadriel whispered, pushing forward so he could see.

The wolf at the end, still shaking, tucked its tail between its legs. It crowded the side of the bridge, chewing at a strand of rope blocking its way.

Weston's growl intensified. The wolves behind him cowered, quickly flattening down to their bellies, but the last wolf edged farther toward the side, its body now against the ropes. It looked like it was fighting itself. Or maybe fighting Weston.

Lucille walked to the area Tamara had just vacated but didn't shift, watching the frightened wolf.

Weston left his post and jogged down the side of the line of wolves, perilously close to the side. He reached the one at the end and cuffed it on the head hard enough to draw blood, his growl rumbling through his chest. It vibrated through my body, and I wasn't even attuned to his animal. He grabbed the scruff of the last wolf's neck and pulled, urging it to walk.

The wolf cowered down a little more. Its head lowered and its ears went out to the sides.

"He's regaining control," Hadriel whispered. "He must've been an alpha of a large pack. He's damn good at his job. I wonder

269

how the demons were able to capture him. He never said."

Numbers, probably. Get one or a few wolves alone, and sacrifice as many demons as it took to bring them in. When you didn't care about your people, you didn't care how many perished to get you what you wanted.

Weston turned, a tricky business, and jogged back along the line, his feet inches away from the side. Back at the front, he slowed and gave a sort of yelp. The wolves behind him rose to standing, heads down as though they were shouldering a great weight, and started moving again, following their leader off the bridge.

As soon as the last had made it across, Lucille erupted into her dragon—a little smaller than Tamara, with glittering, wheat-colored scales. She pulled off the same maneuver, jumping off and catching herself with her wings, beating and tilting them to get to the other side.

Tamara, human again, cleared away, and Lucille hit the landing on the other side. She'd misjudged her fly-hop, however, and her dragon's back foot slipped off. Her tail swooped down to adjust for balance, but the weight shift dragged her body toward the lava.

Micah pushed forward, looking over the edge. It was clear he wanted to help but didn't know what to do.

I watched, breathless, as the dragon's front feet scraped against the stone, her body sliding back. She shifted, down on hands and knees, one leg dangling over the side and her body about ready to pitch over after it.

Tamara darted forward and grabbed her outstretched hand. Someone behind me cried out as Lucille continued to fall. Tamara held on, though, leaning back with a determined face. She backed up, pulling Lucille with her, dragging her back onto the stone.

"Fuck," Hadriel said with a release of breath as Lucille made it, panting, to safety. "Good thing they've worked as a team for so long. That was close."

I had to agree.

"Okay, Hannon, let's start walking people across," I said before I could talk myself out of it.

"You're not affected either?" Hadriel asked.

"I am. But I'll push through it. We have too many people who can't shift for Hannon to take them all. Someone has to help."

I have to push through it, I thought.

Yes. Because if you don't, you will kill us both.

Didn't need to be said.

Sometimes you are dense.

She was a dickhead at the best of times.

Hannon briskly took to the bridge with Jedrek over his shoulder. Almost immediately, Jedrek bucked. He flailed his arms and tried to claw his way out of Hannon's grasp. Clearly he'd been playing dead. It would've been nice if he'd kept it up.

A shimmer of magic preceded Jedrek morphing, hair erupting from his body.

"He's shifting," Hadriel said in an excited hush. "It'll be interesting to see if he succumbs to the call of the alpha."

"What does that mean?" I asked as Hannon twisted and then bent, setting Jedrek's changing form down and then pinning him against the bridge.

"An alpha has an alluring type of magic for a wolf. They are the leaders of the team, and they promise safety and security in exchange for obedience. Unless a wolf is powerful enough, he'll succumb to the magic and fall in line. The amount of power you need to resist is dependent on the alpha, but Weston is incredibly powerful. It would take a *lot* of power to resist him when in wolf form. Jedrek won't have it, bet you. Or maybe he won't even try to resist. Hard to say."

Jedrek finished shifting and snarled, surging up and throwing Hannon off. He lunged, going for Hannon's jugular. I called out, stepping forward to help. Weston was already on the bridge, his teeth bared.

Neither of us made it in time.

Hannon grabbed Jedrek's snout, one hand on the top and the other on the bottom, holding it open. Saliva dripped from Jedrek's sharp teeth. Hannon fell back, the wolf toppling him onto the bridge. Without so much as a flash of rage, Hannon tensed, and then a wicked *crack* rent the air. He'd ripped his hands apart.

I flinched and then watched as Jedrek's form went airborne, Hannon having gotten his feet under the suddenly limp wolf and launched him away. The body hit the rope and then spun away and down, into the lava.

My mouth dropped open.

"Welp," Hadriel said with a crooked grin. "That settles it. Don't fuck with Hannon."

"Thank the goddess *someone* finally dealt with that idiot." Micah walked off to the side, readying to shift. "I'll always think of him as a possum, though."

Weston gave a huff and turned back, quickly getting off the bridge.

Hannon met me back on my side. "Sorry, Finley," he said softly, putting a hand on my shoulder. "I wasn't thinking beyond trying to save myself."

I shook my head slowly. Shock was still my prevalent emotion, but a bit of sadness and guilt were creeping in.

"You had no choice," I said, looking down into the pit. "We should've forced him to shift earlier and had Weston take charge of him."

"You didn't know to do that." Hadriel patted me. "He was a weasel, Finley. You're better off."

Much better off, my dragon said.

But I couldn't help a prickle of guilt. He was seriously the worst, and I hadn't ever liked him, but I should've gotten him out of here, at least. I should've taken better care of the situation. Leaders saved even the assholes. If I wanted to stand at Nyfain's side, I'd need to learn to look after *all* the people, even the Jedreks.

"It was my fault, not yours, Finley," Hannon said, his hand still on my shoulder. He could read me exceptionally well. "He didn't want to leave, anyway. You can't force someone to want to survive. You did what you could, and ultimately, I did what I had to. And you know what? I'm not sorry. He wasn't to be trusted, and you're safer this way."

Hannon was right. It was hard to save someone who didn't want to save themselves.

"If he didn't do it now, I was planning on doing it when you weren't looking," Vemar called, zero remorse.

"Come on." Hadriel patted me again. "We need to get going, or we'll all end up like him."

Yes, we need to get going, my dragon said. *We have to get out of here. He isn't worth us all dying for.*

She was right. They were all right. And in my heart of hearts, I had to own that the guilt wasn't entirely because I'd failed to get him out. It was because a part of me felt relieved. After everything he'd put me through, a part of me hadn't wanted to save him at all. A part of me had wanted to leave him behind. I felt guilty for being relieved that someone else had solved the problem of Jedrek.

I felt guilty for not being a better person.

Eventually I'd conquer my remorse about all this. I'd make peace with it. But right now, I needed to look after the living.

"Okay," I said, taking a deep breath. I pointed at those who couldn't change. "Who wants to go first? I'll tie you up with the dragons' clothes so that it'll be a little easier to take you across."

"I'll shift, milady." Leala handed off her whip to Hadriel, and I was too frazzled to ask *what the fuck?* before she reduced down into a sort of...monkey thing. Or a lemur. She had large brown eyes that looked too big for her face, ringed in black, with a small snout. Her body was brown with white areas, and her small, furry feet ended in little black claws.

"What is she?" I asked as she started slowly for the bridge.

"A slow loris," Hadriel replied, stepping up to me with the whip outstretched. I took it, and he turned around so I could use it to secure his wrists. "Don't let her dainty size fool you. They are one of the most venomous mammals. Their poison can suffocate. Not human-sized creatures so much, but still, a nip would give you a bad day."

She worked her way out onto the bridge and then stopped moving.

"The bitch is, when they sense danger, they often freeze..." His voice trailed off.

Hannon didn't hesitate. Smiling, he stepped onto the bridge and scooped up a frozen Leala. She scampered up his shoulder and clung to his neck.

I secured Hadriel as Vemar shifted into a gorgeous, glittering blue dragon and leapt off like he had no fear of death. Then again, he probably didn't.

I threw Hadriel over my shoulder and marshaled my determination. Vemar landed as Hannon returned to the business end of the bridge and grabbed a pretty little faerie, holding her to his chest. I gave him a head start over the bridge, the faerie thrashing in his arms but not nearly powerful enough to cause him a problem. Leala re-froze on his shoulder.

"Here we go, Hadriel. I hope this isn't the end of our friendship." I started out.

"Ah, you admitted we're friends. That's so great! Except I am a butler, my love, and I am not friends with princesses locked in towers who—"

The magic of the bridge washed over me like a sack of stone. It clawed at my middle and tried to drag my ribs out of my body. My vision blackened then spun. Hadriel jerked and started screaming—or maybe that was me—and struggled to get off my shoulder. He punched my back, scrabbling to get closer to the ropes and likely throw himself over.

I staggered that way. Or maybe I meant to take that step. I wanted to throw myself off with him. To chuck him over and jump in after him.

This is a real gut-bender, folks, I thought desperately, tears streaming down my face. *Will she give in to her baser desires and jump?*

I struggled him closer to the end of the bridge, only to realize I was listing toward the ropes at the side.

Get a grip, my dragon screamed inside my head. *Fight your way back. Use Nyfain. He is our lifeline. Use him to keep you grounded.*

I did. With everything I had, I reached out for him through the bond, desperate. Terrified. Ready to end it all.

Like when I'd been brought to Dolion and his people tried to claw the bond from me, I felt Nyfain reach out. I felt him reel me in possessively, holding me tightly to him. The mark he'd given me burned and then tingled, like he was refreshing it, claiming me body and soul.

Mine, the sentiment seemed to say. *You belong to me. No one and nothing else can have you. Nothing will take you from me.*

The feeling from before, like his dragon's wings spreading over me protectively, eased some of the crippling anxiety and broke through the chaos of my mind.

When I blinked into semiconsciousness, Hadriel was dangling from one of my hands, his feet above the lava, and I was looming over him, one leg bent as if I were about to climb over.

The bridge shook and wobbled, and as I hauled Hadriel back, I saw Hannon hurrying toward me with terror screwing up his expression. He couldn't go too fast, though, or the bridge would shake enough to dump me over.

"It's okay," I said, out of breath, as I dropped onto the safety of the bridge, bending to him. "It's okay, folks. She seems to have narrowly avoided catastrophe."

"What?" Hadriel asked, flailing against me.

Oh great, now everyone *will know you're crazy,* my dragon thought. *And I'll be considered crazy by association.*

"Nothing." I punched Hadriel to get him to stop struggling and then just dragged him behind me. I didn't trust myself to sling him over my shoulder again. "I'm okay."

I wasn't, of course. My vision wobbled, and the desperate urge to jump didn't ease. But Nyfain kept his grip on me and I fell into it, clutching him through the bond and forcing my legs to keep moving.

On the other side, I let Hadriel go, wiped my nose and then cheeks, and started back across.

"Wait, Finley—" Tamara said, but I didn't hang around to see what she'd say. We needed to hurry.

"Many hands make light work," I muttered, over and over, reaching the other side and grabbing the next victim. No one wanted to go with me after seeing Hadriel's near miss with the lava, but time was ticking, and they relented. I took the next, Hannon following me. Then we did it again. And again. We continued on that way until it was done. Each time I crossed, I wished I would die. I was having a hard time dealing with the agony, not of the body—I was used to that by now—but of the soul.

What seemed like hours later but hopefully wasn't, I fell to my hands and knees on the stone on the safe side, sobbing.

"Carry her," someone said. It sounded like Micah.

"I'm a little short on strength right now." Hannon panted. "There was a lot of fight in those last couple of dragons."

"I can't force myself close, not with the power pumping into that alpha's scent," Vemar said, clearly frustrated.

"I'm fine," I said as someone else said, "I can."

I was so twisted up in my thoughts that it took me a moment to register it was Tamara. "I...don't mind the smell," she said, pulling me up and giving me a supportive smile.

I shook my head and put a hand to her shoulder. "I'm good. It's fine."

"We gotta get moving, Strange Lady," Vemar said, and for once, he wasn't smiling. "That took longer than it probably should've."

"It's okay. We started a little ahead of schedule." Calia drifted closer and rubbed my back. "That took great bravery. She deserves a rest."

"No shit it did," Tamara said. "Micah, Vemar, and I all tried to cross to help, but we didn't make it far enough to even congratulate ourselves on the effort. Without our dragons, we would've been more cargo for Hannon."

"Tough as balls." Vemar shook his fist as he grinned at Hannon and me. "Both of them."

"Balls, my ass," Lucille replied. "Balls are the most fragile things I've ever heard of. A small slap is the end of the world to you fuckers."

"Yes, yes, we all wish we had the mighty vagina. Bully for you," Hadriel cut in, rolling his eyes. He stepped closer to me. "Finley, darling, you yourself know that you cannot stay here and rest. Either walk or get carried. Those are your options."

"I'm good." I straightened up and wiped my nose with my sleeve for what was probably the millionth time. "It's fine." I cleared my hoarse throat. "My voice is a little worse for wear, though."

"Well, yeah, you were screaming the entire time you crossed the bridge." Hadriel grabbed my arm and moved me forward. "Okay, love, here we go. This is the part where we need to pay very close attention, or we'll be lost in this accursed dungeon forever."

CHAPTER 23

FINLEY

RELEASING MY DEATH grip on Nyfain's essence through the bond, I pushed myself forward. Power still thrummed within me, but I felt utterly exhausted. I felt the way my brother looked.

The tunnel leading away from the Bridge of Doom didn't take much navigating, so I let Hadriel set the pace, the two of us at the front. Like me, he'd paid attention to the path leading in, so the two of us would need to find the way out.

"We still need to figure out how to get a demon to pilot the boat," I told him as I sucked in air and remembered that, once upon a time, I used to think this place stank so bad it layered my tongue. Now it just smelled like *air*.

Gross.

"There will be one or two demons patrolling the beach near the boats," he said as we reached what looked like a dead end.

"See? Dead end," someone in the back said with a shaky voice. Elex, it sounded like.

Neither Hadriel nor I replied. We couldn't spare the energy.

He reached to the side for the latch and then pushed the skull door open.

"Thank the goddess you paid attention to how the door was opened," I said, putting some pep into my step as I walked through with him. Maybe we weren't being followed, and maybe they didn't even know about our escape, but prisoners were brought in randomly. Hadriel was proof of that. We didn't want a chance meeting with unsuspecting demons. "I was too busy gawking at the skull. Also in pain—they pushed me down the first set of stairs."

"They did? What the fuck?" Hadriel stopped, surveying the walls when the tunnel broke into three separate paths.

I found a familiar marking, and my dragon pointed out the tunnel with the correct smell. I pointed.

He nodded, and we were walking again.

"I thought Dolion wanted to keep you safe to use against Ny-fain?" Hadriel said, reducing his volume.

"At the time, sure. The demon who did it was an idiot."

At the next crossroads, I pointed again. Hadriel nodded.

"You know, when I first got here, I was so sure I could get out—that no prison could hold me," I whispered, coming to the next intersection and pointing. Hadriel paused for a moment, scanning the walls. After a moment, he nodded. "Turns out...nope. If not for you guys, I'm not sure I ever would've gotten free."

He snorted. "Calia said something incredibly similar. It's a lesson in the strength of teamwork and, for me, a lesson in the strength of teams that span the species divide. As I heard it, the dragons, wolves, and faeries have all tried to escape... They faltered because they only cooperated with each other the barest amount. It took someone to bring them all together. It took *you*."

"With the help of my amazing butler, brother, and whip-toting lady's maid…"

"Well, heroes never do it alone, my darling. They just claim they do. Remember that for a drunken storytelling situation."

I chuckled softly.

One of the torches that usually lit the way had guttered out, washing part of the tunnel in darkness. I glanced back at those who were still magically suppressed and/or couldn't see in the dark. Those who could see held on to those who couldn't, guiding them.

We neared what should be the end of our path. The air had cleared dramatically, sweet and refreshing compared to what we'd been breathing. More torches burned against the walls, strangely archaic. I wondered how they stayed going. Magic, perhaps.

Up ahead, it looked like another dead end but for the slips of light and tunnel beyond. Bars cut across the tunnel, an actual door with a real lock.

"Vemar," I whispered, turning to look back. He'd been charged with bringing the tools.

"Yes, Strange Lady, ah…" He looked hard at the bars. "Shit. My tools were in my pocket."

I blinked at him, then looked over his nude body. "Were?"

He met my eyes, frustration burning in his gaze. "I wasn't thinking. I should've given them to Hannon. My clothes went over the side and into the lava. It completely slipped my mind about the lockpicks. It's… I…"

He sagged in misery.

My stomach dropped, and my ass tightened, and I felt like throwing up all at the same time. At the last door, the one where we desperately needed a real key, we didn't have any tools to open it.

"Anyone?" I turned around desperately. "Does anyone have tools?"

Those who weren't naked patted themselves, their faces falling.

"Shit." I turned and grabbed a bar. "Fine. I'll run back. I know the way. I can get across that bridge. Who has tools in their cells?"

A chorus of people gave me an affirmative, and I knew where one of them had been held without needing to ask for further details.

"No—" Hadriel gripped the bars, but he didn't get much farther than that. There was no point in arguing; we needed to get through this door, and lock-picking tools were the only way to do it.

"I'll go too." Hannon pushed through the crowd, stepping out into the space next to me. "I can make sure you get across the bridge."

"No, it's—" I cut myself off for the same reason Hadriel had. It would be safer if Hannon went with me.

With a chuff, five wolves stepped forward.

"The wolves will be going too, if that wasn't obvious," Hadriel said. "And I guess I should come, just in case you forget the way. Vemar, I hold grudges, know that."

"Normally, I'd make fun of you, but in this instance, I don't blame you," Vemar said. "The bridge made me forget anything other than…well, the bridge."

"You might need me if a lock has been engaged." Calia stepped forward with her sister.

"Fine. Let's hurry." I started jogging, my pace labored and my form horrible, but at least I was moving. The others, except the wolves, went about it the same way, all of us malnourished, ridden with anxiety, tired, and now desperate. Trapped.

With the markings and smells fresh in my mind, I led the others through the tunnels without a problem, passing through the skull door and closing in on the bridge.

"Someone is going to have to carry me again, *Hannon*," Hadriel said as the large, glowing room appeared up ahead. "Vemar told me what almost happened. I would rather not be tossed overboard, *Finley*."

Calia giggled, and I didn't need to look to know Hadriel was scowling at her.

I rounded the corner and hurried into the room, smacking off a hard chest and bouncing backward. Growls reverberated behind me. Someone gasped.

I stood face to face with Govam. Behind him, filling half the room, were his guards.

CHAPTER 24
FINLEY

I BUILT POWER to strike, but he rushed forward and wrapped his arms around my waist, spinning me and throwing me to the ground. Denski grabbed Calia, ripping her away from her sister.

"Weston, go!" I yelled. "Get the others! Hurry! Bring the dragons!"

The wolves turned quickly and sped away, not a moment to lose.

"Don't do anything yet, Finley," Govam said very quietly, his lips right next to my ear. "This isn't going to go how you think."

I almost struck out with a killing blow, but Hadriel said, "Finley, wait—"

Govam rolled off me and then yanked me up, now whipping me around. He held my elbows like usual, pointing my front toward the mess of guards in the room. What I saw left me speechless.

The guards were fighting each other! Not with whips or sticks or the usual weapons we were accustomed to, but with swords. Well, some of them had swords, at any rate, and they were rushing the other guards and running them through. Guards fell quickly, yelling and groaning, grabbing their middles.

"I had intended to do this at the boats," Govam said urgently, watching the scene. "You see, the demons who patrol the boats don't know how to work them. It ensures no one can overcome them and escape."

Two quarreling guards stumbled over each other's feet and tipped over the edge into the lava. Another guard was thrown after them. Sonassa, still glammed up in her red dress, slashed down with a dagger and opened the chest of her new enemy. When blood splattered across her face, she smiled.

"You would've been stranded there until another patrol came and found you. Your escape attempt would've ended in the same way as all of the others. Dolion is very good at trapping his prisoners. He's just as good at trapping his subjects."

The melee in the large room slowed, then mostly stopped, the surviving guards breathing hard, only those with swords or daggers left standing. After a beat, a few of them started picking up the fallen and throwing them into the lava.

"This will actually be quite handy for cleanup." Sonassa sauntered forward before brushing her hair off her shoulder. She smiled at me. "Hello, princess. I haven't seen you in a while. I've been monitoring your sad sack of a betrothed. I figured you wouldn't leave without him. I ensured you didn't have to. Forgive me for blaming the change in the parties on you two, but...it was the quickest way to the finish line. You understand."

Govam released me before stepping back quickly.

"What's happening?" I asked softly.

"And you..." Sonassa grinned wickedly at Hadriel. "You and your gal pal." She laughed. "Perfection. You accomplished what should've taken months—years, even—in a matter of weeks. Genius."

"Yes, what is happening?" Hadriel said. "You were always incredibly terrible to us."

"Of course I was. People would notice a leopard without spots."

The sound of pounding feet echoed down the hall. Govam jogged quickly to the other side of me, and Denski let Calia go and did the same.

"Hear me out, Finley," Govam said in the same urgent tone. "Hear me out. If you don't like what I say, then kill me. I know you can. I've never held any pretenses. You've always been the most dangerous of the dragons."

Micah filled the doorway, his olive skin slick with perspiration and his muscles flaring. His deep brown eyes held rage and vengeance and destruction, and his power punched into the room like a solid force, his dragon clearly right at the surface. He stopped when he saw the state of the room as the other dragons and then wolves filled in behind him, ready to burst into the room and do serious damage. They didn't care about the odds—they never had.

Govam raised his hands in the air. The rest of the guards did likewise, except for Sonassa, who stepped back a ways. She alone had the ability to control the faeries and shifters, and she was making it clear that she had no desire to.

"What is happening?" I repeated, louder.

"You said I should work on overthrowing the king," Denski said, a step behind Govam, nearly at the bridge. "We are. We have been. But we can't do it from within. Dolion and his minions are too powerful. We need the other kingdoms to step in. That's where you come in, princess."

"This sounds like a trick," Micah said. "Or a trap."

"They just killed a bunch of guards and threw them into the lava," I told him. It also struck me that they were now using Dolion's name and not his title. To Govam, I said, "Explain, quickly."

He marginally lowered his hands. "The people in your kingdom aren't the only ones who are stuck, Finley. We are trapped"—he gestured to the guards behind him—"within the current king's rule. We are treated as second-class citizens—"

"Second class would be an upgrade," Sonassa mumbled.

"—and we are killed without thought. Our lodgings are sparse, our food tasteless—we take what we are given or we are killed. It is a life without hope. We have always hoped a prisoner escape would lead to Dolion's comeuppance, but it was starting to seem unlikely. Until you came along, Finley."

"Except there have been escape attempts in the past, and you've stopped them," I said.

"Yes. Because we were ordered to." Govam lifted his eyebrows. "You might not see the officers, but they see you. Remember me telling you that? They caught on quickly with past attempts, and they always call the guard first. They'd rather let us die. But this time..." His smile was faint. "How'd you poison them all?"

Denski chuckled. "That was quite the shock when I was taking you back."

"You knew?"

"Yes. I've dealt with them for years. Decades. They do hibernate after the ritual, but even then, they don't look like... Well, like they are dead. On the way back, I checked to make sure."

I shook my head a little, the pieces fitting together. "And the *obice*?"

"Forgotten on purpose," he replied.

"We didn't realize you'd already found a way to take care of that." Govam nodded to Calia. "Very clever. You didn't need our help at all."

"The meeting with Dolion?"

A shadow crossed Govam's face. "And that is where I showed my hand, as it were. He did want to see you. About what, I don't know. I was instructed to get you. You were prepared as request-ed, and then I summoned Denski so I could leave and make an excuse about why you couldn't be seen. I told him the officers had whipped you to the point of incoherence. He has a host of digni-taries coming in tomorrow who will remain for a few days. After they depart, he'll call for you again. That's when he will discover you are gone, the shifters with you, his officers are dead, and half of his best guards servicing the dungeons are missing."

"What about the guards you just killed?" I pointed to the lava. "Won't he notice they're gone?"

"There was a large shake-up after that last party. A great many guards were killed, many more beaten. Several of our people are healing in their rooms... Besides, the guards who are with me, and those who are in there"—he pointed to the lava—"service the dungeons. He won't try to call on us until the guests leave."

He took a deep breath and then continued.

"As of now, I am a dead man walking. Everyone in this room is. If we show up alive, he will either guess we had a hand in this or punish us for not stopping it. Either way, we'd die. Our lives are now in your hands."

"How did you know she was going tonight?" Hadriel asked. "I

put most of those pieces together, but how did you know tonight would be the night?"

Govam's smile was tight. "I know dragons. I know how they operate. I can anticipate them. Finley is a lot more mysterious than most, but I've been watching intently. The only reason she left the golden dragon was to save his kingdom—*her* kingdom. I knew she'd try to escape. I'd thought she'd hit a standstill because she couldn't connect with the other shifters. I was trying to come up with a way to force the issue, but then...her friends showed up." He looked at Hadriel. "And they worked miracles to open the lines of communication. I still wasn't sure how you could bypass the officers, but I saw the look on your face"—his gaze shifted to me—"when I came to get you earlier. Between that and the vibe of the other dragons, I knew you had to have worked something out. I still didn't know how—"

"How did you poison all the officers?" Denski said. "And how did you get everyone across this bridge? And how did you activate the faeries' magic?"

He sounded absolutely mystified.

"It doesn't matter," Govam said, his eyes boring into mine. "We can hopefully discuss that when we are in the boat. You need someone to run it, Finley. You need a certain type of demon. I am that type of demon, and so are those behind me."

"Except for me." Sonassa raised her hand. "I lead the demons of my kind, who are stationed in a few kingdoms Dolion wishes to bring to ruin. They are trapped there, much like you were trapped, Finley. I want to free them as you are trying to free your people. They are not all in line with my way of thinking, but a great many are. If you take me on, I can give you allies on the inside. We both know I can't affect you. I have proven this theory. You are safe from me. You know that I am not trying to get close in order to turn you to my plans."

"Well…you are," Hadriel said. "You're just being up front about it."

Her smile was sultry. "I like you."

"I know. You said. Before you threatened me. Remember?"

"Not especially. I threaten a lot of people."

"We have people on the inside, too," Govam said. He glanced at the lava. "And we just killed several who weren't in line with our thinking. It'll thin the numbers a little, at least."

"So…" I moved my weight from my right foot to my left. "You're basically asking *me*, a prisoner, to help *you*, a guard, escape your own kingdom?"

"And then tear out the current regime and replace it with a more balanced faction of demons, yes," Govam said.

I just stared for a long moment, not knowing what to say, struggling to process this turn of events and expectations.

Hadriel broke the silence. "I say we take them. There are, what, fewer than a dozen? We can kill them if they do something we don't like."

"If the patrolling guards can't work the boats, we'll need at least one of these demons to get out of here," Hannon said, ever practical. "My plan depended on taking someone from the patrol."

"I agree with the others," Micah said. "But they will need to be guarded. They will trade their current supposed cell for one of a different kind."

"I've seen how Finley responds to those who meet her half-way," Govam replied. "You will treat us better than you have been treated. Probably better than we are currently treated. Until you develop trust in us, if you ever do, then I will take your deal."

"It's not a deal. I'm done making deals with demons." I motioned them onward. "You have a key for the final door?"

"Ah. Is that what you came running back for?" Govam asked. "You caught me by surprise. One of many I've experienced when dealing with you."

"The tools ended up in the lava."

"Yes, I have a key."

"Let's go, then. Space yourself out between the dragons and the wolves. We need to move fast to get a head start on Dolion."

I still didn't totally trust them, but we needed them. So we hurried through the tunnels, not even second-guessing the turns at this point.

"How'd you get the map of the tunnels?" Denski asked as he easily kept pace.

No one answered him as we met the others, waiting by the door with anxious expressions. When they saw me running toward them, relief bled through their faces, followed quickly by confusion when they spied the guards.

"Long story," I said as the way cleared and I stepped aside for Govam at the door. I gave him plenty of space, just in case he planned to turn toward me and stick me with a knife.

"What's happening?" someone whispered.

At least I wasn't the only one struggling to get my head around things.

"I knew it. We're all gonna die," Elex whined.

"We're not, but you might if you don't shut your hole," Hadriel grumbled.

"It would be best for you all to pretend to be in our charge," Govam said as he swung open the door and waited for me to go through. "As I said, we were planning to meet you at the boats. The patrol would've assumed we were pursuing you. That would've given you time to kill most of the demons, capture one of them, and realize he or she was useless. It would've given me a better bartering chip."

"We could've just captured you then," I replied, quickly walking forward with him at my side—though still more than an arm's reach away.

"I had considered that. Worst case, at least one of us would be able to leave and try to bring about change."

I shook my head as we reached the stairs leading to the side entrance, mulling that over. I glanced back at Hadriel, who nodded. If the demons pretended they were escorting us outside, it would inspire curiosity, but it wouldn't bring people closer to investigate. It would ensure we didn't have to fight our way to the boats, which would hopefully buy us more time before we were discovered.

One thing was infinitely clear—Govam and his crew really were dooming themselves. Dolion would be furious if he found out they'd failed to capture us. He'd kill them on the spot.

We'd become their lifeline.

"Fine. Hurry." I let him lead us up the stairs, his guards fanning out around us. Except Sonassa, who changed her appearance to look like one of us, beautiful but still bedraggled, malnourished and beaten down. I wondered why she'd bothered with a red dress.

"There won't be anyone out on this side of the castle," Govam said as we reached the magical lock at the top. He stopped and put up his hand, twitching his fingers before pulling the spell away and continuing on. "We can run. When we reach the corner, though, we'll need to walk. It would help if you all hunched a bit."

"What about the wolves?"

He glanced down the stairs. "They should shift. They'll be naked, but that'll be less interesting than being wolves."

I relayed that back to Weston, confident he would take care of it.

Govam's voice dropped, almost like he was talking to himself. "I have no idea what Dolion was thinking, taking away your suppression. I'm obviously glad he did, but it was a shortsighted move. Did he misjudge your power?" He shook his head. "I've been studying him and his strategies for years, and his reasoning completely eludes me."

"He doesn't know shifters like you do," Sonassa said. "He surely misjudged her power, yes. I doubt he thought she would be strong enough—or motivated enough—to free the dragons or do any real damage. He thinks shifters have the intelligence of animals. I've heard he fears the golden dragon and *only* the golden dragon. He doesn't fear any of the other shifters. Not in the same way."

"I don't know about that," Denski said as the wolves shifted back and we jogged along the castle wall. "He had a lot of plans for her before she killed half his guards and two of his most prized magical workers that tried to remove her bond. I think that widened his eyes a little. He kept her at more of a distance after that. That couldn't have been a coincidence."

"True," Govam murmured as we reached the corner. He slowed to a stop, putting up his hand and beckoning me closer. "Time to play the prisoner, Finley. I know that you can kill me. You know that I know that you can kill me. Let's use some civility."

So we put on a show as we made the journey across the rain-soaked and windswept lands. Deep night had fallen, no stars visible in the cloud-choked sky. Two demons walked to our right a ways, hunched against the gale. If they noticed us, they gave no sign.

Near the beach, a handful of demons patrolled the area in pairs, their uniforms decorated with different symbols than the other guards. They did notice us approach, taking us in first and then looking to Govam.

"His highness's orders," Govam said, jerking his head behind him.

"What's that, now?" the other guard replied.

More guards stepped up or walked into the area to figure out what was going on or what might be needed of them.

"His highness's orders," Govam said again, louder, waving his people forward. "He asked that we tell you…" Govam looked at the guards standing back a ways, clearly impatient for them to get within hearing range.

As if pulled by a string, they drifted closer, their eyebrows lifting, their focus on him.

"That you are no longer needed—"

His guards rushed forward, swords out, stabbing or slashing at the guards before they knew anything was amiss. In a blink, they lay silent or groaning on the beach, the rain washing away their blood.

"Now you are really fucked," Vemar said with a laugh.

Govam glanced at the incline behind us, probably to see if anyone else was coming.

"Okay, hurry now." Govam steered me toward the rowboats pulled onto the sand. In the distance, bobbing in the sea like hulking reminders of how I'd gotten here and why, waited the larger demon boats. "Finley, you can take me. And Sonassa, since her magic doesn't affect you."

"Dragons," I said, watching those bobbing vessels, "set fire to the boats we don't use and these rowboats once we're done with them."

"That'll be seen from the castle," Govam said.

"So?" I looked him straight in the face, watching his reactions closely. "They'll figure out we're gone soon enough, and as soon as they do, they'll try to follow us. There's no way to prevent them finding out about the escape, but we can hold them off for a while. I don't see any other boats."

Govam studied me for a moment. "Send one of your drag-ons—preferably one that blends into the night—around the horn of the island." He pointed to where the land rose and turned, jutting into the sea. "Let them tell you how many boats are there."

"Let them tell me...or do you suggest we destroy those too?" I quirked an eyebrow.

Govam pointed the other way. "There are more in the basin at the bottom of the large cliff. If you destroy all of them, which will take time, as the wood is rain-soaked and won't be quick to burn, he can bring out the fleet in production. They are in the caves beneath the castle. Not even I know how to reach those."

"I do," Sonassa said. "But only through the castle. There's no way we could get a dragon in that way without raising questions. We'd be stopped almost immediately."

"Dolion is no fool," Govam said as the rain beat down on us, what he said about the fire catching incredibly poignant. "He knows what he is doing—what he has done—and has the potential to incite rage from many kingdoms. His predecessors were just as bad. They have built themselves a fortress that not even dragons can penetrate. He is a paranoid, cunning ruler, desperate to hold on to his crown. Do not underestimate him as he has done you."

"He's right, Finley, as much as I hate to admit it," Hadriel murmured.

Yes, he was. He could be lying about the caves, but his point about the rain-soaked wood was solid.

"Fine. Let's go."

While the first load of people rowed, the others gathered up the dead guards and carried them out of the way so they wouldn't immediately be noticed.

"Fuck, this is a lot of trust for me to put in someone who's spent the last…however many months imprisoning me," I said as Govam stood at the boat controls, flicking switches and adjusting settings.

"And this is a very precarious position I am putting myself in," Govam replied, "entrusting my life to the very creatures who have been trying to kill me for a lot longer than the few months you were here."

He had a point.

When the last rowboat of people had been loaded into the largest boat, Govam glanced at Denski. He nodded and descended to help the guards tie the rowboats to our larger vessel so that we'd take them out to sea with us.

"Clever," Hadriel said.

"I don't want to be caught any more than you do, Mr. Entertainer," Govam replied as the anchor was lifted and the boat cast off.

As we steered away from the castle, I wondered whether we had just walked into a trap. Or maybe, finally, we were on our way back to Nyfain.

CHAPTER 25

HADRIEL

I DRAPED MY head over the side of the boat as it rose and lurched, climbing up a wave and then plummeting down. No one else seemed to be freaked the fuck out by the violence of the sea. It hadn't been violent when we came. This definitely couldn't be normal.

"Princess, a word."

I wiped my mouth on the back of my hand and struggled to straighten up. That voice belonged to Govam, I knew, the sort of guy who watched more than he spoke. Those types always made me nervous. You never knew what was going on in their heads.

He seemed genuine, that was true enough, but demons were crafty fuckers. He might be trying to overthrow his king, sure, but I didn't for one moment think he cared what happened to us. We were a means to an end. Then again, they were also a means to an end for us.

"I'm not a princess," Finley said as she stood a little way down from me, looking out into the night.

Dragons lounged on the decks, tired from the past few hours

of frolicking in the air above us. The second we were far enough away from the castle, in the wide sea, they'd risen into the sky and tested out their wings. They'd rolled and swooped and spat fire while *some* of us would've liked a little peace and quiet in which to throw up what little had been in our stomachs.

Govam stood at the side of the ship with Finley, Denski having taken the helm, or whatever they called the magical control area.

Govam spoke in an undertone, so naturally my ears pricked up.

"We are at the point where we need to plot a course."

Several others looked their way, including the big alpha dragon and intense alpha wolf, both in their skin forms. Calia drifted a little closer too.

"And?" Finley replied.

"Have you thought about where you will go?"

She gave him a searching look as Hannon walked closer and leaned in next to her. He was the thoughtful and deliberate one of the pair. She'd listen to him. Which was why I'd pulled him aside for a talking-to a bit ago, when she was taking a quick nap.

"My duty has always been to go home to Nyfain and tear down the curse."

The longing in her voice broke my heart. I turned away, a movement that naturally morphed into throwing up over the side of the boat.

I felt a hand on my back. Leala, the woman who never seemed troubled by anything. How the fuck did she do it? She was a rock.

"Of course," Govam replied, clasping his hands behind his back and standing close enough that she could kill him. He was silently communicating that his fate was in her hands. Good work, crafty demon. "Only, I wonder if you have thought it through?"

"What is there to think through?" Now her tone held a very distinct warning. I was glad he was broaching this subject and not me, and also impressed he didn't take a step back.

"Dolion's first order of business when making a deal is to cripple his opponent. I've seen your kingdom. It is on its knees. Forgive me for saying, but so is its prince."

She stayed very still, and now it was just plain stupidity for the demon not to take a step back.

"They can shift now," she replied slowly. "And I've heard that there are more dragons."

"Young dragons, correct? Inexperienced dragons? And, as I understand it…less-than-effective shifters."

I sighed and straightened up, using my shirt as a rag this time.

"Love, listen…" I sidled closer, not straying far from the side of the boat. I clasped my hands in front of me and then pulled them apart and braced them on the railing behind me. "You have a kingdom filled with mediocrity. You know that. The shifters who are left are not very powerful or fierce. You're bringing back a handful that are both of those things, but they're weak from years of imprisonment."

Her eyes narrowed. "What are you saying, Hadriel?"

I scooted away a little. "If we show up now and break the curse—which you'll do as soon as you lay eyes on the master; you won't be able to help yourself—then you'll be opening the door for the demon king to bring all his forces in and destroy what little is left. He'll do it before the master—the prince—can be declared king and take his established place on the council."

She straightened up, clearly frustrated. "The deal was that I would allow Dolion to take me to his kingdom to buy Nyfain time to prepare our people to fight, then I would come back and we'd protect what was ours. You agreed. You helped plan this!"

"Yes, love. I know that. But then I realized how many of those buggers there are—and that the demon king is willing to lose any number of them to get what he wants. We've been shortsighted. We do not have enough people. We don't."

"I will not abandon him, Hadriel. Besides, where else would we go? It's home to more than half the people on this ship. Then there's the fact that Dolion's going to storm Nyfain's castle after he figures out I escaped. When I'm not there—"

"The demon king will have no leg to stand on," Govam cut in. "He can't kill the prince. The curse forbids it."

Finley stared at Govam in mute rage, torment, and frustration. It was clear she didn't know what to say.

"What will likely happen," Govam said in a tone that could only be described as delicate, "is that he will torment the people like usual, bring in more of Sonassa's kind, and post his people throughout the kingdom to make sure you cannot get back in. He will lock the portals and fortify the place as best he can to keep you from Nyfain. He won't be able to stay there long, though. He'll need to get back to his kingdom or risk trouble. But he can leave loyal ambassadors high in power to oversee matters." He paused for a moment in the sudden silence. "This situation seems new and unfamiliar to you, but this is the way demons have operated for centuries. They dominate and control so they can steal and bleed a village, town, city, or kingdom dry."

"I've taken all his prisoners. What if he kidnaps more?" she demanded.

Govam didn't speak for a moment. "Then you will have excellent grounds to go to the council and demand an audience. Given you, yourself, have been in that prison, and you have Dolion's former guards to testify on your behalf…"

"Except we won't be able to get back to Wyvern if he closes the portals. We're running out of time to break the curse."

"We can get you back in," Calia said softly, holding her sister's hand.

Finley looked at them like she was seeing them for the first time. She shook her head.

"You need an army at your back, Finley." Micah got to his feet on the first try, which was pretty miraculous considering the rolling and pitching of this accursed boat. "You need a host of dragons to scrape those filthy demons from your land. I know my people will join me in helping you. It isn't even a question. Not only because they will want vengeance, but because you are a dragon, and we help our own."

"But what if there's been some mistake, and I'm not really a dragon?" she asked in a small, helpless voice.

Suddenly I felt like a real asshole for sabotaging her plans.

"Then we will fight for you anyway, because without you and yours, we would have died in that prison," said the sickly dragon—Beelax or Exlax or something—and I was surprised he was jumping on the gratitude bandwagon after bitching and moaning during our escape.

"My village loves fighting," Vemar said, his eyes sparkling with mirth or madness or probably both. "They will want to help a fellow dragon."

"We will stand with you." Weston stood up, and I caught a wobble in his stance as we hit a wave. That made me feel better. "I don't know what shape my old pack is in, but I will petition the new alpha for aid. I will ask that they help me find vengeance.

First to free you, and then to scour the demon king and all his filth from this world."

I pointed at Govam. "Present company probably not excluded. Offense likely meant."

"It's been sixteen years, milady," Leala said softly. "Waiting another few weeks won't affect them nearly as badly as if we go in without enough support and get killed or worse for our efforts. We've just escaped. Let's make it count when we go back."

"You too, Leala?" Finley asked, her face falling.

"Me too, Finley," Hannon chimed in, delivering the final blow. That guy sure had good timing. "You'll be more help to the prince, and our family, if you can shift. And we absolutely need more people. I had no idea how outnumbered we were until I saw their staff and all their guards. And that was just a portion of them. If he mobilizes against us, this was all for nothing."

Tears welled in her eyes, and her lower lip trembled. "I have to go back. I *have* to. If I don't go back, he'll think I did what he asked and left him. He'll think I'm moving on. I can't let him think that."

"How will he know you've even escaped?" Lucille asked.

"Our bond. He knows. He seems to have gotten very good at reading my emotional cues and knowing how to help. He'll know I'm out, and he'll think I've found a new home. I..." A tear tracked down Finley's cheek. "I can't do that to him. I can't."

Tamara stepped closer to Finley and laid a hand on her arm. "I've known the prince most of my life. He's not easy to bring to heel or break down. He's held up this long, and he'll hold up for a while longer. Let's secure the help these shifters and faeries are willing to give, and then we'll go in as we should—on fire."

"We'll drop everyone off at the docks in the Flamma Kingdom

302

so they can go their separate ways," Micah said. "We'll gather reinforcements at the dragon villages, and then meet again at the port city. I told you I'd secure you a dragon army if you got me off that island, and I intend to. Give me that chance. Let's make this count."

Finley sagged against the side of the boat, another tear falling down her cheek. "In my heart of hearts, I figured it would come to this. I'm not dense. It's just…"

"You're in love with a really lucky motherfucker." Vemar spread his hands. "And you're horny. We get it, Strange Lady. Anyone who orgasms while they are being tortured and masturbates in a dungeon has it bad. But unless you have help, you ain't never gonna ride that cock again, you know? Do it for the cock."

"Wow. That just got super dirty," I said. "I'm impressed."

"I learned from the best." He winked at me, and I felt a little flutter. The guy was as hot as he was batshit crazy. Thank the goddess and her secrets he was not into men, or I might make a terrible mistake.

Wait. He wasn't into men, was he?

Finley threw up her hands, then turned for the stairs and the scant rooms belowdecks.

"I'll go with her," Hannon murmured, and followed.

Tamara wandered closer, watching them go. A little too close, actually. Why the fuck—

I jerked away when she suddenly leaned in toward me.

"Goodness, Hadriel, a little jumpy, huh?" she said, grinning.

"What do you want?"

"To pitch you overboard, but because you helped us out in a major way, I won't. Isn't that nice of me?"

"There is nothing nice about you."

"I love you too." She laughed. "Anyway." She pointed at Hannon's retreating backside. "What's his deal? He's gorgeous. I'm not usually into redheads, but..."

"He's too green for you, that's his deal. He hasn't had demon sex conditioning. You'd probably stick a finger in his butt, and he'd hit the ceiling."

She clucked her tongue. "I'm so excited to spend more time with you." She made a fast motion with her hand, and, annoyingly, I flinched again. She grinned mischievously as my stomach swam from all the movement and standing and leaning. No way was I going to throw up in front of her. I'd made fun of Lucille earlier for doing it on the deck, and now look—fucking karma.

Thankfully, Tamara's expression turned solemn. "Seriously, though, how's the prince? How was he when you left?"

I nearly threw up but held it down. "Not good. He's hanging on by a thread. He needs her back. She made him...as even-tempered as he can possibly be. She restored his past self to him. The good parts. You should see her with plants. I think she's better with them than the queen. I really do. She cured the demon sickness."

Tamara leaned away with a skeptical expression. "What's this now? We aren't the only kingdom that's been cursed with that sickness. A couple of other dragons came in with it. I don't remember where they were from, but it wasn't Wyvern or Flamma. They died...pretty hardcore. The guards and officers both said there was no cure."

Pride welled up from my fucking toes. Along with my stomach.

When I was done throwing up, I turned back around.

"She figured it out. I'm telling you, she's amazing. Well, she's had to be, right? Or else she was destined to see the rest of her family suffer and die. She lost her mother and…grammy or something to it. Sometimes I stop listening out of drunkenness. Anyway, she's great. You'll see."

"Is that why he gave her the sword?"

"I don't honestly know. Neither does she. She was in peril, so he promised to get her some weapons—he was giving her *space* at the time—and he put the sword in a sack in the woods. He was showing her how much she meant to him, and she didn't even realize it."

Tamara shook her head. "I don't know whether to be pissed or swoon."

"I fucking swooned, and don't you dare talk me out of it."

"Goodness…" Tamara turned her lips downward. "You sure have a prickly side when it comes to them."

"Yes, I do. Thank you for noticing. They are going to be crowned king and queen when this bullshit is all over, and they better be good at their fucking jobs. Real good at their fucking jobs. And they better need a mediocre butler because I'm starting to like this gig. Mostly. Kinda."

"You talk nonsense half of the time."

"Only because of your nonsense personality."

She laughed and turned to look out at the sea. "I'm scared to go home. I'm scared of what I'll find."

"Expect the worst. Then sit on that for a moment, imagine something worse than that, and expect *that*. Then have a nightmare about it, really just wallow in that nightmare, and expect *that* as your new reality. Welcome to a nightmare—cheers!"

I put up my hand, thought about a drink, and threw up mostly nothing over the side of the boat.

"And she's common." Tamara sounded distant; she was probably thinking about it through the lens of her past position. She'd been the captain of the queen's guard, a very noble role. Once she got to know Finley better, she'd see her worthiness. I had no doubt about that.

"Poor as fuck. From the worst—or poorest, I should say—village. She has nothing but her talent. And her dragon."

"*If* she's a dragon."

"Oh, she's a fucking dragon. She'll be a helluva fucking dragon, too. You should hear her and the master rage-fuck. Now that is a terrifying situation. Only dragons do that, you know. Normal shifters do not—"

I felt her hand on my shoulder and flinched *again*, before pulling away. You could never be too careful with a dragon from the court.

"They rage-fuck?" she asked softly.

I squinted at her shocked face. "I can't tell if that turns you on or..."

"He has—or had—an extreme temper."

"Oh, you're shocked. Yeah, I know about his temper. I actually panic-sharted a couple months ago, right after she left, when he snapped and yelled at me. It turned her on, though."

"What?" She blinked.

"Panic-sharted. It's a terror-fart that turns into a nasty little surprise in your pants—"

"Not that, you idiot! It...turned her *on*? He had some very tough paramours who'd turn to ice when they felt even a sliver of that temper."

"Well...that seems a bit much. He doesn't usually do anything with it."

"It's the power behind his commands and his bearing and…" She shivered.

I pointed at her. "See? If you said all that to Finley, she would have shivered with arousal. They are true mates. He has claimed her. They fit, trust me. She's hard as hell, and she won't give him an inch. He needs that."

"Yes, he does." She let silence drift over us for a moment. "Was he pissed that the true mate bond was held by a commoner?"

"I have no idea. But they were very hot and cold at first, so possibly. She kept resisting his commands, which pissed him off, but it also turned them both on… My job was miserable there for a bit, but then I almost died and—"

She lowered her hand to my shoulder again. Another flinch! Damn it! I had to stop. It amused dragons when they made people flinch.

"She resisted his commands?"

I rolled my eyes and contemplated throwing up. "She can kill people with her will alone, Tamara. Yes, she can resist his commands. To a point. And he can resist hers…to a point. What does the term 'true mates' mean to you if not a couple equal in power and temperament? They were literally made for each other. And thanks so much for asking about how I almost died. Very caring."

She blew out a breath and shook her head. The silence lengthened, and it occurred to me that some of the changes in our kingdom had actually been for the better. Finley wouldn't be subjected to the same ridicule and judgment as she would've been before the curse. She'd be judged mostly on her merits.

Tamara stayed put, and just as I was starting to wonder whether her boredom would turn to violence, she said, "I never really spoke to him. The prince, I mean. I had high standing as the captain of the queen's guard, but..." She shrugged. "There was a way things were done in the castle, and I didn't have business with him. But I watched the queen in the fields more times than I can count. I watched her with him, too. Those were her happiest times, tending the fields with him."

"He found that again with her. With Finley. I mean, obviously it wasn't the same feeling, because that would be weird, but—"

"She always told me, 'Don't call him "the prince" around me. Call him "your son," because he's not like the princes before him. He won't be like the kings of the recent past. Or the present. He'll change this kingdom. He'll summon the dragons from all the small villages and towns in other parts of the world and consolidate them, like in the days of old. Give them a proper home. As it should be. He isn't a prince when he's with me—he's *my son*.'"

"And then she told him to flee."

"I think she recognized a losing battle. His happiness meant more to her than turning a falling kingdom around. It wasn't the demons who did that place in; they just took advantage of the rot already there."

"Clearly. And after sending him away, she gave in to the long night."

"She didn't have anything left to live for, Hadriel. You have no idea what she was enduring."

I nodded, because she was right. I didn't.

"Anyway." She pushed off the banister and wandered away.

"No worries. Don't ask about my stuff or anything," I called after her.

She stopped and looked over her shoulder.

I grimaced and hunched next to the banister, then went back

to minding my own business. You could only taunt a dragon so much. I really needed to learn my lesson.

"I know why you—"

"Oh fuck!" I jumped, jiggled, sidled away, and threw up. "Fuck!"

Weston stood behind me, naked, each muscle clearly defined. He somehow still looked robust and godly despite having been starved. Fucking alpha males. They were my one weakness.

"I know why you didn't shift," he said, watching me with the intent gaze of a wolf assessing his surroundings. "On the bridge."

"Oh yeah?"

He stared for a moment, and this time I half thought I should put my ass over the side. He made my bowels a bit watery. Quite the weakness! I would never survive a romance with one of these bastards.

"You knew you would fall in line with the pack," he said, one hand on the banister, probably really annoyed he needed to hang on, since the alpha dragon did not.

He waited for a moment, but I didn't comment. I knew he didn't expect a response.

"Even though it would've granted you safe passage," he said, "you stayed in human form so that you could stay true to the…Finley."

"She's a dragon," I spat out. "Wait until she shifts. You'll see."

He jerked his head downward, his version of a nod. "I commend that. It took courage, doing what you did. It shows loyalty. She has a good wolf in you. A real good wolf."

I couldn't help beaming with pride. That was an incredible accolade coming from an alpha like him.

"How'd they get you?" I asked.

Normal people would've blown out a breath and looked out at the sea. Or inhaled. Or done something other than stare a hole into my head. But as alpha of what was probably a very large pack, he was not normal people.

"They got one of our younger wolves. He was running in the water past curfew. He didn't know the repercussions of being on the beach that late. His mother had two younger children to look after, and the father was absent. She had gone home to feed the younger ones, telling the young man what time to come home. When he didn't show up, she asked a neighbor to watch the kids so she could go look. I went instead."

The muscle in his jaw jumped, and this time he did look out at the ocean.

"They were loading him into a net when I got there." He shook his head. "It was a fool's mission, I knew that. But I couldn't bear the thought of doing nothing. I couldn't bear the thought of seeing his mother's expression when I delivered the news that he had been taken. So I tried to get to him."

"And were taken as a result."

"Yes."

"And he…"

"Didn't make the trip. They piled a couple of other captives on top of him. I was on the bottom of the shuffle as well, but…"

"You're built like a brick wall, yeah." I stared out at the lightening sky. "You had curfews?"

"We were having a lot of disappearances down by the water. We hunted the area a few times, but the water washed away most of the scents. We weren't entirely sure what was causing it, so I'd enforced a curfew."

"I guess you figured it out."

"Yes," he growled. "I will need power in order to claim vengeance, however. The demon king is wealthy and influential. My king and queen might hesitate in declaring war."

"Well, there is one future king and queen who will not hesitate. Not for a moment. They'll overturn the goddess's own bed to bring him down."

Weston turned and leaned against the railing, an alpha in repose, a very rare occurrence. "That is what I'm banking on. I will back her with everything I have to see that it is done."

CHAPTER 26

FINLEY

TWO DAYS OF travel later, we docked in the Flamma Kingdom, and I clutched Calia with sudden terror. If she left and didn't return, my path to Nyfain would be cut off. If something happened to her, I wouldn't have a way to get back to him, not if the demon king closed those portals.

"I will be back, I promise," she said, hugging me. "I will be back, and I'll have warriors with me. We will cleave our way to your prince if we have to, okay? You have my word."

Still, my heart was in my stomach as I watched her walk up the docks, in search of travel arrangements that would take her and her sister to their home in the Narva Kingdom.

Weston left next, taking all the wolves but Hadriel. He'd hired a boat that didn't need demon magic and would make sure anyone who lived elsewhere would get home. The goodbye he offered us was similar to Calia's. He'd amass more strength and meet us back here.

"They mean it," Hadriel said, rubbing my back. "They're going to come back. This is the right way."

It didn't feel like the right way. As we traveled into the mountains, moving toward the dragon villages and farther and farther away from Nyfain, it felt like I was betraying him. He needed me. The kingdom needed me. And while I did see the wisdom in collecting a host of allies before we took on Dolion, the doing of it was slicing into my heart. If not for Hannon and the other members of our group who were making the same sacrifice, I couldn't have managed.

My heart wasn't in the smiles I offered people as we came upon the first dragon villages. My curiosity was only mildly sparked at the prospect of seeing how other villages lived. And when it was decided that we would accompany Micah to his village, one of fifteen in the dragon-occupied mountains, I couldn't muster any excitement at the prospect of a much-needed rest after the long journey.

"I will see you soon, Strange Lady," Vemar said as we parted ways. He gripped my upper arms and peered down into my eyes, all seriousness. "We will have a rest, we will organize, and we will free your kingdom as you have freed us. This I swear. Learn to fly, and by the time you have mastered it, we will be leaving again."

"My village isn't far," Micah told us as we kept moving up the wide, rocky road.

We rode in horse-drawn carts and carriages. While the magical world had found many ways to magically pilfer various modern conveniences from the neighboring but oblivious human world, like electricity and radio, we'd never advanced enough for things like automobiles. Traders did cross the magical barrier between our worlds to acquire and bring back other commodities, like various types of steel or specialized tools and machines, but their efforts were limited by travel.

I assumed as much, anyway. My knowledge was passed down from my parents and the few books our small, never-changing library had about the neighboring world. Having been caught in the curse since I was seven, I had a shallow knowledge of modernity, at best. And while I wanted to learn more, I had other concerns at the moment.

Overhead, a dragon soared through the sky, its purple scales sparkling within the glow of the late afternoon sun.

"What color do you think your dragon's scales are?" Hannon asked, his voice heavy with fatigue.

"I haven't thought about it," I murmured, watching the dragon cut through the blue above. "I feel like I've known her forever, but since she's never taken an actual physical form, I don't think about it much. Maybe if we'd grown up with people actually shifting I'd be more curious, but…"

I'm curious as all fuck, my dragon thought. *I hope I'm not shit brown. That would be embarrassing.*

Another dragon soared overhead, this one a lighter shade of blue than the backdrop. Its great wings beat at the sky, its flight straight, no frills or embellishments. It had somewhere to be.

Micah glanced back and caught me looking. A knowing gleam flashed in his eyes.

"We'll get you up there tomorrow," he said. "With someone to guide you through your first shift, you shouldn't have any problems. And when you grow tired of flying, we'll find something else to get your mind off things until we're ready to act."

"Like learning how to use that sword," Tamara said with a grin, peering into the trees to either side of us before looking skyward and watching the dragon until it was out of sight.

"All I really know how to do is work with plants and hunt," I said, noticing the healthy trees and plant life around us. The air was crisp and clean, a soft breeze mussing my hair. "I've never really had downtime."

"Reading," Hannon said. "You can do some reading."

"Should we see if they have watercolor painting?" Hadriel waggled his eyebrows at me.

"There used to be a couple of very knowledgeable women who worked with healing plants in my village," Micah said. "The whole collection of villages sought their aid in the infirmary. They used to be very selective about who worked with them, but if they are still around, I'm sure I could put in a good word for you. I have a lot of sway in these villages."

I could hear the note of pride in his voice. The confident swagger. He was probably one of the most powerful dragons, and that gave him clout.

Little dwellings came into view. Micah slowed before stopping and sucked in a deep breath. He let it out slowly. "I've been away from home for so long. I'm both nervous and dying with anticipation."

He started forward again, falling quiet.

"My dragon is anxious to get airborne," Tamara murmured as we neared the edge of the village. Small fences enclosed little patches of land outside homes, the yards within flattened and cleared of rocks and dirt mounds.

"Mine too," Lucille added.

"I'm surprised you guys didn't do more flying on the way here." I peered through a window as we passed, not able to see into the dark interior.

"We didn't want you to take off running back toward the boat with your demon friends," Lucille said, her tone light and teasing.

My mind was so scattered that I hadn't even thought about the pack of demons holding up the rear. It had been decided that they'd stay with us for now, surrounded by the protection of dragons. Given they had essentially exiled themselves from their kingdom, they didn't really have anywhere else to go.

At the edge of town, where the paths narrowed, too small for the carriages and carts, we climbed down and left them behind to be tended to after we found a place to rest.

Micah led us down a couple of really cute cobblestone streets, the houses beside us modest but well kept. We emerged into what must've passed for their town center, with a little park to the right and a winding path that led in front of little shops with glass doors or large windows. Flower boxes dotted the way and everlass grew in cracks or along the pathways, wild but mostly pruned.

I smiled down at one of the plants before bending to strip away a few leaves that were floundering on it.

"*Micah?*" we heard.

I stood, seeing two middle-aged women walking down the path arm in arm, their eyes widening. One of them lifted her fingertips to her breastplate.

"Micah, is that you?"

"Desiree." He smiled at her as all the blood drained from her face.

"But...we thought you were dead..." Her gaze traveled his body, clothed in ill-fitting pants and a shirt he had grabbed after we docked. Thankfully, Govam and the other demons had thought to bring some gold. "They made inquiries and found out that you'd never made it to the merchant in Fiddler's Green."

"Demons captured me on my way there," he replied, walking toward them slowly. It looked like he didn't want to spook them, which was probably wise. They looked like they were staring at a ghost. "They took me back to their castle and imprisoned me in a dungeon. It's a story I only want to tell once, the details of which are cause for war. I'll want to see the elders. For now, though, I need to find lodgings for my friends and take a hot bath—"

"Goddess bless you!" Tears in her eyes, she ran at him, slamming into him and wrapping her arms around him. The other woman piled on, crying.

The rest of us scooted back awkwardly, some with half-smiles and others clearly uncomfortable, probably wondering if anyone from their old life was left.

Micah was greeted like that throughout the town, everyone running to see him again as word spread. It was clear he was someone with a lot of status, and they'd missed him terribly. It wasn't until evening was kissing the sky that he was finally able to get people to listen for long enough to explain our needs. After that, they wasted no time in finding us lodging, even the demons. We were treated to a delicious, fresh meal, hot baths, and soft beds in the local tavern.

The next day, I found myself listless and edgy. Any shifting lessons were put off because the village elders had wanted to see Micah as soon as possible, and the dragons from my kingdom were too wary of our power differences to attempt to guide me through the shift. Basically, they'd figured out my dragon was a temperamental ass-bag and decided I'd do best with a powerful alpha. So we had nothing to do but wander the paths and check out our surroundings.

It was a lovely place, full of blooming flowers, well-tended walkways, and smiling people who made Hadriel incredibly nervous. He didn't like being cooped up in a village with so many dragons. And *I* didn't like being away from home. Nyfain had started to distance himself from the bond, I could tell. His emotions seemed like they were going dormant. He knew I'd gotten out, he knew I wasn't in danger, and he was letting me go. If he were right in front of me, I'd kick the living shit out of him for it…then fuck his brains out.

Since he was hundreds of miles away, the thought filled me with terror, and my impatience to get to him turned my dragon listless.

"I'm going to go for a walk," I announced too loudly the next morning.

We sat at a large round table in the tavern common room—we, meaning the people from my kingdom. The demons had decided to stick to their rooms whenever possible, not liking the narrow-eyed looks they got from the locals.

"I thought we could get in some sword work today," Tamara said, eyeing the weapon on my hip. I had no idea why I'd put it on that morning. Force of habit, perhaps. Or maybe the weight of it on my hip reminded me of him. It kept him close to me as the feeling of the bond receded.

"Sure." I pushed back my chair and stood as a brown-haired server whisked my plate away.

"Do you want company?" Hadriel leaned forward, pausing in the motion to push his own chair back.

"I'll go." Hannon blotted his mouth and stood. "I could use the walk."

"Good." Hadriel relaxed. "I don't like the way people here eyeball me. It's like they are about to yank my head off at any moment."

"They're all incredibly pleasant," Jade, the green-eyed dragon, replied.

Hadriel pointed at her. "You just can't see it because you're as crazy as they are."

"You're just being paranoid," Leala said, smiling and shaking her head.

"You don't have to go, Hannon," I said, pushing in my chair. "Micah made it very clear that we're safe here."

My brother shrugged. "You can find trouble at the best of times."

I rolled my eyes but waited for him to come around the table before walking out.

"Just find me when you're ready to learn that sword," Tamara called after me.

I definitely needed to, but I just didn't feel like sucking at something right now. I wanted a distraction. A bit of comfort, even if it was fleeting.

Hannon didn't say a word as we walked through the center of town. We got smiles and nods and more than one stare, especially as people got close enough to smell me. No one said anything, though.

"He's trying to forget me," I said softly, knowing exactly where I was going. I'd spotted a large everlass field at the very edge of the village yesterday. There'd been an enticing fragrance piping from it. Someone was making elixirs, I just knew it. If I really wanted a distraction, that was where I would find it. "He's trying to distance himself from me."

"He won't move on," Hannon replied, his voice just as subdued. "He won't ever forget you, Finley. You know that. And we won't be gone long enough for him to do something stupid, like get himself killed. Keep thinking of him. Keep trying to emotionally connect with him however you can manage it. He'll catch on that you're not gone forever."

I let out a breath, my heart aching. "I just don't know, Hannon."

"I do. I feel it. This is a necessary stop, and then we'll go back and finish this."

Once we reached the outskirts of the village, I immediately spotted the everlass. Without a word, we skirted around the trees and emerged in the field, which was almost an extension of someone's backyard. In the distance, I could just make out an herb garden and a couple of rosebushes, vibrant and healthy. It made me wonder if the ones Hadriel and I had tended in the castle were still flourishing, or if Nyfain had let them grow wild, distancing himself from them because they reminded him of me.

A large pot hung over a smoldering fire, releasing ash-gray smoke into the clear sky above. Beside it, two smaller pots sat on a little stove, although I couldn't tell if there was any heat beneath those.

"They are set up to work the plants," I murmured, wandering into the everlass field. "These are well tended." I stopped beside a crowded plant, pointing at it for no reason. Hannon knew better than to mess around in the garden unless he was expressly asked for something.

"Micah mentioned the women who helped the infirmary." Hannon put his hand up to block the glare of the sun as he looked at the house. "Maybe they live there?"

"Hello?" A middle-aged woman with brown skin and shiny jet-black hair emerged from the wood with a basket tucked under her arm and an apron tied around her middle. She was very pretty and had an air of confidence and command about her, like she was picking plants today but might waltz into battle tomorrow.

Her expression creased into one of puzzlement as she looked from me to Hannon.

"I don't think I know you…" She walked within the plants as though she'd been tending this field all her life. Maybe she had.

"Is that your house?" I pointed at the backyard.

"No, but I help out there. Can I help you?"

I opened my mouth to answer, but I really wasn't sure what to say. *Hi, I would like to invite myself into your world, take over your operation, and not get any grief from you about it. That cool?*

Hannon came to the rescue.

"We're delayed in the village for a time. We came with Micah…"

He waited for the name to register and wasn't disappointed.

"Oh," she said on a release of breath, peering a little closer at our faces. "You were imprisoned with him? What village are you from?"

"We're from…a forgotten kingdom," Hannon said softly. "You probably haven't heard of it."

Her shapely eyebrows pinched together. "Try me."

"We're from Wyvern," I replied. "It has a curse—"

"Wyvern?" She went back to studying my face for a long moment, then Hannon's. "I've heard of it. Forgotten is right. All I know is the name at this point."

Hannon nodded. "If it isn't too much trouble, my sister would like to work the plants. Maybe I can help inside the house if you need assistance. We're not used to being idle."

"Well." She hesitated as though weighing the pros and cons. Finally, she said, "You better come in, then." She passed us, taking the lead back toward the house. "Do you have any experience tending a garden or working with everlass?"

"A lot, yes," I replied.

"She is exceptional," Hannon said.

I scowled at him as she glanced back at us with humor in her brown eyes. "Exceptional, huh? Hmm. We shall see."

She looked down for a moment, probably catching a glimmer as the sun sparkled off my sword, and then did a double take.

"Quite a sword," she said, scowling. "Warriors wear swords like that. Rich folk."

"It was a gift," I replied, feeling a little defensive for reasons I couldn't explain.

"What is your name?"

"Finley. This is Hannon."

"Some gift. Are you expecting trouble, Finley?"

"No. I just…" I touched the hilt, and an honest answer blurted out of me. "I want to remember the man who gave it to me."

She continued to study me, as though searching for something. Maybe a better explanation. Or maybe she wanted to judge whether I was lying and planned to stab her in the back. After a moment, though, she gave me a curt nod and continued along without a word.

"Ami," she called after going through a little gate in the waist-high picket fence surrounding the backyard. "Ami, you have visitors."

We stopped at the fence, not quite sure about crossing the threshold unless specifically invited.

A woman emerged from the back door with a basket of her own. Probably edging in on fifty years old, she had wheat-colored hair tinged with red and a lovely face with soft lines in it. She wore plain clothes, but the way she carried herself seemed almost regal, like she was stuck in a simple life now but would one day rise to a lofty perch. Her apron was the same style as the other woman's, smeared with whatever she'd been working on.

"This girl over here—Finley—has a mighty fine sword." The woman who had led us over set her basket by the wall. "Says she's from Wyvern. Came in with Micah's group. Her brother Hannon says she is *exceptional* with everlass."

Ami's expression remained unchanged as she took all of this in. She pulled up her apron and wiped her hands as she walked toward us.

"Wyvern," she said, looking at the sword. "I haven't heard that name spoken in a long time. Yes, that is a very fine sword indeed. We don't have that kind of workmanship here in this collection of villages. Swords are considered more ornamental. We fight with claws and teeth. Are you a—"

She tensed when she got close, her eyes turning intense. She must've caught Nyfain's scent.

"Are you a dragon, Finley?" she finished with a tight jaw.

"Yes…we think. My true mate is a dragon, but I haven't shifted yet—it's a long story. Micah is supposed to help me, but he's been delayed."

"Micah is very powerful. Nearly as powerful as that scent you wear. But you do not need a powerful teacher—you just need one with experience. Claudile and I have plenty." Her clear blue eyes flicked to Hannon. "And you, Hannon? Have you shifted?"

"No. I tried but couldn't."

"And you think you are a dragon as well?"

He shrugged. "We don't know what I am. Our parents were both wolves, but…Wyvern has fallen on desperate times, and there is an element of surprise in people's animals of late."

"Myths becoming reality." Ami smoothed her apron. "Well then. Since you are delayed, and are exceptional with everlass, maybe you'll tell me this long story as we work the plants, hmm? We can always use an extra pair of hands. After that, we'll see about shifting. I'm sure you're eager to learn the color of your scales."

Tell that story fast, my dragon thought. *I want to finally be set free. I'm sick of being at the mercy of your invisible friends and dumb decisions. It's time for this bad bitch to fly.*

I didn't tell the story fast, but the words flowed out of me. Our family's trials. My background with the everlass. How I'd met Nyfain and discovered he was my true mate. They'd heard about the dungeon, so they didn't ask me to recount much of that except for a few questions about how we'd escaped. They both smiled when I told them about killing the officers with the crowded everlass, but otherwise they just let my words tumble out freely as they tended to the garden and the steaming elixirs. I worked with them, pruning.

When I'd finished, silence stretched for a long moment, the soft breeze drying my tears and my heart still aching for what I feared I was losing. For this delay that was keeping me from my love and my family.

"It sounds like you've had a hard life," Ami finally said as she glided over to collect the herbs I was cutting.

"I'm still alive. It's worth the struggle to save those I love."

"And what of this true mate you speak of?" Claudile asked. "He is sacrificing for you, it sounds like. He wants you to leave and not return. To save yourself and be happy. Would you not consider it?"

Anger poured into me. I gave her a direct stare as power rose in and around me. "Men often think they know what's best for women, when in reality they rarely even know what's best for themselves. No, I will not consider it. Not for a moment. I didn't do all of this to save myself. I did it to help my family, my mate, and my kingdom. I will see this job through if it kills me."

"I will not let it kill you," Hannon said softly, seated in the corner of the yard, out of the way.

"Well then." Ami deposited the tray she'd taken from me to the side and started untying her apron. "Since you have battle in your future, we'd best make sure you have the most efficient way to fight. Take off the decorative sword. That won't help you now. It's time to meet your dragon."

My stomach rolled and filled with butterflies, and my dragon's anticipation and excitement rose as the women led me past the everlass field and into the trees. Hannon followed us but kept back, letting me have this moment.

Take it easy on the first flight, okay? I thought as we found a clearing and stopped to step out of our clothes.

Sure, sure. And if not, at least you have your invisible people to keep you company.

"Damn it. Why did I get stuck with such an asshole animal?" I muttered as I walked behind them into the clearing.

"The most powerful dragons tend to be quite temperamental in their youth," Ami said. "Possessive, dominant, fearless."

"Foolish," Claudile murmured, and I had a feeling she'd be right about my dragon.

I'd heard an alpha needed to help with the first shift. Micah had been pretty adamant that I should shift with him first, and the other Wyverners hadn't argued with him. I worried these women wouldn't be enough. That my dragon would get confused, I'd try to help, and we'd get stuck mid-shift and die.

We wouldn't be the first to go that way.

"Calm yourself, little dragon," Ami said in a low tone, clearly reading my body language. Power infused her words, but they didn't come through as a command. Instead, they wove through me like a gentle breeze caressing my face, completely in harmony with our surroundings. Her will, like mine, carried magic.

That wasn't what immediately calmed me, though. The thing that washed through my middle and wiped away all of my apprehension was her choice of words. The same ones Nyfain had used in his letters.

I wanted him to be here with us. I wanted *him* to guide us, not them.

I wanted him to quit fucking pushing us away.

Ami and Claudile's questions had shaken something loose in me. I didn't give a shit what kind of life Nyfain wanted for me. I'd always pursued the things I wanted, the opinions of others be damned. I would not sacrifice that now. Not even for him.

One day, somehow, I *would* fly with him. The curse might have stripped him of his wings, but there had to be a way to undo what had been done. There *had* to be a way to heal him.

That was all in the future, though. For now, I would need to settle for him being with me in spirit.

My dragon reached out through the bond even as I did, both of us leaning deeply across the distance he was trying to put between us to yank him back. I clutched him to me in an iron grip, feeding him the rage he'd so often shoved at me. Pissed that he was stupid enough to assume that I'd gone through everything—finding a cure for the illness, allowing the demon king to imprison me, enduring torture—just to leave him behind. To leave *my family* behind.

Did he even know me?

I pumped rage into the bond even as I pulled power from him.

His answering swirl of mirth made my stomach flutter. My rage made him smile, just as *his* rage always turned me on.

My dragon was feeding them her own collection of emotions: excitement, anticipation, impatience.

They likely knew what was about to happen. Nyfain's dragon did, at any rate, because in a moment I felt a different sort of power flow through the bond. A controlled gush, tingling and alive.

My stomach dropped out, as though I had just jumped off a mountain and was free-falling.

"Fuck, here we go," I murmured, eyes squeezed shut. "What do I do?"

"If you'd just wait a moment, we'll explain—"

Ami cut Claudile off. "No. She isn't talking to us."

Damn right she isn't, my dragon thought, giddy now. *Get ready to move out of my way. I'm going to follow the dragon's prompting and surge to the surface. His power will guide us...I think. I'll figure it out. But when I make a move, you make a move, get it? If you fuck up and don't relinquish control in time, we'll die horribly.*

Nice melodrama, asshole.

Thanks. Sometimes I have to go overboard to get through to you.

I rolled my eyes while I still had the power to do so. Soon she'd be in charge of all body mechanics. Soon we'd be in the air.

Oh fuck.

Nervousness and adrenaline rippled through me, followed by

another surge of Nyfain's mirth. He was either feeling joy at being here with me through the bond, helping from a distance, or he was laughing at me. Maybe both. Next, though, I felt a surge of unwavering support and confidence from him. He had complete faith this would go fine.

Power pulsed within me now, hot and then cold. Hard thrusts, followed by a trickle. The tingling increased. Butterflies filled my stomach. I could feel Nyfain through the bond as distinctly as if he were right beside me, holding my hand at the edge of a great precipice. In my mind's eye, he was looking over at me, the wind ruffling his unruly hair, the sun glinting off his sharp cheekbones. His golden eyes sparkled as he willed me to jump. Willed me to follow his lead, put my faith in my dragon, and take the leap.

Ready? my dragon asked.

I took a deep breath. I thought of Nyfain's gorgeous golden eyes, with the flares of deep orange streaking from the pupil. I felt his confidence, and yes, his joy. His happiness to be with me, even like this, during my first shift. During my first flight.

You better not fucking kill us!

I relinquished control. I left myself open for her to surge up and push me out of the way. It wasn't like it would be the first time, only this time I wouldn't claw my way back to the surface.

Barely able to breathe, I waited as she built power, heeding the dragon's guidance. She pulsed it *just so*. She feathered it. And then, in a blinding flash, she surged out.

Two lines of pain erupted down each side of my back, less painful than the officers' whip cracks but covering slightly more ground. My scales, I knew.

My stomach flipped, and then it wasn't my stomach anymore. My dragon exploded to the surface and, with her, the essence of

Nyfain's dragon. More pain crackled along my skin.

Child's play, my dragon thought, and it was. We'd learned a new meaning of pain in Dolion's castle.

My middle grew warm and then throbbed as I felt Nyfain's dragon shove him away and rise. They were shifting with us. Nyfain and I both sank, it felt like, deep into the darkness, holding each other as we did so.

My dragon's body grew through the clearing, up and up, until Ami and Claudile were peering at me with widened eyes. Hannon stood off in the trees, watching us with a small smile on his face.

"Fuck, we're huge—" Only, I wasn't in control of our mouth. Or our large maw with long, sharp teeth that felt weird touching with our large, long tongue.

Our mate is much bigger. He will still dominate us, my dragon thought with a purr.

I was glad I got that last eye-roll in.

She ruffled our wings as she looked down at our body. I sucked in a startled breath.

This is much better than shit brown, she thought, and then she pumped our wings and lifted into the air.

CHAPTER 27

FINLEY

*O*H *SHIT! OH shit! Oh shit!*

Three days of attempted flying later, I squeezed my eyes shut, but of course I wasn't in control of the huge dragon body that was currently beating its wings frantically to stay in the air.

I've got this, my dragon thought, following another huge dragon body glittering azure blue.

The mountain face rushed toward us. The dragon in front—Ami—banked and began pumping her wings before catching an updraft and soaring toward the mountain peak.

Do not try that, you shit-hamper, I thought-yelled at my dragon. *Don't try it! We're not experienced enough. Remember last time? We fucking crashed last time. We've only been doing this for three da-ays—*

My stupid dragon never listened to me. She was getting back at me for all those times she wanted to go to Nyfain and I refused to let her. Except those instances hadn't been life-threatening, and these—

She banked like the dragon in front, beat her wings…and

caught the underside of the updraft. Rather than lifting us above the peak, it shoved us into the mountain.

I screamed inside her head as she swore and tried to shove my presence down. Our chest scraped against the rock, and our knees buckled with the onslaught. Gravity grabbed hold, and then we were falling, rolling down the hill and knocking our body and limbs as we did so.

Give me back control, I begged, wanting to teach her how to fall gracefully, if nothing else.

I'd begged to help off and on since we'd haphazardly risen into the sky that first time. Thank the goddess Claudile and Ami had quickly shifted and met us up there, or we would've downed at least three trees with a sudden crash landing.

This time, though, it seemed she was tired of my nagging.

You want control? Fine, have control.

Suddenly my presence embodied this new, enormous shape covered in glittering scales reflecting sun. Four legs rather than two, ending in claws instead of toes. A weight off our back in the form of a long, spiked tail. We fell fast toward the side of the mountain. If I didn't find some kind of purchase, we were going to be dead as fuck.

I made a weird sort of *maaarrr* sound as I attempted to scream—first instinct—and then our ass hit the mountain. My legs—*too many fucking legs!*—scrabbled for purchase.

Just…need…the…first…couple… I worked my front legs, digging into the rocky dirt to slow the slide. Then, with effort, my back.

The mountain face slid loose beneath my claws, dumping me down the steep slide.

That wasn't my fault, I thought, shoving off with both feet and twisting in the air.

What are you doing?

Flying!

You don't know how to work the wings!

I've never really tried, have I?

I worked them like I might my arms, waving them in the air as gravity once again took hold. Except they didn't work like arms. Not even close. The muscle at the top of the wing spiderwebbed through the rest of it, connecting with bones and sinew and veins and all this other shit that I didn't know how to deal with. I probably looked like a kid jumping off a roof with a kite strapped to each arm. Eventually I'd hit the ground and break my leg. Or head.

Okay, okay, hurry! I relinquished control to her, getting the hell out of the way.

The dragon filled the space immediately, taking over our wings. They caught the air and worked frantically, trying to stop our downward plummet. The side of the mountain came to meet us, but there was no wind to shove us around, so she pushed off with our legs, and we were in the air again, flying out to meet Ami, Claudile, and their friend Gunduin, our flight instructors for the day.

Ami had been a merciless instructor. She'd started fast and challenged us immediately, even when there was a very real threat of crash-landing into trees...or the side of the mountain. She'd had incredibly high expectations and given us almost zero room for error.

We weren't the type to back down from a challenge. Even a harebrained one.

Again, my dragon thought, not following the others back toward the village. *We almost had it.*

We didn't come close to having it! We just didn't crash as hard. You're welcome.

You know what they say...

She didn't finish her thought as she approached the updraft again.

No, seriously! I thought desperately. *Maybe let them show us one more time!*

Nah, I got this. This is going to work, my dragon thought. *You'll see.*

Yeah, I'd see as we crashed into the side of the fucking mountain.

A COUPLE OF hours and a few crashes later, we finally allowed Ami and friends to fly us to the wood where we could touch down and shift back into human form. Dragons weren't supposed to be in the village proper, given there were plenty of things—and people—to trample. So when the townsfolk wanted to fly, they walked out to the wood and shifted there.

I sat down onto the ground heavily, my body dripping with fatigue. Flying was hard work.

"You're fearless." Gunduin grinned at me, showing straight white teeth in a ruggedly handsome face. He was about Ami's age, maybe a little older, with crystal-clear green eyes and sandy-blond hair.

"That or crazy." Claudile bent to grab my clothes from the base of the tree, throwing them at me. She hesitated at the sword, reaching out to grab it but stopping short of touching it. "Tell me again why you cart this thing everywhere? There's no need for it here."

Panting, I pushed to standing and quickly pulled on my clothes. I retrieved the sword out from under her hand. "It reminds me of someone I miss."

"It's a keepsake from her loved one." Ami pulled on her shirt. "Or maybe she stole it and intends to sell it."

I strapped the sword around my hips. "I'm also training with it."

"Who's training you?" Claudile gave me some side-eye as we headed back to the everlass field. Hannon, who'd waited there patiently for our return, gave us a slight nod, but didn't move to join us as we entered the rows of plants. Ami had tried to help him shift, but no luck. In the end, the three dragons had ruled that Hannon wasn't one of us. The nature of his animal remained to be seen.

"Someone from the queen's guard from my kingdom. She knows what she's doing."

"Does she?" Claudile asked. "*I* know what *I'm* doing. Maybe you'd like to spar with me?"

"Not hardly. You'd probably stab me in the leg and tell me it was a learning experience." I lifted my brows. "I know, why don't *you* spar with *her*? That would help me out. I'm tired of sucking at it. Just give me a dagger and send me on my way. A sword is a genteel sort of weapon, and I'm not genteel."

"Then why were you given a sword?" Gunduin asked.

I ran my hands over the leaves of the everlass plants, closing my eyes and soaking up the glow of the day.

"She has told her story already, Gunduin," Ami said as she and the others fanned out through the field. "It's not one she probably wants to repeat. I'll fill you in another time."

He shrugged as he bent to prune one of the plants. And that

was how we passed another hour, working in quiet, or mostly quiet, harmony. Ami or Claudile sang to the plants occasionally in another language I didn't know and not many seemed to use, and I muttered to them. Even though the women still seemed distant and sometimes a bit cold (Claudile especially), it lifted my spirits and relieved my mind to feel camaraderie with people who gave everlass the respect and care it cherished. We had found one commonality, and we didn't need to be friends to appreciate it.

Hannon waited patiently, whittling something out of a sliver of log or gazing into the healthy wood surrounding us. It was a pleasant sort of place, without the pressures and demands of a curse, demons, and people dying.

A while later, as Hannon and I were preparing to leave to meet the others from Wyvern, Claudile beckoned to me. "Finley, I wanted to get your *exceptional* opinion on this elixir."

I ignored the sarcastic dig.

She led me to the backyard and stopped beside a simmering pot, the steam curling up into the sky, carrying with it a spicy-sweet fragrance. A spoon and a smattering of ingredients lay on a table beside the hanging pot, and she picked up the spoon and dipped it into the contents.

"What do you think about this?" She handed me the spoon with the liquid pooling inside it.

I watched her for a moment, wondering if she'd give me any clues as to what it was for. No. Apparently this was some sort of test.

I didn't really care what these people thought of me—if they thought I was good with the plants and elixirs or not—but I did love a challenge, particularly *this* challenge. I knew what she was asking me. She wanted me to guess what they'd made and, if I could, come up with a way to make it better. Improving formulas was something I'd always had to do on my own—it was exhilarating to do it with others.

I smelled the brew before touching it to my lips. It took me a moment to identify each of the flavors in the symphony of taste, then another to categorize them. I thought for a long moment, running through what each ingredient was good for. There were a few possibilities, but none perfectly matched.

I grunted softly and shook my head. That was frustrating.

The only thing I did know was that the balance was off. The taste was much too tart. It nearly scratched the back of my throat as it went down. A large cup of this would likely start a countdown, at the end of which I'd need to sprint to the washroom. More than that in a twenty-four-hour period? Forget it.

"A petal of calla lily, one and a half max, would stop the raging diarrhea this probably causes." I gave her back the spoon.

Hannon smirked and shaved another chunk off the wood he'd been handling. Claudile studied me for a long moment, as did Ami, standing on the other side of the backyard.

"Calla lily negates the best effects of everlass," Claudile finally said. "It deadens it. It's best used to temper the effects of the crowded plant."

I tilted my head at her. "Oh yeah? I didn't know that about the crowded plant. I'm still learning. Huh. That'll be incredibly useful." I looked at Hannon.

"You wouldn't have needed it with the sickness we were facing," Hannon said. "But I'm sure that'll be helpful if you need to do something other than poison someone in the future."

I barked out a laugh, thinking of the officers.

"You've given the crowded plant to people without knowing

the risks?" Ami's voice dripped with disapproval.

"All due respect, ma'am," Hannon said, his tone calm. "You clearly don't understand the kind of life we were living. Finley cured a kingdom. The serum might have killed people, but what was the alternative? To let them die slowly? And it worked. She cured them, starting with our father. I administered the elixir myself, and I knew the risks. She only uses that plant if the alternative is dire—"

"It's fine, Hannon," I murmured. "I get why she's asking. It would have been reckless if they weren't about to die anyway."

"Why were they about to die?" Gunduin asked, sitting in a chair in the corner. "What do you mean she cured a kingdom?"

Everyone ignored him, and I picked my conversation with Claudile back up.

"Calla lily negates the effects of the everlass, sure, but only when too much is used or it's with other base-type ingredients. Everlass runs a bit acidic, so too much base will deaden it. But given how acidic this elixir tastes, one petal for a pot this size will cut down on the acid without affecting the elixir too much. It'll still do the job...though I don't recognize this concoction. What are you trying to do?"

"You can't tell from—"

"Severe joint ache caused by age," Ami cut in. "A patient in the infirmary suffers from habitual joint ache when he flies too much. He doesn't want to deal with the side effects of our healing elixir, though."

"Raging diarrhea, yeah. I don't blame him." I nodded, resting my hands on my hips. "Well, the calla lily will certainly help, but I have a great remedy for arthritis that has no side effects. It'll help the joint pain, no problem. The symptoms are basically the same, right? I ran into the diarrhea problem as well, but it wasn't an option for me to ignore it. People barely had enough food—they couldn't afford to lose it that way."

"Show me," Ami said, coming over.

I got to work, finding most of the things I needed in her well-stocked and -maintained garden and the rest in the wood. It was an arduous concoction; one needed to pound certain things, grind others, and mix them in a way that the ingredients all harmonized together. Thankfully, Ami and Claudile were great help, needing very little instruction. Gunduin and Hannon helped when needed or asked, both of them working peacefully with us until a large pot was set above the fire to simmer slowly.

"I don't see how this will work," Claudile said, looking down into the murky liquid. "No one is going to want to drink that."

I held up a finger as a shape caught my attention out of the corner of my eye. Micah stepped in close to the side fence, having just left the road. I was late for my sword training with Tamara, and he'd clearly wanted to make sure I was okay.

I ignored him for a moment. "The trick is to simmer it very lightly. If it boils, it's ruined. In fact, if it even brushes up against a boil, it won't work nearly as well. You need to keep it on very low heat for three hours, give or take. The murkiness will clear, and the water will turn a lovely lavender color and smell really nice. Take it off the heat then, let it cool, and then serve it. Don't serve it hot, though, or else it'll have a punch of sourness and people will bitch. I mean, it'll still work, but people who ache all the time are already cranky as all hell. It's easy to push them over the edge. Then they yell at Hannon."

"It's not pleasant," Hannon murmured.

Ami quirked a brow.

I smiled. "I'm not good with people. Hannon administers the elixirs. I couldn't be arsed. He helped a guy down the way from our house and…well, I could hear the yelling from my backyard."

"Old man Fortety is miserable at the best of times," Hannon grumbled. "I still hold a grudge that you sent me down with that elixir, knowing it was too hot."

I laughed; I couldn't help it. It had been a dick move, but sometimes I liked seeing Hannon get all riled up.

"Finley, it's time to head back to the others," Micah said, checking me over. "You have a gash on your arm." His eyes flashed menace as he glanced at Ami. An annoying little flutter tickled my belly, something that had happened a couple of times in his presence at the demons' castle, and more often these last few days. "You're pushing her too hard. From now on, she'll practice with the other newly shifted. It's a better place for her to learn."

"All due respect, alpha," Ami replied, "but *she* is pushing herself. She nearly has the hang of that updraft. We showed her once. She chooses to go back, over and over, trying to best it. What would you have us do, fight her to keep her away?"

I'll take that fight, my dragon thought. She would, too, and we'd get stomped on by these women. They weren't as powerful as us, but they were wily and experienced and sometimes downright vicious. They'd smack us down and call it a lesson.

That lesson would likely hurt something fierce.

Gunduin grinned, always seemingly happy-go-lucky. You couldn't help but like the guy. "She's a fire starter. Training her like the other newly shifted would waste her time."

Micah's hard gaze settled on Gunduin for a moment, and I could practically see the power curling from Micah, heavy and thick. Gunduin picked up the vibe, an obvious challenge, and held the stare for a long moment. Then something flickered in his eyes, and he dropped them.

A hot and uncomfortable feeling unfurled in my middle. Micah turned to Ami, but I was already reacting. I would not tolerate someone browbeating people who were helping me.

"Enough," I barked, and a surge of my power cut through the backyard. Leaves tumbled across the ground, caught up in the force of my will. The pots swung and bumped, and Ami took a step back with widened eyes.

I took a deep breath and laid my hand on Micah's arm.

"Sorry, I know you're trying to do what's best for me, but I'm fine. It's not them, it's my dragon. She's a shithead at the best of times, and her new goal is apparently to master flying in just a few days. It's nearly impossible to control her. If you paired us with new people, we'd get everyone in trouble and probably end up with a bunch of dead kid-dragons. She's not to be trusted."

He shook his head slowly. "At least bring Tamara and Lucille up with you." He looked to Ami. "They'll have a little more care to keep you safe."

"I have no desire to bring strange dragons into the sky with me," Ami said loftily. "I took her up simply because I was curious, and now I find it humorous. We fly, and then we work the plants. There is no cause for alarm."

That was a white lie, since my dragon repeatedly smashing into the side of a mountain and then tumbling nearly to the ground was *some* cause for alarm, but I didn't mention it. Micah was already riled up enough.

This place was what we both needed right now.

I untied my apron and handed it over to Ami. "Thanks, for

both your curiosity and your good humor. I don't much care why you've helped me—I'm grateful for it."

Ami took the apron slowly. Her gaze flicked to Micah and then back. Something sparked in her eyes. A sort of hunger for excitement. For challenge.

"You know…" she said softly. "I happen to have a practice dagger lying around. And a few practice swords. If you think that dragon of yours wants to let out a little rage, I'm sure Claudile and I could spark you up a bit tomorrow. I'm interested to see what a scrappy little dragon who grew up in a hard life can do when pushed."

Something about the look in her eyes and the power curling around her made my heart speed up and excitement drum through me. My dragon pushed closer to the surface, straining to get out, liking what she heard.

A little smile curved Ami's lips. She nodded, almost imperceptibly.

"Waste of time," Claudile grumbled, but I could hear the excitement in her tone, too. The eagerness to get fighting. To draw blood.

Maybe dragons *were* crazy, but fuck it if I didn't want to play.

I couldn't keep the grin from my face as Hannon rose from his chair and met me at the gate.

"Don't bring anyone," Ami called as we left and joined Micah on the lane. "Just you. And your brother."

Micah shook his head a little as we headed back to the village center. "I wonder what her interest is in you. She's known to everyone, but the three of them usually keep to themselves, and Ami only trains and flies beside a select few dragons. Allowing you two in is…unusual." He glanced back, his expression troubled.

I shrugged. "I kinda forced my company on her."

"Tending the plants, yeah." Micah scratched his chin. "That's probably it. She has a higher regard for those who do it well, and she is generally thought to be the best. She's a good person to learn from."

I crinkled my nose, indignation running through me. Regardless of my comparative youth, I was a master, same as them. I'd had to be.

Not like he would have any way of knowing that, I supposed. Before meeting me, he hadn't known what crowded everlass could do. He hadn't realized the significance of me knowing about it, and how even that set me apart from other dragons.

"Any news?" Hannon asked Micah.

"Not yet. They've heard my story, and the other escapees are spreading the same tale in their villages. Word is circulating, and there can be no doubt we're telling the truth. There can be no doubt that the demons pose a problem to all of us, but we're not the authority in this kingdom. To get the kingdom behind us, we need to appeal to the king and queen, and that will take weeks. Their deliberation will take even longer."

"We don't have weeks," I said.

"We don't, no." Micah looked down on me as we neared the tavern. He stopped. "They are discussing two courses of action. The first is to send a representative to the king and queen to tell our story, and Elex has stepped forward. Given the look of him, he's good for the role. The second is to help you. We've been spreading word that we're going to help a fallen dragon kingdom in the clutches of sex-trafficking demons, and all volunteers are welcome. They've been warned that it will be dangerous."

"That warning was probably a highlight for them," Hannon said.

Micah laughed. "For many it was, yes. Vemar has not been quiet about his experiences. He's taking Hadriel's approach to the whole thing and shocking everyone with his directness. When they get over their shock, they listen, and surprise turns to rage."

"What's our timeline?" I asked.

Micah shook his head. "I don't know yet. You have to remember that this is all new information for everyone here. We've only been here a few days, and most can't seem to focus on the name Wyvern. *I* can't. The curse or the magic is making it hard for us to discuss the situation. But we are mobilizing. You will have aid from us as well as the wolves and faeries. They'll turn up."

"Worst case," Hannon said, "we force Govam to take down the magical locks on the portals and go that way."

"If Dolion hasn't gotten rid of the portals entirely. The officers aren't around to make him new creations to send through. Why keep them open?"

"Because he needs a doorway, and that is it," Hannon replied. "Otherwise he'd have to strip all the magic keeping Wyvern separate, and then what good is a curse?"

He was right. I knew he was right.

I nearly turned and went back to the everlass field and Ami's house. I wanted to check on the elixir and then ask if they needed help with anything else. Anything to take my mind off my current situation.

Micah's comforting hand drifted to my shoulder. "It'll be okay," he said softly. Shivers coated my body. "We'll get through this. We'll save your kingdom." He hesitated for a moment. "If you want to come by my house...to get your mind off things, you're welcome. It was left vacant. It's still a little dusty, but it must be nicer than a tavern. I can make you a hot meal, and you can stretch out near the fire."

Heat sparked in his eyes. Warmth soaked into my flesh from where his hand rested on my shoulder and then wormed through my body. My stomach fluttered and my heart started to quicken, making it a little difficult to breathe.

I blinked up at him, confused, shaken by my body's reaction to his proximity and the heat pulsing off him. His power flirted with my dragon, drawing her closer to the surface, making her purr in appreciation.

A moment later, a strange feeling trickled through the bond, a mix of rage and understanding. Nyfain and his dragon sensed our reaction and knew it was to another man—his possessive dragon wanted to squash the threat to his claim.

Alarm replaced the heat, and I stepped back, dislodging the hand on my shoulder.

In another situation, sure, I would have been happy to get to know Micah. He seemed steadfast and loyal, and he clearly had the potential to excite my dragon. But Nyfain had my heart, and so I had zero interest in anyone else. I didn't understand the stomach fluttering or the heat worming through my veins. I didn't get why my body was reacting so differently than my head and heart.

A troubling thought occurred to me. Weren't my head and heart opposed to Nyfain at the beginning, too? I hadn't even wanted to get to know the guy at first. I'd wanted nothing more than to get away! But my body and dragon had kept yanking me toward him.

I blew out a breath. Before I could gently turn Micah down, he murmured, "Think about it," then continued on.

Hannon edged closer. "He's strong and capable."

I furrowed my brow, watching the large dragon's confident strut as he disappeared into the heart of the village. People nodded at him with smiles or bent their heads in respect.

"And?"

"And should you see a fork in the road, romantically speaking, he'd be a good choice."

Anger rose, hot and heavy. I squished it down before I did something I would regret. Hannon could certainly handle violence, but he really only engaged in it to protect his family or friends. It was a tool for him, not a crutch. He didn't reach for it to cover tumultuous emotions like I did. Like the other dragons seemed to. He used words.

I made a disgruntled sound and kicked the dirt for a little release. Unfortunately, I only succeeded in hurting my toe.

"It's just…" I gritted my teeth, hating to even admit to this. "Okay, here's the thing. I'm not interested. I'm not! Only…my stomach flutters, and sometimes I get tingly, and just now there was some heat happening…" I popped out a hip, uncomfortable with the situation, with myself, and also with Micah. My mixed-up feelings scared me. "At first my dragon had a lot to say about the attention he was giving us. She was pissed, and steadfast, and gleeful when Nyfain's dragon rose through the bond, pulsing out power and rage and dominance. But…not anymore, for some reason. She just fucking purred! I don't want Micah, and *she* didn't want Micah, but my body is betraying my mind. I just don't get it. He's not our true mate. He's not Nyfain. I love *Nyfain*, unquestioningly. Unconditionally. He's it for me. He's all I want. So what the fuck is happening with my fucking body, you know?"

"You've been away from Nyfain longer than you were with him. Your love didn't have a chance to really flower. And now you find yourself spending all of this time around another powerful alpha dragon. You were in dangerous situations with Micah, and he did his best to help and protect you. There's a strong trust there. I'm sure your dragon realizes that he could take her on, and it probably confuses her that she wants to rise to the challenge. Dragons seem to really love challenges, yours more than most. And maybe you just want some companionship after this hard road..."

He's very wise, my dragon thought. *He's also correct. Micah's dragon keeps blasting me with this sort of...erotic challenge. I don't want to meet that challenge because of our mate, but...I do want to meet that challenge. I want to rage-fuck. We need a big cock between our thighs or rammed down our throat. He'll do for now.*

Heat pounded through me. I swayed, grabbed by Hannon, and quickly shook him off. I did not need my brother touching me when this feeling was pumping straight to my core.

No, you disloyal cuntcicle, I thought, clenching my teeth, *he will not do for now. We were claimed. We consented to a mate. I will not betray our mate because you're horny and want to answer some sort of weird sex challenge. Nyfain is more than just sex. He's more than a challenge.*

But Micah doesn't need to be more than sex, she thought. *Soak up some of that big-dick energy right now, and when we go back, our mate can kill him for infringing on his claim. His rage will be so incredibly intense. Just think about all that rage when he dominates us and re-stakes his claim?*

She shivered. So did I; I couldn't help it. That did sound like a wild time.

Don't worry, she went on, *after he has re-staked his claim, he'll forget all about it. Other than staying close to make sure no one touches us again. But that'll be hot, too.*

A fierce tingle crawled across my flesh and soaked into my core. That also sounded like a good time, yes. Something about Nyfain being protective and possessive lit a weird fire in me. He would stop any unwelcome advances like the one Micah had just given me. He'd cut out any threats from delusional fuckwits like Jedrek (I still hadn't allowed myself more time to feel guilty about how that had played out). He'd be my incredibly hot, bad-tempered bodyguard, shoving away advances I had never wanted anyway.

He will do that regardless, I told her. *He did that before he claimed me. He's always acted like I was his. Because even though it took me a while to realize it, I always was. And will continue to be. Not to mention the fact that we are not going to set Micah up to die. What is wrong with you?*

When two alphas fight over a claim, one usually dies. It's logic.

I wanted to strangle her. Then I wanted to strangle all memory of my body's stupid reactions to Micah. Then I wanted to stay far, *far* away from him so that it didn't happen again.

Fucking Micah is out of the question. It is not going to happen. Do I make myself clear?

We'll see...

I balled up my fists in anger and let out a shout of frustration. "I wish you were standing beside me so I could punch you in the stupid face!"

I started forward.

"Done arguing with your dragon?" Hannon asked, keeping

pace.

"Only for now, since she is probably going to try to throw her-self at Micah, the fuckface."

We met the others inside the tavern, Hadriel and Leala giving us beaming smiles.

"Ready to train?" Tamara asked me, and Lucille stood from her chair.

"Ah, man, does that mean I have to keep watch over the de-mons?" Hadriel hooked a thumb toward the stairs. "The dragons are very rowdy now that they heard what was done to Micah and them. It's going to be hard to get the demons some food."

"I'll help," Leala said, shifting the whip coiled in her lap.

I grinned and shook my head, then checked on the demons. One of them always stayed in the room in case they were needed, but the others took turns taking walks and getting air. We had an understanding—try to get away, and we would find them and kill them. Stick around and keep a low profile, and they could have their freedom. I hadn't realized the dragons were getting anxious about their presence, although it made sense.

Thankfully, they seemed to take the news in stride, and Leala really was a wonder with that whip.

In the days that followed, I spent more and more time keeping busy with Ami, Claudile, and Gunduin, while the others took a chilled-out break.

There was always a calm before the storm.

CHAPTER 28

NYFAIN

I SAT ON the bed in the tower room, looking out at the bright sunlight, only a few clouds rolling through the sky. My attention was focused inward, though, on my bond with Finley. I'd been checking in more often since feeling her reaction to the other alpha, presumably the same one who'd tried to dominate her when she was in the demon dungeon. I knew what he was doing. I could feel it in her confusion, in her dragon's rising interest.

It was forbidden, what he did. It was also unfair to her, given she didn't understand what was happening and probably didn't even know it was possible.

He was fucking toying with my mate.

Rage coiled in my gut. Desperation to get to her, to protect her and defend my claim, blotted out my reason for a moment. Before I knew it, I was up and pacing, my hands curled into fists.

You told her to leave, my dragon accused me, power pumping through us. *You did this. You put the idea in her head, and now she has found exactly what you told her to—someone who can lay a claim over ours. Her dragon is responding to his magic and power as any dragon would, and it's your fault.*

White-hot rage stole my breath, but I didn't deny it. She *should* replace us. She should find happiness outside of our cursed kingdom. I wanted that for her. I'd given her that opportunity, and when she headed into the mountains rather than coming straight here, I'd figured that fate would be on her horizon. Sure, I could feel her misery, but that didn't change the fact that she was headed for freedom. For a new life. And while she might not like the idea at first, eventually it would grow on her.

But then she'd yanked me back to her, anchoring me so thoroughly to her that I was helpless to pull away. She'd made her choice—*me*—and *insisted* that I honor it.

She was mine. She would always belong to me.

And I knew now that she would come back. She wasn't going to listen to me any more than she'd ever listened to anyone else who'd tried to govern her life. She was a woman who knew her own mind and desires, which was part of the reason I'd been drawn to her in the first place.

I felt guilt about my immense relief. Guilt…and also a surge of incredible rage at the thought of another dragon trying to lay his mark over mine. Of another dragon trying to infringe on my territory.

With sheer determination, I forced myself back down onto the bed and took a deep, steadying breath. A thrill sang through the bond as Finley flew.

I smiled, leaning forward, wishing I could be there with her. Fly with her. There was nothing more thrilling than twisting through the sky and outmaneuvering your peers. My dragon and I had loved flight training, loved being challenged to do things most others couldn't and nailing it. Loved the danger…but also the tranquility of a lazy afternoon flight, soaring with the air currents and letting one's mind wander. While I didn't regret the sacrifice I'd made to protect my people, I did miss my wings.

Adrenaline fueled Finley, and her stomach fluttered. They were trying something they'd been failing at since their first flying session last week. I wondered what it was. Usually it ended in the dragon and human wrestling for control, followed by pain and frustration.

I laughed every time, and my dragon settled in near the bond, purring in delight. I could envision the struggle they were having. Mostly because my dragon and I had been through the same thing—the push to conquer the challenge, the annoyance that it wasn't happening, and the blame pinging between human and dragon. Then the rage, the fights, the wrestle for control and, in the end, victory.

Fuck, those had been good times.

She probably had everyone worried she'd kill herself. And when they told her to stop, she'd just keep on trying until she finally mastered whatever she'd set her mind to. I doubted anyone was crazy enough to push her to her limit. It would take someone who understood her true potential to do that—someone who perceived her strength and would turn a blind eye when she faced death over and over.

Pain rolled through the bond, then more frustration. She'd failed again. That would really burn her.

I saw movement through the trees.

My smile dripped away as I caught sight of forms stepping out of the trees. Black clothing. Graceful movements. They could only be the demons. That they were here in daylight meant they were high in power.

Dolion had brought reinforcements. He clearly knew Finley had escaped. Once he realized she wasn't here, he'd lock this place down tight. Then he'd probably start killing my people out of spite.

It was time to choose a path. Either I trusted Finley to come back and help us, or I pushed the issue and traded myself for the kingdom's safety.

I wondered if holding out for her was even an option. I'd seen Dolion in a rage. He couldn't kill me or break me, but he could do both to the people in my kingdom. He'd wiped out the whole court of dragons in a rage.

"Sir." Urien, my valet, poked his head through the door opening. "Sir, the demons have come. They have the castle surrounded."

"Get everyone inside and out of sight. Keep them to their rooms, if you can."

"Yes, sir." He paused. "Sir, I know you have plans, but…"

Although the staff knew Finley had escaped from the dungeon, I hadn't shared anything else with them. They didn't know she intended to come back. What Urien did know was that I intended to make a deal with Dolion. He probably thought the time had come.

Maybe it had.

"I've heard this through the staff quarters," he said, "and within the halls—we hope to fight, sir."

I tilted my head. "What's that?"

"We hope to fight. Hadriel—the strange little butler stand-in—made it clear that he and Leala would be back with Finley. We wish to wait for them, and to fight."

I thought about clearing the air, but another part of me wanted to give my people a way out. They weren't warriors. None of them were in a position to fight off a demon horde. They had courage, but I didn't want them to die for nothing. If the worst-case scenario came and I'd need to make the ultimate sacrifice, I didn't want a lot of people to lose their lives beforehand.

"They've moved on," I told him, not actually believing it. "If they had wanted to come back, they would be here now."

"Well, sir," he said, "Hadriel fancied himself a strategist. He was the best chess player in the castle, even before...all of this. And it is widely held that Finley wouldn't leave us forever. They think she'll be back, and they wish to wait."

Even though my father had put them through hell they didn't want to see me sacrifice myself. They wanted to fight with me, *for* me.

I couldn't help my heart swelling at their continued allegiance, after all these years of torture. My people didn't deserve this.

I watched through the window as the demons advanced. What I wouldn't give for my wings and my court. What I wouldn't give to take Dolion and his kingdom on. To teach them what it meant to stand against dragons.

"I'll stay to my room this evening and let Dolion...wander, as he does. Send dinner."

"Yes, sir."

I watched for a while longer, rage burning brightly. My dragon did the equivalent of pacing within me, desperate to fight, to get out of his skin cage.

I locked the tower room behind me and took the stairs down.

"Sir." Jessab, the cook, waited on the third-floor landing. He made a fist. "She will be back soon, sir. Her sister says so. We will fight." He shook his fist.

I furrowed my brow at him, wondering when he might've spoken to her sister.

Down the next stairs I went, only to find more servants shaking their fists on the next landing. Anger lit their eyes.

"I'll fight."

"We'll fight."

"Wait for her, and we'll fight."

"I will fight." Eliza, the plump and lovely seamstress, shook her fist. Her face turned red, and spittle flew from her mouth. "I will kill!"

Great goddess, my dragon thought. *I didn't know she had it in her.*

I spied a group of people standing in a cluster, nodding and fisting their hands.

"The demons are coming. Get to your rooms," I barked as I passed by, power swirling around me.

They straightened, one and all, looking back with wide eyes before scattering through the hall. A girl was left on her own with a spattering of freckles across her fair features. At fourteen, she was all knees and elbows, thinner than she probably should be, but her face wore a hard, determined expression.

"Sable?" I asked, taken aback. It was Finley's sister. Here, in the castle, as the demons advanced on us. "Sable, damn it!"

I lurched forward and grabbed her, running her up the stairs and to the tower before she could squawk an objection. I fumbled with the key, thrust open the door, and quickly dropped her to the bed. I shut the door behind me, my heart racing and sweat coating my brow.

"Sable, what are you doing here?" I demanded.

She screwed up her face and crawled off the bed, anger showing clearly in her movements. "No you don't! You are not going to lock me in the tower like you did my sister. I heard the whole story. Even if I were your age, you would *not* be my type. I expect a little rationality from my men."

I opened and closed my mouth for a moment, blindsided, then shook my head to clear it.

"Sable, the demons have come. It isn't safe for you here. Why aren't you with your family in safety?"

As soon as Finley escaped, I'd relocated her family. Dolion would want to take his rage out on someone, and her blood would likely be his first choice. I didn't want to give him that opportunity.

She didn't answer, defiant to the last. She reminded me of her sister.

"We're going to have to keep you locked in this tower," I said, "until we can get you out of here."

"As if anywhere in this kingdom would be safe." She stomped up to me. "Everyone knows what you're planning to do. Make a deal, right? In case it hasn't crossed your mind, that didn't go so great for your father or the kingdom, did it? Nyfain—sir—I know my sister. And while she can make strange decisions, she always comes through. My brother's the same way. Hannon would not have left if he didn't think he was coming back. They *will* be back. I am absolutely sure of this. I feel it in my bones in that way I do. If you leave before then, she will just try to follow you."

"You're right," I said, because I knew she was. "Except we are out of time. If I don't do something now, there won't be a kingdom to come back to."

She grabbed my forearm. "Please. Stall. Give her a chance."

I let out a breath and pulled my arm away. "I'm going to have to lock you in this room until we can safely get you out of the castle."

"But—"

I closed the door tightly and locked it behind me. I just hoped Dolion didn't try to go in.

Finley is common, my dragon thought. *She is from poor stock. She is a nobody. And yet, in such a short time, she is the hope of the kingdom. We need to buy her time to get back to us. And we need to feed her thoughts to hurry her along.*

Yes we did. The problem was that I wasn't so sure how much time Dolion would give us to wait for aid. My guess was *not much.*

CHAPTER 29

FINLEY

MY DRAGON HIT the ground running, and I shifted before she'd taken three full steps. I raced to the tree where I'd left my clothes and quickly began throwing them on.

"Why are you in such a hurry?" Claudile said with a smirk as she caught up.

"Something's happening. He's out of time." Tears fogged my eyes, and desperation clawed at my throat. I hated that we were so far away from him. A couple of days by boat, at least. "If we don't get back to the kingdom soon, he's going to do something stupid, I just know it."

"What did you say, girl?" A hand grabbed my arm and swung me back.

Ami stared into my eyes, searching.

"Who is going to do something stupid?" Claudile asked, her smile fading.

I yanked my hand out of Ami's grasp. "The prince of Wyvern. My mate." I gathered up the sword but didn't bother strapping it on. There would be no practice today. "Thanks for…the distraction. It's time that I fight for my home now."

I turned and started jogging, making it to the everlass field in no time.

"Wait." Ami and Claudile jogged up behind me. Gunduin wasn't here today. "Wait." Ami caught me when I was almost to Hannon. "How can you be sure?"

"Because I know him. Because I *feel* it. He will think it is his duty to sacrifice himself for the bloody kingdom, because he's a fucking idiot. Hannon, come on!"

Hannon looked up from his chair and the wooden spoon he'd been whittling. He stood immediately, dropping the spoon to the side.

"What's wrong?" He looked me over, probably thinking I'd pitched out of the sky or finally fallen off the mountain face.

"Nyfain. Something is happening. He's getting that impatient...desperate...resigned feeling. Time is up. We need to get to him."

"Do you think the demon king has reached him?" Hannon asked.

"If you just wait a little longer, there will be a host to join you," Ami said, shadowing me.

"I don't have a little longer. It'll take a couple days just to get to him, maybe more." I started to jog, Hannon at my side. To Hannon, I said, "Probably, right? It's been a couple weeks. I'm surprised he didn't get there before now."

"Which means it took him a while to figure out we were gone, or he was organizing a large force."

"We need to ask Govam. He seems pretty knowledgeable about how the demons operate. I would really like to say it was the former, but my bad luck tells me it is probably the latter."

The tavern common room was empty. I didn't waste time looking for everyone, not yet.

At the top of the stairs, I turned right toward the end of the corridor and knocked on Govam's door. Denski answered, his clothes rumpled but his eyes looking fresh and alert. When he saw me, he immediately pushed the door wider, stepping out of the way.

Govam stood from a chair in the corner, lowering the book in his hand. He took one look at me and stood. "Dolion has moved on the kingdom."

I quickly explained what I was feeling and what it probably meant.

Govam nodded, laying the book on a small chest. "He's taken some time to plan his next move. You're an extreme liability for him, and he's in damage-control mode. His first move is to determine whether you are with the golden prince, working on breaking the curse. Since you are not, he will want to cripple your kingdom forever. He would've done so already if not for the gold and the shifters he's been kidnapping. Neither of those conditions will stop him now. He obviously can't risk taking more shifters for fear someone from the council will ask to inspect his dungeons, and some of Wyvern's gold has proven inaccessible to him. It's magically protected, and none of his attempts to access it have worked. With this new pressure, he'll give up. He's out of time. He can't let the council discover what he's done to your kingdom. It'll make them question his other dealings, and those have been less than savory."

My blood pumped hot and cold, fear and anger churning together.

"So basically, we need to hurry our asses," I surmised.

"If you want to save your kingdom, yes. Hopefully your golden dragon can stand in Dolion's way long enough to give you a chance." He gave me a long look, then added, "He is the most ruthless, stubborn dragon I've ever seen, and given my past position, that's saying something. He is your greatest hope of stalling long enough to reach them in time. Your only hope."

I pointed at him. "Don't think I didn't notice the *you* and *your* instead of *we* and *our*."

"That curse is your fight. It will be *our* fight once it is broken."

"Fine." I turned. "Get ready to leave. We'll waste no time."

I jogged back down the stairs with Hannon in my wake, needing to find the others. Hadriel and Leala stood out back, watching Tamara and Lucille spar. He noticed me immediately, turning my way.

"What's happened?" he asked.

I quickly explained what I was feeling from Nyfain, along with what Govam had told me.

Hadriel swore but then seemed to gather himself. "It's fine. This is fine. Let's not go to pieces. We expected this."

"We're just not incredibly ready for it," Leala said.

"Leala, my darling, you are not fucking helping."

She smiled sweetly at him. "Suck a toe."

"We're headed back to the castle. I probably will if we can't sort this out. And I hate feet."

I glanced at Hannon. "I'll round up the others and find Micah. You get our things ready."

He nodded and jogged into the tavern.

"There's a meeting the next village over," Tamara said, dropping their wooden practice swords to the side. "Micah will be there. It won't take us long to fly."

Hadriel stared at me for a moment. "I cannot believe I am asking this, but...can you take me in your mouth?"

"Bad idea." Tamara shook her head. "She'd accidentally clench and bite you in half."

"Well then...would one of you..."

Tamara shook her head again. "Same goes for us. None of us have that kind of control."

"The master carried Finley a bunch of times," he said.

"The prince is in a league of his own, Hadriel, you know that," she replied.

"You can round up the others," I told him, "while we go get Micah."

"Balls," Hadriel said.

"I'll keep them from picking on you," Leala told him, her face screwing up in determination.

"As if that's fucking possible," he grumbled.

I followed Tamara and Lucille, jogging quickly out of the village and into the woods. When we reached a clearing, we quickly stripped. Lucille shifted first and took to the sky, her wheat-colored scales shining in the late-morning sun. Tamara shifted next, and the two of them hovered in the sky, waiting for me.

My dragon took over, the shift making me feel, for a moment, like my bones were being broken and my skin peeled off. The others had told me it would get easier the more I did it. The white-hot pain from the two tears that had opened down my back—lines of goldish-red scales taking the place of skin—had already faded.

My dragon rose a little haphazardly, accidentally slipping forward and slicing the side of Tamara with a claw on one of our wings.

Shit, sorry! I tried to call before I remembered I didn't have access to our mouth, and even if I had, we couldn't speak.

They know we're learning. It's fine. We'll blame the teacher.

I didn't bother responding as we flew after them, inexperienced and still fairly shit at flying, but requiring very little effort to keep up.

The next village was super close, and we'd started jogging into it before my mind caught up to the fact that we had no clothes, something I pointed out with a red face.

"We're shifters—get used to it," Lucille said as she slowed near the periphery of the village. "Besides, you're super hot. You have nothing to worry about."

"Except maybe my enormous lady beard," I murmured, taking the lead and running along the paths until I found my way into the village center. Once there, we asked around until we found the location of the little meeting house where the elders were apparently chatting about who was going to do what. I barged in, zero regard for decorum, and interrupted a woman with more wrinkles than face.

"Sorry for the interruption," I said, not at all sorry. I looked around the circle of people. Micah stepped forward from the side, as did Vemar and a few others from the dungeon. Some of them had left our group to spread word to other villages, so presumably they had messages to convey.

Hopefully it wasn't bad news.

"Guys, it's time," I said quickly, making a circle in the air with my finger. "Something's happening and I have to go. You are welcome to come or stay, but I'm leaving."

"Now, wait a minute, young lady," said a man with a brown-spotted, balding head and wispy white hair. "We understand your haste, but we have much to organize—"

"I'm sorry, truly," I said, still not selling it. "But I'm fairly certain the demon king has stormed my kingdom and intends to devastate it. We have precious little time. I need to get back and help. *Now*. I cannot wait for you to continue organizing. I'll be taking my people and leaving."

"I'm with you." Vemar stepped forward. "I have a host ready to leave at a moment's notice. We're gonna fry that fucker alive. The wolves should be waiting in the town near the docks by now, and the faeries will be joining them soon. We were never meant to stay in the villages longer than this. We should have enough of a force to band with your kingdom. And if we don't...fuck it, we all gotta die sometime. This fight will be worth it." He winked and smiled at me. "I'm ready for a little vengeance."

"Let me...talk to her." Micah put his arms out as though to shepherd me. "Let me just talk to her for a moment, please. I'm sure we can reach an understanding."

"I'm sorry, Micah"—*goddess, please help me actually sound sorry*—"but there's no need to shepherd me outside. When I step out there next, it'll be to finish preparing to leave."

"But we need more time," one of the circle called out in a voice shaky with age. "We don't have all the plans in motion."

Micah glanced at the circle as he stepped forward again, trying to block my way. "I realize that. Let me talk to her."

My fear of a delay boiled over, turning quickly to anger. Power throbbed through me, and I released a surge of it, knocking Micah away without touching him. I stepped close to the circle. When I spoke, my voice was low and rough, power still throbbing around me. "I will leave tomorrow at dawn. That's the most I can compromise. You will either join me or you will stay here. As far as the wolf king and queen go—by the time they make a decision, we'll either be victorious or dead. No hard feelings if you choose to stand down."

The room was silent as I left, all except for Vemar's low chuckling.

I stormed out of the room, but Micah met me outside before I made it too far.

"Finley, please, wait." I stopped, and he hurried around me. "Let me talk to them. I'm sure I can speed them up."

"I just talked to them, Micah. We leave tomorrow. You're coming or you're not—it's that simple."

"People need a chance to pack and say goodbye to their families. You can at least allow them that. We'll get to the docks faster, since we're all flying."

"But Hannon and the others can't fly."

He gave me a knowing smile. "It is going to test your mediocre butler's nerves, and certainly the demons' gumption, but we have a workaround. There's something we use to carry the little ones." He gripped my upper arms, his heat spreading across my flesh and his power flirting erotically with mine. His gaze skimmed Nyfain's mark, a challenge and desire flashing in his eyes. "I promise I will gather a big enough force to make a real difference. Give me a little more time to put it all together."

He was issuing me a command. He was trying to dominate me.

Only one man was allowed that privilege, however. Only one man had earned it.

I stepped back, and his hands fell away. I wasn't good at following orders, and it was better that he learned that now rather than in the heat of battle when it really mattered.

"Tomorrow at dawn. Be there...or don't. Time is up."

With that, I turned and strode away, Tamara and Lucille just behind.

"You handled that perfectly," Tamara said softly. "I expected you—*everyone* probably expected you to fall in line."

"Fall in line with whom?"

"With Micah, for one. He is the most powerful dragon in this collection of villages. He's their uncrowned leader and holds great sway with their elders. He's been setting this up as *his* mission, and you just walked in and showed them all who is really the boss. You shoved him to the side with a will stronger than anyone has probably ever seen. The queen didn't even have a will that strong, and she was regarded as the mightiest female in our kingdom."

"Why didn't I know any of this?" I asked.

"About him? Because you didn't ask, and we didn't think it was relevant," Tamara said.

"Because you don't care." Lucille laughed. "You didn't answer to the rulers in the demon kingdom, and it sounds like you gave the golden prince hell on a regular basis... Why would you care about the ruling setup of these villages?"

She had a point.

I jogged into the wood and shifted. Arrangements needed to be made, and then I wanted to take some time to try to communicate with Nyfain through the bond.

I needed him to know we were coming.

I needed him to do everything in his power to stall Dolion's advance.

CHAPTER 30

FINLEY

O UR WINGS FELT like lead weights as we pumped them
through the crisp air. The sun was high in the sky; it was
probably noon or a little past. The sea yawned before us, the
glittering waves moving into the busy harbor.

Two dragons flew to either side of me, and another three doz-
en flew behind us. Apparently the turnout would've been higher if
there had been more time, but this was more than I'd hoped for.
Even without the wolves, this many fire breathers would make a
serious dent in the enemy host.

We just had to get there in time.

It had only taken us half a day to fly at this breakneck speed.
The dragons who had spent many long years in the dungeons
were exhausted, I could tell. Their heads drooped and their
tongues lolled out of their mouths. My dragon was tired too, for
that matter. She'd been setting a pace that she couldn't hope to
continue for much longer. But just a little farther, and we'd make
it to the boat.

"No, you bastard!" Hadriel hollered, his voice hoarse from all the yelling. He hung from a sling around Vemar's neck. Despite his fatigue, Vemar was doing his best to dip and tilt and swing Hadriel around, much to Hadriel's continued dismay. It turned out my mediocre butler wasn't terribly fond of heights. Not while manically swinging through the air below a slightly mad dragon, at any rate. "Just fly normal for one fucking second!"

Micah, beside me, tilted his wings down and looked over. He'd basically been my dragon's flight instructor all day, subtly showing us various tactics for not dying as we flew out of the mountains and down to sea level.

My dragon matched his movements, and we descended slowly, gliding to save a little energy.

Rage blistered through the bond, followed by intense pain. My stomach pinched, and I wished I knew if I should distract Nyfain with pleasure, as he'd done for me countless times, or leave him to push through it. So far I'd opted for leaving him be, mostly because we'd spent all day in the air, but also because I had a feeling he was in a battle of wills with Dolion. He would want his mind to remain clear.

Hurry, I thought for the millionth time.

The dragon has not thought goodbye yet, she told me as we continued to descend, waiting for somewhere to land. *He's full of rage and brimstone. The fight is not out of him.*

Nyfain's dragon was always the last to give in, though. He held on to hope when all was lost. He'd hold on much longer than Nyfain the man. Maybe that would be our saving grace.

As we steadily neared the ground, Micah looked over, tilting his wings just so. My dragon didn't take the hint.

You're going to hit too hard, I thought, tensing.

Her wings did tilt then, but too much, catching the wind and dramatically slowing us down. She overcorrected, exhausted, and we dove, the ground swinging up in a rush now. She tilted her wings again, catching air, then folded them up.

We dropped from the sky like a stone.

Oh shi-it! I thought-yelled.

We hit with a solid thud and then bounced forward, landing on our chest and head.

Give me back control, I thought. *I'm more skilled at falling than you are!*

Thankfully she relented, magic blossoming around us until my human arms and limbs were flung around, and my body rolled along weeds and dirt.

I tucked and spun, gaining control before stopping the tumble. As I slid to a stop, strong hands found me and pulled me up. A thick arm bent around my lower back, keeping me upright.

"Are you okay?" Micah's worried face swam into sight.

"Nice spill, Strange Lady," Vemar called, laughing. "I've done something similar a time or two."

"I've got her." Hannon braced one hand on Micah's shoulder and pulled me away with the other. "Can you stand on your own, Finley?"

I rubbed my eyes and sagged but stayed standing. "Yeah. I'm exhausted, though."

"Me too." Vemar walked closer, a little wobble in his step.

"You wouldn't be so exhausted if you'd flown straight and not tried to scare the piss out of me," said Hadriel, staggering behind him.

Vemar laughed. "Worth it. You sure can scream, little man."

"Oh, don't worry, no offense taken, you giant wankstain," Hadriel muttered.

Vemar turned back slowly, a mad gleam in his eyes.

Hadriel scowled at him. "Finley, I'll be down by the docks asking after the faeries and wolves. Keep that crazy fucker on a leash, would you?"

Tamara and Lucille walked over with grins as they watched Hadriel stagger toward the docks.

"He should've known better than to accept a ride from Vemar," Tamara said, bending over and bracing her hands on her knees.

Leala joined us, her hair windswept and stars in her eyes. "I think he figured they had some sort of rapport, and a dragon he knew was better than one he didn't."

"We *do* have a rapport." Vemar rubbed a hand down his face. "One I probably appreciate more than he does. He's fun to taunt."

"We've always thought so," Lucille replied.

"Okay." I straightened up and nodded at Micah. "Thanks for helping us get here."

"Of course," he replied. "I have to warn you again, though, this port doesn't typically like to deal with dragons. It might be harder than you expect to get a vessel."

He'd told me that yesterday, while we were finishing our preparations. He'd relented on leaving at dawn but attempted to convince me to fly to the larger, busier port to the south, which would be easier for dragons to use. It would have taken us twice as long to get there, though, and time was one thing we didn't have.

"We'll make it work." I took a slip from Leala and pulled it over my head. The non-fliers had been in charge of the clothes. We were keeping them simple, however, in case we had to fly again.

I turned and put a hand to Hannon's arm so that he would

step out of the way. The demons waited in a tense cluster, a few of them darting furtive looks at the dragons standing very close. It was one thing to allow the demons to wander a bit while in the mountains surrounded by nothing but dragons, but here, where there were plenty of escape routes, they were being watched closely. I was sure that was Micah's doing, and it was a good call.

"Govam, with me," I called, pushing aside my worry for Nyfain and refocusing on the challenges of the moment. Govam stepped away from the others without changing expression, stopping by my side expectantly. "Let's go see what we're up against."

"Our boat is still here if needed," he said as we made it out of the tall grass and weeds and onto a path that led down to the docks. It would merge with a path lined with the stalls and stands of merchants selling their goods.

"I'd rather not use a thing only you can operate," I told him, watching Hadriel at one of the stalls nearest the village, up the slow rise. My stomach fluttered. Had the wolves returned as promised? And the faeries? "What are the chances that Dolion has closed down the portals?"

Govam took a deep breath and paused for a moment, probably thinking it through. "Unlikely. If he applies the *obice*, he won't have to worry about anyone but my kind breaking in. He'll post powerful demons to guard them in case there is such a breach. With this collection of dragons, we'd be able to get through them, but we might suffer losses, and it would certainly take more time. It would be best to avoid it if possible."

I remembered to breathe as we made our way to the docks. My stomach was in knots. We could do without the wolves if we had to. We could even do without Calia if absolutely necessary.

But each absence would stack the odds further in Dolion's favor.

"How is this going to go down for you?" I asked, eyeing the various vessels bobbing in the sea. "We're about to confront your people. Your king."

Govam nodded as Hadriel glanced back at us. He turned again, staring at the vessels lining the water before shifting to look out at the village. Oh goddess, I hoped that was good news. Even just one of the two would greatly help our cause.

"Do you plan to fight with us?" I asked.

"There are a great many of Dolion's supporters whom I would absolutely help you kill. But there are just as many who are simply trying to survive. They are the ones I would like to call on to help turn this tide."

Regardless, the people in our kingdom wouldn't know he was on our side. Which meant he'd have to be kept away from the actual fighting. He had knowledge that Nyfain could surely use. I didn't want to risk him accidentally being killed, not to mention I still didn't totally trust him. Only a fool would.

Hadriel hurried back down the path, scanning the docks again.

"Weston is here with a host of wolves…" He glanced around. "About this size. Good wolves, too. Strong and fast." He smiled, his chest puffing out. "It's a good turnout. They have a boat or ship or whatever docked, ready to take them, but it's not huge. We'll need to get our own."

An incredible wave of relief washed through me. Worst case, we went through the portals. We'd have the numbers to clear the way.

"Good news, Hadriel—"

"Wait. Finley."

I glanced over my shoulder, surprised to see Gunduin jogging down the docks behind us.

"Who is that guy?" Hadriel murmured.

"I didn't know you'd come," I told Gunduin. "I didn't see you with the others from Micah's village."

Gunduin's smile was sly. "You were too busy leading, I think. We fell to the back in case there were any stragglers."

"We? Are Ami and Claudile here?" I asked. I would've thought they'd be happy to see the back of me.

"Of course! They wouldn't miss a fight like this. Come, Finley. As I understand it, we don't have any time to lose. I will be helping you procure a craft. It was felt that dragons should pay for the vessel, not..." He gave Govam some side-eye.

Govam took the cue and stepped back.

I didn't care who was paying. Time was wasting. "Fine. Let's go. I hear they don't like dealing with dragons. Maybe Hadriel will need to do the talking."

"We should've probably asked Weston for help," Hadriel said as I slowed in approaching a ruddy-faced man with red cheeks and a bulbous, pockmarked nose. Wispy gray hair flew out from under his cap. His blue eyes narrowed when he saw me looking, and then his brows dipped when he caught sight of Gunduin.

"How do they know you're even a dragon?" I asked, grimacing as another shock of pain roiled through me from Nyfain. He was still fighting, whatever he was doing. He was enduring Dolion's treatment.

Not for long, I don't think, my dragon thought. *Something is worrying the dragon. Hurry!*

I nodded, putting a little pep in my step.

"It's the manic look in your eyes," Hadriel responded. "You all have it."

"We are typically larger in stature than other shifters," Gunduin said. "More menacing. And more competent on the battlefield."

"Arrogant, I think you meant to say. More arrogant," Hadriel intoned.

Gunduin laughed. "Possibly so, yes. Or maybe it is because we are the favorite choice of their women…"

"Enough," I said quietly, stopping in front of another couple of ruddy-faced men with a little less weight around their middles. One leaned his large, grizzled hand against a thick wooden pole keeping the docks in place. He didn't bat an eye at us, unlike the two men beside him. I knew it wasn't because he liked the look of us any more than they did, however. His bearing gave off a *fuck off, or I'll make an example of you* vibe, backed by confidence and hard-earned experience. The body language of the others suggested they looked up to him. Which meant he probably had the best boat and most money of any of them.

"Sir, we'd like to hire a boat," I said.

The man glanced at each of us in turn, settling on Hadriel for a moment. "What are you doing with a bunch of dragons?"

"Hating my life, mostly. Constantly looking over my shoulder…"

The man grunted out a laugh, and the other two chuckled.

"Sir, please, this is urgent," I said, threading power into my voice.

He slowly turned back to me, his eyes narrowing. He pulled his hand off the pole and crossed his arms over his chest like the others.

"Are you trying to magic me, dragon?" he asked. The other

two grumbled their outrage, moving their hands to their hips.

He said *magic* as if it had a couple additional consonants tacked on the end. Was he looking for a challenge or something?

I ignored it. "Can you take us? We can pay."

"Yeah? Well, turns out I don't need a dragon's money, so you can bluster and blow as much as you want—it makes no difference to me. You'll get no ships here, dragon. Fly, if you're so inclined. Or swim."

The two guys beside him snickered.

"What's the problem here?" Weston's heavy boots thunked against the wood as he made his way closer, two hard-eyed guys behind him. I hadn't seen them before, but they bristled with muscle and might. These fuckers would be a handful in a fight.

The captain clearly came to the same conclusion, taking a step back and suddenly not sure what to do with his hands. The other men looked like they were ready to haul ass to get out of the area. Hadriel preened as if they were his own personal bodyguards.

"We don't take dragons," the captain said. "No self-respecting wolf would do their bidding. Not in this port."

Weston tilted his head. "No? And why is that?" he growled. "They are paying customers. Is it not your job to do the bidding of your paying customers?"

The captain's eyes narrowed, and his lip curled. "You must not be from around here. What are you, a mountain wolf? Need them to take care of you, do you? Well, we don't hold with dragons around these parts. We don't need their kind. Take your business to the Anglian port. I hear they'll hire out to anyone."

Weston bristled, staring hard at the man. "Finley, I think he needs a lesson in compromise."

The small hairs on the back of my neck stood up.

"Dragon magic don't bother me," the man said hastily, visibly uncomfortable in Weston's cross hairs. Dragon magic might not trouble him, but Weston's certainly did.

"Maybe you just haven't experienced *this* dragon's magic," Weston said softly, the words rumbling through him.

"You cannot touch him, Finley, or you will be imprisoned," Gunduin said quickly. "You must threaten him with power and menace alone."

I furrowed my brow and looked his way. "Are you all kidding? That's what you think dragon magic is, blowing and blustering to get what you want?"

"It has worked very well for the master for a very long time," Hadriel murmured. "Except on you, but you're a headcase. That's why you don't understand."

"Hell, I'll take ya," someone down at the way said, and then spat into the ocean. "Any dragon who's got a team of wolves and a demon hanging around must have a good story."

We all turned to look his way, and Weston gave the newcomer the full brunt of his intensity. He was wiry, dressed in threadbare clothes hanging off his frame.

The guy waved the alpha away, which was pretty brave, considering his scrawny stature. "No need for any of that. I ain't looking for trouble. You need a boat? I got a ship. You need two ships? I got a buddy. It's yours for a price."

"And what price would that be?" Gunduin asked.

The man spat again and licked his chapped lip where a bulge made it protrude. He looked us all over. "More than some, cheaper than others."

"We have three dozen dragons and a few odds and ends," I said, walking his way.

"A few odds and ends, huh?" He looked up the way, spying our people and probably the demons. "You're gonna need my buddy, I reckon, and you are gonna need to personally ensure those demons mind their manners. I don't have no cause for fearin' dragons, but demons are another story. They turn pirate more often than not."

"We'll ensure these demons aren't a threat. Moreover, we'll kill any others we see on the sea," I replied.

He pushed up the lip of his cap and scratched his messy hair. "I should tell ya, that's illegal."

"Only if you get caught. I've always heard that boats sink after they're burned to a crisp…"

He tilted his head. "That's about the way of it. They had a bonfire here the other night with a demon boat that was tied up. Probably not right, but I don't blame them."

Well, there went Govam's offer.

"Can we leave soon, sir?" I asked. "Within a couple hours?"

"Where ya headed?"

"Wyvern. You've probably never heard of it, but—"

His eyes lit up. "Well, now. That *is* interesting. It's on the maps, and the land is there, but some force repels anyone from entering. A few that I know have tried. Why do you want to go there?"

"Because we know a way in."

He spat before licking at his lip. "For the right price, I'll take you."

Gunduin put his hand on my arm, and I knew he was thinking what I was—the captain would accept a lower price now than five minutes ago. Curiosity would ensure it.

"I'll take care of this," Gunduin said softly. "You get everyone ready."

"Why is he paying?" Hadriel asked quietly as we made our way to the others.

"I honestly don't know, but I don't intend to look a horse in the mouth. Did you hear anything about the faeries?"

"Gift horse, love. Don't look a gift horse in the mouth. You can look—Never mind. The faeries haven't shown up yet. Weston has been here for a few days, and there's been no sign of them."

My stomach churned as waves of pain rolled through the bond. I held Nyfain tightly within me, feeding him the warmth of my love and support, feeding him my assurance that we'd make it through this. I was coming.

"We can't wait anymore. Govam can get us through the portals. We'll have to fight our way in. With Weston's help, we can do it. I know we can."

When I reached Micah and Hannon, Hannon's face showing a small scowl, I opened my mouth to deliver the news. But then someone gasped, and everyone on the docks turned to look out at the sea. Looking with them, unable to help it, I felt pure joy well up through me.

A lovely boat with fresh paint and clean sails was slowly making its way into the harbor. Painted on the white wood of the bow was the royal symbol for Narva.

Calia had arrived just in time.

CHAPTER 31

NYFAIN

D OLION SPOKE THROUGH his teeth. "Where is she?"

I gritted my teeth against his hot, stinging magic slicing through me. The demon king had been at this for a little over two days, trying to force information out of me or maybe just abuse me for fun. I didn't show any sign of its effects. I would endure the pain forever if I had to, waiting for Finley.

Except this time, he had me by the balls.

His demons had found Finley's father and brother. Now Dolion was looking for Sable so that he could torture them all together while I watched. He thought that would spur my cooperation.

He was right.

We stood on the grounds, the moon showering us in its glow. My people watched from the windows of the castle, peering down at the grisly scene.

Demons held Finley's father and youngest brother between them, knives at their throats, shallow wounds already gouged into their flesh. One of them shook Dash, and my blood curdled to watch it. Dash didn't cry, though, just stared straight ahead stoically, refusing to fall to pieces.

"Please don't hurt them," their father wailed, reaching for his son. "Don't hurt them! They are innocent."

The whole kingdom was innocent. That wouldn't save them.

Dolion flicked his hand, and one of the demons bashed Finley's dad in the head.

The older man grunted and his knees buckled, dropping him down to the ground. The same guard kicked him in the stomach, rolled him over, and then kicked him once more to stop his struggling.

My chest squeezed. Tears leaked out of Dash's eyes.

"Where is she?" Dolion asked again.

After I'd snuck Sable out of the castle, I'd stashed her in Finley's favorite everlass field, near the birch. It was all I could think to do. The demons had focused their attention on the villages, and they weren't watching that part of the wood closely. I'd left her with food and water and a means to keep warm, but that wouldn't last her forever.

After Dolion gruesomely killed Finley's family, he'd start on the rest of the kingdom. His patience, in as much as he'd ever had any, had run out.

Dolion's power speared through me again, making it feel like my head was being cleaved in two. That I could resist. The pain was nothing. It was the knife at Dash's throat that loosened my lips. The drop of blood running down his skin.

I gritted my teeth for a moment as my dragon crouched within me. It was time for him to say goodbye to Finley's dragon, and he knew it. I couldn't wait anymore. Not if it would spare her family and our people.

"She's hidden," I finally said, and Dash looked up at me like I'd betrayed him. Like he would've happily gone to the beyond rather than give up his sister's whereabouts. "Let them go."

A wicked smile crept up Dolion's blue face. "Let them go? Why would I want to do that? No, I think I will still kill them slowly unless you tell me where the girl is. If you do that, I will do them the mercy of killing them swiftly."

I didn't believe him for a moment.

"Spare their lives, and I'll make a deal with you," I ground out.

"A deal? What do you have to offer? You are a prince of ruin. Conquered. I've taken all I want from this place. You have no other dragons left. No powerful shifters. Unless you can unlock the magic surrounding that gold, nothing you have could tempt me."

The gold.

That was the reason I'd been able to stall for the last couple of days. Dolion had taken everything he could from the gold reserves, but some sort of magic protected the rest from his greedy hands. Mine too—he'd forced me down to the mines to see if I could unseal it.

I'd refused to try, of course, despite his attempts to beat and maim and torture me into submission.

As if that would work. Without the suppression, something he didn't think to reapply for some reason, I had access to all of my magic. Even with the curse to help him control me, he wasn't powerful enough to force my compliance.

But then Dash had tried to sneak out of hiding to find his sister, his dad running after him to haul him back, and they'd been found by the demons. So I'd tried to free up the gold and failed. Dolion was giving up on it, which meant he was ready to start his *fuck you* tour of the kingdom, starting with Finley's family.

We'd run out of time.

"You can have me," I said in a growl. "Me for them."

Dolion's eyes sparked with interest.

CHAPTER 32
FINLEY

HEART IN MY throat, I stood in the wood just outside my kingdom, a sheet of leathery air cutting me off from what lay inside. The ships that had brought us to this point—large vessels with daring and curious captains—were anchored just off a sandy beach about three hundred yards away. The rowboats had likely finished shuttling the rest of the first wave to shore by now. The Wyverners and the most powerful wolves had been transported first. The rest of the dragons and wolves would arrive shortly. We'd been hurrying to catch up to the faeries, who'd reached the sandy shores ahead of us. Their ship was sleek and swift, always ahead of us.

Thank the goddess, because they'd clearly needed plenty of time to do their part.

Ten of them spanned out in a lazy arc with Calia at their head, each touching the shoulder of the one slightly ahead of him or her, until the last in line, whose hands rested on Calia's shoulders. Her sister stood beside her, head bowed, eyes closed, and a man with a pleasing face stood on her other side in the same position. They hadn't brought warriors, after all, just those who would boost Calia's magic. The warriors were preparing for something bigger, she'd said. They were preparing to mount a larger attack on the demons, and it seemed like she hoped to ally with our kingdom to do it. We had Govam, after all, and the ruthlessness to kill him if he got out of line. With his knowledge and our combined strength, we stood a chance at doing what no one else had yet accomplished.

Calia stood with her hands raised and eyes shut, palms facing the leather wall of demon magic. Sweat coated her face and ran from her temples.

"I can't work through all of this magic," she said in a wispy voice. "It's…too vast. I can't pull all of it down."

Fear and adrenaline beat a drum in my chest. Tumultuous emotions rolled through the bond from Nyfain, and I knew he was coming to a decision that might damn us all. I could feel it. I could feel his decision cutting through my gut like a hot knife. I knew if he went through with whatever he was currently doing, I'd lose him forever.

Hot tears coated my eyes. "Can you do…*anything*? Anything at all? Slice through it, cut a hole…anything?"

She pulled her hands away, and I ran through how long it would take us to backtrack and then work around the kingdom to the area where the portals let out.

As if hearing my thoughts, she turned slightly, looking behind me to where the demons stood in a cluster, watchful and silent.

"I can use their magic to fuel me. Borrowing a demon's magic feels a little like…wading through sludge, and it's hard to hold on to, but I can use it for a time to open a sort of doorway." Her indigo eyes landed on me. "I will have to physically hold the door open while you run through. It will tax all of those connected to me, so you'll have to hurry. Then, when we can't hold it anymore, we'll be locked out."

"If I can't release that curse, you'll be glad for it."

I looked behind me at the dragons landing and the wolves running toward us. Hannon, Hadriel, and Leala jogged my way. They'd been part of the first wave, but they were slower on their two legs. I wasn't sure why Hadriel wouldn't change, but I knew Leala wouldn't have been any faster in her other form, and Hannon still hadn't figured out how to release his animal. I wondered if he'd be stunted forever.

The next words out of my mouth nearly killed me.

"We'll wait for the rest to arrive. When we've assembled, let's do it."

Hannon stopped next to me, out of breath. "They're coming," he said. "They're almost here. Not long now."

More dragons landed as he scanned my face. A line formed between his brows. He nodded but didn't comment. He could read me well, and he knew the stakes. We had precious little time.

"Finley, you will never believe this…" Hadriel shook his head and bent down to rest his hands on his knees. Tamara glanced at me, standing with the Wyvern dragons in the flesh, waiting for an opening to unleash hell. "I swear I saw…" He gulped down air. "It's impossible, I know that. But I *swear* I saw… Fuck, my wolf is clamoring to get out. That fucking alpha—No offense, sir. Anyway, I first saw her belowdecks when I was checking on people— before Vemar started running his mouth. That guy is not right in the head, Finley. And then just now… I mean, she had a cloak, and her face was all shadowed, so maybe she's just a look-alike, but I swear to the goddess she looked just like—"

"Goddess help me, Hadriel, do you ever shut up?" Jade barked. "Get your head right. We're heading into battle."

He nodded, straightening up, and I saw the fear lining his face. He wasn't built for battle.

I put my hand on his shoulder and gave him my undivided attention for a moment.

He swallowed, his gaze latching on to mine like a drowning man might grab a piece of driftwood.

"You're going to be okay, okay?" I told him softly. "Stick with Hannon. He'll make sure you don't come to any harm. He might seem calm and gentle, but he will rise to the occasion when he has to. He's a Mosgrove—my family was built tough."

He nodded, his face somewhat slack. "I know. I stole him a really nice chef's knife and a good axe from the tavern, so he's armed."

I let the smile touch my eyes, if only briefly. "Perfect. His favorite weapons."

"I'll make sure our family is okay," Hannon told me. "I'll go to them first."

I released Hadriel and looked at my brother, my heart swelling. I nodded. "Hide them. Don't let Father fight or Dash get any crazy ideas and sneak out. Hide them until this is all over."

Micah landed not far away, having stayed to the air to watch the progress of the others while the faeries worked. He stalked up to me, large slabs of lethal muscle shining in the new night. His dark brown eyes took me in, chasing away some of my fears and doubts and alighting my fierce determination. The alpha commander had stepped onto the battlefield, and regardless of his unwanted and very confusing effects on me, I had to admit that he owned his mantle. He was a good guy to have on our side.

"The last of them are minutes away—a few of the…more seasoned dragons and the smaller wolves."

More seasoned dragons—he probably meant Gunduin, Ami, and Claudile. I hadn't seen even a glimpse of the latter two, who'd apparently stayed belowdecks and out of everyone's way, but Gunduin had checked on me a few times. I felt more comfortable having some experience in the ranks.

I gave him a curt nod, glanced back their way, thought I saw the moonlight sparkle off azure scales, and turned to Calia. She was watching me steadily, waiting for the signal.

"Go," I said before turning around to face everyone else. I addressed the alphas, who had the best working knowledge of their people. "Tamara, Micah, Weston…organize your people. We'll get a doorway for a brief time. We need to get through it quickly and efficiently and then get out of the way for those coming in behind us. Organize now, and then keep your people organized on the other side. As soon as enough of us are through, we'll move. Kill any and all demons you see. Govam and his demons will stay on this side for the time being, so you don't have to worry about killing the wrong creatures. The enemy demons will stand out—they'll all be wearing pleated black pants with bad hair, probably." I felt my heart thumping in my chest as I lifted my voice to address everyone else. "They've stolen our people. They've clapped us in chains. They've whipped us, tortured us, subjected us to unspeakable acts, and now we will claim revenge. First we will free this kingdom from their clutches, and then we'll free the magical world. Dolion's reign is at an end, starting now! Rise up and fight. This night will be our victory!"

Weston shifted into wolf form before throwing back his head and sending up a loud, clear wolf song. The feeling of it tore right through me, promising the thrill of the hunt. The triumph of a fresh kill. The joy of working together to bring down a common enemy.

Hadriel shook and doubled down, clutching his clothes in a fist, clearly fighting his animal's desire to heed the call.

I couldn't wonder at it for long, because Tamara and Micah both stepped away to get more space, shifted, and sent up roars that nearly froze my blood. Their dragons' roars rang with vicious energy, rage, and the thrill of meeting the challenge and crushing it.

I grabbed Hannon's forearm and gave him a long look. He was calm, even now. Unruffled but ready for anything, always dependable.

"Keep yourself safe, Hannon. Please. Don't leave this world tonight. I can't win back one and lose another."

"I was never the risk taker, Finley. You keep *yourself*...well, alive if not safe. Leave me enough of you to patch back together."

My eyes glossed over again, and I nodded before cutting off all sentimentally, not letting the fear of what was to come claw at me. Nyfain would be okay. He *had* to be okay. I couldn't consider anything else. Not now. Now, I could only think about getting to him and saving the motherfucking day.

"Dragons," I called as the faeries continued their work. The demons stepped up closer, Govam watching Calia intensely, obviously feeling her use his magic. "The rest of you will run through before you shift. Here we go!" I made a small gesture and turned, my intent clear. It was time to add my battle roar to the mix.

I sure hoped we could fucking roar. It hadn't gone well in practice flights.

I got this, my dragon thought, power pumping through us.

Everyone scattered out of the way, reading my intention, but Hadriel called out, "More room—she's huge," pushing and shoving at people to make room.

The pain barely registered through the adrenaline as the dragon form took over. Calia was moving her arms now, weaving them through the air like a dance. Those around her bowed under the strain, lending their power and strength to her efforts. Even the demons started to wilt from the strain. We wouldn't have much time.

Roar, I thought like a whip crack. *Now!*

My dragon tilted back her head. The vibration started low and then built up through us, one clear directive blasting out with an incredible surge of power, all our own.

Fight!

Everyone around us shivered and shuddered. The wolves shifted as Weston tipped his head back again and added his song to our roar. Micah and Tamara added their roars as well, calling for action. Calling for vengeance!

"Go!" Calia said, pushing her hands wide. "Go! Hurry!"

The leathery substance peeled away, high enough to fly through, wide enough for one dragon with extended wings. Plenty big, in other words.

My dragon took to the sky immediately, moving through the doorway and into the very edges of the Forbidden Wood, beautiful on one side and twisting and crackling on the other. My rage fanned higher at this evidence of what the demons had done to us. To this kingdom.

I stayed in the air as Tamara came through next, followed by Micah. Below them, dragons in human form sprinted through on one side and the wolves streamed through on the other, peeling away in organized groups or shifting and taking to the sky and flying out a ways to make room.

When enough of us were through, we banked and turned to face the castle. I didn't need a map to know where to find it. From the first time I was taken there, it had been stored in my heart, along with the rest of the kingdom. Along with the rest of my home.

My dragon roared again, the sound booming and reverberating through the air. Way up ahead, shapes popped out of the shadows, startled. They waited between the trees, weapons strapped to their bodies, keeping watch even way out here.

Demons.

Kill them all, I growled.

My dragon didn't need to be told twice. No one did. We all shot forward as one, the dragons and wolves and those on two legs.

My dragon was first, though, on them in a heartbeat but blocked by the accursed trees.

Fire, I thought, anxious to get to them. Wanting to be the one who smote them from my home.

I'm fucking trying! It won't come.

We'd never been able to do it in practice. Ami had said it took time to learn. Usually a dragon could only summon fire if they were utterly secure in their flying ability and at max power.

But fuck it if I didn't need to get this knocked out a lot sooner.

My dragon flew low, just above the treetops, our mouth open and the desire to blast the demons strong. Still, nothing came. Not from us, anyway. The results were better when Micah and Tamara gave it a go.

A blast of delicious heat coated our sides and underside as streams of fire tore through the night, raking over the demons and burning them alive. Those gathered in front of me, sparse because we were so far on the edge of the kingdom, pulled up their bows and nocked their arrows.

Oh shit—

If I'd been in charge, I would've flinched or ducked and thrown my hands over my head. Arrows flew right at us, their aim perfect, the points gleaming in the moonlight. My dragon roared with rage as the arrows struck...and bounced off.

Oh shit, I thought again. *How'd you know we were arrow-proof?*

If we can slam against mountain sides and land on rocks or get pummeled by a rock fall and not take any damage, what's a measly arrow? To our body, anyway. I don't have such high hopes about our wings.

Still, we flew on, nearing one of the villages now. My glance behind revealed dragons spanning out behind us, creating a V formation and spitting fire down at or enemies. What demons they missed, the wolves found. They ran through the trees like wraiths and around brambles with no problem, working with us as one cohesive force. I only wished I could've gotten to see how the graceful faerie warriors would've fit into our ranks.

Well, if we can't blow fire, what the fuck good are we? I asked, frustrated. *If only I had a dagger, I could at least do* something.

We are doing something. We're leading. Why don't you talk to your invisible people and let me work?

It occurred to me that I hadn't rolled out that bit of neurosis in...a while. I didn't even know how long. And I didn't want to now. I wanted to take control and do something rather than just sit around watch everything unfold.

Yeah, how does it feel, fucker? my dragon thought as the tree space opened up a bit.

She swooped suddenly, and if I'd had a stomach, I would've lost it. She nearly scraped the ground with her head as she clamped her jaws around a demon that was running toward the nearest village. The vicious crunch of a body between our teeth made me inwardly grimace, and then she was pulling up again. Our legs skidded against the dirt. The trees caught us as we lifted out of the dive, crackling and breaking as we barreled through.

Fire lit up more demons beside us as she shook her head and body parts ripped off. She flung the body and let out the largest, most triumphant, most vicious roar I'd ever heard. She'd finally been let out of her dark cage, and she was about to go fucking crazy.

CHAPTER 33

FINLEY

Y DRAGON VEERED left, toward the village, coming up hot on demons scattering for cover. She scooped up another and lifted into the air before ramming into the side of the first dwelling. Chomping the demon, she sent blood spraying across the ground.

Rise, her roar said, calling to the people of the village. *Fight with us. Rise!*

Demons ran out of not just pubs but houses, and our vision went red. She swooped down, hit the ground running, and started grabbing them at will, chomping and throwing and grabbing more. She stomped and kicked, flinging around her tail and hitting anyone she could.

Wolves and other animals ran down the streets, the villagers starting to shift. Teeth bared and hackles raised, they launched into the demons throughout the village and then ran toward the wood. Small, slim, seemingly young dragons rose into the sky around the village. Those had to be the kids, responding to my call.

Incite them, I thought, my purpose suddenly clear. *Get to Nyfain, but as you go, summon them. Bring them to our cause.*

My dragon jumped up before pumping our wings, getting above the rooftops and lifting higher into the sky. She made a slow turn, since she still didn't know how to bank very well, then put on a burst of speed. Her roar filled the hearts and minds of the villagers, all of them running out, shedding their clothes in the streets, and changing into their animals.

Over the Forbidden Wood we flew, toward the castle but at a diagonal, aiming to hit the next village. I had faith Hannon would get to ours in time to help our people, and there wasn't any time to circle back. Nyfain needed me.

Tamara flew at my wingtip with the rest of the Wyverners in tow, but Micah separated. Somehow my dragon instinctively knew, or maybe sensed from his body language, that he would finish up here and keep battering the demons in the wood. We had a lot of ground to cover and not enough people to do it quickly. I needed to get the rest of the kingdom helping.

I just hoped to hell I'd be in time.

HADRIEL

LEALA CRACKED HER whip as we ran behind Hannon. She had practiced when we were in the dragon village and was now very good at it. It made me incredibly nervous.

But not as nervous as all the demons that randomly popped out from behind trees as we made our way to Hannon's village. Wolves flanked us, growling and snarling. The alpha's call for aid beat throughout my chest, yanking constantly at my wolf. Each time my wolf felt it, he struggled to break free and join the pack, to find our place and belong for once.

But I couldn't. If I did, I knew I wouldn't want to go back to Finley. I wouldn't want to stay. I'd leave with Weston and maybe never see her again. Wolves like Weston didn't settle with dragons, they just didn't, and I couldn't bear to leave Finley behind. Or Leala or Hannon or any of those crazy fuckers I'd been through hell with in the castle. I'd stay a misfit forever if it meant I could remain with my newfound family.

A light-skinned demon—gray in the moonlight—darted toward Hannon from the side as we neared a clearing of sorts. He met the attack with a very lazy duck, followed by a very fierce uppercut with his knife into his enemy's sternum. He shoved the demon off nonchalantly, glanced back at me to make sure I was okay, and continued on. The guy always checked on Leala and me after he slayed a demon. He was like some sort of lethal babysitter. Why was that so hot?

A whip cracked and a girl screamed, almost at the same time. I looked at Leala in confusion as she snapped her whip again, wrapping the end around the neck of a demon and yanking. The demon tried to grab the whip, choking, and was tackled in the back by a lunging wolf.

Leala released the whip as the cry sounded again.

So not Leala, then.

"What's..." I glanced left, into the field, and saw a demon haul out a little girl. Three other demons fell in around her, like they were taking her hostage.

Hannon looked at the same time, then froze for a moment. A shock of color burst out around him, like a glimmering aura, before he exploded into action. He ran in the girl's direction, axe in one hand and knife in the other.

A demon launched at him, out of nowhere. It latched on to his back and slashed with claws, tearing across flesh.

Leala cracked her whip, slicing the demon in the side and making it convulse. It was all the time Hannon needed to throw the thing off and chop down with his axe.

Bye-bye, demon head. Or near enough.

Another burst of light and color shone around Hannon, like no magic I'd ever seen. No animal I'd ever heard of. He tore his fragment of a shirt away, exposing a tableau of rippled and bruised and slashed muscle, having taken a lot of damage and not shown one ounce of pain.

He jogged now, moving through what I recognized as everlass plants, Leala and I trailing behind him. The demons dragged the kicking and flailing girl farther into the field before stopping and raising a knife to her throat. In a moment, I saw who it was.

Sable. Hannon's sister.

Why the fuck was she all the way out here?

One of the demons said something, but I didn't catch it as Leala murmured, "Closer, Hannon. I'm out of range."

Hannon held out his hands, one weapon in each, bending a little like he might put them down. He slowed to walking—almost creeping—his movements slow and thoughtful, underplaying the threat he posed.

"Closer," Leala whispered as we walked.

"Hannon!" Sable shouted before the knife tip was pushed against the front of her throat. She winced but didn't stop. "I'd heard the roars and wanted to go check on Dash and Daddy. I didn't want to sit here if they were in danger—"

The demon shook her, and light leaked from around Hannon,

curling and misting. The moonlight filtered through his wild hair like it was glowing, sparkling through that strangely pulsing aura.

"Let her go." Hannon kept creeping forward, slow and methodical, as though he were just looking for a place to sit and take a rest. "Let her go, and I'll put these down. I can't shift. I'll have no defense against you."

He bent as if to do just that, then—

"Okay." Leala's voice was a soft hum. Her whip made a sharp *crack.*

It hit before they'd registered she was moving. Dead on target, slashing against the demon's hand that held Sable. The demon hissed and pulled back, turning his body a little to pull his wrist to his chest.

Hannon exploded into action, that bend he'd been doing turning into a lunge, his big body aimed right for Sable. Her eyes didn't widen. Instead, her brow pinched in concentration. She ducked at the last second, then rolled out of the way.

Hannon crashed into the demon, his knife already working.

Leala pulled back her whip for another strike, but the jumble of bodies didn't give her a clear shot.

I jumped to the rescue, shit with a knife but really good at breaking up fights and sex-capades gone wrong. I slapped at hands and peeled a demon away from Hannon as he shot out his axe and got that demon in the upper chest. He turned in a smooth movement, stabbed another through the belly, and then turned and sliced his knife across the third demon. Leala hit the first with her whip, but he was long dead, and soon they all were.

"I'm pretty sure I helped," I said, out of breath. "Pretty sure."

Sable scrabbled up and grabbed Hannon, hugging him hard.

"Come on, let's go check on Dash and Dad, okay?" Hannon

said comfortingly, as though he hadn't just gruesomely killed three demons.

"You missed your calling, bud," I told him as he turned and stuck out his hands, offering to carry his sister piggyback. "You should've been a librarian. No, no, let me carry her. I'm not doing anything else anyway—"

Three dragons flew directly overhead, heading in the same direction we were about to go, off to help the villages while Finley stormed the castle. My mouth dropped open, and my heart froze.

I *knew* that dragon. The whole kingdom knew that dragon. She would be azure in the day, nearly matching the color of the sky, but her glimmering scales would give her away. She was so graceful and silky smooth in flight. I'd watched her in fascination throughout my youth.

"That's—"

It was at that moment, when I was awestruck and confused and not paying attention, that Weston's wolf song rose in the distance. The wolves near us took up the call. The music rolled over my flesh and down my spine before reaching in and grabbing my wolf in a hard grip.

Before I knew it—before I could stop it—my wolf surged forward and overcame me. He forced the shift, in control. He tilted his head back, easily falling into the pack, and I knew I was lost.

CHAPTER 34

NYFAIN

T HE DEAL HUNG heavy between the demon king and me as I put out my hand to seal it. It wouldn't ensure the kingdom was completely safe—Dolion was nothing if not cunning and great at bargaining—but it would give my people time. They would be able to get out, at least, and find somewhere else to go. Finley could lead them and help them find a future away from this accursed place. As soon as they scattered, Dolion would lose interest.

My fate, however, was about to be sealed.

My dragon continued to roar inside my head, drowning out my thoughts. He tore at me, trying to steal control, trying to stop me. He was urging me to wait just a little bit longer. Finley's dragon hadn't accepted his goodbye. He thought that meant something.

Little Dash stood just off to the side, tears of pain streaming down his face and blood dripping from the blade at his throat. They were slowly sawing at his neck. His father lay at his feet, barely moving, his head bleeding profusely.

I'd stalled all I could, and they were paying the price. My time was up.

Dolion's greasy smile curved his blue lips. "I'd say I won't be too hard on you, but why lie? The entire castle will hear your screams…and then watch your pleasure as you suck my cock."

I took a deep breath and moved my hand forward. She was worth it. They were all worth it. This was my duty. Dying for them was the least I could do after what my father had done to them. I would do it without regret, but I'd still do everything in my power to try to drag Dolion straight to hell with me.

The roaring sped up my heart. Drowned out everything around me.

And yet my dragon had stilled within me…

Confusion seeped in as I realized those roars hadn't been coming from my dragon at all.

The demons who'd gathered around, watching in glee with satisfied smiles, suddenly flinched and ducked and looked right.

My dragon's anguish and agony had turned to smug pride and a desperation to rise into the sky. To fight. *Right now.*

And then I saw her.

I knew it was her the instant I laid eyes on her.

Beating her wings for more speed, soaring out over the Royal Wood, she bore down on Dolion's party with such unspeakable rage that it made my stomach flutter and a grin tug at my lips. The demons around me, including Dolion, cowered in fear…

Finley. Her dragon.

I couldn't do anything but stare, locked in time like my castle, struck dumb by her majestic beauty and glittering rage.

She was the most stunning dragon I'd ever seen, and she took my breath away.

Even in the moonlight I could tell her scales shone a deep burgundy, glimmering and sparkling. A light dusting of gold coated her, shining yellow in the low light. I'd never seen anything like her color.

And I knew, without a doubt, that the gold dusting would match the color of my once-dragon. She was my true mate in heart, body, and soul. And it didn't matter that I stood in a kingdom of ruin. She would always fight to be with me—and then fight at my side.

She was my princess. One day she'd be my queen.

And she'd proven that she would walk through hell and come out on fire to make me her damsel. The woman sure knew how to get her way.

"Sorry, Dolion." I yanked my hand back before he could shake off his stupor and grab it. "Time's up."

I reached for his neck as Finley swooped low, right for us. Her wings tilted wildly, her body positioning all wrong. She had no finesse with flying.

She also clearly didn't give a fuck.

She slammed into the demons gathered around, crashing down on top of some and rolling over others. Then she shifted, the change happening faster than I'd ever seen, and hopped up, naked and covered in blood. She grabbed a dagger out of a demon's hand, not worried that the rest of him seemed to be absent, before slashing her way toward me.

Dolion's eyes widened. My fingers began to curl around his neck, but the next instant they moved through nothing but air. He'd teleported away, a magic only the most powerful of demons possessed.

"Fuck," I grunted. No time to go after him. Not until Finley's family was safe.

I spun and grabbed the arm of the demon that held Dash. I wrenched, and a fierce *crack* preceded her howl of pain. I yanked her forward, took the knife, and stabbed her in the throat. I got out of the way, and my dragon took over, shifting and growing in front of the boy and his father, shielding them as Finley cut her way to us.

More dragons flew in, some familiar, belching fire and carving through the air. My mouth would've dropped open if I'd been in human form. My dragon paused in shock.

Tamara. Lucille. Jade. Xavier. More. I'd thought they were dead. Long dead. Where had they—

Wolves burst through the trees, growling and snarling. And although we had wolves, plenty of them, I already knew these wolves weren't from our kingdom. A great alpha led them, running onto the dead grass, his pack fanning out behind him in perfect harmony. It was the sort of pack that would be legendary throughout a wolf kingdom—the sort of alpha who didn't usually like the idea of working with dragons.

Fire scoured the ground, blistering over demon bodies as they attempted to flee like cowards. They'd brought in a huge host, filling every inch of the kingdom. They should've had the upper hand. And yet...

Finley's dragon swelled into being. As she came closer, she saw who was at my feet, and rage roiled through her. She swung her tail and took out three demons before bending and snatching another in her mouth. She chomped at him aggressively, shook his dead form, spun the limbs off him, and then knocked over two other demons when she flung the remains.

Any demons who'd held out turned and ran.

My heart swelled as I adjusted to keep Dash protected between my feet, kicking a demon who ran too close. My dragon swung our tail and cleaved through two other demons trying to get away. Finley fought with me, even though it meant staying on the ground.

Fuck, I loved this woman.

The grounds cleared in no time—the demons who could teleport away from the castle had and the rest had run, now being tracked and taken down by the wolves.

Finley shifted back into her human form, hurrying to her family at my feet. I stepped away, leaving her to it. We couldn't have a reunion yet. Not until our people were secured.

I quickly checked the bodies littering the ground. No Dolion. That bastard had seen what was coming and gotten out. He couldn't teleport across the entire kingdom, though. Maybe when he popped into being, someone would be there to grab him.

I ran to the edge of the clearing, the dragons remaining in the air above me, the alpha wolf waiting patiently for direction. He was putting himself under my charge—because of Finley, I had no doubt. A debt, maybe. Something owed. As soon as his duty here was done, he'd be leaving. The fact that he'd come at all showed he had honor. He was someone to respect, not overlook.

I'd kiss his ass for it later. Right now, we had a job to finish.

Shifting into my human form, I stopped just long enough to give directions.

"The demon king has fled. Find him if you can. Those of you who are unable to trail, scour the wood and the villages for demons. Kill every last one you come across. If you find wounded, help the locals take them to a central location within each village so they can be treated. Let's lock this kingdom down from the inside so that we can break the curse once and for all."

My stomach dropped and then fluttered as desire spiraled through me. I wanted to break the curse right now. I wanted to turn around, run full speed at Finley, throw her down, and claim her all over again. This time she'd be claiming me as well. This time, there would be no tea afterward to prevent getting her with child. She was my forever, and I wanted it to start as soon as possible.

But I would not break the curse and put her in further danger. Not until I was sure we could succeed.

Back in my dragon form, we ran, and we refused to look up to see what the dragons of the old court thought of us. Ground-bound. Dull, murky scales. Wings ripped off my back. They probably didn't think we counted as a dragon anymore. I couldn't bear seeing my disgrace in their eyes.

We cut through the trees with the wolves on our tail, not as fast as us but much more agile. My dragon caught a demon running. Watched him duck behind a tree. Smelled another, hiding in the brambles. He was used to tracking down their kind in these woods. We knew all of the fastest ways to kill them and their creatures.

We passed the first, attacking it with our tail as we ducked behind the tree and snatched the head off the other. My non-dragon people jogged through the wood in various places, on hunts of their own, in groups. They weren't strong, and they knew it—they were playing the odds. Good.

Near the other end of the kingdom, close enough to where the portals were, my dragon scented Dolion's passing. A great many demons had fled through here recently, I could tell. They hadn't planned on a battle, and the surprise of it made them run like cowards.

The portals had been removed, locking us in. Locking all these other demons in here with us.

My dragon turned and huffed, letting them know this was a dead end. Our heart started thumping; we knew what—or rather who—awaited us when we got back to the castle.

But I still had to check on my people. I still had a loose end to tie up.

Release them to the hunt, I told my dragon. He'd know how to relay that through sounds, body posturing, and positioning. That alpha wolf would have no trouble picking up on my signs. *We need to secure Sable and check on the wounded.*

My dragon lost no time. The dragons above kept pace, flying so slowly that they probably wondered if they'd drop out of the sky.

Hollowness filled my chest. I might be a prince in title, but what would happen if I assumed the crown? Would my own council still recognize me as a dragon, or would I be some sort of abomination?

Would they snicker or shake their heads behind my back and stare right past me?

And Finley. Poor Finley. How would she, so majestic, so beautiful, cope with having a monster by her side? A once-dragon, now just a beast.

At the everlass field, we saw the disturbance among the plants, many of them wilting and starting to die. Someone had done battle within them. On the edges, I caught Sable's scent, and then Hannon, Hadriel, and Leala, mingled with demon blood. Hannon had found his sister and retrieved her, that much was clear.

Thankful for something else to focus on other than our deformity within the eyes of our peers, we made our way to a newer path. They'd probably gone and checked their home before heading toward the castle. Once they discovered it was empty, they'd be on the way to Finley.

My mind churned as we followed the scent, getting close enough to the castle to gauge that they'd made it. Instead of following them in, I went to the villages to check in and get reports.

A moment ago, I'd been ready to claim my princess and start our future. But those were just blind emotions. She drew me in a way that I struggled to understand. She stayed in my mind always and played on my heart without remorse. In her presence, I was confused, bewildered, and delighted. In rapture.

But cold logic always crept in. Since the beginning, the reality of my situation had never been far from my thoughts.

Now, I couldn't bear to see her. I couldn't bear the reminder of what I'd become—and how she'd be forced to endure it beside me. I'd sent her away to spare her. Maybe to spare myself. But there could be no hiding now. She'd see contempt on the faces of the members of my old court. She'd hear it in their voices. They might show respect for the crown, but how could they possibly show respect for what I'd become? For what I'd allowed this kingdom to become?

She might not realize it now, but she would eventually.

All I would do was continually bring her ruin.

CHAPTER 35

FINLEY

SOMETHING IS WRONG *with the man again,* my dragon said as I hurried into the shed by the everlass field on the castle grounds.

Ami and Claudile were working inside, creating healing brews for the wounded. Obviously they'd been delighted to see the everlass field as I had left it, complete with a working shed nearby, ready to be used. They'd asked not to be disturbed, knowing no one in their collection of villages could work the everlass well enough to be of use in a time of great haste, and correctly assuming the people of Wyvern were better at fighting than healing. I got the feeling the women didn't make friends all that easily. Not that I could blame them. They were basically me, only there were two of them. Well, three, if you counted Gunduin guarding the door.

I'd relented but made it very clear that they were the visitors here, not me. They would make way for me or they'd find somewhere else to be.

I checked in with the bond, feeling Nyfain's emotions roiling.

Then smiled.

He's a broody fucker. That's what he does. If he's swinging from one extreme to the other, he's doing just fine.

But he seems to be avoiding us. He's finding other things to do.

His dragon is impatient, that's all. He has the right idea—we have to make sure the wounded are looked after.

I wished he could be in here working with me, but he needed to see to his people. That was his duty.

Gunduin let me enter the shed, and Ami gave me a look but didn't attempt to intervene as I stopped by the first in a row of pots, this one at a rolling boil. I stuck my head into the steam and smelled, closing my eyes as the various notes hit my senses. Working almost on autopilot, I added the few herbs it needed, gave it a quick stir, and moved on to the next.

"What was that?" Claudile furrowed her brow and stepped up quickly to look in the pot. "This elixir will work without your add-ins."

"I've spent my life dealing with people on death's door," I said as I stuck my face in the next pot and breathed in. This was for my father. He had a concussion and was hard to rouse. The elixir should bring him around without any lingering effects. I was fully confident that he'd be fine.

I was not so confident about what would become of the kingdom when all our help left us.

"When a person is plagued with a demon sickness, any other ailment or wound can kill them quickly. So I've never been able to settle for *it works*."

I sprinkled a little bit of rosemary into my father's elixir before stepping past a few other pots and hauling the last of them off the stove. This elixir was for the shifters who were currently fanned out outside of the shed, resting. None of them were hurt too badly, but our brew would speed up their natural healing ability and ease the ache.

I took the pot out to Hannon, standing by with Sable and Dash, ready to distribute it. They could do that while keeping an eye on Father, lying under a nearby tent.

"You need to break the curse, Finley," Hannon said as he waved his hand over the cooling pot. "With Jedrek dead, the demon king is free to re-enact the suppression magic."

"I know, Hannon, but we need to tend to the wounded."

"You've made something to help the worst of them. Ami and Claudile can handle the others' needs. You need to deal with the curse."

I sighed and left him to it, heading back in the shed.

"He's right," Ami said, slowly stirring one of the elixirs she'd devised. It was to slow blood loss and had some very interesting components. "We have this handled. You need to reunite with m—" Her voice hitched and she turned to the side to cough into her elbow. She patted her throat. "Sorry, burr in my throat. You need to reunite with the curse holder and free these people."

I agree, my dragon thought. *Claim him. This bullshit with the hot and cold is well beyond old. Claim him, mark him, and imprint. Get that big alpha dick deep inside you.*

I rolled my eyes. It had been so nice when she turned her attention, temporarily, to demons and whips. Here we went again with alpha dicks. Next she'd be asking me to get all that jizz so we could get with his child.

You know me so well, she thought.

"He's busy," I said, checking the smell on another of Claudile's elixirs. I tilted my head, catching a fragrance I wasn't quite expecting. "Is that—"

"He's probably stalling," Ami said. "He—men like him, I mean, tend to stall when they know a serious obligation is on the line, and they don't think they have all it takes. They convince themselves they aren't good enough. That they aren't *enough*, period."

I didn't know about men like him in general—was there more than one guy like him? I wasn't sure the world could handle it— but that *did* sound like him. He'd worry his kingdom was in ashes. That he still couldn't protect me. All sorts of crap.

Butterflies swarmed my belly. He was overthinking things, obviously. I'd given myself to the fucking demon king, for the goddess's sake—nothing else was going to faze me.

I took a moment to look around. Things were in hand for the healers, for the most part. The shifters who were still alive would claw their way back to health, my father included. He had access to his animal now, so he was already slowly improving. My remedy would only speed up his recovery.

I took it off the fire to cool.

Besides, I wasn't on my own anymore. For the first time I had help outside of my family. I said as much.

"It'll be good for you to have a community," Ami said. "To rely on others."

"Maybe." I pulled off the apron I'd worn out of habit, revealing a crappy pair of clothes I'd retrieved from the bundle that had been dropped just outside of our entry point. Someone had retrieved it, venturing close enough to hear the faeries and demons through the barrier, still waiting. That was probably a good thing, since if the demons had gotten through, they probably would've been killed by accident.

"Or maybe I'll get bored," I murmured.

Claudile huffed out a laugh. "Likely."

I picked up my sword with one hand and went to grab the elixir for my father with the other. Hannon would do what he did best and nurse. It was time I fulfilled my other duty.

More butterflies took flight in my chest, this time accompanied by a low, throbbing burn deep in my core. My heart sped up. I wanted Nyfain now. I wanted our reunion. I wanted to finish what we'd started...and then keep going with it.

"Aren't you going to wear that?" Ami asked with a note of suspicion in her voice. She probably still half thought I'd stolen it. "Why would you carry it if you could put on the belt?"

"No. After a battle and dealing with demons, he'll probably have random spurts of rage. The leather belt is getting a little worse for wear, given all it's been through. I don't want him to rip it off without thinking."

"You know him very well," Ami murmured, and her tone struck me as odd. Kind of whimsical. Like she'd known a man like that once and longed for him.

"Finally," Dash said as I walked out, taking a quick peek at Father. He had a thick bandage around his neck with no blood running through. He'd be fine, too, thank the goddess for her protection.

No, actually, thank Nyfain for his protection. I'd gotten my family into this mess. Nyfain had nearly sacrificed himself to save them, even though he must've known I was coming to get them out.

The heat in my core throbbed harder. I felt his dragon stir, and their answering desire for us. He wouldn't be able to avoid me forever. He never could resist me for long. I'd never minded the way that truth enraged him.

"Finley." Weston walked through his smattering of shifters either drinking the elixir or lying back to rest and recuperate. None of them had bothered with the trampled clothes.

I waited for him to reach me, spying Micah heading toward the shed on foot by way of the castle. I didn't want to see him right now. My core throbbed for Nyfain. I needed to put in the face time with these guys, and probably Tamara and the others— they'd *saved* us—but...I had to be filthily honest, I wanted to get that big alpha dick up in my cumquat.

My dragon preened. *Told you.*

Weston stopped in front of me, oozing power and authority and confidence. His presence prickled my skin in not totally unpleasant ways, but this was definitely not a man you wanted behind your back. He could surely be dangerous if he wanted to be. His prowess at keeping his pack in line showed that much.

"Thank you for helping with this, Weston," I said, keeping eye contact, refusing to be distracted by Nyfain's pounding desire pumping through the bond. "We were outnumbered even with the help from your pack and the extra dragons. If not for your superb leadership and ferocity, we wouldn't have been able to pry this kingdom away from Dolion."

Weston studied me for a moment. "I'm anxious for you to break the curse everyone speaks of. I want my memories of this place back. For the demon king to have such an incredible interest in it, it must have been mighty once. I suspect it will be mighty once again."

I lightly shook my head and looked at the castle, noticing Micah slowing, stalling, waiting for me.

"I don't know. We've lost so many people. Some were taken,

as you know, but I think a great many more were either killed or died from the sickness. I'm not sure we will become much of anything, even if Dolion doesn't return and finish what he started."

"About that. Listen, I knew you weren't like normal dragons when I first saw you in that cage. I've come across a lot of dragons in my days, and while some were rougher than others, like those in Vemar and Micah's villages, they all have a certain pride. A certain sense of superiority. They aren't easy to work with. They aren't pack animals, though I now realize they *can* work together quite well. It's obvious they don't much *want* to work with wolves or other animal shifters."

I remembered what Nyfain had said about the uselessness of "dogs" and his passing negative comments about bear shifters. He did tend to look down on other shifters. Before, having put dragons on a pedestal most of my life, I might've gone along with it. But I felt differently after working with the faeries and the wolves. We were much stronger with them.

"I saw something different in you," he went on. "As did Calia. We saw the glue that could bring us all together and get us out of that awful place. So did Govam, if I'm honest. What I didn't see until later was the respect and loyalty you engender in those closest to you. I can see why now. You are willing to sacrifice yourself for the wellbeing of others. You did it for this kingdom, and you did it again after the battle. Instead of getting back to your dragon prince, you came here to help the ailing." He put his fist to his heart. "You have my loyalty, Finley. You are a friend of my pack. We will always help you in times of need."

My eyes prickled with heat.

"All I know is survival," I told him, bracing my hands on my hips to keep from throwing them around his neck and sobbing uncontrollably. It seemed I was a little fragile at the moment. "To survive, you must pull together as a community. I wasn't raised a dragon. So no, I'm not like them. And I'm not like the people in my community either. They're mostly wolves, although I'm not sure about all of them. I always felt different, though. I never fit in. I'm a dragon in wolves' clothing, maybe." I shrugged, wishing I was half as eloquent as he was. "You didn't need to put yourself in danger to bail out a kingdom you couldn't remember, yet you put yourself—and your pack—on the line. That took a lot of guts and trust. I don't have a pack, or really much of anything, but if you ever need help, I'll come. I have no fucking idea how, but I'll make it happen."

His smile was slight. "You seem like a person who never knows the how of things when she starts something but always gets where she wants to go anyway." He paused for a moment. "You can hug me, if you want. It's not really something we do in the pack with non-mates, but…you're a dragon, so I'm sure it'll be fine."

"How'd you…" I didn't bother finishing the question before I wrapped my arms around his shoulders, squeezing him tightly for a moment, so fucking grateful to him. I didn't let myself cry, though. I had to have some respect, after all.

Thank fuck for that, my dragon thought drolly.

After I pulled back, Weston glanced at the castle. "I don't know much about the prince, but I know a strong leader when I see one. A capable leader. What happened to his wings?"

"He wouldn't let the demon suppression magic keep him from his dragon. Fighting it muddied his scales and ripped the wings from his back. It stole half his strength. But he held on. He used his dragon to protect his kingdom against the creations Dolion kept releasing to kill everyone off. He never said die."

Fuck my eyes. The waterworks were threatening. All the emotion of being home, the close call with my family, and getting to see Nyfain again were starting to get to me.

Weston didn't show any signs that he'd even heard me, just continued to stare at me after I'd stopped talking. I felt my eyebrows creep up my forehead.

"That's why his human form bears scars?" he finally asked.

"Yes. He didn't have much access to his healing ability, and he didn't know me yet. I would've kept him looking much prettier."

He studied me a bit longer, nodded, and walked away. No goodbye or any indication he was done with the conversation.

"Okay, then." I turned, meeting Micah next. I'd have to make this short, though. I could feel Nyfain's longing for me pulsing through the bond. He was finally on his way; I knew he was. He had met his threshold of resistance, and he was coming for me.

And then I'd make him come for me.

"Hey, Micah," I said. Out of the corner of my eye, I could see Hannon drifting closer. He wasn't hurrying, though. He clearly wasn't worried about my dragon being a cheating dickface at the moment. "I need to go tear down this curse, but thank you for helping us free the kingdom. You and Weston and your people didn't have to put yourself in danger, especially for a kingdom you couldn't remember, but I'm so thankful you did."

He looked down at me, his eyes open and inviting. I leaned back a little, put off by his intensity.

"Of course I came, Finley," he said quietly, and a little shiver danced down my spine. "I didn't do it for your kingdom, though. You have to know that by now. I did it for you."

Unease coiled through me. I put out my hand to push him back a little, needing some distance. Needing not to do this now.

"Look, Micah—"

He shook his head and put a warm finger to my lips. With his other hand, he grabbed my outstretched hand and pulled it closer to his heart.

Before I could say or do anything, he was talking urgently, leaning much too close.

"I know about your duty to this kingdom. I know you have to claim the other alpha. But all that doesn't mean you are trapped. I will accept the challenge of his scent. I can overcome it and lay my own atop it. There aren't many others who could. Don't give up flying with your mate because of a curse that wasn't your fault. Don't give up your chance at real happiness with a *complete* dragon to save your people. You don't have to settle."

I stared at him dumbly for a moment, shock roiling through me at his use of the word *complete*. At what he meant.

That *bastard*.

So it took me a moment to register my dragon's excited flurry. Then another moment to understand the rage pounding through the bond. The uncontrolled aggression. The alpha who saw another infringing on his claim and intended to protect what was his.

"I—"

Micah's body was ripped away in a rush of brutal violence. He flew to the side and hit the ground rolling.

Nyfain stood just behind where Micah had been, enormous and terrible to behold. His height might've been a shade less than Micah's, but his girth was wider, his body stacked with layer upon layer of hard-earned muscle streaked with scars and ink. His chest heaved like he'd just run a mile, and rage billowed off him in heavy waves.

My dragon purred in delight. I fought to keep from rubbing my thighs together in uncontrolled desire. Holy shit, he was hot when he was worked up.

Told you, she purred.

But this wasn't the time. He couldn't upset the balance of the dragons, not when we needed their cooperation so badly.

"Nyfain, wait—"

Hannon grabbed my arm and whipped me back, cutting me off as Nyfain stalked toward Micah, emanating strength and power and incredible fury.

"No, Finley," Hannon said, his voice soothing but holding traces of anger. "Micah knew what he was doing. He would know this is the response he'd get."

It was true, but still…

Micah burst into his dragon form, ripping his clothes as he did so, and Nyfain shifted a moment later, his dragon larger, more muscular, and—I knew this for an absolute fact—much, *much* meaner. Micah should've stuck to a human-on-human combat. Nyfain's dragon was fucking nuts.

"Tamara said that Micah was using erotic pulses with you," Hannon said, watching Nyfain prowl closer to Micah. "I couldn't feel anything, but apparently it's something dragons do to excite their chosen mate. I guess it was always forbidden here, but Vemar said the rules are different in the villages. If the tactic is used on someone of equal or better power, it's a dragon's way of showing interest."

"Why equal or better power?"

"Because it can influence those of lesser power into doing

something they might not want to do."

I remembered the feel of his power, the flutters of my stomach, the confusion of my dragon. It now made a lot more sense. We just hadn't realized there was any magical influence at work.

"We need those dragons, though," I murmured.

"A strong showing from the alpha will probably help."

Damn it, Hannon was right again. He'd learned an awful lot about dragons in a very short amount of time. I said as much.

"It didn't seem like a short time when we were sitting in that dungeon," he replied.

Micah rose into the sky. Nyfain lifted his head to watch, and Micah circled him lazily, taunting him, showing him what he lacked as a dragon.

Pain vibrated through the bond from Nyfain. My heart lurched for him. My dragon bristled. I couldn't fight this battle for him, though. That much I knew.

"He's drawing a crowd," Hannon said softly.

Dragons hovered in the air, beating their mighty wings, watching. Others, including the wolves, watched from the ground as the alphas faced off...except only one was participating. The other was watching, unable to engage.

"Fight back, damn you," I said through clenched teeth, power pounding through me. "Get mad. Where is your rage?"

The pain continued to throb in the bond, worsening, blackening. And suddenly, I *saw*.

All of Nyfain's fears were coming true. Micah was mocking him in front of their peers, rubbing his changed appearance in his face.

"I cannot abide by this," I said through angry tears. I'd never been mocked for what I looked like, but it had *always* overshadowed my accomplishments. I'd never been seen for *me*, all of me, including my oddities. Until Nyfain came along.

I loved him—faults, hang-ups, and all—and I'd never gotten the chance to tell him. Nor could I tell him now.

"Micah is doing this to show you what you'd be missing," Hannon murmured sadly. He felt bad for Nyfain. "I heard what he said to you, and now he's proving it. That was probably his intention all along."

"How do I fix this?" I asked Hannon.

"How do you usually fix him? You're the only one who seems capable of it, from what Hadriel says."

Rage.

Rouse his dragon, I told my dragon. *Rouse him. He's letting the man's fears muddy his mind. Shove down the man so they can win this fight. Win this battle and claim us as their mate.*

My dragon surged up unexpectedly and shifted, her pain and anguish at watching Nyfain's shame fueling her haste to do as I said.

Don't battle for him, though, I cried in desperation. She got crazy when it was time to battle; I'd just seen that firsthand.

I'm not an idiot.

I often beg to differ.

She waited for Hannon to scrabble backward, his eyes wide, before she beat her wings two times, hard. It lifted us up off the ground, and we hovered there for a long moment, gathering everyone's attention, before she curled her wings in with a snap and slammed down onto the ground. With a mighty roar, she set the ground to trembling.

Weston, to the side, shifted into his wolf. The other wolves around him followed suit. And then he lay down, his head on his paws. The wolves behind him, as one, did the same. Sable and Dash sat down next to Father, their eyes hard. In the sky, the Wyvern dragons dropped gracefully, stopping at about the height my dragon had reached before snapping in their wings and dropping as well.

For a moment, no one moved beyond treading air, the dragons from the villages contemplating their choice. They either sided with one of their own, a powerful alpha, or a foreign prince who had lost his identity as a dragon in trying to keep his people safe.

Movement caught our eye.

Across the field, Vemar walked forward with a powerful strut. He stopped with a hard expression, staring straight at me, then shifted and rose exactly like I had. He hovered for a long moment, like he was debating whether to continue into the sky to support Micah's treatment of Nyfain. Then he snapped his wings, slammed down onto the ground, and sent up a savage roar.

One by one, the dragons in the sky lowered, some slower than others. Most didn't make a show of it, touching down on the ground and then closing up their wings, but a few did. A few added their roars to Vemar's, showing their disappointment in the man they knew.

Finally, the pain and suffering within Nyfain eased a little, letting his dragon have more space to take matters into his own hands, as it were.

Rage built, hard and hot. Power leached from us, his dragon taking from us after all those times it had done nothing but give. I added some heady pleasure into the mix so Nyfain would know I was here for him, eager to help in any way that I could—the equivalent of a little kiss on his way to work.

Micah didn't give up his circling, though he dipped in his flight a little now, just out of reach.

I knew Nyfain wanted to leap off the ground to try to grab him, but he held still. And built. And built. My dragon kept supplying power, feeding him all we had.

Silence drifted through the spectators. The ruffle of Micah's wings filled the vast space.

And then Nyfain exploded with a roar so loud, so intense, that it seemed to freeze the air. Micah wobbled, his wings flapping like those of a startled bird, and tilted dramatically. Nyfain launched up, higher than Micah could've ever expected, I was sure, plucking the other dragon out of the air and pulling him back down to the ground. He was on Micah the next moment in a vicious attack that churned my stomach even as it sent desire flaming through my blood.

Nyfain ripped scales off Micah's side with his sharp, well-used claws. He tore lumps out of his flesh with a practiced jaw. And although Micah fought his way to standing, Nyfain quickly swung his tail and sent spikes into the other dragon's side.

Nyfain's savagery was unparalleled. This was a showcase of his constant fighting for the last sixteen years. He was brutal. Feral. He knew no rules. He'd long since abandoned decorum for the sake of survival.

His prowess showed and then some.

In a moment, it was over. Nyfain stood over the bleeding form of his opponent, stopping short of killing him, and sent up a thunderous roar in victory. The ground quaked. My blood froze. Desire flooded me.

Shift, I thought, as though tapping her shoulder so she'd notice me. *Shift!*

I want to take that dragon right now.

He can't fly, and watching two dragons trying to hump in a field will add insult to injury. Besides, I need to claim him. Shift! *Hopefully breaking the curse will give him his wings back. Then...no, I don't want to be a part of that. Never touch his dragon.*

Sure, yeah. Let's pretend I'm going to listen to you.

She relented, giving me free rein. Before I could push the shift, though, Nyfain expanded his chest and sent a huge jet of fire blistering into the sky. It could've been directed at Micah. I knew from the others that fire wouldn't kill a dragon, but it could blind them, suffocate them if directed at them for too long. Or, if the blast were strong enough, it could punch through their wings.

That blast would've been plenty strong enough.

The dragon showed restraint in their battle, my dragon said, dripping with gooey love and devotion. *He could've disfigured the other dragon with a blast like that. It was in his right to kill, but he withheld. Why?*

I knew why. Because even though Nyfain thought Micah crossed a line when it came to his female, Micah had also come to Nyfain's aid. He might've done it for me, or said he did, but he still did it. Nyfain clearly thought that was worth sparing the other dragon's life, and I agreed.

I shifted, walking forward, my clothes in tatters on the ground behind me. I didn't care. All I saw was the dragon and, in a moment, the man. *My* man.

He didn't spare anyone else a glance. He didn't look back at his fallen enemy. He only saw me, his emotions raging from victory to pain, love to loss. He reached me in a rush, and I grabbed his hair in two fists and dragged his mouth down to mine.

His taste swept me away, at once familiar and exotic, comforting and so fucking arousing.

"Fuck me, Nyfain," I murmured against his lips.

"As you command, my princess," he replied.

CHAPTER 36

FINLEY

N YFAIN SWEPT ME up into his arms and walked me past all the standing dragons and into the rear of the castle. I held on to him tightly, almost not believing I was in his arms again.

I'd finally made it back to my dragon.

"Nyfain, I lo—"

"No," he said, not taking the stairs up to the tower but instead bringing us into the back where the salons were located. "Don't say that yet. I can't…"

Heavy emotion wove through his tone and the bond, a kaleidoscope of intense feeling that hammered into my heart and melted me against him. As we reached the outer door to the salon lobby, he put me down and leaned me against the doorframe, opening the door with one hand and keeping me put with the other.

"For a moment, I thought I'd lost you," he whispered, his voice ragged. "You shouldn't be back here. You shouldn't have come back. But…"

His mouth crashed onto mine and he picked me up again, carrying me through the doors, into the hallway, and into the last room in the corridor, the one we'd used before.

"This is a quick stop," he said by way of explanation as he pushed past the curtain and walked me into the tranquil waters of the bath. "I just want to wash the blood and grime off us. I want us to have a semblance of cleanliness for our first time."

"Our first time?"

His golden eyes pinned mine as he lowered us into the warm water.

"You've never experienced what it's like with scales."

He ran his lips along my jaw as he grabbed the soap and made quick work of washing my body, his hands gliding over my fevered flesh in a kiss of pleasure.

"And it'll be the first time," he whispered, "that you tell me how you feel. I'm desperate to hear it and dreading it at the same time."

"Is the broody guy just around the corner?" I teased, and then sucked in a breath as he ran his thumb over a taut nipple.

"Maybe, but it won't matter. You can handle my rage as easily as you handle my sentimentality."

He slowed his ministrations as we sat together, his eyes drinking me in, roaming my face.

"Fuck, how I've missed you, Finley," he murmured, running his fingers down my neck. "I shouldn't allow you to stay. I shouldn't relish in the fact that you're back. But I can't resist you...and I can't bring myself to give you up."

I rested my hand against his cheek as he quickly cleaned himself. I let my other hand drape down his chest and then take hold of his large, straining cock.

He jolted like lightning had run through him and then

grabbed my hair in a hard fist and yanked my head back. He ran his teeth along my neck before sinking them into my flesh, over his bite. My stomach swirled, and hot, sweet pleasure ripped through me. He ran his tongue over the tingling mark before he pulled my hair harder, making me lean back, and sucked in a hard nipple.

"I'm going to fuck you so hard you forget your name," he growled, kissing up my chest and pulling me in toward him, taking control. "You're mine, little dragon, and I mean to prove it. Over and over."

His kiss was dominant and intense and erotic as he pulled me up to standing, trapping his cock between us. He grabbed hold of my jaw with one hand, the fingers of the other curling though my hair. Heat throbbed in my core. His eyes shone like those of a predator looking over his prey. His power curled around us, dangerous and wild but not a threat to me. Never a threat to me. No, he was only a threat to my enemies.

I knew Nyfain would always protect me, even if it cost him his life or his sanity. I'd broken him a little, I knew, needing to feel his pleasure when I was suffused with pain. But he'd never faltered. He'd never pulled back. I knew he never would.

"Take me," I said in a husky whisper.

"No, princess." He gripped me through the bond, pulling me into that place we'd found where nothing could reach me but him. "Now *you* will take *me*. You will mark me as yours."

He scooped me up into his arms again, water splashing around us, and walked us out of the now-murky water. Without covering up, he took me through the castle, still deathly quiet. The space was totally empty. The others were giving us time and distance, hoping we'd do what only we could—break the curse.

Free them.

My heart hammered. Nervousness peaked inside of me.

Nyfain climbed the stairs to the tower, and the second he pushed his way inside, I knew this had been his home when I was gone. He'd stayed here, with my smell around him. He'd forced himself into a dungeon of his own, trapped with my memory. He'd never planned to move on. Not for a moment.

Desperation overcame me as he set me down, but I didn't rush. I didn't jump him. Instead, I peeled back the covers and slipped into the silky sheets. He came in after me, watching my every movement, taking my cues. I could feel his anticipation growing, and mine with it, but he didn't let it show. He didn't rush me.

I reached for him, running my hand over his shoulder and across the top of his back, gently urging him closer. Closer still. His hot flesh brushed against me as he put one of those large, strong arms to the other side of my body, holding himself off me a little as he moved his body over mine. His delicious chest, cut with battle and muscle and branded with ink, rubbed against the hard peaks of my breasts. My eyes fluttered shut as I ran my hands across his skin and my thighs up the sides of his hips.

"I envisioned this, when you were feeding me pleasure and power through the bond," I whispered, fighting the memories. "But it wasn't the same. I didn't feel your heat. My memories of your strength were only a pale echo compared to actually being with you."

I pulled him down until he was flush with me, large and heavy and hard, pushing me down into the soft mattress. His lips found mine softly, and then a little harder, until he was filling my world with his taste. With his body.

"You saved me," I said, wrapping my arms around him, my eyes squeezed shut, all the pain and fear I'd held back in the demon prison now flowing out of me. Tears fell down my cheeks. "By claiming me, you saved me from...the worst of things. The worst of everything."

I shook with sobs, still gripping him tightly. This wasn't why we were here, but I didn't want to go any further until I got this out. Until I exposed the dark places of my soul and let him wrap me up in his safety.

"You saved us all," he murmured.

"Hadriel, Leala, and Hannon saved us all."

"No, they helped you get out of the dungeon. But it is your blind love that will save us all."

I opened my glassy eyes and met his golden gaze, so beautiful. So full of emotion. And suddenly I needed him inside me with a desperation the likes of which I couldn't remember experiencing before.

I pushed his hips back, and he caught on to what I needed immediately. His lips crashed down onto mine, and he dragged his big cock down my slippery folds. The blunt tip prodded my opening, and then he thrust. Color and light flashed behind my closed eyes, the feeling of him better than anything I could remember. Anything my (very vivid) imagination had conjured. He held himself fully seated for a moment, his arms wrapped around me, holding me tightly.

I turned my head until my lips were right near his ear and whispered, "I love you."

He sucked in a breath, and a dam of emotion burst within him. He pulled back and thrust into me powerfully, the slide of him so fucking good. I rocked my hips up to meet him, clinging to his back as he strove, all his fear and misery and yearning in each thrust. I met each of them, working through my own darkness with every crash of our bodies. Exposing it and showing it to the light.

We struggled to get closer. To get deeper. To meet each other in this place of fear and uncertainty and fuse ourselves together so that we didn't have to endure it alone ever again. I raked my teeth down his neck, and he shuddered in ecstasy.

Not yet, my dragon said, basking in the feeling of his body filling mine, of his power swirling within ours. The bond locked me in, cradling me in his strength and power. I knew I needed to give him the same connection. I needed to create a safe place for him to retreat to—a place within himself, and me, that he could hide without the world knowing he needed to.

He rose a little, allowing more movement, bending to continue our kiss, to deepen it. The friction, his power, the slick slide of his cock pounding into my pussy—

An orgasm tore through me, making me cry out into his kiss. He didn't stop, daring me to come harder. His dragon daring me to build more power.

They were showing us the way to claim.

Still he strained, the sounds of my groans and our sex filling the room. The bed creaked under our movement. His hips slapped against mine. I built again, higher this time, harder, the power between us throbbing.

"I love you," I said again, arching back as he worked, pushing my legs wider now, needing him deeper. Needing more.

"You are everything," he replied, bracing on his palms on the bed as he ground into me.

I gripped his shoulders then grabbed his hair, about to pull him to me again for a bite.

Not yet, my dragon said, her power flirting with Nyfain's dragon. Coaxing him. Playing. *Wait until we start to wrestle.*

Nyfain's hips jerked in intense thrusts, branding me with pleasure, doing as he'd promised and ruining me for any other man. How stupid Micah had been to think I would walk away from this. To think my love was so shallow that I cared about the color of Nyfain's scales or the absence of his wings.

How stupid I'd been, confused by a fluttering belly and the intensity of Micah's presence. He could never compare to Nyfain. I'd found where I fit, and I did not plan to ever let go.

I came again, unexpectedly. Then, again, the waves of pleasure rolled through me, spiraling with the victory of coming home. Of defeating the demons. My high was met and built upon by his body, by the hard push of his cock.

"Yes, baby," I said, moving against him, my pleasure escalating higher and higher. "Fuck—"

I gritted my teeth as another orgasm took hold of me. The dragons shoved power between each other now, turning more aggressive.

Fuck him hard, my dragon said, the push and pull of our animals spilling over into us.

I shoved at Nyfain with my will, trying to roll him over so I could climb on. He resisted, splintering my efforts. His dark chuckle raked across my heated flesh.

"Try harder, princess. I'm not like the dragons you're clearly used to pushing around."

I yanked his hair for a little violence before building more power and shoving again. I felt the mirth of his dragon, resisting my efforts, then the explosion of power through us as my dragon lent me aid.

This time my shove was hard and ruthless, ripping him off me and splaying him across the end of the bed.

"Good," he growled, grabbing my ankle and dragging me closer. "Never go easy with me. It's beneath you. It's beneath us both."

He pulled me closer, and I climbed onto him, slippery with sweat and wet with desire. I sat onto his hard length, grabbing a fistful of his hair and looking into his eyes as I started a fast pace. I used the other hand to massage my clit, the pleasure driving my breath out of me in fast pants.

"Yes, princess," he said, his eyes on fire. "Use me. I am yours."

The power between us throbbed, the feeling expanding through my ribcage. The extra stimulation made me come again, and again, my breathing ragged, my pleasure still building as my dragon wrestled with his for more power. As our bodies waged war with each other, fighting to get closer. To fuck harder.

I cried out with the orgasm, and this time fire burned through my body.

Now, my dragon thought, and I ripped his head to the side and bit down on his neck, allowing my dragon right near the surface. Together, we felt the hot liquid rush across our tongue in sweet satisfaction as he groaned beneath me, gripping my hips and slamming me down onto him. He shuddered his release as the power within us mixed with love and lust and yearning and forever. It washed through him, then back, and settled into the bite I'd ripped into his flesh.

His groan continued, and he pumped his release into me still, feeling this on a level I could well remember. I jerked my hips and continued to work my clit, hitting another high before he finally came down.

He held me close as our breathing slowed and our scents mixed, his on me and mine now on him. But that was all that had changed. I didn't feel anything different.

"What does imprinting feel like?" I asked, pulling back a little to look out the glowing window. The day looked back.

"We didn't imprint," he replied softly, and regret dribbled through the bond.

Fear and pain lanced my heart.

"Am I not..." I swallowed. "Am I not your true mate, then?"

"You know you are. You've read enough about the subject, I know you have. The bond is proof."

"Then why..." Only one other explanation came to me. "Do you not really love me?" I choked out, my eyes overflowing with fresh tears, and these weren't because of what I had endured in the past.

These were because of what I was enduring now.

CHAPTER 37

FINLEY

H<small>E PUSHED MY</small> hair out of my face and tucked it down beside my cheek.

"I love you with all that I am," he said. "I think the problem is that I don't love myself. And I'm finding it hard to see how anyone else could. I don't belong with the dragons anymore. I don't belong with anyone. Even though I want you more than is probably healthy, I…I'm struggling against the compulsion because I don't want to force you into this half-life with me."

My heart twisted and then broke in half. I leaned toward him and touched my forehead to his. If it weren't for seeing his battle with Micah, I wouldn't truly understand the gravity of what he'd just said.

But I had, and I did. I'd seen his suffering and his fear of what the future might hold.

I looped my arms around his neck and lightly traced the pad of my finger down one of his scars.

He shivered as I said, "You belong with me. And I have news for you: you're not the odd one in this pair. I have never fit in—

with any crowd—and I'm not suddenly going to start because I have some scales and a pair of wings and a real asshole dragon yammering in my head."

Suck rocks, my dragon thought.

"I'll be the one who stands out, not you," I continued. "I didn't grow up knowing anything about dragons. I still don't. I won't act like one—Weston already told me that. He thought it was a good thing, but I'm sure other dragons won't agree. Nyfain, I didn't even know the names of the royal family! That's how removed we were from court. I'll stand out at every formal dinner, civilized meeting of the social elite, and...important function or whatever it is you all do. In a bad way. In the ways that matter most in this world, *you* will fit in, and *I* will be out of place. They'll say, 'There goes that powerful dragon with the weird mate,' and it won't be me they are pointing at."

"You can change all of that. That stuff is teachable."

I stroked his face and traced the scar near his lip. He didn't pull away. "And wearing your scars proudly will teach others about the suffering you've endured. It'll show them that you triumphed despite it. They'll see the scars where the wings were ripped off your back and know the power and perseverance of a prince who wouldn't bow down to a tyrant. They'll see, with their own eyes, the pain you went through to protect your people. We'll match in that way."

I pushed off him and turned, showing him the scars the whips had left on my back. Pain and rage tore through the bond.

When I turned back around, climbing into his lap, he shook his head, tortured.

I snuggled close to him and laid my head on his wide shoulder. "Remember what you said to me when you were in my room?"

I went back to slowly tracing the scale scars down his back. He shuddered in physical pleasure mixed with internal pain. It was the opposite of what I'd experienced in the dungeons, but no less damaging.

"You said, 'I see you, Finley. I see all of you, and I am in rapture.' I fell in love with you in that moment. I didn't know it at the time, but I know it now. And then you kept chiseling away at my heart with your letters and your actions until I was lost to you. Until you ruined me, just like you'd promised. Only it wasn't in the way you promised. You only ruined me for other men. Because *I* see *you*, Nyfain. I see all of *you*. I see the scars you wear—and those you hide. I see your temper and rage...and your loyalty and love. I see your power and strength, and your kindness and tenderness. I see it all."

"Others will not see past my deformity." He clutched me, the pain overwhelming him in that moment.

I held him tightly. "It's not a deformity unless *you* see it as one. It is a badge of pride that you didn't give up. It is proof of your strength."

We sat quietly for a moment as I continued to stroke down his scar, tempering the pain with pleasure.

"I love you despite your best efforts to push me away," I said softly. "And I'll continue loving you forever. So take as much time as you need to be comfortable with who you are and who you've become. I'll be waiting right beside you. I've chosen my place. It wasn't our dragons' bond, and it wasn't the curse—*I* chose you. And I'll continue choosing you. Forever."

He pulled back, looking at me with glossy eyes filled with incredulity. He shook his head and kissed me, love and longing filling our bond.

"You have zero sense," he finally said.

"Hannon has mentioned that a time or two. Now. You promised me a first." I pulled my hair over my shoulder and turned, showing him the two lines of scales down my back. "I want it, please."

Instead he ran a finger down a line in the middle of my back, and I knew he was tracing one of my scars.

"Someday soon, I will hear every detail of your time away from me." He traced another scar. "And before I die, I will make Dolion pay in a way no one has ever paid in the history of the world."

"I think you'll have to get in line. He took shifters from all over for his dungeons. Faeries too. They will want their own vengeance. He's even pissing off his own kind enough to rise against him."

"I spoke to Tamara and the others. I was shocked to see them. Though...I probably shouldn't have been. It makes sense he'd covet their power. We'll talk about that later, though. We'll talk about all of it later."

He clearly knew he wouldn't like the details he'd receive.

His lips touched down on my nape before his hands landed on my shoulders. He turned me and gently pushed me forward.

"Grab a pillow," he murmured, getting me to crawl a bit to grab one and then putting it under my hips so that my butt was raised in the air a little.

A hand on each thigh, he spread them wider before running a finger down the seam of my pussy. The bed moved as I lay on my stomach, and then I sucked in a breath and closed my eyes as he followed his finger with his tongue.

"I'd prefer it if you'd not take the tea, and obviously our drag-ons agree." His voice was low and husky, and a furious shiver crawled up my spine and spun around in my stomach. He was fine with the idea of getting me with child. Welcomed it.

My heart sped up a little, and my dragon purred in delight.

"Okay," I said in a breathy whisper.

"I should warn you, though." He pushed apart my thighs a little more so that he could wiggle his tongue across my clit before sucking it in and pulsing for a moment. "Imprinting often sets off a dragon's heat. If I can get out of my own way and imprint with you, which I don't think will be a problem anymore, then it might set you off. You'll want to be bred. Not fucked, not made love to—hardcore bred." A smile entered his voice. "I know how much it weirds you out, using that kind of language."

But it didn't feel weird at the moment. I wanted it. So bad. I wanted his cock deep inside my cunt. The prospect sent a crazy sort of thrill through me. It felt right. All of this felt so right. We'd fought to get here. We'd earned our happy ending, goddammit.

"Nyfain," I begged as he licked up my pussy. He put two fingers inside of me and started to pump them in and out.

"You'll want me to ravage you," he said, bending his fingers in the perfect way. I clutched the mattress, moaning, on the verge of begging for his cock. "The feeling will be so intense that you won't have much reason under its sway. Neither will I. This is just what I've heard, but everyone seems to agree. Our dragons will be insane. *I* will be insane, I think. A child usually results from it. If you aren't ready…then now is not a good time to stop that tea."

He let the comment linger, and I took a deep breath before answering. "I'm ready. Probably. I don't know, but—"

You're fucking ready, my dragon butted in. *You're past fucking ready. Let's get this imprint going and get fucked and ruined and destroyed or whatever the fuck this dragon has promised us. Let's get it all.*

"I don't think my dragon would allow me *not* to be ready," I said with a nervous laugh. Why did all of this suddenly seem so much more intense? So new, like I'd never been with anyone before.

Because you know he is finally ready, my dragon said. *And you are ready. It's about fucking time for that happy ending, I agree. Let's start with coming. Goddess above, I sure wish they could fly. I want to get it on in my scales as we tumble through the sky. I want the dragon to get me with child, not the man. It's fine, though; we can probably figure out how to ground-hump or whatever.*

"Get going, Nyfain. My dragon is starting to get…a bit much."

You like it, she thought.

He licked up my pussy again before running his hands across my butt and down the sides of my waist.

"I already want to fuck you again," he murmured, kissing up the center of my back. "Good thing I can do that and work your scales at the same time. I've never done this with someone, so you'll have to teach me what you like best. I'm not sure whether I'll instinctively know…"

I was so wet that I could feel it dribbling out of me, along with our combined release. He eased his girth into my cunt, nice and slow, as a whisper of touch feathered up my right scales.

"Holy—" I clamped down on a scream of pleasure so pure that I didn't even know how to describe it. "That's good," I said, pushing back into him.

"Hmm, I like this," he said as he shoved his hips forward and hit me deep. "I'm going to fuck the cum out of you and then fill you up again."

He was so wickedly filthy, and I was fucking here for it.

"Yes, Nyfain," I said, moving my hips forward before pushing back into him.

He grabbed my hips, pulling back as he rammed in with a wet slap. He groaned, and then that whisper of a touch was back along the other scales.

"No, holy—"

He eased back out, and then slammed in, his cock punching into my wet cunt, his teeth lightly scraping against a scale.

"*Fuck!*" I blasted apart, blown up with pleasure, pieces of me probably all over the room.

I shuddered as he hammered his cock into me again, then again, hard and fast and obviously out of control.

"Yes, Finley, again," he said, stroking up one scale with his nail.

"No—no! It's too...good. Oh fuck—too much! *Too much—fuuuuck.*" I screamed with it this time, the pleasure pounding through. "Is this...what it always...feels like...for you?"

"No." He was breathing hard, slamming into me, holding me down to keep me put so he could go harder. Wilder. Losing himself in it.

I was right there with him. It felt like I was outside my body, nothing but pleasure. Nothing but the feel of his skin on mine and his cock inside me.

He said a word with each pound of his unrelenting cock.

"Proper-mating-with-a-double-claim-is-supposed-to-make-it-more-intense." He was breathing hard. I was grunting so loudly that I could barely hear him. "Imprinting-is—*Oh fuck!*"

The orgasm ripped through my body, and this one didn't need

the scales. He yelled out unintelligible words as he shuddered against me with a few more thrusts.

And then a new feeling settled over me. No—over *us*. A feeling of peace, and a connection deeper than before. It almost felt like we'd joined together as one. One heart, one soul, one being.

He pulled out, yanked away the pillow, flipped me over, and then re-entered me in lightning-fast movements before kissing me deeply, wrapping me in his arms.

"It's happening," he whispered, and swiped his tongue through my mouth before tangling it with mine.

It almost felt like the goddess herself was blessing our union.

"Just this once, I wish we were like the wolves and could knot," he murmured against my lips, his hold on me insistent, both with his arms and the bond.

I'd read about that in passing but had been skimming. I wasn't sure I wanted to know the logistics. At least not right now.

And then magic curled around us, pulling tight one moment and snapping the next. A strange sort of filth seemed to gather in the air, drawn from everything within the room, and then it seeped out, leaving everything lighter, somehow. Fluffier. Almost like the air had been scrubbed clean with a fresh rain.

Nyfain pulled back to look at me, his eyes filled with wonder and pride. He smiled.

"We did it," he whispered. "We lifted the curse." He laughed, a relieved sound. "If you had any doubts about being my true mate, now you know for sure. You're *mine*."

He kissed me again, pure joy in the touch. I lost myself to the feel of him, relieved and thankful, knowing nothing but how I felt in this moment.

After what could've been a moment or an hour, something

occurred to me.

"Your scales?" I reached around him, but before I could touch them to see if they'd been restored, a knock at the door stole my focus.

"Sire—master—" Quieter, as though in an aside, Hadriel said, "I don't even know what the fuck to call him…"

"Is he for real?" Nyfain muttered. The way he said it, like he was so routinely annoyed by Hadriel that he'd become resigned to it, made me laugh. "Does he want to die?"

"Call him sire now, right?" Leala whispered on the other side of the door, not nearly quiet enough for the conversation to stay between the two of them. "The curse has been lifted—*we did it!* Or we helped do it. Anyway, it's lifted, so he's back to being a prince."

"He was always a prince."

"I mean…now we don't have to hide it because the demons are gone. We're a real kingdom again!"

"Love, now is not the time to squeal and freak out. We are interrupting the master—Fuck! I'm going to fuck this up. We're interrupting a sex session, which is probably very intense, and he probably wants to kill me. Lifting the curse isn't going to suddenly make him more bearable."

"Fine. Okay, go."

Hadriel raised his voice again. "Sire." He knocked. "Sire, I know you're in there. I'm coming in. It's urgent."

"Oh my—" I scrabbled across the bed and quickly climbed under the covers so he didn't see me in the throes of sex. I was getting used to being naked in front of people, but that would be a step too far.

Hadriel stuck his head in and caught sight of me in the bed and then Nyfain rising up onto his knees, his erection prominent.

"Get out, Hadriel," Nyfain commanded with such malice that I felt a shiver go through me, followed by another wave of lust. I'd stopped thinking it odd that he could both scare and arouse me at the same time.

Hadriel didn't share the sentiment. He jerked, clunking his head against the doorframe before visibly shaking in his boots.

"Yes, mas—sire," he replied, his voice quavering. I could just see Leala backing away a little more. "In literally every other instance I would, sire. I think I just pissed myself a little because of your yelling, so that needs looking after, but this one time, you need to come. You'll *want* to come. It's urgent."

"I intend to come, Hadriel. Get out so I can."

"Funny, master—sire. Ha-ha." He grimaced. "But it's imperative that you come with me first. You've been requested, and this is really one of those things that you wouldn't forgive us for not telling you about. And you'll want to…" He stuck in a shaking hand and made circles with his pointer finger. "You'll want clothes, sire. You won't want to show that—rather impressive, excuse my saying so—erection for this. Not to her."

"Not to whom?" Nyfain growled.

"Well…" Hadriel coughed into his fist. "Your mother, sire. The queen. She lives, it seems, and she's here. Now that the curse has been broken, her fellow villagers know her for who she is. They just remembered, as though they'd always known. So then they told the former members of the court, who sought her out… It's actually kind of a mess, at this point. Because now there's some question of who rules, and…"

He trailed away, his gaze growing intense as he watched Nyfain's face. Confusion and continued annoyance bled through the bond, probably from both of us.

"Hadriel, I have never appreciated your humor," Nyfain said in a low, rough voice.

"No, sire. I am well aware. But…" Hadriel put up his hands in defeat.

"My father is the one who told me she died," Nyfain went on. "He blamed me. His grief was clear. Grief like that couldn't have been faked. I was at the funeral."

"I…" Hadriel shook his head. "I don't know what to say, sire. It was a closed casket. She died nearly a week before you returned to the castle. No one saw her body—king's orders."

"But his *grief*," Nyfain yelled.

Hadriel jumped. "Yes, sire. I remember him being very distraught. And there was a lot of confusion around the whole thing. Then the curse took effect, and…" He opened the door a little wider. "She's here now. I saw her with my own eyes. I saw her before…" His gaze darted to me, and guilt surfaced on his face. Sadness. Another silent message quickened my heart: farewell. "Tamara and the others bowed to her. It's *her*."

Anger washed over Nyfain. Frustration. Grief.

He got off the bed and, almost as an afterthought, put out his hand to me. I pushed the covers back and took it, getting up, still firmly in the land of disbelief. There was no way the queen was still alive and here, of all things! How could she have escaped all of those years ago? And how could she have come back? Other than the faeries, we'd all traveled on the same two boats from the villages. I wouldn't have recognized her, but others in her court surely would have. And if not on the boat, then at least flying into battle.

"Wait, sir. Sire." Leala bustled in, gave an apologetic curtsey, and went to the wardrobe. She took out a slip for me, no better than a nightgown, and a pair of threadbare jeans for him. "We'll just cover up a smidge, like Hadriel said. Just a smidge, no biggie. You'll thank us, sire. And soon we can open lines of trade and get modern things and even some light bulbs. We should get the human electricity through the portals again, right?" A smile stretched across her face. "The magic that lets us pilfer things like that from the human world should be active again. We just need to get reestablished, that's all. Why we smashed all the light bulbs in year six is beyond me…"

"Leala, love, you're rambling," Hadriel murmured.

"Yes. Sorry," she replied.

Unease rolled through the bond now, but Nyfain didn't show it on his face. He stepped into the jeans. I slipped on the bit of fabric as Hadriel stepped out into the hall, his eyes large and sorrowful, trained on me again.

"What is it?" I asked him as we passed. He wasn't acting like his usual self.

Was the queen's return terrible news for me for some reason? Why was he acting like this was it for me and he wouldn't see me again?

He shook his head as we passed. Barefoot, Nyfain walked beside me down the stairs.

"She's out front, sire," Hadriel said as we made it to the second-floor landing. "She wanted to be as formal as possible, given the circumstances."

"If this is some sort of joke, Hadriel…" Nyfain said, anger rising, grief riding the tide.

"I would never joke about this, sire," Hadriel replied. "I know what you'd do to me."

He made it to the door where Urien waited in a pressed suit

with only a little speck of dirt marring the side of his neck. He looked at Nyfain for a solid beat before moving to the door and grasping the handle.

"I will await further instructions," he said as he opened the door.

A swell of nervousness rolled through the bond. Anger simmered. Nyfain wasn't sure what to think.

My heart started beating faster. And then, when we walked outside onto the stoop and I saw who waited there, my heart leapt into my throat.

Ami stood there, Claudile just behind her, and Gunduin last in line. She couldn't have aged in the last sixteen years, otherwise she would've been too young to bear Nyfain. Time must've stopped for her like it had the court.

But how was that possible if she hadn't been here? And she hadn't, because I was at her house.

I was at her house!

When I saw what was in her hand, my stomach curdled.

She held my—*her*—sword.

Suddenly a million memories came back to me. They'd always reacted strangely to that sword, keeping tabs on it, asking about it. Still, they'd never taken it. They'd never asked for it.

They'd never mentioned that she was my fucking queen! I wouldn't have been like the others in that village. I would've held on to that piece of information.

"Nyfain," Ami said, her head held high and her bearing straight, regal even with crumpled clothes and messy hair.

Insecurity thrummed through me.

She'd often been so cold to me in the village. Distant. And Claudile had acted like she didn't trust me. They must've smelled

Nyfain on me, and they would've known his scent. Hell, I'd told them whose scent it was. I'd filled them in about everything.

They'd been judging me the whole time. Clearly they'd found me wanting.

And now they were here to claim their old life back. A life I didn't fit into. A role that fate had handed me instead of my family lineage.

"Mother," Nyfain said on a release of breath, so many emotions tumbling through the bond that I couldn't catch them all. His tone was stiff. "How is this possible?"

Guilt crossed her expression before she could wrestle it under control. In that brief moment, she'd let down her guard. She'd shown the truth of her situation.

And he'd caught it.

One emotion radiated through the bond now.

Betrayal.

Did she have a hand in the curse? If not, how had she escaped it?

Everyone had thought she'd died. The king had grieved and then damned the kingdom, blaming it all on his son for leaving.

Whatever the reason, she was here now. She'd hidden from her people, but now she stood before them, regal, as though she'd never left.

We'd finally released ourselves of the curse, only to be confronted with old haunts. Haunts who still commanded loyalty in the court, not to mention the villages. Haunts who could make my life hell. *All* of our lives hell. Because she was still technically the queen, in charge of this kingdom we'd just freed.

THE END.

About the Author

K.F. Breene is a Wall Street Journal, USA Today, Washington Post, Amazon Most Sold Charts and #1 Kindle Store bestselling author of paranormal romance, urban fantasy and fantasy novels. With millions of books sold, when she's not penning stories about magic and what goes bump in the night, she's sipping wine and planning shenanigans. She lives in Northern California with her husband, two children, and out of work treadmill.

Sign up for her newsletter to hear about the latest news and receive free bonus content.

www.kfbreene.com